THE
TAPESTRY
OF
TIME

Also by Kate Heartfield

The Chatelaine
The Embroidered Book
The Valkyrie

THE
TAPESTRY
OF
TIME

KATE HEARTFIELD

HARPER
Voyager

Harper*Voyager*
An imprint of
HarperCollins*Publishers* Ltd
1 London Bridge Street
London SE1 9GF

www.harpercollins.co.uk

HarperCollins*Publishers*
Macken House,
39/40 Mayor Street Upper,
Dublin 1
D01 C9W8
Ireland

First published by HarperCollins*Publishers* Ltd 2024

1

A catalogue record for this book is available from the British Library.

ISBN: 978-0-00-856781-1 (HB)
ISBN: 978-0-00-856780-4 (TPB)

Typeset in Meridien by Palimpsest Book Production Ltd, Falkirk, Stirlingshire

Printed and bound in the UK using 100% Renewable
Electricity by CPI Group (UK) Ltd

In memory of my grandparents,
Arthur and Emily Heartfield

PART 1

JUNE 1944

CHAPTER 1

Kit

Halfway between the Louvre and the canteen for Nazi soldiers, Kit becomes uneasy. Like cold fingers fumbling up her arms; like the jangling of a piano that hasn't been tuned since before the war.

And why shouldn't she be uneasy, in the evening light, in this too-quiet Paris? Pedestrians with their heads down, cyclists slipping past. Her mind, like the city, is occupied. Checkpoints. Shortages and queues. Occasionally, an outcry. People running. Soldiers with guns. Markets full of women trying to fill their children's woeful rations. A hand-painted sign. Yellow stars. A grandmother sitting on the pavement, her legs splayed, her hands empty, her gaze absent. Buses and trains rumble and smoke, carrying people away. Every moment, some piece of the city implodes and dies, leaving scar tissue.

The two women walking in front of Kit have painted their legs to look like stockings, with a careful seam drawn with grease pencil. They murmur to each other about practical things. Kit is one in a line of women, walking home late from work, as life carries on.

Her gaze breaks free, across the Rue de Clichy.

A woman is standing on the pavement, staring across the street, her arms at her sides.

She looks like Ivy – no, she *is* Ivy.

It's impossible; Ivy is at home now, in England. But Kit knows her youngest sister's face. That defiant expression, the hint of a pout, like Betty Grable looking at a camera no one else can see. Every blonde curl pinned perfectly.

Kit's running across the road, yelling Ivy's name, trying to get her attention, when a bicycle screeches, its rider yells, and Kit, startled, sees the bicycle as it stops a few inches from her. People are staring at her, warily, wondering what she was running towards.

Because there is no one standing where she saw Ivy a moment ago. The figure of her sister is burned into her mind, like a negative image.

Kit looks all the way up and down that side of the street. Rooted, she turns in a circle, searching for her sister, until the cyclist tells her, not unkindly, to *get out of the traffic, for the love of heaven*. There is no one in the spot where Ivy was standing. No alley nearby, no store to duck into. A few steps to the south there's a massive apartment block, with a concierge standing just inside the door. He takes a long time before answering Kit's question, but eventually seems to decide that there's no harm in telling her that no, he did not just admit a young blonde woman. No one has entered for the last half-hour.

Back out in the evening light, she gathers herself. Whoever she saw, it must have been a stranger. Someone she mistook for Ivy. A trick of the mind.

Kit walks north towards her flat, the palm of one hand pressed to her temple.

It's the war, it's the damned war. Maybe it's the possibility of peace. Hope cracking all her defences like a weed in the pavement.

Yesterday, the Allies landed on the beaches of Normandy. The opening notes of Beethoven's Fifth Symphony have echoed in her mind, in the city's mind, all day. The notes that open the broadcasts of Radio Londres every night: three short and one long, Morse for the letter V, for victory. Then come the coded messages. And the news from the Free French in London, announcing that the long-expected invasion has begun. D-Day has come.

It's natural, to think about family at a time like this. To think of Ivy here. There must have been a hundred evenings when they walked together on this street, when Ivy, too, lived in Paris.

Kit trips over nothing and lurches forward, into the arms of a young German soldier, who calls her *mademoiselle* and asks if she is all right. The smell of his cologne, like rotten oranges, as she rights herself and gets her bearings. A sign in faded blackletter type dominates the Place de Clichy: *Soldatenheim.* The canteen for German soldiers. She usually gives the place a wide berth, but she was distracted. She picks her way through grey uniforms and smart skirts, through an obscene minefield of careful, light conversations.

Paris is a vacant museum, the void in every gilt frame stacked against the walls. Eyes of stone, like that sculpture of a nun's head she packed for sending away in the last days before the invasion, when the Louvre was being emptied. The mournful expression between stone wimple and stone chin-strap, the nose knocked off. Artist unknown. Not terribly interesting or unusual; but on that desperate day, it spoke to her, and she wrapped it in shredded cardboard and found a place for it in a crate full of precious things.

Everyone in the city has that mournful, absent expression in their eyes now. Eyes of stone would be a blessing. Nobody wants to see anything. But all the same, when she finally reaches her flat on the Rue des Dames she feels that she's being watched. Just the glare of the concierge. Dust motes swirl over the staircase in the last rays of the evening, filtered through a grimy window, as she climbs the three flights of stairs to her flat.

The familiar smell of yesterday's cabbage and her own cigarettes, a whiff of grease and metal from her bicycle by the door.

But something is wrong.

In the darkness, with one hand gripping the cold doorknob, she reaches a finger to the light switch. Nothing. No power, again. She stands very still, breathing shallow, letting her eyes adjust, interpreting the shadows.

In the far corner of the room, cigarette smoke rises into the moonlight from the window. She feels a twinge of disappointment at seeing the lithe silhouette and cloud of golden hair. No – she's not disappointed to see her lover, just surprised. Evelyn Larsen hates Montmartre and hardly ever comes to Kit's flat. And they made no plans tonight.

Kit walks in and flops on to the sofa opposite.

'You're late, sweetheart,' Evelyn says. She gives it an extra American drawl; she knows Kit thinks this makes her sound like a movie star. 'You're too talented to be stuck in that basement with your files and pencils until sunset.'

'I wouldn't have dawdled if I'd known you'd be here.' She moves her leg to brush Evelyn's, in greeting. Unlike the women on the street, Evelyn has real stockings on her long and glorious calves.

'I had business in the neighbourhood, and curfew is coming.'

Business. The German soldiers in the Place de Clichy; or perhaps at the Moulin Rouge. Every woman has to make her choices in Paris. Evelyn has always been honest with Kit about her choice to play the Germans for fools, to take her revenge in protection for her friends, in papers and useful

6

information. But this transactional resistance – if it even can be called resistance any more – is not something Kit chooses to witness up close.

Is there even a way to get close to Evelyn Larsen? She seemed unapproachable when Kit met her on a dig in Arabia in 1937. Impossibly ethereal. Kit, on the other hand, always seemed to have sweaty armpits and trousers baggy at the knees.

Kit hated archaeology, as Father had always said she would. It was overwhelming, disorientating. She got headaches all the time, from the sun. Stubbornly, she stuck with it for months, until she finally admitted, in a letter to her friend Maxine, that she was miserable. Max said she was about to take a flat in Paris; why shouldn't Kit join her there for a while? Kit jumped at the chance to study art history at the École du Louvre, and get her bearings.

What a glorious moment, when Kit walked into Le Monocle in Paris the following year and saw Evelyn dancing with friends, saw her turn and smile, recognize her, call her by name.

How beautiful Evelyn was, but how beautiful everyone was then – the girls with their high collars and tuxedos and sleek Marcel-waved hair. When the Occupation came, the club was boarded up; everyone knew what Nazis thought of inverts, and what they might do to a club full of them.

But Kit and Evelyn had something more in common. Evelyn was a private research assistant for an archaeologist in Paris, and Kit had taken a job at the Louvre as a research assistant to one of the experts on medieval sculpture. She and Evelyn had coffee, and then they had sex, and Evelyn said she was finding ways to help people however she could. She offered to get a letter through Vichy France to Kit's family, and for a year or so Kit was able to write to them, and to get letters back.

It has been several years, now, since the last letter. She does not know who is dead and who is alive. She has tried, very hard, to stop wondering. And she does not believe in ghosts.

Evelyn is looking at her with concern. 'You're working too hard,' she says.

Kit snorts. 'Not hard enough. It's difficult to do one's research in an empty museum. I get the journal published every quarter, and I arrange my notes and files for my monograph, but I can't write it until I can get my hands on things. And of course, I do my part to placate the Nazis when they come. They always want to see the little we left behind when we got everything out in 1940.'

Evelyn stubs out her cigarette. 'About that. I wonder whether some of the items might be safer if they were returned to the Louvre now, what with the invasion in Normandy. What about the Bayeux Tapestry? I know it's special to you, because of your dad.'

She is right about that. Even though Kit hasn't spoken to her father in years, even though there is bitterness between them, she still reveres his life's work: the eleventh-century embroidery that shows the story leading up to the Norman invasion of England in 1066. He is an expert on it – or he was, before he started embarrassing himself with crackpot theories.

The D-Day landings were not far from Bayeux, but Kit knows the tapestry isn't in immediate danger, because it's no longer there. A few years ago, it was moved to a small château farther south and deep in the countryside, under the protection of the Louvre.

'I don't think the tapestry's in any immediate danger from the invasion,' Kit says, more curtly than she intends.

'Himmler might disagree. He wants it, you know.'

Kit snorts. 'Himmler wants everything. I'm sure he would

love to hang it in his castle, along with everything else he steals. We've managed to keep it from him so far.'

'Yes, but he has a special interest in this. He says it's an important part of German cultural history. Because William the Conqueror was a Norman, and the Normans were Vikings, hence north Germanic. He's worked it all out.'

Of course he has. Heinrich Himmler, the man who runs the security forces of the Nazi empire, is building a master race. People say that his recruits for the array of paramilitary organizations known as the SS were chosen based on so-called Nordic characteristics: blond hair, blue eyes, measurements of eyes and noses and foreheads. But it isn't enough to breed a superior nation; they have been taught to believe in their superiority.

So the Nazis need a history they can believe in too, a history that tells the story they want it to tell. All the little fair-haired girls and boys must learn that they are descended from greatness: that every great achievement of humanity can be traced back to Germanic tribes, somehow. Kit had read Nazi research claiming Norse influence in South America, in India. One of the ghouls who made life difficult for French museums was an archaeologist who had made his name excavating Viking sites. It was no wonder they would claim a connection to William the Conqueror, who was a direct descendant of a band of Scandinavian warriors.

And it was no wonder they'd take an interest in a tapestry showing the conquest of England.

Then again, Nazi researchers could find an Aryan connection to anything they thought might look better in a Berlin museum. Kit had heard something about a team of them photographing the tapestry, a few years ago, but had never heard that it was a priority for them, unlike the beautiful objects claimed by some officer or other. Most of the Nazi researchers arrogantly assumed that there would be plenty of time for moving artefacts where they wanted them, when the final victory came.

Kit shudders. She asks, 'How do you know what Himmler thinks about the tapestry?'

Evelyn laughs. 'You know me. I know everyone in the Ahnenerbe. I know everyone everywhere.'

Kit first encountered the Ahnenerbe, Himmler's research institute, on the dig in Aden. There was one archaeologist who'd been on a dig in Italy that had purportedly found Norse carvings that showed the Roman Empire was attributable to the influence of Nordic travellers; it was ludicrous, and Kit had made an enemy by saying so. Another researcher she'd met had a theory about a matriarchal society in the frozen north from which all humans had sprung; the sinking of Atlantis was wrapped up with it somehow. These were intelligent, educated people who had begun, most of them, with just wanting to get their research funded, and they'd willingly transformed into zealots for the most outlandish theories, all in service of the idea that some humans had more right to live than others. She'd had no desire to get to know any of them better.

'I don't know how you can talk to those snakes. My God, Evelyn, do you know what Himmler would do to you and me, if he could? You know he has a theory that bodies in bogs are evidence that people used to execute homosexuals that way. That's what he would do to you and me: drown us in a bog.'

Evelyn shrugs. 'Nobody's perfect. There's theory and there's practice, Kit. In practice, they don't care who I sleep with. They think I'm useful to them.'

'Until you're not.'

'Let me worry about that.'

Unlike Evelyn, Kit doesn't have the instinct to get what she needs from people. She likes her records and files. Yes, her war work has consisted of moving artefacts and shuffling paperwork, writing interminable articles based on other articles, attacking theories and then arguing against those attacks, while making life a little more difficult for the occupiers than it needs to be, counting every minor incompetence a victory. She and her colleagues have kept some things safe and some things hidden.

But not everything, and certainly not everyone. If the Bayeux Tapestry ends up in German hands, it will join a long list of thefts that Kit has not been able to stop. If they're coming for the tapestry, they'll be coming for more. The war will have to end eventually – everyone says that – but it's hard to imagine that end will be anything but bloody. What will liberation look like? Who will be saved, and what will have to burn?

The chignon at the nape of her neck is too tight; it's giving her a headache. She pulls it out, runs her hands through her hair. 'Thank you for telling me about the tapestry, Evelyn. I'm not sure what we can do about it, but we'll try.'

Evelyn gives a mock bow with a fluttering hand. 'I do my best.'

Kit kicks off her shoes and goes to the few square feet that might, with some imagination, be called the kitchen. It's a one-room flat: there's a sitting area with a chair, a sofa where Ivy used to sleep, and a kitchen counter. The flat is on the corner of the building, and it bends into another area, the bedroom. A curtain separates the bedroom from the sitting room, but once there was a curtain down the middle, too, to separate Kit's bed from the one occupied by her old friend Max. The good old days, which she tries not to think about.

Out of instinct, she tries the stove, but she's missed the window for gas, if there was any today. It's all right; she isn't really hungry anyway, though she would have liked a cup of tea. She puts her hand on her beloved copper kettle, sighs, and lights a candle instead.

When she turns, holding the candle in its wine bottle, Evelyn is standing in the kitchen too. She looks tired in the candlelight. But exhaustion, somehow, makes Evelyn look even more like a movie star. She leans against the wall, with a bottle of cognac hanging from each perfect hand. Her knitted top sweeps across her shoulders, her collarbone catching the light.

'Spoils of war,' she says, in answer to Kit's expression. 'Trust me, I earned it.'

Kit takes the bottles from her hands, intending to open one, but instead is kissing Evelyn against the wall. Evelyn once told her that she 'got' red lipstick the way some people get religion, and that, coming from Minot, North Dakota, it was bound to be one or the other. It smells like a drugstore and tastes like a drug.

They fall on to the sofa, Kit on top of Evelyn, settling down on to the familiar topography of her body. She bunches her lover's honey hair in her hand, pulls her head back to expose her swan neck. Smears her lipstick with her thumb. They are careful with their stockings but not with each other. By the time they end up on the cold floor beside the table, the candle has gone out.

Half-naked on her back, Evelyn's arm draped possessively across her hips, Kit stares at the ceiling, knowing the pattern of the cracks in the plaster even though she can't see them in the dark.

CHAPTER 2

Kit

Kit wakes too early, in and out of bad dreams.

Evelyn's mention of the Bayeux Tapestry has thrown her back into an old memory, of the time in 1928 when Father took the whole family to see the replica, on display in Reading. Kit must have been nearly twelve.

She can see herself and her sisters in that hall, each of them gazing at a part of the long tapestry. Father had explained that it was not actually a tapestry at all, as the images were not woven, but embroidered. All the same, everyone called it a tapestry. The replica, unlike the original, was divided into framed sections. So they each took a piece and made it their favourite.

Her sister Helen, the oldest of the Sharp girls, standing awkwardly near the beginning, as if she wasn't sure what she was supposed to be doing. She liked the parts with the horses and dogs. Helen liked animals. Two of the horses were blue, and one of the blue horses had a red stocking, and the other a striped orange one. She seemed to find this puzzling, fascinating or disturbing – Kit wasn't sure which.

Ivy, the youngest Sharp sister, thought it was hilarious that the Victorian embroiderers had put clothes on the naked men when they made their replica. She went right up close and pointed at them.

Rose, the quiet one, stood at the end with her hands behind her back. Kit overheard Father telling her that scholars thought the final panels must show the triumphant William at his coronation, but they didn't really know, because that part had been missing for centuries.

All of them found mysteries to love in it, perhaps because they could see how much Father enjoyed it. It wasn't his life's work yet, but he already had photographs of the tapestry on the wall of his study, and books about it on his shelf.

For Kit, the most fascinating part of the tapestry, then as now, was Aelfgyva. A woman with a name but no story; she just appeared, during the part when Harold swore his oaths to William, in Normandy. Father explained that Aelfgyva was then a common name, so there were many candidates for this one. Some scholars thought she wasn't there in Normandy at the time at all, that the embroiderers put her in to show that the men were talking about bloodlines. Father told them his own theory: that Aelfgyva was really what the English called a foreign woman named Agatha, whose son Edgar had the best right to the throne, though he never took it.

'Perhaps she was in Normandy trying to get William on her side, or make a deal,' Father said. 'See how the cleric, here, is touching her face? He might be blessing her cause.' He chuckled. 'Or it might be something else altogether. Nobody knows. But it's so odd, isn't it? The way the sentence just stops. Can you read the Latin?'

Kit did her best. 'Where Aelfgyva and a certain cleric.'

'Yes. But then it stops! Where Aelfgyva and the cleric . . . what? Was it too dangerous to say?' He sighed. 'The embroiderers must be trying to tell us something, something we can't understand. I wish I knew. I don't have much evidence for my Agatha hunch.'

How exciting she found it, knowing there was a mystery that all the scholars of all the universities had not yet solved. Back then, Kit was ready to believe that Father's hunches were the height of brilliance. And she knew then that she wanted to investigate history too, the way he did. That moment, with Aelfgyva, was the reason she went on to study archaeology, and then art history – and the reason she eventually became estranged from her father.

Something about the quality of morning light on her bed's white sheet, draped over Evelyn's sleeping body, reminds Kit of that painting by Toulouse-Lautrec: two women in a bed, a sheet up to their chins. It makes her think of Ivy, at an exhibition years after the tapestry one, with a different look on her face. She'd taken Ivy to the Louvre soon after she came to Paris, and known from Ivy's face at first sight of that painting that it wouldn't be as difficult to explain her lesbianism to her little sister as Kit had feared. For a while, they had been happy, Ivy and Kit and Max, three young women sharing a flat in Paris. Until that, too, went sour.

Kit sits up, slowly so as not to wake Evelyn. Then she freezes.

There is someone else in the room.

If she turns her head a little, she knows she'll see . . . she can't think it. She balls the sheet in both hands and makes herself look towards the window.

Ivy is there. Standing with her back to Kit, looking out. She is standing perfectly still, impossibly still, and Kit can see the wall through her legs.

Kit does not believe in ghosts. She has never put much stock in the old family stories about the Second Sight, which Aunt Kathleen transmitted fervently on every visit to her nephew and his children. She doesn't believe in the supernatural at all. But she does believe that the mind plays tricks. She takes a deep breath, and chokes on it, noisily, a horrid wet violence.

Evelyn's hand on her arm. 'What is it, darling?'

By now, from her position, with her eyes open, Evelyn should have seen Ivy. She isn't there for Evelyn, which is not entirely a relief. Because Kit can still see her, pale and ghostly as a double exposure but undeniably present.

The image does not turn at the sound of their voices.

'Nothing,' Kit says, shuddering. 'A bad dream.'

She doesn't want Evelyn's hand touching her skin, suddenly. How to shake it off, without causing hurt and tension? Kit pushes herself out of the bed, strides with terrible desperation to the window.

When she has reached the place where Ivy was, there is, of course, nothing there. The image dissolved as she approached.

'I just need air,' Kit says.

She goes to the window in her nightgown. Lifts the sash and lets in cool air and the muted jumble of morning sounds – and stops with her hands still on the window, her body turned to ice.

Down on the street, standing next to a man behind a newspaper cart. Ivy – if it is Ivy – is looking up at the window, with the same blank expression she had inside, and on the street yesterday. She looks solid and ordinary enough, now.

Damn it, is she going to be haunted by her sister at every moment? No, not haunted, not haunted. But what, then? *Of course one has to take care not to end up in the county asylum,* said Aunt Kathleen once, knitting away merrily, when they were still girls, and she was telling them about dead sailors appearing to their wives before their wives knew they were shipwrecked.

Ivy on the Rue de Clichy. Ivy in her flat. Ivy on the Rue

des Dames. Kit pulls a plaid skirt and cotton blouse from her chest of drawers, gets dressed and throws her cardigan over her shoulders, mumbles something to Evelyn and goes out and down the stairs, ignoring the concierge, into the cool morning.

Kit remembers, this time, to look for cars and bicycles, to the right and left. Before she reaches the far side of the street, she is already sickeningly aware that her sister is not where she seemed to be. Ivy has vanished, again.

An urge overtakes her to sit down on the pavement, ball up her hands and cry like a toddler. Instead, she stands where her sister was a moment ago. Damn Ivy, always wanting attention, even . . . even now. If it's a game, then Kit will play it. She plants herself on the pavement next to the newspaper seller and looks around, waiting for the next moment she'll jump out of her skin.

It comes as a hand on her shoulder.

She whirls and sees, not Ivy, but Maxine Yardley.

The sharp face framed by dark curls. The brown eyes wary.

Kit nearly collapses under the weight of emotions she can't name. She puts her hands on Max's upper arms. A real woman, not a vision. But she has not seen Max in four years. Max, like Ivy, is supposed to be in England. In fact it was Max who got Ivy safely out of France, in 1940. That was the last time Kit saw either of them, and she's only had a handful of letters since, years ago.

Finally, Kit manages, 'Are you really here?'

At that, a familiar wry ripple crosses Max's expression.

'Depends on who you ask. Come on, let's go somewhere where we can talk. Can we go up to the flat?'

God, Evelyn's probably still in bed, still not dressed. Flustered, Kit says, 'I don't want the concierge to ask questions,' which is not a lie.

Max frowns. 'Is it the same man who worked there when I lived here? He was nice enough, I thought.'

'He turned in three Jewish families in '42.'

'The bastard! Which ones? Not the little girls.'

'Yes, the little girls.' Kit looks up and down the street one more time, but sees no one that could be Ivy.

It's hard to concentrate when Max is looking at her, her gaze steady and her eyes too bright. Kit grabs her arm and leads her into a side street where there's a stone step in the entranceway of a law office, closed at this hour. It's chilly in the shade; the June sun hasn't had a chance to warm up the day yet. She pulls her cardigan tighter.

Max looks older, and it suits her. Confident, from the crease in her wide trousers to the smart lapels of her loose, tawny jacket. A dark blue blouse beneath. The long dark curl over one dark eye. But her cheeks are gaunt, and there are new lines on either side of her mouth, and between her perfectly imperfect eyebrows.

'How long have you been here?' Kit asks. 'Here in Paris, I mean.'

'A while.' Max looks around, but there's no one nearby. 'I need to ask you something, Kit. And I want the truth. You can trust me.'

Kit makes a face. 'When have I ever not trusted you?'

Max is still not looking at her. 'I need to know whether you've seen Ivy.'

A sharp intake of breath, and then a half-gasp, half-sob. It's the only answer she can muster at first, and it's enough to make Max look straight at her.

'You *have*,' Max whispers hoarsely.

'I thought it was my imagination. She was . . . like a ghost.' She hadn't dared to think the word, until now. 'There one moment, and gone the next.'

'What do you mean? You haven't spoken to her, then?'

Kit shakes her head. 'Last night I thought I saw her on the street, on my way home from work. Then, this morning, I had a funny feeling in my room, and thought I saw her – and then when I looked out of the window she was standing on the street. That's why I rushed out.'

Max frowns. 'I thought it was me you saw. I was staring up at your window long enough. Where did you see Ivy?'

'Standing right beside the newspaper seller,' Kit says, pointing. 'Just before I came out. But then she was gone again.'

Max shakes her head. 'I've been standing right here for the past twenty minutes, trying to get up the nerve to go and knock on your door.' She smirks at her own embarrassment. 'A few people came up and bought newspapers, but I would have seen if one of them was Ivy.'

The morning is cold; the world is cold. To mistake a woman seen on the street for a loved one once isn't so strange, but to do it twice? And then what was that vision in the flat?

'I don't understand,' Kit says weakly.

'Neither do I,' Max agrees, and buries her head in her hands, rumpling her hair. Then she looks up. 'I'm going to tell you something I probably shouldn't, but I need your help, and I can't think what else to do. It might be a dangerous thing to know.'

'Oh, Max, what sort of trouble have you got yourself into?'

'I'm an agent of His Majesty's Government, I'll have you know. One hundred per cent sanctioned trouble. I'm here to help the Resistance.'

This raises a million questions, but they'll have to get in line. 'What has all this to do with Ivy? I thought she was in England!'

'She was, until a month ago. I've just learned she was supposed to make contact with a network in another part of France. But that network was broken, compromised, right around the time she dropped. There's no sign of her. So I thought, well, maybe she came to Paris, and maybe she couldn't make contact with any agents here. Maybe she tried to get help from you instead. I don't know.'

Kit hears this as if through a tunnel. When she speaks, her voice sounds high and odd. 'What do you mean, "the time she dropped"?'

'By parachute, about a month ago. The last full moon before this one.'

Kit's brain is stalling like an engine. 'Surely this is a joke. Can you really see my little sister parachuting out of a plane? *Ivy*, of all people?'

'Yes, I can. You never gave her enough credit.'

Kit notices the past tense, and bites her lip. She squeezes her eyes shut, tries to think. 'All right. My little sister Ivy dropped behind enemy lines by parachute. But when people do that, don't they have someone waiting to greet them?'

'Not always. It was probably a blind drop. I don't know the details. All I know is that Ivy, or an agent going by her code name, missed her contact. It doesn't mean she's captured, or worse. Not necessarily. But there's no sign of her.'

'Who's looking for her? How can we help?'

Max hesitates. 'I don't think anyone's looking for her. Agents go missing all the time. They fall out of touch for weeks, or months, and then they turn up somewhere. Or they don't. And right now, with the invasion, there is a lot of activity, of course. Many agents working in and around the fighting. I don't think London will be able to do much for Ivy.'

Kit tries to absorb this. 'Do you know where she . . . dropped?'

'Not officially.' Max pauses. 'But I know which network she was making contact with. I'm on my way back out of the city, and I'm going to see what I can find out. There is no way in hell I'm giving up on Ivy. I'll give you an address in Paris. Will you send word there, right away please, if Ivy does show up? I'll give you a code phrase.'

Kit shakes her head violently. 'Absolutely not. I'm coming with you.'

'Kit, no. You can't.'

'I can and I will.'

Max frowns. 'Listen. You thought you saw her. Maybe you did. Maybe she is in Paris, and being followed, and just hasn't had a chance to make contact yet.'

Kit remembers her sudden conviction that if she just turned her head . . . 'I don't think it was her at all. Just my mind playing tricks on me. I even thought she was in my flat this morning, but she wasn't, of course. It's just that imagination of mine getting me into trouble again, that's all.'

Max looks at her curiously, but not affectionately. She has never looked at Kit this way before; it's a hard expression, one acquaintance looking at another. The war has desecrated everything. But truth be told, this is an older wound, and this is preferable to the way Max looked at her the last time they saw each other. It will never be as easy between them as it used to be. Not ever again.

Kit feels the weird absence of affection keenly in this moment, when she is trying not to panic about her sister. She wants to sniffle on Max's shoulder, to wail, to pace and come up with a plan. Instead, she feels frozen in place. If Max goes and leaves her here, she might stop breathing.

'I don't have false papers for you,' Max says, uncertainly. 'If we're stopped, I don't want them to make any connection between us and Ivy, nothing that could give them any information about her.'

Kit thinks, with a twinge, of Evelyn, who has used her

connections to make sure Kit will be safe no matter what. 'I have false papers. Good ones.'

'Hmpf,' says Max. 'We'll have to come up with a cover story. I sell cosmetics, you see; that's my cover. Explains why I travel. But, with two of us, we'll need something different. Do you still have your bicycle?'

'Of course.'

'It's a long ride. A day just to get there, probably several days before you can get back to the city. And what happens when you don't turn up for work?'

'I can say I'm going on a research trip. I'm writing a monograph on women in Romanesque sculpture.'

'Of course you are.'

'Max, please. It's Ivy.'

Max closes her eyes, annoyed, but says, 'Damn it. Yes. You know her better than anyone. I have a feeling you might be useful.'

'There's always a first time.' Kit looks up at the flat, at the window where she saw her sister. 'Stay here. I'll get my papers out of the flat and be back in ten minutes.'

She worries that Max will object, insist on coming with her, but Max just looks at her and nods, rubbing her bottom lip.

Evelyn is already dressed in last night's top and skirt, making something that approximates coffee on Kit's stove.

'The gas is back, then,' Kit says at the door.

Evelyn turns to her with a brilliant smile. 'Don't you know that I can work miracles? Come and have some. It is arguably better than nothing.'

'I can't just now. I have to go and help a friend. I might be gone a few days.'

Evelyn's expression doesn't change. 'Gone? You're leaving Paris?'

'Just to check up on an old friend. Make sure she's all right.'

Evelyn knows Max from the old days, and Max knows Evelyn. Yet here is Kit trying to keep them from finding out about each other, as though she's a teenager again, hiding her relationships with girls from her parents. There is no reason to hide anything from Max, except to spare feelings that Max, no doubt, lost years ago.

But of course, there is another reason to keep Max's activities secret. Somehow, it doesn't surprise her that Maxine Yardley has found a way to do the most difficult and dangerous work she could. She never did anything by halves, not even practical jokes or games. She used to get what Aunt Kathleen called 'the light of the fairies' in her eyes.

Evelyn takes a few steps towards Kit, walking like a model. There is no light in Evelyn's eyes, just heady depths. 'You have that look about you, darling.'

'What look?'

'You used to get it when you had an idea. All quiet and private, as if no one could get in.' Evelyn is close to her now, looking at her curiously. 'You had it in Aden, the day you found the temple. You were so stubborn about wanting to extend that trench, even though there was nothing in it.'

Kit remembers everything: the glitter of the sun in the sand, the smell of sweat, the headache she had from reading Father's most recent letter to her. Chastising her, taking issue with everything she believed. The feel of stone beneath her fingers.

Evelyn puts one red fingernail to Kit's own cheek. 'You kept insisting that if you could just extend the trench a few more inches, the wall would be there. Gertrude was so sour about it, do you recall? Called it a waste of time. But then there it was. The wall. Exactly where you said it would be. You do have a way of quietly puzzling things out and then astonishing everyone.'

It was nothing more than an instinct. Everyone has those kinds of feelings from time to time: a conviction not to take the usual bus to work, or the confidence to make an aggressive bid in a game of bridge. These were the sorts of coincidences that led to the family tradition that the Sharps had the Second Sight; some ancestor must have had some combination of cleverness, good instincts and luck, and then his or her descendants found it useful to pretend to have some strange power.

But Kit is an educated woman, a sceptic by nature, and she knows there must have been something speaking to her subconscious mind that day. Some shadow or bump. The moisture of the earth under her fingers.

Anyway, today she has no such feeling, and she isn't puzzling anything out. If only she could. If only Ivy would appear in reality. If only Kit had some idea where to find her.

She chews her lip.

'I like to be astonished,' Evelyn declares. 'I hope you'll tell me what you find this time.'

Kit kisses her because she can't think of a response. Then she says, 'I'll have to find a telephone, to let the Louvre know.'

'No need. I'll go there and tell them myself. What shall I say?'

'You really don't mind?'

'I've got an errand to run near there anyway.'

'Then tell them I'm off doing research, that something's come to light in a small church that bears on my monograph, but you don't know where.'

'Which route are you taking?' Evelyn asks, watching her.

Kit shakes her head. 'I hadn't thought about it yet.'

'The Porte de Clichy tends to get overwhelmed, and they won't have anyone there with two scruples to rub together, especially not today with so many heading to the front. Here, take the cognac.' She strides over to the kitchen table and takes the unopened bottle, hands it to Kit.

'I can't take this.'

'It might come in handy. Don't worry, there's more where that came from. And be careful out there, for God's sake. No, forget him. For *my* sake.'

Evelyn is a force of nature. 'I don't deserve you,' Kit says, and kisses her cheek.

She remembers the nun's head she packed away, the weight of it in her hands. She doesn't know where that particular truckload of the Louvre's treasures ended up, but somehow she is certain that the nun's head is safe, still in darkness, still nestled against other work by other hands. She can almost hear the feet of rats, the silence, as they packed up the arte-facts to wait out the war. Who was that nun, in her day? Not necessarily a nun; any medieval woman might have worn a wimple like that. But Kit thinks of her as a nun. An abbess or someone important, no doubt. She would have found the stone too smooth a medium, nothing like the pockmark on her forehead, the web of red veins on her cheek. A lie before God. She might resent being saved, being hidden away, as she resented the maker of that sculpture, as the maker resented her, for wanting something impossible from his art. As Kit resents Evelyn for loving something Kit is not.

Evelyn kisses her mouth, breaking Kit's spiral into imagi-nation. The kiss makes Kit think that perhaps Evelyn does see her, that perhaps this affair is not, as she always assumes, some inexplicable lark on Evelyn's part. That maybe she won't be gone forever some morning, on to a new amuse-ment. It makes her shiver.

She occupies herself with taking her false papers out of a drawer and pulling her bicycle away from the wall. 'Will you lock up for me?'

'Of course,' Evelyn says. 'I'll just tidy up here first.'

Kit gives her one last smile as she leaves. Evelyn doesn't tell Kit to stay safe. Kit doesn't tell Evelyn not to worry.

CHAPTER 3

Kit

Max puts the bottle of cognac in her bicycle basket, not asking where Kit got it. She also doesn't ask why Kit says they should take the Porte de Clichy route, just nods and says it's as good as any other.

Kit has taken a few day trips out of the capital during the war, for the very research she told Max about. Women in Romanesque sculpture. There are many interesting churches around Paris. But the truth is, she has all the examples she needs. It's only a matter of making sense of it, of writing the thing. Sometimes Evelyn says that Kit doesn't want to get the monograph done, and maybe she's right. But Kit can't seem to get hold of it, of the idea that she knows is there, connecting all these nameless, wimpled women who have withstood a thousand years of wind and rain.

They ride north towards the Porte de Clichy, where a gate once stood in the old city wall. Kit's legs revel in the movement, and the cool morning breeze calms her face. It's something of a relief that she and Max can't really talk as they bicycle through the streets. What would they say?

Everything used to be natural between the two of them. They were best friends, for as long as Kit can remember. Then came the night Max decided to try to make their friendship into something else, and Kit had to tell her she didn't feel the same. That chilly night in 1940, something broke that Kit fears can never be repaired.

Paris was still free, then. Kit and Max were walking home from Le Monocle, arm in arm. Ivy was back at the flat with a cold, so it was just the two of them, and they'd both had champagne. Kit was laughing so hard it hurt, as Max told stories about all the lesbians of their acquaintance.

When Kit had caught her breath, she said, 'I never imagined it could be like this, back home. I knew I was different, but I had to come to Paris to know that it was all right. That there were so many of us.'

'I knew how it could be, even if there weren't any more of us,' Max said. There was a long pause, just their two sets of footsteps on some quiet side street at two o'clock in the morning. Then Max said, 'You knew it, too.'

'Well, I suppose I had heard stories.'

'You knew it that night of the May Ball. When I asked you to dance with me and you ran away.'

Kit stopped, her face still flushed from laughter and champagne. She felt accused of something, put on the spot, and she didn't know what. 'I only worried we would look childish.'

'Since when have you ever cared about decorum? You used to run around in trousers—'

'So I should have known I was a dangerous woman, is that it?' Kit grinned, tried to turn it back into teasing. But she thought, *It's Max who is dangerous, Max with that look, that could destroy everything.*

'You should have known that I—'

'No, Max. Please.'

There had been hints before. Once, Max had made some joke about noting the way to Kit's heart, when Kit was rapt about an old book. A gallant compliment here and there, when they were getting ready to go out. Kit had just deflected these volleys, disarmed them, pretending not to see them for what they were. She chose to believe that Paris had taught Max how to flirt, and that was all. Max always liked to play with things until they broke, but Kit was not willing to take that chance. She couldn't believe Max would risk everything they had just because she couldn't see a cliff without wanting to drive off it. Loving Max as a friend was all right; nobody would bother them about it, and it would never go wrong. But, if they became lovers, Max would find Kit disappointing, as she found everything disappointing. She would put Kit in the box with all the other clandestine romances that only interested her because they would have made her father rage.

The one thing Kit couldn't understand – the painful mystery she could not solve – was why Max didn't see this herself. Why she insisted on driving off that cliff. Could it be that Max didn't feel as she did? That she could bear the thought of losing Kit to boredom or recriminations or shame?

It seemed so. The moment came, inexorable. The moment when Kit lost Max anyway, despite all her efforts at passive defence. There, at night, on the street.

She can still hear Max saying those rash words. 'I can't do it any more, Kit. I can't pretend I'm not in love with you.'

Max could fall in love as a lark; Kit couldn't. It might be an experiment for Max; it would consume Kit entirely.

So Kit had told Max she was being ridiculous, that she valued her as a friend. Setting things straight, making things clear, every sentence more horrible than the one before until they were walking in silence, their footsteps like gunshots. Back to the flat where Ivy, sniffling and coughing, didn't understand the looks on their faces and felt left out, making everything worse.

Now Max has moved on, to do astonishing things, as Kit always knew she would. She has become the woman she was always going to be: daring, brilliant, glamorous. Kit, bookish, quiet Kit, is now just someone Max used to know, a role she always knew she must occupy one day. And, by pushing Max away that night, Kit kept her own heart safe in the process. But she couldn't save the friendship. It broke in 1940, before the war tore them apart.

Convoys of German soldiers in trucks and tanks pass by, on their way to the front, paying no mind to two women on bicycles. Kit is eager to get out and gone, and feels no nervousness when they encounter the checkpoint, only four years' worth of dull rage.

A pile of sandbags and plywood at the old gate out of the city. A couple of motorcycles. Half a dozen Wehrmacht in uniforms and helmets, some men in grey suits – Gestapo? And a few members of the Milice, the French fascist collaborators. So eager to fight for the Fatherland. How Kit hates the word, in all languages.

The young man checking papers is a *milicien*. Fighting against his own country, although surely he must believe otherwise. He must see De Gaulle's Free French and the Resistance as the traitors, interfering with the march of fascism across Europe, opening the door to Bolshevism, tolerating the continued existence of Jews and everyone else deemed incompatible with the Nazi utopia. The *milicien* is thin, round-shouldered, pointy-faced, his beret incongruously jaunty. But he has a gun and he believes in it, just as he believes women shouldn't smoke or wear trousers. Or, presumably, sleep with other women. His Paris is not her Paris, but his Paris snakes through hers, unavoidable, an ever-shifting scar drawn with sandbags.

Max stops her bicycle in front of him.

'Name?' barks the *milicien*.

'Laure Dieudonné,' Max lies. Her French sounds native in a way that Kit's does not, even after all these years. When Max was a child, she used to spend the summers in France. It always seemed like a terrible punishment to Max, and to Kit and her sisters: an enforced separation. Max always came back to England with presents and stories about how boring and terrible life in the château had been, stories that Kit had known even then were embroidered for the sake of the Sharp sisters, whose summer holidays were spent in chilly Scotland with Aunt Kathleen.

The *milicien* grabs Max's identity card. 'You're going to . . . ?'

'Chambly.'

'Not far. You should have no difficulty in getting back well before nightfall. Visiting family?'

Max turns to Kit. 'We're going to see an old schoolfriend. She moved out there before the war.'

The *milicien*'s glare is hard. 'You all went to school together?'

'Yes.' Kit's mouth is dry as sand. She keeps her answer short, to hide her trace of an accent.

'And the name of this friend?'

The more Kit thinks about how she must not pause, not even for an instant, the more she worries that haste will betray the fact that they rehearsed. 'Marianne Larocque.'

'She's married?'

'Widowed,' says Max, and somehow manages to make it sound like a threat.

The *milicien* puts out his hand impatiently for Kit's identity card, and Kit leans forward over her bicycle basket to give it to him. His fingers on it are busy, flicking the edges, rolling the corners, as though he can feel the lies.

'You're bringing her a gift?' He smirks at the bottle of cognac in Max's basket.

'We thought we might find some vegetables for her in the town market. She's nursing a baby and her milk is drying up.' Max's voice is almost scolding now. 'Her own garden won't be ready for some time. Not ever, if we can't help her.'

It's utterly shameless. The breastfeeding mother. The name 'Marianne', the spirit of France. The whole story is such obvious pap.

But this boy in a uniform wants to be fed nonsense. He wants to believe in Marianne Laroque and her friends with the strong legs pedalling their bicycles, tying their hair up in the garden to make sure the baby gets enough milk. He wants these women to be out there in the sun and dirt, or inside Paris on his arm. Otherwise, they are no good to him at all. And certainly no threat.

He hands back Kit's identity card. 'Bring me back some peas in the pod,' he jokes with an ordinary smile, and it makes Kit cold and sick all over. She nods, not trusting her voice, and stuffs her card back into her coat pocket, and pushes hard on the pedal. Too hard, so her foot slips and the pedal scrapes her calf. The *milicien*'s smile vanishes but Kit doesn't pause. She pedals hard after Max, nearly colliding with her back tyre. They are through the checkpoint. They are out.

About half an hour outside Paris, on a road lined with houses and busy with horse-carts and bicycles, Max stops at a cross-roads. Kit pulls up beside her.

'Another two hours to Chambly, would you say?' Kit says.

'You're hurt,' Max says, pointing to the line of dried blood on Kit's leg. 'Why didn't you say something?'

'Oh, it's nothing, just the pedal. I was nervous. I thought that *milicien* wasn't going to let us through.'

'Ha.' Max kicks the stand on her bicycle, wets her fingers at the neck of her canteen, then squats and wipes the blood off Kit's leg. She does it roughly, hastily. Kit looks down at her curly head, suddenly weirdly grateful for the cut on her leg that's given Max the chance to reach through the new, invisible barrier between them.

Max says, 'The checkpoint was easier than I expected. Better than the one I hit yesterday on the way in. You were right about Porte de Clichy. They're watching the western ways out of the city more, watching for people going to join the Resistance.'

'You came to Paris only yesterday?'

Max shrugs. 'I go in and out. We all had instructions before D-Day, things to do. I had to bring some things into Paris, things that were dropped out in the country. Money, mainly, this time.'

There's so much Kit doesn't understand about Max, even though they've known each other all their lives. She doesn't understand how Max can always be so fearless, so brazen about everything she does. How can someone learn to be like that, in the village of Stoke Damson? It was Max who first told Kit about a fairly chaste affair she'd had at boarding school, with another girl. Max who, with that one late-night story over a bottle of brandy stolen from her father's study, had made things clear to Kit in a way they'd never been clear before. She understood, at last, why she was always thinking about a girl in her own class, why she found teasing about boys slightly irritating. By the time Kit went off to Edinburgh for university she was ready for affairs of her own, chaste and otherwise. It was a secret she and Max shared, and they compared notes and commiserated with every holiday or family visit.

But Max had not been content to keep it a secret. She'd told her father, straight out, that she was in love with a girl.

(By this time, it was a girl in London, named Alice, who had sleek bobbed hair and wore long, straight jumpers. Kit had seen a photograph. She secretly disliked Alice, but she was glad Max was happy.) Mr Yardley had cut off Max's money, written something horrible to Alice's parents, and forbidden Max from seeing her again. Max, of course, took no heed of this, and went haring off back to London to run away with Alice, only to find that Alice was really rather boring.

So Max had found herself a job at a Paris newspaper. And it was only when the war came, when Ivy needed someone to get her out, that Max had gone back to England. By then, of course, she had another reason to leave: she and Kit and the awful night.

Kit would like to ask Max how it was, seeing her father again, whether they are on speaking terms now. She herself has never told her parents about her inclinations, only her sisters. But she managed to create a rift with her own father anyway. She would like to talk to Max about all of it. But it's all tangled up with things she does not want Max to say, with expressions she does not want to see on Max's face.

'I hope we don't encounter Germans,' Kit says. She takes the canteen from Max, takes a sip of the cool water, hands it back. 'On their way to the coast to fight.'

Max screws the cap back on the canteen and returns it to her bicycle basket. She throws her leg over, puts one foot on the pedal. 'We aren't going north,' she says mischievously. 'We aren't going to Chambly. That was just the story. So yes, I think it's very likely we will encounter Germans.' And she cycles off leftwards on to the road that leads to the west.

Dusty roads take them past rustic fences and hedges, the odd farmhouse. Max turns frequently, so they avoid even the tiniest villages. Even so, they pass farm-horses and other bicyclists, and once, proving her right, a convoy of German soldiers' rides past them, stirring up dust and leaving a smell of exhaust in the air. But they pay them no more mind here than they did in the city.

There is so much sameness of landscape that Kit starts imagining something that would break through that horizon. An image in her mind: something like Mont St-Michel breaking out of the sand and water. No, not that – a great rocky crag with a castle on top of it. Perhaps it's a Crusader castle, she imagines. Perhaps something out of Walter Scott. A castle full of the kinds of treasures she has been cataloguing, moving around, keeping out of Nazi hands as much as possible. Or perhaps it's a castle like the one they say Himmler has in Westphalia, already stuffed full of paintings and tapestries that once hung in the homes of Jewish families or country churches.

By the time they stop, Kit has lost all sense of direction, and the sun is in the middle of the sky.

They flop down on the verge under a brambly bank, amid a scattering of yellow-and-white flowers. They each drink from Max's canteen. Max pulls a loaf of heavy bread out of her pack, and tears off a piece for Kit.

Kit is used to being hungry; it fades into a dull, foggy ache throughout her body, for the most part. But today, after bicycling for hours, she is ravenous. Her stomach gurgles loudly with the first bite. Max politely says nothing; once, she would have burst into laughter.

Staring out at the road, Max says. 'Another few hours and we'll reach a safe house, where I might be able to find news of Ivy.'

Kit has not seen a vision of Ivy since she met up with Max, and a sinking feeling comes to her, that she should have stayed in the city after all.

'Stay quiet when we get to the safe house,' Max continues. 'You are not supposed to know anything about this.'

'I *don't* know anything about it.'

'You know enough to get someone killed.'

'Well, I certainly don't have a clue where we are.' There's a low, messy hedge on the far side of the road, and a faint smell of manure in the air. The steady hum of insects seems loud to her ears. 'I hope you do.'

Max says nothing for a while, resting her elbow on her knee and gazing down the road in the direction they came. 'Yes. Navigating these country roads is much more relaxing when I don't have gelignite strapped to my chest, I must say.' She winks, as though it's a joke, the first glimmer of the old Max that Kit has seen today. 'I've been in France for over a year, and working as a courier all that time, so I know many roads within a day's ride of Paris.'

'A year,' Kit says, and whistles. A year in which Max has been in and out of Paris, and she has not come to see Kit in all that time. Of course she hasn't; she has good reasons not to.

'Yes, I've lasted longer than most agents,' says Max, looking down at her hands. 'We never rely on any one person. If I'm captured, the work goes on. I've been lucky. The W/Ts – the wireless operators – they have it worst, if you ask me. Moving from place to place with a suitcase full of evidence, signalling their location to the enemy. We've lost so many of them.'

'And what is Ivy's role?' Kit asks.

Max shakes her head. 'I don't know. I'm not even meant to know that she's here. I just happen to know her code name. If I had to guess, I'd say she has a particular job to do here. Maybe she's off doing it, and it came down to a choice between getting it done and making contact. What do you think?'

Kit knits her brows. 'I have no idea. How could I?'

'When's the last time you had a letter from her? Or from anyone at home?'

'Not for years. At first, the occasional letter got through Vichy territory. I had your two letters, thank you. A letter from Mother all about her volunteer work. And one from Helen telling me that she was going into the Women's Land Army.'

She doesn't mention the odd letter from her father about the tapestry.

'Ah, yes. So I suppose you don't know. Helen had a baby. She's living back at home with your parents now.'

'A baby!' Kit is astonished. 'Is it – it's George's, of course?'

'Yes. They plan to marry, when he comes home. A baby girl. I went off to training just after she was born, so I haven't met her, but Helen came through the birth without any trouble.'

'Goodness, Max. What else do you know? Mother's letter only said that Rose was going to be a typist and Ivy was driving some sort of military vehicle, which I found astounding. If only I'd known.'

'She was driving majors around, based in Sheffield, for a while,' Max murmurs. 'Before she joined the same service I'm with.'

'That was the only letter that mentioned Ivy. Then in '41 there was a letter from Mother through the Red Cross service, saying that Aunt Kathleen had died. Nothing since.'

She tries, and fails, to keep the tightness out of her voice. She had always been close to Aunt Kathleen, who was crotchety in a way that Kit appreciated. She had once been close to her father, too. It stung that Father hadn't been the one to write about Aunt Kathleen, since she was *his* aunt, really, and great-aunt to the girls, although they never called her that. He couldn't even bring himself to write a few personal lines to Kit, not even about that. Only his excitement about his crackpot theory.

When Kit first went to Edinburgh to attend the university,

she wrote to her father every few days about what her professors were saying, what books she was reading. It felt, at first, as though she had an advantage, being raised by a professor of history at Cambridge.

And he was so interested to hear about her field work on Iron Age settlements. He'd already been working on his unpublished book for several years by then, trying to pull everything he'd learned about the Bayeux Tapestry into a grand theory, something about the power of predictive stories in shaping history. Over the years, their arguing became less amicable, especially during Kit's visits home. But he was no less proud, no less enthusiastic about her work. Or rather, her potential. He asked Kit to write a chapter in his book about the petrospheres she'd excavated in Scotland – strange carved rocks that nobody quite understood. To her father, they were clear evidence of the development of what he called 'the narrative inheritance'. To Kit, they were the work of a single pair of hands, and evidence of a given history in a given time and place. The idea that civilizations all followed the same course was old-fashioned – and even dangerous. She would tell him that nobody thought of culture that way any more, like grades in school; that he was imposing a false and even bigoted narrative on history. He said she just hadn't taken the time to understand his ideas; she said that his ideas sounded no different from what the fascists were peddling. At that, he went red in the face, and they never spoke again. A few brief, polite letters, after she went to Aden, and then even those dried up entirely.

After a long silence, the last one from him came in 1941, the last letter from any of her family. Telling her that he'd decided that parts of the tapestry must have been made before 1066; that it was a tool for prediction, not a record of events as they were. A tool for prediction! It was ridiculous on the face of it. Surely not even Rupert Sharp, so eager to make sweeping connections, would come up with a theory that would get him laughed out of Cambridge?

Kit read that letter over and over again, painfully touched that he would feel compelled to share his theory with her, as if with a colleague. She felt pity for him, and, on the third or fourth read of the letter, started to see how it had taken shape in his mind. His fascination with Aelfgyva, the way her story broke off mid-sentence, as if the embroiderer was uncertain what, exactly, the woman did.

Kit kept that letter, in her dresser drawer. She sat down to respond to it, more than once. She could never think of what to say. He never wrote again.

Max, with her hands in her pockets, is staring not at Kit but out at the road. 'Did you hear anything? Just now?'

'Hmm? No, I don't think so. Wait, yes. A car, maybe.'

'Yes, that's what I mean. A car. I think it stopped. It hasn't passed us.'

'It must have turned. Or reached its destination.'

'Probably. But it's time we were going.'

It is more exhausting to start up again, but Kit relishes the fatigue. She can feel the numbness of the last few years dissipating with every push of her legs. Her eyes sting with tears that the wind dries immediately. Hope, fear and love are creeping into her like pins and needles. From time to time, they hear a distant rumble: the fighting on the coast.

The sun is low, gilding the world. She keeps catching distant glimpses of something on the horizon that isn't there: the castle she kept imagining on the ride, earlier. A great block of stone on a hill. She's building castles in the sky, as her mother would say.

CHAPTER 4

Helen

Helen is trying to arrange a family picnic, and no one is co-operating. Perhaps she's restless because of the news of the landings in Normandy, the Allied push into France. Such a great relief to see it happening at last, and so terrifying, thinking of Kit in Paris. Helen had thought at least Mother would be enthusiastic about the picnic idea – it's a lovely June day and she is always evangelizing about the benefits of fresh air – but Mother is in her happily frantic mode, preparing for the afternoon's knitting and sewing circle. She has covered the kitchen table with supplies: piles of wool unpicked from various unwanted garments, tins of buttons, baskets of thread.

'I think it's important to get Father out of the house,' Helen argues.

Mother starts winding some wool into a ball. 'Oh, he's perfectly happy puttering in his study. A nice break for him to have a day to himself – he's been so miserable teaching those cadets.'

'Yes, but all the more reason he should be out in the sunshine, playing with his granddaughter.'

Mother smiles at her affectionately, then glances over to the floor where baby Celia is crawling with determination towards a spider. Helen darts over and plucks the spider away, and Celia's face crumples. She's in Helen's arms before the wailing starts, but the wailing is loud and sustained nonetheless.

'Why don't you take her for a walk yourself?' Mother suggests.

'I just think it would be good for all of us to get out,' Helen says, bouncing the baby to soothe her. 'The boys will come home hungry from wherever they're playing soon enough. Instead of eating lunch here, we can all enjoy the day.'

The Sharp family home has never been a quiet one. Before the war, there was Helen and her three younger sisters. But she's the only one left; Kit has been gone for years, off in occupied France, which Helen doesn't like to think about. Ivy's driving army vehicles at a signalling facility somewhere in England, and Rose is typing in Wolverton. Helen was never good at driving or typing, so she went off to be a Land Girl, and she'd enjoyed it. But when she got pregnant she came home, to raise her baby in a house without a husband. A loving house all the same; a busy house, with the two refugee boys from Germany, and Mother and Father.

'Another day,' Mother says. 'I promise. When things aren't so busy, we'll have a lovely picnic.'

'I think Father should get out of the house. Today.'

The baby stops crying, as if she and everything else in the house is silent, listening, watching, wondering what is wrong with Helen. This is not a question Helen knows the answer to, any more than she knows why she feels it is so important that Father not be in the house today.

Helen puts the baby down, and rubs her temple.

'Are the headaches back?' Mother asks gently.

'A little. I suppose I'm out of sorts.'

'If you're worried about your father, why don't you take him a cup of tea and check in on him? He'll like that. Celia can help me wind the wool, can't you, darling? Yes, you clever thing, but don't put it in your mouth.'

Even after her father calls out a 'Yes?' to her knock, Helen opens the door to his little study gingerly. Inside, it's dim; there are no windows and he's only turned on one table lamp.

This room was always a little terrifying to her, as a child. Bookshelves line the bottom halves of the walls; over them hang framed sections of photographs of the Bayeux Tapestry, and the figures seem to stare down at her, to move in the lamplight.

She's not a little girl any more, and not afraid of this room. But conversation has been delicate with Father ever since she told him that she was going to have a child. George's child; and George was already gone to the front, and no chance to be married. A kindly gossip in the village put it around that George and Helen had married in secret, before he shipped out, but Helen and her parents know the truth. She can still see, in her mind's eye, her father's face, perfectly still but getting more purple with each passing second. He never said a word more about it after that day. He is an affectionate grandfather, though.

Now, his face when he looks up at her is kindly, but tired and worn. She supposes that must be why he's been on her mind, why she's had an urge all morning to get him out into the sunshine. It can't be good for him, sitting in this dim, stuffy room with his books and papers when he isn't at the university, with other books and papers.

He has a paper now, in fact, on his lap. He's holding it with his left hand and stroking it with his right, as if there's some texture on it.

'Am I interrupting your work?' Helen asks, uncertainly.

He looks down at the paper. 'What? Oh, no, I was just reading this letter from Ivy. The one that came a few days ago.'

'There wasn't much to read, was there?'

'No.' He sighs. 'As usual, only a few lines, saying that she's well, that she is busy at the signalling facility, that she misses us. Somehow it has made me worry about her. I always did worry about Ivy the most of any of you. It's odd, isn't it, given that Rose was always so shy and delicate? But Rose knows who she is. Still waters run deep, I suppose. And as for you, well, you have such a head on your shoulders. I knew you'd be all right.'

She doesn't give him time to realize the irony of his words, to remember that she is the one who had to come home in disgrace – or for the silence to fill with unspoken mentions of Kit. She rushes in with, 'Sometimes I wish I didn't have this particular head.'

'Is it aching again? I wonder whether the doctor can give you anything better.'

She shakes her head, which makes it reverberate. 'I just need a good night's sleep. I had the most terrible dream last night – about Ivy, as a matter of fact.'

'About Ivy? Do you remember anything about it?'

She hesitates. It's there, in the back of her mind, but she doesn't want to remember it. 'Just something horrid.'

'It's become worse for you the last few years, hasn't it? These dreams, these headaches?'

'It's the war. All our terrible imaginings won't leave us alone, even when we sleep.'

'Yes, very likely.' He looks at his desk, at the piles of papers there. 'I don't suppose you had any occasion to, well, to touch anything in here? Even some time ago? Dusting, or looking for a stamp?'

43

It's an odd turn. 'Are you missing something? I could ask Mother and the boys. I haven't been in here without you since – well, ever, really.' She laughs nervously.

'No, I'm not missing anything. I am sorry, Helen.'

She isn't sure what to make of this. She and her father never seem to be in the same conversation at the same time.

'I think an hour in the sunshine would do us all some good,' she says brightly. 'I've come to invite you to a picnic with the children. Mother's busy preparing for the sewing circle, but she'll be grateful to have us all out from underfoot. And it will make it so much more special for the children if you're there.'

There it is, that sense of terrible urgency, that she has to get Father out now, that if they stay in this oppressive room a minute longer . . . what? She can't finish the thought, but every muscle in her body wants to pull him towards her. And he is just sitting there, looking at her quizzically, holding a letter from another of his daughters, a daughter who no doubt would be as surprised as any of them to learn her father was thinking of her at all.

Voices from the kitchen. Mother's, and a man's.

Father says, 'Ah. That sounds like Gregory.'

That breaks the spell at last, and pulls Father out of his chair, out of his room, and into the sunlit kitchen. As always when he gets up after sitting for a long time, his slight limp, a legacy of the last war, is more pronounced.

He was right. Gregory Yardley, who lives across the stream, is standing just inside the door with his hat in his hand. Helen stands up straight and picks up Celia, noticing as she does so that her daughter's little dress is stained. She was not thinking about company, much less about the wealthy Member of Parliament who has always made her feel dowdy and silly. She never felt comfortable going over there to play with his daughter Max, not unless at least one of her sisters was with her. That was why Kit and Max grew up best friends, climbing trees and imagining secret passageways in some fairyland of their own, and Helen was always more likely to go off with some group of girls from the village. And, eventually, with George.

Father is on friendly terms with Mr Yardley, especially in the last few years. They sometimes drink scotch or tea together in the sitting room in the evenings, although it's more usual for Father to go to the Yardley house.

And it isn't usual at all for Mr Yardley simply to turn up in their kitchen on a Thursday morning.

His expression is unusual, too: grave and almost stern. From the moment Helen notices this, she keeps bouncing the baby, her movements artificial and out of rhythm, waiting for the news to come. Someone is dead; George, could it be George? No, surely Mr Yardley would not be the one to bring that news. Some terrible development in the war. Invasion of Britain, at last.

'Rupert, do you have a moment?' Mr Yardley says mildly.

Father nods and the two of them go into the sitting room. Mother puts the kettle on, then returns to packing a sewing basket, her mouth taut and her expression uninviting. She's worried too, but neither of them can hear anything through the sitting-room door. They'll have to wait and see what Father chooses to tell them, or what they read in the news-papers themselves.

Celia starts to fuss, and Helen takes her up to her bedroom, so that she won't disturb the men. It's only as she's halfway up the stairs that she remembers that the fireplace in her parents' room is a wonderful spot to overhear what's happening in the sitting room below. She pushes open the door to that room guiltily, putting Celia down to crawl so that it might look as if Helen's followed her wayward daughter in, if she's caught.

The men's voices drift up.

Mr Yardley sounds more forthright and terse than she's ever heard him. Perhaps men sound different when they talk to each other, without women around. He is talking about something that Father wrote: a letter.

'I told you I had it all in hand,' Mr Yardley says. 'I told you that it would be more dangerous this time. Once is a coincidence. Twice? I can't make a case for you, Rupert.'

Father replies, 'I couldn't just sit on this information. I see them, Gregory. I see them now, in my mind, the stars falling – I thought they were comets, from the tapestry – but you know as well as I do—'

Mr Yardley's voice is higher when he breaks in, almost angry. 'I know nothing that I can't prove. And you would do well to adopt that position. If not for your own sake, then for your daughters'.'

There's a long pause. Helen doesn't want to know who Father's written to, and she doesn't want to know what it's about. She only wants to know what Mr Yardley is warning him about. She realizes she's biting her nails – an old habit. She tucks her hand under her armpit and looks out of the window. On the road from the village, two men in military uniforms are walking towards the house.

There is Father's voice, at last, quiet. His voice always goes quieter when he's angry. 'What do my daughters have to do with it?'

Another pause, shorter this time. 'The whole house will be under suspicion, Rupert. You've invited scrutiny. That part, I think, I can help you with. I'll look after Dorothy and the girls, direct attention elsewhere. I'll do my best.'

'I'm happy to answer any questions. They'll find no evidence that I've done anything wrong.'

If only Kit were here. Someone brighter than Helen, someone who could understand all this and would know what to do.

There's a knock on the front door, and Helen nearly jumps out of her skin. She goes to the bedroom window, scooping Celia up. The two men stand there. One uniform looks like Royal Air Force, and she doesn't recognize the other. She knows that they have come to take her father away.

She watches him walking away from the house, not turning back, and she has the feeling she's seen this before.

CHAPTER 5

Kit

The afternoon is waning when Max and Kit turn on to a farm track, where the trees block the rays of sun, mercifully. Max pulls over to a weathered fence where a teenage boy is leaning, watching them. He wears a wide-brimmed hat and his clothes hang loosely. Behind him, a ramshackle barn, crowned with a weathercock in the shape of a fleur-de-lys. Beyond, a small farmhouse.

'Good evening,' the boy says in French, speaking to Max but peering warily at Kit.

'This is a friend,' Max says. She wipes the back of her hand across her forehead, leaving a dirty streak. 'We'd like to stay here for the night.'

'Then you'd better come and see Lucienne.'

Lucienne, it turns out, is a wiry middle-aged woman in straight-legged trousers with short, gunmetal-grey hair. She bears no family resemblance to the boy, Jean-Pierre, who deposits Kit and Max in the parlour of the farmhouse and leaves again.

White plaster walls, chairs of various kinds and colours, and a low table. It smells, strongly and incongruously, of fresh bread. Why should that be incongruous? There is something odd or unsettling about the place, Kit thinks. Something that reminds her yet again of the empty eyes of the stone nun's head. Why does she keep thinking about that piece, out of all the bits of stone, wood and canvas that she helped to move, in the days before the Germans came?

In the Louvre, Kit found her calling at last. She didn't want to pull things out of the earth and send them to distant museums. She wanted to solve mysteries that were hiding in plain sight, all the evidence laid out for the world, if only someone could come along and see it properly. Mysteries like the identity of Aelfgyva in the Bayeux Tapestry. She wanted to do what the art historian Meyer Schapiro had done, in bringing all sorts of evidence to bear in an analysis of a medieval sculpture, demonstrating its significance, seeing it in a way that no one ever had before. Or to gaze at the markings on the Rosetta Stone as Young and Champollion had done a century ago, and resolve it into language.

But she has not been able to make sense of her own small research, not in all these years of war, when she has had little else to do in her empty museum. She can't see the shape of the thing properly when she looks right at it; she only gets a tantalising sense of it, sometimes, and doesn't feel clever enough to catch that and write it down. Just as she isn't clever enough to make sense of why she thought she saw Ivy in Paris, and where she might be now.

Kit glances across the hall into another sitting room, where she realizes with a start that a man is lying on a sofa, looking at them. His head is bandaged.

'Stop disturbing him!' Lucienne barks, as if Kit looking at him were a disturbance. She leads them into the kitchen, and puts two plates of smoked herring and farm bread on to a table and, most wonderful of all, a dish of raspberries. Lucienne has keen eyes and red knuckles. She looks as though she has done a lot of washing-up in her life.

Kit sits down and begins to eat, hungrily. The smell of baking bread has woken up her stomach. But Max takes Lucienne aside and they talk in low voices, Lucienne glancing at Kit from time to time.

Then Kit realizes what is strange: the house has nothing personal in it. No needlepoint or family photographs on the walls, no treasured ugly vases or china dogs, no piano, no old lace or linen. She peers into the parlour through which they entered. Other than the chairs, there is a clock on the mantel, and a radio on the table. This is not a place where people live; it is a place they pass through.

And a place where Max was probably not supposed to bring a stranger.

Out in the garden, a dog barks, startling Kit, who hadn't seen it when they came in.

'Our mutual friend here tells me you're working on our side and you need help,' Lucienne says to Kit, accusingly.

Before Kit can come up with an answer to this extraordinary statement, Max breaks in, and says, 'We're looking for the same person. Someone code-named Juliet.'

'I don't know any Juliet,' Lucienne says.

Max continues, 'Neither do I. That's the problem. But we should.'

'What makes you say that?'

'You're not going to like it,' Max says.

Lucienne folds her arms and waits.

Max explains, 'After the rest of the Mechanic circuit was taken, their W/T managed to get to Paris, and left a note in a letterbox, in case the Gestapo got him next. Which they did.'

'It is against protocol to create points of contact between

networks, particularly contaminated ones,' Lucienne snaps.

'Which is why I didn't check that letterbox for weeks after they were caught. But I had reason to check it yesterday, and found his note. One of the things he passed along was that London had told Mechanic to expect an agent named Juliet.' Lucienne looks at Kit, and Max adds, 'She knows Juliet.'

'Then she knows more than I do,' Lucienne replies brusquely.

'Juliet must have been trying to contact Mechanic,' Max pushes on. 'But it was broken just before she dropped. If she couldn't make contact with them, where would she go?'

Lucienne raises an eyebrow. 'You're following a lead left for us by a member of a circuit that we know was compromised? You know better than that. Bad enough that London keeps ignoring the signs when W/Ts get captured, keeps sending more agents directly into Nazi hands. Waste after waste after waste. Even if this particular W/T were still safe, even if this came direct from London, London is easily fooled. Whatever information you think you have, I would question it. It sounds to me as if the Gestapo are trying to set us up to accept a spy.'

She looks at Kit, again, in a way that makes Kit wonder about the odds that she'll let her leave the house alive.

Outside, the dog barks again, loudly enough that Kit jumps. But nobody makes a move to silence it. The soldier in the next room groans, and Lucienne straightens her posture, as though remembering her many duties.

'You will stay here tonight, and make yourselves useful. It'll be dark soon. Have a wash. Tomorrow I'll tell our W/T to ask London about Juliet in our next schedule. We'll have to wait for a response in a later communication. But maybe they'll be able to tell us something.'

'Thank you,' Max says, and Kit echoes her, feeling useless and ignorant.

'Just remember,' Lucienne says gruffly, 'even if this agent was dropped, even if it's not just a Gestapo joke, the most likely reason we have not heard from her is that she's dead. People die and go missing every day, and we have enough work to do.'

They spend the evening helping Lucienne bake. She's making a dozen loaves, in batches in the single oven, so that she can put explosives in three of them. The basket of bread will be delivered to a German factory tomorrow.

Kit's job is to knead, shape and punch. They don't speak much during this work. Neither Kit nor Max talks about their next steps; they wait until they're alone. Over and over, Kit thinks about Ivy, about all the possibilities. Kit has always been a person who takes comfort in planning for everything, including for the worst. If Ivy is dead, Kit must confirm that, and bring her body home if she can. She must save her parents, and her sisters Helen and Rose, from that hideous uncertainty. If Ivy is hurt, or captured, then Kit must get help to her, as soon as possible. The heavy curtains at the dark windows seem to mock her: night-time, creating delay. Tomorrow there might be news from London, or some other clue, and they can be on their way to wherever Ivy is.

And if Ivy is perfectly well and just going about her business somewhere, Kit will berate her, and laugh, and hold her close.

Kit doesn't think through the possible explanations that might explain the visions back in Paris. She's already been over those, and she doesn't like any of them. She doesn't trust the easiest answers: that she was tired and anxious; that she had some clue she did not notice with her conscious mind. The other answers terrify her, because there is no planning for those. If the vision was a ghost, then it means not only that Ivy is dead but that reality is not to be trusted.

If it was a hallucination, it means Kit's *mind* is not to be trusted.

There – she has thought about it after all. Uselessly. She looks down at her hands, as if there is some comfort to be found there.

When the loaves are all baked and cooled, Lucienne uses a thin file to make holes in them, and carefully puts sticks of something terrible into the holes. Max explains that a factory worker on the side of the Resistance will conceal the explosives inside the factory during the day, then set the fuses after hours once everything is in place.

Lucienne pours everyone a sip of wine and they make small talk for a few minutes. The dog is still barking, on and off, and Kit is relieved when Max tells her to follow her up a narrow flight of stairs to where they'll sleep.

It is a small room, with two narrow beds, each with a different quilt. Max throws her shoulder bag on one bed, as if automatically. Of course: she must sleep here, at least some of the time. But there's nothing here that betrays that fact. An old dresser in the corner doubles as a washstand, holding a white pitcher and basin with a long brown crack in it. The narrow window between the beds is covered with yellowed lace curtains.

Max pulls two pairs of pyjamas out of the top drawer of the dresser, and tosses one set to Kit, then goes into another room to change. It's an oddly intimate thing, wearing Max's pyjamas, Kit thinks, and then realizes that these probably belonged to someone else and were left behind, or they're the spare set that belongs to the house. She is probably not the only person to turn up here with nothing to sleep in but their clothes. She hadn't packed anything, since their story was that they'd return to Paris the same day they left.

The blue pyjama trousers and shirt are old, and the cotton is worn soft. There's a spot on the cuff so thin it's nearly a small hole, and the hems have been taken up, so that, when Kit pulls them on, they're a bit too short.

Max comes back in pale orange pyjamas just as Kit is rearranging her hair in a loose plait for the night. She hands Kit a sliver of soap and toothbrushes and toothpaste. Kit arranges everything on the washstand, absently.

'Kit, I'm not going to give up on Ivy,' Max says, flopping on her bed with one knee bent and the other leg crossed over it. Her pyjamas are the right length for her; the hem of the crossed leg rises a little to reveal her trim ankle. 'You do know that, don't you? I have to put my own war work first – of course I do, especially right now, when everything depends on us – but I will keep asking, keep looking. No matter what we hear tomorrow, or what we don't.'

'You don't sound as if you have much hope we'll hear anything.'

Max hesitates. 'I don't think London is likely to know what happened to Ivy. If she had been able to contact them, she'd also have been able to contact one of the networks here, and I'd probably have heard her name by now. Or I would have heard about someone new, someone who might be her. Despite the protocol Lucienne chastised me about, a lot of information changes hands, especially among couriers. It has to.'

Vertigo overtakes Kit out of nowhere. She grabs on to the dresser so hard that the basin rocks. Turning her gaze towards the window, she is suddenly convinced that if she goes and pulls that lace curtain aside, peers into the blackness, she'll find that she's not in the second storey of a farmhouse but instead in the turret of a castle, atop a craggy hillside, and that she will see not the void of a blackout but the lights of a town laid out around the castle. What is wrong with her? Perhaps it's just her imagination, reacting to the shock of the last twenty-four hours. She's taking refuge in the parts of her mind that can't be occupied: the medieval places in her books and photographs.

'I should have brought up a snack,' Max says.

'You and your snacks,' Kit murmurs, grateful to be distracted.

'It's not my fault I can eat so much. Do you remember that enormous leg of lamb I cooked, in Paris? Whose birthday was it? I don't even remember.'

Kit turns from the dresser, wiping her hands on the little brown towel. Max looks concerned; she thinks they've reached a dead end, that they won't find Ivy, and she's trying to take Kit's mind off of it. She's wishing she hadn't involved Kit in this, wishing that she'd done her the mercy of letting her find out that her sister is dead through a telegram and a moment of private grief. Kit understands all of this; she knows Max. She knows how Max curses herself.

She wants to say that she doesn't blame Max at all; that it is so much better to face this with her, and to be doing something. To be trying.

Instead, she says, 'I remember we came back from Le Monocle to find you drunker than we were. But the lamb was delicious. I liked the mint sauce.' Kit pauses. 'I don't bother cooking much, with just me in the flat, and food so short, not to mention the electricity and gas. I keep hats in the oven now.'

Max sighs and throws one arm over her forehead. 'The first thing I will do, after the war is over, is hold a ridiculous party. I miss that more than anything, I think. What about you? What will you do, when you can do *anything*?'

Kit imagines walking into the Louvre and seeing it full of art and objects again. Walking into the national library to find it full of books. She wants any person to be able to walk into any institution of culture and history and be surrounded only by wonder, not by questions about the official suitability of the people or the books or the art. But she doesn't want to talk about any of that, because it makes her angry, not happy.

How wonderful it would be to pack in around the wobbly table at the back of Le Monocle and settle in for a brandy and an argument. But if Le Monocle reopened, it would not be the same. No one would feel safe, and every corner would be haunted by the dead and the treasonous.

When else had Kit been happy? A quiet morning in the old house with her sisters – but that thought is not possible now either.

She wants to see Ivy, but that may require a greater miracle than the end of the war.

'I'll come to your ridiculous party, of course,' Kit says at last, and throws the hand towel playfully at Max.

'Yes,' Max says, holding the towel and looking down at it as if it's somehow revelatory, her face serious.

Then her eyes gaze up at Kit, with the same expression that scared Kit down to her marrow four years ago. Desperate, unflinching, serious in a way that Max is never serious. All of the usual animation in her face stripped away, to something so intense it ought to be illegal.

A bomb resounds in the distance, then another, like thunder. It shakes Kit out of the memory of the night she turned Max down, and, mercifully, shakes the dangerous look out of Max's eyes.

It doesn't sound very far away. In the city Kit felt buried alive; here, she feels exposed.

The urge to look out, to see the world from her castle turret, overwhelms her. Like scratching an itch, she takes a few steps to the window and pulls the lace aside. The night is not as fully dark as she'd thought; the sky is still purple, the June sun not quite finished with the world yet. And of course she is not in a castle, and there are no town lights below. Just an old barn, and overgrown fields.

'Kit,' Max says, in an urgent tone.

She says something after that, but Kit is barely listening. She is looking at the figure standing on the grass below. A woman in white, just visible in the near-darkness. Standing and staring up at the window.

Kit presses her face to the glass to get a better look, but she knows in her gut. There's no mistaking her, not this time.

'She's outside now,' she whispers.

'Who?' Max stands up.

'Ivy,' Kit says, grabbing her yellow cardigan from where she'd thrown it on the bed, and bursting out of the bedroom door.

Kit is crying already, before she even gets to the empty patch of ground where Ivy is not standing, of course. There is no one here. Just that damn dog, wherever it is, tied up probably. Barking away now, at the sight of Kit running into the night. She crumples, falls to her knees, the weeds scratching her palms. There is no explanation now other than the most terrible one: that Kit has seen some image of her sister that no one else can see.

Max is there, putting an arm around her. 'What is it?'

'Ivy,' Kit says, choking on her sobs. 'Ivy was here. I saw her, Max. I really did.'

A bright light falls over them, making them both flinch and shield their eyes, but it's only Lucienne with a torch, telling them to come in, foolish girls, they'll catch their deaths.

CHAPTER 6

Kit

Lucienne pours brandy into cups of cocoa and they all sit around the scuffed kitchen table.

'Now, let's hear it,' she says gruffly.

'It's all right,' Kit says, her tears dry now. 'It's nothing. I apologize for alarming you.'

Lucienne just stares at her for a moment. Then she says, 'I have to know everything that happens in this house. Surely you see that. You might as well talk about it here with me, rather than upstairs. The walls in this house are thin. It's why I never give couples the room I gave the two of you. It's next to mine.'

Kit's face goes hot. 'It's really nothing. I thought I saw something outside, and rushed out.'

'What? What did you see? Why were you crying?'

Kit rides a pendulum between two horrific possibilities: that the image she saw existed outside her mind, but came and went on the wind; or, that what she saw did not exist in the world outside her mind at all. She is clasping her hands so tightly that her knuckles are white.

Lucienne says, quietly but not softly, 'I've sent Jean-Pierre out beating the bushes for stray bits of parachute or spies in the middle of the night, so you will please tell me exactly what you saw.'

Kit raises her eyes to meet her gaze. 'It wasn't a parachute or a spy. I saw her very clearly, but then she was gone. My sister.'

Lucienne leans back, her expression calculating. She glances at Max, to confirm that the sister is the missing agent. Then she shrugs. 'I suppose that's natural. You're worried about her, and in a strange place. I wouldn't discount the bit of parachute, or something of that kind. Even an animal. You may have seen something, and for a moment your mind—'

Max is shaking her head. 'But Lucienne, she saw her in Paris, too. Before I spoke to her. Before she even knew that her sister was in trouble. Before she even knew she was an agent. It's damned odd, don't you think?'

Lucienne is looking into the distance as Max talks; she's thinking.

Kit wishes Max would just let it go. There's no point in talking about it. Either of the two possibilities is useless to help Ivy, surely. If Kit is imagining it, that's nothing to do with anyone. And if there is something out there, something that looks like her sister – but that's ridiculous.

'It was all in my head, I'm sure, but it seemed so real,' she says. 'I have always been someone who imagines things. A bad habit I've tried to curb, since I was a child. I only looked out of the window in the first place because . . . '

'Because of what?' Max presses her.

'Because I kept imagining I was in a castle,' she says with a nervous chuckle. 'I had been daydreaming about it during the ride yesterday, from a distance, and I suppose it was still in my mind. Very silly.'

But neither Lucienne nor Max is smiling. Lucienne gets up, her chair scraping on the floor. Kit winces, thinking it will wake the wounded soldier in the parlour. Then the damned dog starts barking again, which will definitely rouse the soldier.

Lucienne walks to a kitchen drawer and pulls out a scrap of paper and a pencil stub. She puts both on the table in front of Kit. 'Draw your castle,' she commands.

'What?'

She taps the paper. 'I want to see what this castle looks like, in your mind.'

Kit's hand is shaking a bit, but it's easy enough to draw: a large cube, with a smaller cube beside it, and then a large round turret to the side, the whole thing on top of a hill. She thinks for a moment, then adds a wall leading away from the turret. Really, it looks like a child's conception of a castle. She pushes it towards Lucienne.

'There. Is this meant to clear it from my head?' What relief that would be: a clear head.

Max is looking at it over Lucienne's shoulder. 'I feel I've seen this.'

'That's because it looks like every castle in every storybook,' Kit retorts.

'It's the castle of William the Conqueror.' Lucienne looks back at Kit. 'In Falaise. Have you been there?'

Kit shakes her head. 'I've seen paintings and photographs of it. You're right, but really, I think it's just what the concept of a castle is in my mind, that's all. It looks like a sandcastle as much as anything.'

'No, it doesn't,' Max objects. 'You always put four turrets on a sandcastle, one on each corner. Not just a single turret.'

'You're suggesting I'm seeing some sort of vision connected with Ivy? Max, be serious.'

Ignoring her, Max turns to Lucienne. 'Falaise is not too far from here.'

Lucienne's expression is unreadable. 'Yes, it is not too far from here. And yesterday, the Allies bombed it into dust. The boy had a message from one of our people, who lost his whole family. So many are displaced, and being cared for in various places. Of course it's possible your sister was there, but if she's still alive she's probably not there now. Unless you know where to look, you'd be chasing ghosts and putting yourselves in danger.'

Kit nods, her mouth tight, trying not to cry. 'The whole thing is ridiculous. I clearly imagined it.'

Lucienne peers at her in a way that makes her uncomfortable. 'So you keep protesting, but I don't think you believe that. In your heart, you believe you saw your sister, don't you?'

Kit looks at Max.

'Don't look at your friend,' Lucienne snaps. 'She clearly believes you're God, or at least Joan of Arc. You're going to get yourself and others killed if you don't learn to examine *how* you know what you think you know.'

Kit is almost grateful to feel a shiver of resentment, to feel anything other than fear and grief. 'You don't have to lecture me on that, believe me. I am not a superstitious person.'

Lucienne raises an eyebrow. She says, 'Superstition is what happens when we refuse to test our knowledge. If we give priority to our intuition over our information, then we get mistakes like, oh, shall we say, some genius in London deciding a wireless operator's strange behaviour must be caused by atmospheric interference.'

'But sometimes, intuition is simply our subconscious mind at work,' Max bursts out. 'Surely you've seen it: an agent doesn't walk into a trap because of a shadow over the door, or something. Some feeling the agent couldn't put into words.'

'And sometimes it means they're a double agent, and that's

why they can't put it into words,' Lucienne says drily. 'We remember the times we avoided danger, but not the times we didn't. And it's even worse than that,' she adds, her voice strained with emotion. 'If we allow for "knowing" without information, then we accept all forms of bigotry and ignorance. All one has to do, to justify one's hatred, one's violence, is to say, ah, everyone *knows*, *those people* are dangerous to keep around. Isn't that so?'

'That's not fair—' Max begins.

'If the subconscious mind is at work, then that is testable,' Lucienne barks. She leans back and counts on her fingers. 'So what are our possible explanations for an impossible vision? We know it could be an illness of the brain. We know that it could be the subconscious mind, interpreting true facts in a way the conscious mind has not. We know it could be justification for false belief. Is there another possibility? We can't discount anything. We can't afford to dismiss anything; we are fighting for our lives. If knowing is something the brain can do without gathering information through the five senses we have names for, is it just possible that your brain could obtain that knowledge in some other way?'

'A sixth sense,' Kit says, with a heavy feeling in her stomach. 'It's the family superstition.'

A superstition passed down by Aunt Kathleen, who earnestly and wholeheartedly ascribed every strange occurrence to the Second Sight. Father's late aunt was the only one left in her generation of the family. She lived in a little old house in a village just south of Glasgow, and only used to see the family in Stoke Damson at Christmas. In the summers, the family always went up to her house for a fortnight, by train since all four girls and their parents couldn't fit in Father's Morris Minor. He barely used that car, not even to go into work at Cambridge University.

Kit remembers a Saturday in June 1934. Her last summer

in Stoke Damson before she went away to university. Father had been up on the roof, repairing a loose tile, when the sound of a motorcycle broke through the afternoon. Helen ran out, because she was in love with the telegram boy. George Bodley came around the wooded lane on his new motorcycle, wearing his General Post Office uniform. Kit and Mother were in the kitchen, making pressed tongue sandwiches for lunch. And there was Helen, standing at the gate, reading the telegram up to Father.

Then Father came down to lunch, and did not go back up on to the roof. Helen showed Kit the telegram:

AVOID HIGH PLACES STOP DREAMT OF RUPERT
FALLING STOP

It was from Aunt Kathleen, who had no way of knowing her nephew would be up on the roof that day. She was adamant about not having a telephone. The following day, Father hired a man to mend the roof, and was very particular about his safety equipment.

Had he ever told Aunt Kathleen that her intuition had been timely?

Kit hadn't mentioned it to Father or Aunt Kathleen. She was soon spending some weekends at Aunt Kathleen's house, when she was studying at the University of Edinburgh, as she could get to Glasgow by train and then by bus to the village.

The house itself was outside the village, a brisk walk. Aunt Kathleen said it was built in Elizabethan times by their ancestor Malcolm Sharpe, a bookbinder by trade. Malcolm had predicted that the village was going to suffer a terrible fire, right down to the month and year. Nobody had listened to his warnings, so he'd protected himself and his family by moving them to a new house far enough away to avoid any stray spark. But when the village did burn, precisely when he'd said it would, someone had blamed him and taken revenge by trying to burn his new house down. Malcolm had known right away and put it out, but Aunt Kathleen pointed to the scorch marks on the stone walls. The old bookbinding workshop was full of Aunt Kathleen's botanical sketches and baskets full of oddments she'd picked up on her walks: stones with holes in them, dried bundles of flowers, little skulls. There were a few of Malcolm's books, too, with lovely Tudor frontispieces. They were all books about nature; Aunt Kathleen had inherited that interest from him.

Another of Aunt Kathleen's treasures was a seventeenth-century French gold coin, which came with a story. Malcolm had predicted that one day his family would need a hiding place, and so he built it into his house. The knowledge of it was passed down to his children and his grandchildren, along with the location. The children were sworn to secrecy. After a few generations, the location of the hiding spot was lost, but the story was not. Aunt Kathleen's aunt Mary had a dream, as a child, that there was a man hiding in the wall of her bedroom. As Mary's father was a man with a love of history, he dismantled the wall – much to his wife's dismay – and they found an opening and signs that a Jacobite had once hidden there, with the gold he'd brought from allies on the Continent. Aunt Kathleen showed Kit the coin and the hiding spot, complete with graffiti looking forward to the victory of Bonnie Prince Charlie.

Kit did wonder how people with the Second Sight could know they'd need a hiding spot for Jacobites but not know that Bonnie Prince Charlie would not win, but she didn't say that.

She listened to all the stories, and even wrote some of them down in notebooks; she'd always had a recording instinct. She didn't contradict Aunt Kathleen either; her stories were true in the way of stories, not in the way of facts. Her warning to Father had seemed private, somehow. And Kit, who believed it was a coincidence, wasn't sure how to broach it in a way that was both honest and respectful.

There were other coincidences, less dramatic ones. Once, when Aunt Kathleen was visiting, Father mentioned a cousin being dead, only to correct himself a moment later, saying of course, he was still alive, what was he thinking? Later, they learned the cousin had died that day, and to Aunt Kathleen that was firm evidence of the Sight. She compared it to the time her great-grandmother saw her great-grandfather in his winding-sheet, laid out in the parlour, three days before his death. These things ran in the family, she said; perhaps some distant ancestor had been to fairyland and come home with the Gift. When Aunt Kathleen was a girl, people used to come to their house to ask her father for advice about their livestock and her mother for advice about their pregnancies, even though her father was a schoolteacher, and her mother had no midwifery training at all. Her grandmother knew all the town secrets and used to have a quiet chat with any landlord who needed the fear of God put into him. In the old days, Aunt Kathleen said, the power was stronger.

Kit's mother, who was a religious woman, would invariably respond by murmuring 'more things in heaven and earth', and seem to give it no more thought. Whenever she misplaced something, such as her keys or reading glasses, she'd ask her husband or one of her daughters where it might be, and usually their first guess was the right one. Once, Ivy casually guessed at breakfast that Mother had dropped her keys outside in the garden by the hollyhocks, and was correct. This caused Helen to go white, and Kit suspected Ivy of having seen the keys there and pretending to guess, just to cause Helen alarm and get attention for herself. But Mother thanked Ivy soberly and didn't ask how she knew.

Sometimes, Father would tell Kit to trust her instincts in a tone that seemed more portentous than it ought to be – when she didn't want to go to the seaside one year, or when she was uncertain about studying archaeology. In one of his last letters – the brief ones, after they argued – he wrote that he had an odd feeling that she would find useful information for her architectural research in a particular obscure nineteenth-century journal about folk-lore, and she found a paper there on precisely the subject she'd been missing. This was, of course, only the instinct of a historian, but, like the temple she'd found in Aden, it was hard to see exactly what train of thought might have led him there.

Rose absorbed the stories as she absorbed everything about the world, swallowing it whole, accepting whatever anyone told her. Helen hated the stories and would find an excuse to leave the room. Ivy, though, found it fascinating. And all four of the girls accepted it to the extent that they worked it into their games, ordinary games like guessing when floating sticks would pass under bridges, or when the light at a railway crossing would change . . .

'You don't believe it.' Lucienne's expression, turned on her again now, is hard to read.

Of course she doesn't believe it. It's just Aunt Kathleen's conviction and a few ordinary coincidences and funny feel-ings. When they were children, Kit's job was to calm Ivy's nightmares on the nights when Aunt Kathleen told them the stories. Kit's role in the family was to help and protect, to earn a living by her wits, by her reason. Like Father. But she failed to keep anyone safe, and argued with Father, and the best way she found to protect them all from pain was to keep herself far away. Or so she thought. But even that sacrifice wasn't enough.

Kit says, her voice shaky, 'If this is the Second Sight making an appearance all of a sudden, it is clearly not much use, or I would know where to find my sister.'

'Have you tried?' Lucienne asks.

Kit furrows her brow. 'Tried?'

Lucienne shrugs. 'I have told you the reasons why we should distrust a certainty that comes without evidence. So, then, I flip it around. I say, as any woman of science would: find me the evidence. This is, shall we say, a long-time interest of mine.'

Kit closes her eyes and tries to gather herself. She wonders about the life Lucienne led before all this started. So many wasted lives in this war: sculptors, doctors, writers, seamstresses, singers, mothers, daughters and little babies, all snatched from the living world. It has to end, some time, doesn't it? Everyone says the Allied invasion will succeed, although how long that will take or how far it will go, no one knows. The Allies will push and push, slowly and painfully, until there is nothing left to push against, no rubble left to bomb.

What will Lucienne do, if she survives? Somewhere she must have had books; perhaps she still does. She must have had people she cared about. A reason for talking so openly and so desperately tonight with a stranger who could be a spy.

Kit takes a breath, and opens her eyes. 'Then you do believe in it? The Second Sight, the sixth sense, whatever you want to call it?'

'Oh, I believe in all kinds of nonsense. Everything seems like nonsense until you have an explanation for it. I believe information travels invisibly and at great distances, and we can catch it in a little device if we hold a wire up to the sky. I believe that in that sky there are people in flying machines. If my great-grandmother could see our world, she would believe we had found magic. Isn't it possible that something that seems like magic to us now will be science to later generations, who learn to understand it? So go ahead. Try your best to see your sister again. Or just to get a feeling about her. It can't hurt. I won't let you do anything dangerous. You have permission to be foolish. Isn't that what science is?'

Kit looks at Max, who is staring at her so earnestly that Kit shrugs, downs her cooling cocoa with the brandy bite, and focuses her eyes on the yellow-flowered wallpaper.

She thinks about Ivy.

Ivy was always watching, when they were little. Whenever Father would tell a story, the girls would gather around his chair. Helen, on the carpet with her knees bent to one side, her elbow on the coffee table. Kit, draped on the floor in some haphazard way. Rose, sitting in her favourite old chair, leaning forward with her hands clasped on her knees. And Ivy, lying on the braided carpet with her chin in her hands, watching them all. She never seemed to be listening to Father so much as she was watching the scene of everyone else listening to Father.

Or, in the garden, Ivy would be sketching while the others worked. She would stand in the doorway during arguments, and make everything worse with the detached interest she seemed to take.

But it was Ivy who always knew when Kit was miserable. The day that Kit told Father she wasn't going to take the job with his old friend, that she was going away to an excavation in Arabia instead, Ivy found Kit down by the stream with her eyes red, sitting on her favourite rock. The lumpy old boulder that was always warm from the sun. Ivy had known where to find her. And she had known what to say.

There was a dog – no. There was no dog. The dog is here, barking, barking incessantly.

'Can't you get that boy to do something about the dog?'

Kit asks, frustrated. She focuses on Lucienne again. 'It must be almost midnight. If it's a guard dog, it's doing a horrible job. If it barks at every leaf, how will you know if the Gestapo come?'

Lucienne and Max look at each other.

Lucienne says, 'What dog?'

Kit pulls the thin blanket over her head, acutely aware of Max in the other bed, not sleeping either, and wondering all the same things. An arm's length away. Like Parliament, with the benches two swords' lengths apart – although, when Father had told her that story, he'd also told her he suspected it was invented after the fact. Father was always so scrupulous about evidence and reason. Surely he couldn't really have believed all those old family stories.

If Aunt Kathleen were still alive, she'd no doubt assign some great significance to the visions Kit is seeing of Ivy, to the dog she heard barking, to the image of the castle at Falaise.

But in so many of Aunt Kathleen's stories, visions of loved ones meant the loved one was dead.

Kit shivers under the blanket. Nothing can be done until tomorrow, Lucienne says. She will ask about Falaise, and she will ask London for news. At least, now, Lucienne seems to be interested in the problem of Ivy.

A sound like castanets from outside. At first Kit thinks it is the war. But it is rain, growing louder, and a clap of thunder. If Ivy is alive, she is out there somewhere, hurt or captured. It is too awful. Kit doesn't think she will ever sleep.

But she must do, because she wakes some time later, in the murkiest depth of the now quiet and moonless night, hearing voices downstairs, loud male voices, speaking French with a German accent.

PART 2

1940 TO 1944

CHAPTER 7

Ivy

How frustrated Ivy felt in 1940, coming home from Paris before it could work a transformation on her. Not sophisticated or worldly but the same old Ivy, a failure in every way. She could not rid herself of the feeling that she had used up her life's one visit to the wide world, while Kit had somehow found a way to make the wide world her home. Kit had her research and her friends and had made someone fall in love with her, without even trying. Ivy had minor affairs and admirers but, at the end of the day, she always felt like someone's younger sister: naive, round-cheeked, patronized, tolerated.

Max took her home like luggage. That long journey to Nantes, walking most of the way, with half of Paris walking with them. They were both sick on the crossing, on a cargo ship. Ivy asked Max about Kit, several times on the way home, but Max didn't ever want to talk about it. And then Max deposited Ivy at her family home in Stoke Damson, where her father came running – imagine Mr Yardley, running! – over the little bridge to wrap his daughter in his arms, to Max's evident discombobulation.

Though Ivy had not changed during her sojourn in Paris, England had. There were sirens every day, and a bomb shelter in the garden. The bombs killed people in Cambridge, and for the first time in their lives Helen, Rose and Ivy lost all sense of resentment at living so far outside the city. Even their little village was shadowed by passing aircraft, and the local boys cheered the Spitfires.

She'd returned to a family in which everyone seemed to have something important to do. Mother was organizing placements for children: first the refugee children from Germany, then the evacuees from London. And Father was busier than ever at the university, since many of the undergraduates were too young to be called up, but many faculty were called away to war work of various kinds.

Even Rose, who had always had a terror of leaving home, said she might try to work as a typist for some branch of the military. Helen had failed her typing class, and Ivy never bothered to take one. But they would have to do something.

The order for women to join up would not come until December of 1941, but everyone knew it was coming, and it seemed better to get ahead of it and have some choice in the matter. Besides, Ivy didn't like to feel useless, and she didn't like the idea of hanging around at home helping Mother with her tedious committee meetings. Her first attempt to go out and make something of herself had failed; maybe the war would give her another.

But what would she join? One of the auxiliary military services? Which one, and to do what? There were so many tasks required, from packing parachutes to cooking. Her only skill was painting, and she hadn't done that in years.

Helen joined the Women's Land Army, and for about a day Ivy considered doing the same. They would billet her on a farm or in a timber camp, maybe even the same farm as Helen. Ivy didn't mind hard work. She didn't even mind the ugly uniform.

But she was terrified of cows. Always had been. And, once you joined the Land Army, could they send you somewhere with cows at a moment's notice? She thought they probably could.

And so, for that secret shallow reason, Ivy applied for the First Aid Nursing Yeomanry.

There was another secret shallow reason, which was that she had an impression that the best sorts of girls, girls of good family and pragmatic ambition, would join the FANY. Max had joined it, after all, and Max was the daughter of a wealthy member of Parliament. It might be a place to make good connections. Paris had, indeed, not changed her. She was still a schoolgirl trying desperately to fit in somewhere. She knew that about herself, though she hated that it was true.

She had vaguely hoped to drive ambulances, but instead she was posted to Sheffield and drove military men around the surrounding area, to various meetings and hotels. She was lonely and miserable.

In the spring of 1941, she had a letter from Mother saying that Aunt Kathleen had been taken ill, and Father had gone up to Scotland to be with her. At one time it would have been a moment for the family to gather, to comfort each other, to tell old stories and sort photographs.

To occupy herself when she wasn't driving or fending off advances, Ivy made a sketchbook out of scrap paper and amused herself by drawing the various captains and commanders into little cartoons. She showed them to the two girls who were billeted with her, to make them laugh, and they did laugh, but they didn't become her friends.

Those cartoons were the trigger for Ivy to take up painting again. She still had the old oil paints Aunt Kathleen had given her years ago, but that seemed a bother, and she didn't have any canvas, just her cobbled-together sketchbooks. So she bought herself a cheap watercolour set.

If she hadn't gone to Sheffield rather than the farm, she might never have taken up painting again, which made all the difference. But she didn't know that yet.

CHAPTER 8

Rose

By the spring of 1941, Rose was the only Sharp girl still at home. Father was working at the university, teaching cadets as well as the ordinary students who hadn't joined up. Mother was always busy, running to a meeting or going off to convince someone of something. She often took her own refugee charges with her, nine-year-old Karl and six-year-old Kurt. Or she left them with one of the neighbours, most of whom had taken in children too.

As for Rose, she had decided what she would do. She was always good at typing, perhaps because she had so many years of experience playing the piano. All that remained was to put forward her name somewhere, but every day seemed to bring a fresh reason to delay that. Little Kurt caught a cold, then Mother needed help with a letter-writing campaign, and then Father was planning one of his Jesus College gatherings and asked Rose if she would be sure to be home that evening – a pro forma request, she thought, since Rose never went out if she could help it. She said she was happy to help him with the drinks and sandwiches, and keep the boys out of the way.

'And you'll play piano, won't you, as you used to do?'

'If you think anyone will want that.'

'Why wouldn't they? Yardley's coming, and you know how he loves to hear you play.'

Mr Yardley had always been very complimentary about her playing when she was a child, but now that she was twenty-three there was nothing laudable about the fact that she could get through a piece of Bach without mistakes. She was a very ordinary pianist, as she was ordinary in every sense, and she didn't mind that at all. The less that people noticed her, the better. But Father wanted her to play, and playing was the one thing she didn't mind doing around other people. By the third or fourth note, she usually forgot they were there.

Mr Yardley arrived first, saying he had come early on purpose, because he had something for Father.

'Tell me you're not still trying to convince me to read Yeats,' Father said drily, as Rose brought in their drinks. The two men were in their customary chairs in the sitting room.

'Ha, not this time. It's an oddity that I happened across in an auction, and I knew you'd appreciate it.' He pulled a small, framed artwork out of his briefcase, and passed it to Father.

As Rose walked past, she sneaked a glance. It wasn't a piece of art at all, but a square scrap of fabric, perhaps two inches on each side, on a black background, behind glass.

'Is this – it's not from the tapestry, is it?' Father's voice was odd as he held the frame with both hands.

'It is indeed. A Victorian amateur snipped it off and it came down through his family. I've checked the provenance.'

'What terrible instincts they had in those days,' Father said quietly. 'To harm such a thing, out of greed, and call it love.'

After a short silence, Mr Yardley coughed. 'Yes, well, it can't be reattached, more's the pity. There's no embroidery on that but you can see some markings, ink of some kind. Perhaps you'll be able to ascertain what part it came from.'

'I'm sure I will,' Father said, amiably, and handed Rose the frame. 'Will you put this in my study, Rose?'

The frame slipped a little in her hand, and she got a grip on it, but not before it banged against the end table. Smashed glass fell on to the carpet, and Rose went to her hands and knees to pick up the bits.

The precious piece of tapestry lay on the faded carpet among the glass shards. She reached for it, and then stopped, uncertain whether one ought to touch such an artefact or not. As if she would profane it, somehow.

Self-conscious, she turned her hand over and examined her fingers for any cuts from the glass, to make sure she wouldn't stain the tapestry. Father stood over her, then bent down and plucked up the piece of cloth himself.

'I'm so sorry,' she said.

'It's only the frame,' Mr Yardley assured her. 'Nothing that can't be replaced. The cloth itself is all right, isn't it, Rupert?'

Father was holding it in the palm of one hand, staring down at it as if he could read something on it. 'How odd,' he said softly.

'What is it?' Mr Yardley came closer, nearly stepping on a bit of glass Rose had missed.

'Nothing. Just a passing fancy. A sense of connection to the women who made this, centuries ago. Rose, do be careful – those pieces are sharp.'

Later, when the room was full of stale smoke and stale conversations, Father asked Rose to play. She started with 'Skye Boat Song', one of Aunt Kathleen's favourites, and 'The Minstrel Boy'. The mood got more melancholy as she went. How was it possible that every song that sprang to mind was about war, or beloved people being far away?

What about 'Red Sails in the Sunset'? No, no good at all. In desperation, she launched into 'It's a Long Way to Tipperary', which at least had the benefit of being a singalong, but it was also a marching song, and the men's faces just grew more grim. They all had someone to miss, and their own reasons for not being overseas themselves.

A man leaned his elbow on the top of her piano. She didn't know him; he was younger than most of Father's friends, and had kind eyes, and a brown moustache that looked as though it needed a comb.

'Do you know "Lambeth Walk"?' he asked.

'I've heard it, of course, but never played it.'

He started singing, with a bad mock Cockney accent, and made everyone laugh. Rose picked it up quickly, and by the end they'd sped up, as everyone sang along. She ended with a *glissando*, to applause.

Everyone was laughing, then, but nobody asked her to play anything else, which was just as well because she was flushed and tired. She slipped out of the room to the back porch, where it was cool, and leaned on the railings, looking out into the darkness.

'Don't let me startle you,' she heard someone say, and turned to see the silhouette of the man who'd sung with her, against the light from the open door. Then the door closed behind him, and they were in darkness.

'I'm Harry Frederick,' he said, and they shook hands. 'I wanted to thank you for accompanying me. I'm not the world's best singer.'

'I thought you sang very well. Are you a historian, like Father?'

'No, a mathematician. A friend invited me. I don't know most of the people here.'

'Half of them fought in the Great War, like Father, and have been coming here ever since.'

Mr Frederick laughed, but she hadn't meant to be funny. 'How did you learn to play so well?'

'That's kind of you to say,' she told him. 'I'm always getting notes wrong. I'm quick at picking up new songs, at least. I can always hear a song in my head, straight away, just by looking at the notes. And I always hear what comes next. But I'm afraid my fingers are slower than my ear.'

Harry Frederick nodded, and stubbed out his cigarette, regarding her carefully. 'You have instincts. Some people say mathematical ability and musical ability are cousins. A certain way of seeing patterns. Tell me, Rose, have you got a position anywhere? Are you joining a service?'

'Not yet. I will soon, though. I'm good at typing. I suppose there is somewhere they could use me. I'm a little afraid to go to London, I have to admit.'

'I think I might be able to find you something more interesting than typing, and not far from home.'

'Oh, I would be so grateful,' she said sincerely.

'But you can't tell anyone about it,' he said. 'Not even anyone in there. Not your own family. Though I dare say you'll see some familiar faces. We have a few Cambridge people.'

He smiled, and it was wonderful, in that moment, to feel like a person who could do whatever she chose. No longer Rose the daughter, or Rose the sister, but someone nobody had met yet.

Mr Frederick said, 'All you have to do is write to the Foreign Office, and then go down to London for an interview.'

The bubble burst. The whole idea suddenly sounded like a silly fantasy. She'd never been to London on her own – never been anywhere on her own – and she was terrified by the photographs of London these days, the wreckage from the bombing. How did one write to the Foreign Office, anyway? To whom would she address the letter? It was ridiculous. She must have given him a false impression of her abilities.

But she didn't want to say so, and be reassured, so she nodded politely and said, 'Perhaps I will.'

After everyone left, and Mother came home from her meeting and went up to tuck in the boys, Rose went to help her father collect the glasses and ashtrays. She found they were already cleared, and Father was in his study, holding the scrap of tapestry in two cupped hands, looking down at it like a wounded creature in his care.

'I'll pay for a new frame,' she said, standing in the doorway.

'Oh, not to worry. I'll find a safe place for it. I don't really want it on the wall anyway, and this gives me an excuse. I didn't want to offend Yardley – he meant well – but it makes me sad.'

'Because someone took a pair of scissors to something unique?'

'Yes.' He looked up at her. 'I have to admit, though, touching it has sparked my imagination. So much of what seemed dark to me, about the story of this piece of cloth – I feel I can see them, those women who made this. I can see why they made it the way that they did. Do you ever get the feeling, when you're putting a puzzle together, that you need to hold a piece in your hand to know where it goes?'

This was a phenomenon Rose recognized, though she'd never put it into words. Jigsaw puzzles were one thing she'd always been good at, and they used to do them together, the whole family, on New Year's Day.

'It's a little like that,' her father said, with a spark in his eyes. 'It's as if the puzzle is becoming clear to me now.' His expression changed, and he cocked his head a little, looking at her. 'Harry Frederick talked to you.'

It wasn't quite a question, and Rose wasn't sure how to respond.

'He's a good fellow,' Father added. 'You're a thoughtful girl, Rose, and prudent, I know. But it's all right to trust your instincts, once in a while. If there's one thing the war has taught all of us, it's that life is short.'

She realized that he might have thought that Mr Frederick was flirting with her. Even worse: Mr Frederick might have thought the same. Rose had never had any interest in romance, and she tended to forget that other people did. Surely he wouldn't recruit her to a position just to have a chance to court her? She was embarrassed, and tried to remember everything he'd said, but none of it came back to her. All she could hear was the piano, the song they'd sung together. If only life were like music; if only she could guess what came next.

She nodded, and said goodnight.

Rose hardly saw Father for days after that; when he was home he was working all the time, writing and writing.

A week later, while she was planting carrots, Father came and stood over her, shading his eyes.

'I have to go to Scotland,' he said. 'Aunt Kathleen isn't doing well.'

She straightened up and brushed the soil off her gloves. 'I'm sorry to hear that. Is it anything serious?'

'Just her nerves.'

'She must be very unwell, to ask for help. She's so stubborn.'

'She didn't ask,' he said, looking off into the distance. He was freshly shaved, his skin red and bumpy. There were lines around his eyes now that weren't there when she was a child.

'Oh. But in her letter, did she—'

'What letter?' He looked back at her, his expression

confused, and then it cleared. 'Oh, of course. Well, it's a difficult thing for any of us, to live in times like these, and she's an old woman. She can't stop thinking . . . she can't stop herself worrying about . . . '

'The aeroplane,' Rose finished his sentence. A cold feeling came over her.

His eyes widened. 'What aeroplane? Rose, what do you know?'

She shook her head. 'Nothing. I just . . . I thought that was what you were going to say. I don't know why. I suppose it would trigger her nerves, hearing them overhead, wouldn't it?'

He stared at her for a long time. 'It's not good for anyone being at home and idle during all of this. It makes one feel powerless. Perhaps it's not good for you, being here with me. With only me for company so much of the time, I mean. Have you decided what you'll do?'

The way he was looking at her made her feel like an irritant, a problem. She wasn't idle, not at all. She was planting the garden, and later she had washing to do, and she helped him and Mother and the boys all the time. But the last thing she wanted was to be in anyone's way.

'I'm going to write to the Foreign Office,' she said.

Rose told her parents she had been given a typing position at the old railway works in Wolverton, halfway between Cambridge and Oxford.

The factory there was indeed involved in war manufacturing, and she was indeed living near it, but she was working somewhere else: the so-called Government Code and Cypher School. Her first night was spent finding her way in utter blackness from the draughty old train station to her billet with a nasty, pinch-faced old woman who had a very narrow house. After Rose had done that, she thought, *That's as much finding my own way as I'm capable of doing, and more than I ever thought I could do.*

But the following day she found the bus to the country estate called Bletchley Park. Some of the men and women on the bus were in uniform, but many were in ordinary frocks or trousers. They arrived at a country estate, where a big old house sat looking forlornly at a collection of ugly sheds. A woman with a clipboard sent her to Hut 6, and for a few minutes Rose stood with a small group of women as nervous as she was. She gathered from their chatter that they had all been to university; maybe she was in the wrong place.

Another woman came to talk to them. She was middle-aged, and pretty, in a smart Wren's uniform. She asked them all to come into the hut, where several desks bore bulky, odd-looking typewriters.

'You've all signed the Official Secrets Act,' she began. 'Remember that in every moment. You will say nothing about your work here, not to your families, not to the people you're staying with, not even to each other except as the work requires. The penalties for breaking this rule will be severe. Lives depend on our utmost secrecy.'

She looked at each of them, then, as if satisfied with what she saw in their faces, gestured at the odd typewriters.

'These are replicas of the Enigma machines, which the Germans use to encode their messages to each other. Every day, they change the settings on the machines. When we intercept their data, we have a number of methods for figuring out those settings. It will be your task to key the messages into the machines, and see what you get. All right?'

Rose was so exhausted at the end of every day that she hardly had time to be homesick. A letter arrived from Mother saying that Aunt Kathleen had died. It swam in front of her eyes, as if she was trying to decode a message from another world. It seemed impossible that such a formidable old woman could ever die. Poor Father; he had always been so fond of her. Mother said that he was staying in Scotland for a while, to see to her affairs.

Tired though she was, Rose lay in her cold, lumpy bed for a long time that night, remembering Father's expression when he'd told her he was going up to Scotland. About how she had finished a thought for him, the wrong way. Just as she sometimes finished thoughts in the messages she typed. She was getting an instinct for seeing patterns, and suggesting possibilities to the analysts. But she couldn't really say how she did it. It was trial and error, and luck, and maintaining her state of mind. It all happened so quickly, with so many messages coming in, that she didn't really stop to think. It was like playing Bach: so long as she didn't fall out of the pattern, everything would tick along as it ought to. The moment she stopped to wonder how she was doing it, she wouldn't be able to any more.

In December the Americans joined the war, and there were more and more breakthroughs at Bletchley, and it seemed that, if everyone just worked hard enough, victory might be possible. Rose was given the option to return home for Christmas, or to stay on at Bletchley Park through the holidays. To her own surprise, she decided to stay and keep working.

CHAPTER 9

Ivy

That Christmas Eve of 1941, the moment before everything changed, Helen and Ivy sat in the kitchen, making paper chains out of old newspapers. Ivy was painting the strips red, brushing it on with more care than necessary. Helen was sitting opposite, waiting for another strip to dry so she could glue it into a chain.

They'd both arrived back home in Stoke Damson that morning, and now they were alone in the house. Mother had said she would be out late, and the boys were with a neighbour. She had given her daughters a task in the meantime: to put up the Christmas decorations. Which they had, lovingly placing the chipped chalkware Nativity scene on the sideboard, and hanging a few baubles from lamps and window handles, because no one had cut a tree for the house this year.

The paper garlands were all torn and ragged, though, so they'd set about making something new using Ivy's watercolours and the newspapers Mother always kept in a box beside the coal bin. Some of them were from before the war, and it was strange and wonderful to cut through a story about a cricket match.

'You do look smart in your FANY uniform,' Helen said, with a sigh. 'The tailoring shows off your figure. Those corduroy trousers we have to wear are so bulky. And I always have dirt under my fingernails and they're always broken.'

'I'm sure George doesn't mind your fingernails,' Ivy teased.

Helen regarded her paste pot with a secretive smile. 'Well, he doesn't have much else to compare me to, at least. All the other girls at the dances are Land Girls too. I have a feeling you would have managed to make even corduroy look stylish, though I can't blame you for deciding against it.'

Ivy held up the damp strip of red newsprint. 'I'm afraid you can still see a bit of Mussolini's face, through the paint.'

Helen took it from her. 'I'll be sure to make a join on that part. Don't worry. It's going to look very pretty when it's finished.'

'I hope so. Have you got any presents for Kurt and Karl? I wasn't sure whether to get them anything, as they don't celebrate Christmas, do they? But they could be late gifts for Hanukkah. Or just because. But they aren't anything much. Just some comics I drew. My poor attempt to copy *The Beano*.'

Helen grimaced. 'I wish I had a talent like yours. My presents are terrible. I have a jar of jam for Mother and soap for everyone else. Oh, now I've spoiled the surprise.' She rolled her eyes.

'Oh, but I do need soap! And Mother loves jam. That's wonderful. I only have my little drawings for everyone.'

Everyone including Father, though his present would stay wrapped. He was away in Scotland for the sixth time in as many months, still dealing with Aunt Kathleen's affairs, he said. It seemed impossible that an old lady could have left much for him to do, other than the house to sell. Sometimes she wondered whether Father was actually off doing some secret war work, although what use His Majesty's Government could have for a fifty-year-old history professor with a gammy leg from the last war, Ivy could not imagine. Mother seemed worried, though of course she wouldn't admit that. She was distracting herself as she usually did, by keeping herself busy, running all over the country with the Women's Voluntary Service and the Cambridge Volunteer Committee.

Rose wasn't even coming home for Christmas. Rose, who loved nothing better than being at home with her family. And Kit, of course – nobody knew whether Kit was alive or dead, so nobody talked about her, which was the wrongest thing of all. Ivy felt like crawling out of her skin.

'Mother said we could make ham sandwiches,' Helen said. 'If you really don't want to go to the Yardleys'. Max is home, you know. Don't you want to see her?'

They had a paper invitation to Mr Yardley's annual carol-singing party. The whole family used to go to it every Christmas Eve, when they were children. But Ivy didn't want to go this year. Seeing Max would make her worry about Kit.

'I'm just tired,' Ivy said. 'Too tired for a party.'

'Well, if we aren't doing anything tonight, perhaps I'll make something to send to George – some biscuits or something. I didn't have time to make him anything and I didn't want to give him soap. I hate to think he'll have nothing from me at Christmas.'

'Oh, I'm sure even a letter from you would send George into transports of joy.'

It came out strangely sharp, and Helen looked at her quizzically.

'I just mean that all George has ever wanted was for you to give him some hope,' Ivy added weakly. 'He only wants *you*. He doesn't care about presents, I'm sure.'

Helen was looking down at the two halves of a paper chain, one in each hand, suddenly frozen.

'Oh, dear, I didn't mean to snap,' Ivy said. 'I'm just out of sorts, with everything—'

'It's all right. It isn't that. Ivy, can you keep a secret?'

'Of course!'

'He asked me to wait for him.'

Ivy took this in. 'Is he being sent over, then?'

Helen nodded. 'In those first few days after Dunkirk, when we had no word of him, I thought – I really thought he'd bought it. And I thought, what a ninny I'd been, not to tell him how I felt. And then he turned up on our doorstep and I felt we'd been given a second chance. I was so grateful, you know? I didn't really think beyond that. And then, when he was stationed in Yorkshire, I thought he was safe, but now he *is* going over and he asked me to wait for him and oh, Ivy, I can't help but feel that means he's going to die. I have an awful premonition about it.'

Ivy didn't know what to say. 'You've given him a reason to come home.' Then she thought for a moment. 'You did say yes?'

'Of course! I even – well, I wanted us to get married before he went. Because we can't know what will happen, and I want to have been his wife, no matter what. But he said he wanted to talk to Father first, and Father's up in Scotland again.'

Helen seldom cried, and, when she did, she didn't sob the way Ivy would. A terrible contortion came over her face, and her eyes went red and filled up. It was exactly the way Mother cried.

Ivy went around the table and wrapped her arms around her sister. 'It's going to be all right.'

'I'm sorry. It's just everything – Father being away, and Christmas—'

'I think we should go to the party,' Ivy declared. 'Of course we're going to have the glums, sitting around here on Christmas Eve with our ham sandwiches.'

'No, Ivy. I'll be all right.'

'I insist. You go and wash your face, and I'll see if that blue dress of Rose's fits me now that I'm thinner. I always wanted to borrow it, and there's nothing she can say about it now, is there?'

The dress fitted perfectly, and they had Christmas cards made by the boys to take to Mr Yardley. But Ivy had no gift for Max.

She went to her sketchbook and flipped through her little scenes. None of them was any good. She stopped on a still life, a bowl of pears in front of a window. She had intended the curtain to be a study of Toulouse-Lautrec, which was why the colour was flat, but she was not at all sure she had brought it off. The shadows were terribly black, and she didn't know how to do the light the way he did.

She had known nothing about Toulouse-Lautrec until one day in Paris in 1939, when she had gone with Max to meet Kit at the Louvre, and Kit had shown her some French paintings, including one called *Le Lit*. Ivy could see it still, in her mind: the covers pulled up, the two faces just visible under rumpled short dark hair. One woman with her eyes just closed, a smile on her lips, turned towards her lover. The other woman gazing at her through her lashes.

That they were women, Ivy had no doubt. She'd never seen womanhood portrayed so clearly, though little was visible save their cheeks, their noses, the topography of the blanket. That they were lovers, she also had no doubt, though she hadn't quite considered such possibilities until that moment. Looking at the painting, she knew painfully that she was looking at everything she wanted. She wanted to be able to paint that honest clear daylight, with those quick, sure strokes. And she wanted to lie in bed with someone she loved, and smile like that.

Kit and Max had poked each other, seeing her face, and Max had teased her. 'You know they're women, yes?'

Ivy had looked at Kit, and their childhood passed unspoken between them. They were only an occasional church family, but still, there were certain expectations. Kit looked apprehensive, as if seeking Ivy's approval in some way. And Ivy said, in the most world-weary way she could muster, 'Of course.'

After that, they took her along to Le Monocle, and Ivy wore her hair short with her blonde curls precisely arranged on her temples, and had several brief flirtations, most of them with women. For months, she watched the way a man flicked his cigarette lighter, the way a woman held her handbag. She thought she might be able to fall in love with anyone and everyone.

And then, one night, Max and Kit came home, and she saw their faces, and she realized she hadn't understood love at all. It had been right in front of her face and she had been naive. The only one not in on the secret.

But then the war had come, and Mother and Father had wanted her home, and she hadn't argued. Kit didn't argue either. She just did what she wanted, and stayed.

Ivy put down the still life. It was a total failure, a childish attempt at something she had the imagination to admire but not the skill to achieve. She was just an ordinary girl from an ordinary village who didn't have her father's brains or her mother's virtue.

She went to the window of the bedroom she had once shared with Rose. She swept the curtain aside with two fingers and looked out, across the ground dusted with snow, across the creek where the willows were all brown and grey, to the big house where Max and her father lived.

An image came into Ivy's mind, of a dark-haired woman with a grim mouth and hard eyes. A painting she had done some months before, of this very scene, but with the pattern of light and dark made by the river and trees just nudged and emphasized in such a way that it made a woman's face. She'd painted it here, on one of her brief windows of leave, not in Sheffield. Ivy had been looking out at that scene, and thinking about the future, and how dismal it was, how there was nothing in England for her.

It was probably terrible. But she had to see it, now that she'd thought of it.

After some rummaging in an old steamer trunk where she kept things she didn't want to lose, she found it, rumpled and stiff from the watercolours. It wasn't a pretty painting, or an easy one. The woman Ivy thought of as the future stared out of it, her eyes like black smoke, her clothing a mere hint of olive green. A warlike painting, in its way. But it was the best thing Ivy had ever made. Worthy of one of her oldest friends.

The drawing room at the Yardley house was a picture post-card, with holly on the mantel and the smell of rum and fruit and something roasting. How they had managed it all so beautifully, Ivy couldn't think, but Mr Yardley was presumably able to perform miracles as a member of Parliament.

Even though she'd come to this house many times as a child, she never felt comfortable there. Gregory Yardley and Rupert Sharp had worked together in the last war; the girls didn't know quite what that work had entailed, but it was something after Rupert had been injured, and they all suspected it had something to do with intelligence. They'd been friends since, and indeed it was Mr Yardley who had told Father when a house was up for sale in the village of Stoke Damson, just across the stream from his own larger property. Over the years, Father's love of history had worn off on his friend, it seemed; the Yardley house was full of old pots and statues, in glass cases.

Ivy recalled the scrap of the Bayeux Tapestry Mr Yardley had given Father, several months ago, not long before Aunt Kathleen died. One evening, Ivy had come upon Father sitting in his chair and gazing at it, just holding it in his palm, and he'd told her what it was. It was behind glass, he said, when Mr Yardley gave it to him, but the frame broke. Father had looked a little awed by the tiny square of cloth in his hand, and a little guilty. She wondered now why he hadn't put it into a new frame.

There were several neighbours there, the old and the young, mostly women. Everyone was cheerful; it was Christmas, after all, and the Americans were in the war now, and surely everything would change for the better soon.

Helen was ushered into a circle of people who knew Mother from the Women's Voluntary Service, and Ivy managed to escape by pretending there was something wrong with the heel of her shoe and ducking into a hallway.

And there was Max, walking towards her, wearing her hair pinned back at the sides and a comradely smile.

'How are you?' Max said, in her ear, as they embraced. 'How is everyone?'

'Helen is here, in the other room. She'll tell you all about farming if you let her. Rose couldn't be home for Christmas, but she writes like clockwork. Father's been away quite often lately. Mother is busy with the boys – have you met Kurt and Karl?'

Max shook her head. 'Not yet. I've been home for a few weeks, but I came home because I caught influenza, and I've only just recovered.'

'I'm sorry to hear you've been unwell,' Ivy said. There was a silence, and Ivy, seeing that Max was not going to ask what she most wanted to know, decided to take pity. 'We haven't had a letter from Kit, not for several months now. She doesn't say much in her letters anyway.'

'No, she never did, which always struck me as funny, given that she was always scribbling away at something as a child.' Max sighed, looking away.

'Oh, how I miss all of my sisters,' Ivy said, desperately. 'I want to be ridiculous and childish with someone. My room-mates are very serious and very tiresome.'

'But your cartoons about them make me laugh so much.'

'I only wish they thought so. Not that I show them *those* caricatures, of course, but I can't make them smile about anything. And of course, "FANYs must at all times conduct themselves like ladies". Are you still stationed in Grendon Underwood?'

'Yes.'

'Lucky to be so close. You can come home to visit easily.'

Max laughed bitterly. 'It's too close. Father and I don't see eye to eye, you know. We haven't for some time. Oh, we've patched things up enough, but to be frank I'm hoping for a chance to go overseas. With the Red Cross, perhaps.'

'Oh, Max, I hope you don't. After all the trouble we took to get home!'

'I'll be careful,' Max said with a wicked smile. 'Probably just as safe as anyone driving with you would be. How on Earth did you get into that?'

'God only knows. During my training, I was leaning out to be able to see out of the ambulance when I reversed, and I fell right out! I think that's why they don't have me on ambulances now. I'm driving these terrible officers around from one meeting to another.'

At that, Max grinned. 'There can't be that many terrible officers in Sheffield.'

'There are at least three,' Ivy said darkly. 'I wish I could do something that felt as if it was any help at all to – anyone.'

Ivy gestured in the general direction of the continent.

Max pointed at the paper in Ivy's hand, rolled up with a red ribbon tied around it. 'And what have you brought me? Is that a painting? Oh, tell me it is. I used to love your sketches.'

Ivy handed it over shyly.

She couldn't read Max's face at all as she unrolled it and looked at it, holding it at several distances from her eyes.

'Don't you like it? It's a bit gloomy, I know.'

'I adore it,' Max said, looking up at last. 'I haven't ever seen you paint anything like this. I suppose it's to be expected, now that you're grown up, that you'd paint differently.'

There was the sound of a door opening, and a few moments of louder noise from conversation nearby as Mr Yardley came through the door from the drawing room. 'Ah, there you are. I'm sure the two of you want to catch up, but the carol-singing is about to start.'

'We'll come now. But, Father, look at this painting Ivy's given me.'

Mr Yardley had always made Ivy nervous, with his habit of saying clever things very abruptly, and a face that never revealed whether he was joking when he said them. He was a big, broad-chested man with a thick head of wavy grey hair, and a moustache to match. When he was close enough that she could smell the remnants of his most recent cigar, he plucked the painting out of his daughter's hand.

'Isn't it remarkable?' Max said proudly. 'It's so atmospheric.'

'What do you mean by it?' He turned and glared at Ivy. One hand held the edge of the paper so hard that it buckled, while his finger poked at the image. 'Why did you paint this woman?'

'It came to me, just out of my imagination, as I was

painting. I suppose I thought – it is a bit modern in style. A bit beyond my skills.'

He stared at it for a moment more, then his bottom lip pushed out a bit, appraising. 'Nonsense. It's a very good picture. Let me put it away somewhere safe, and, Max, do go out and say hello to your cousin Beatrice and try to cheer her up if you can. We'll start with "The Holly and the Ivy" in a few minutes.'

They nodded, even though they had always started with 'The Holly and the Ivy', and walked towards the drawing room. Ivy felt about ten years old.

'I love the painting,' Max said, walking beside her.

She was interrupted by Mr Yardley, calling after them. 'Oh, Ivy, will you come and see me for a moment? I have something I want to ask you about your mother and the refugees. Max, you go on, please, and make sure there are enough glasses for everyone.'

Max gave her a sympathetic look, and then Ivy was left alone, walking back to Mr Yardley. He was smiling now.

'I wonder, Ivy, would you be available to come and see me the day after tomorrow?'

She was startled. 'Of course. About the refugees? Helen might know better than I would.'

'Just you. I have a proposal for you. But it's very secret. Don't mention it even to Max. It's about war work, and something I think you might be suited for. I'll expect you at two o'clock.'

CHAPTER 10

Ivy

Mr Yardley's study had always been off limits when the girls were young, running around the house with Max. Ivy had imagined it with high shelves packed with leather-bound volumes, and busts of Greek philosophers on pedestals. She felt almost disappointed to find it reminded her of her father's study, only slightly less cramped. The books were all a-jumble, including many plain thick volumes with cheap bindings and boring titles. And instead of a bust, the only thing on a pedestal was an old war helmet with a long nose-piece.

He shook her hand when she walked in, and wished her a happy Christmas, and asked whether she'd enjoyed the carol-singing party.

Ivy had never had a conversation alone with him before. Where was Max? She must be out of the house this afternoon; the housekeeper had shown Ivy to the study. She just nodded and smiled. Mr Yardley gestured for her to sit in a studded leather chair on one side of his desk, while he sat behind it.

'I'm sorry I startled you with my reaction to your painting,' he said.

'It is a rather gloomy and strange painting. Not at all right for Christmas.'

'It's a very interesting piece of work. Ambitious and evocative. I was unaware you had such talent.'

'I don't have much chance to practise.'

'They keep you busy driving cars, I understand. I wonder that you didn't go into the Land Army. Such an excellent initiative. I want to see it continue after the war. A healthy and productive way for young people to contribute. We will need that sort of energy for the future.'

'Helen seems to enjoy it,' Ivy said, wondering whether she was going to have to explain her fear of cows to Mr Yardley.

But he had moved on. He opened a desk drawer and pulled out a photograph. It was not framed. He passed it over to her.

She suddenly had trouble drawing breath.

The woman in the photograph was the woman she had painted. The same face that had emerged from the shadows in the trees and the ripples on the water: it was all there. A face she'd thought she had invented.

'Do you know this woman?'

Ivy shook her head. 'I don't believe so.'

'Yet you painted her into this scene.'

'A coincidence, I expect. Is she a family member of yours? Perhaps we met here, and I've forgotten.'

'You never met her here.'

'Perhaps we passed in a railway station or post office, then, and it stuck in my mind.'

'Do you believe that?'

Ivy hesitated. 'I'm not sure I understand, sir. What else could it be?' She felt defensive, without any reason to.

He put the photograph back in the drawer and took out another piece of paper. With a shock, Ivy recognized one of the silly caricatures she had sent to Max: a sketch of a bulbous-nosed major telling a subordinate that he'd need supplies for Operation Alice. She couldn't think how it had ended up in Mr Yardley's hands.

As if guessing her thoughts, he said, 'After I was so impressed with your painting, I asked Max whether you'd sent her anything else. I'm afraid I gave her the impression I might be able to further your artistic career. She did not betray your trust; she is very proud of you. As she should be. You are a talented young woman.'

'Thank you, sir.'

'You know this man?'

Ivy's nerves turned to cold fear. Was it treason to make fun of an officer? 'I drive for him, when he comes to Sheffield. I wouldn't say I know him.'

'But you know that his mistress is named Alice, do you?'

Now the words wouldn't come; Ivy's throat closed.

'I'm not accusing you of anything, Ivy,' Mr Yardley said, kindly. 'I understand that gossip happens. Is that how you learned his mistress's name? There will be no consequences if so.'

'I'm sorry, Mr Yardley. I don't know. I don't think so. It just popped into my head. I don't believe I even knew he had a mistress.'

'Another coincidence, then.'

He stood up, and went to a side table, and poured two glasses of sherry. She was grateful to take one, as much to moisten her throat as anything.

'The truth is that, as real as your artistic talents are, it's another sort of talent that interests me. But you have to keep this very secret. You can do that, can't you?'

Ivy nodded, frowning.

Mr Yardley walked over to the window, looking out on to the brown December scene: the little river between his house and her own family's. The same scene Ivy had painted, but from the opposite direction.

'Do you remember when Maxine fell through the ice, when you were children, and you came running here to get help?'

'Of course,' Ivy said, shivering with remembered terror. Max had been crossing the stream to visit them.

'You said afterwards that you'd had a vision of her drowning; that that was how you knew, even though you were not on the ice. We all assumed you'd been looking out of a window.'

Ivy froze. She remembered it well enough, the vision and all. But she'd been so young. And memory was unreliable. 'My great-aunt used to tell us stories, you know, of the Second Sight and other superstitions. Children latch on to these things.'

'And did your sisters latch on to it too?'

'Oh, when we were little. We may have convinced ourselves we had inherited some sort of power – you know, just as some girls play at séances and things.'

'But that all stopped, did it?'

'Oh, years ago.'

'No strange occurrences in your family, then? Nothing that would give credence to your great-aunt's stories about the Second Sight?'

'Well, there was the time that she sent us a telegram, when Father was up on the roof. She'd had a dream of him falling. I think he was rather spooked by it.'

'Yes,' Mr Yardley said thoughtfully. 'I know he was. Have you spoken with him about it recently, by any chance?'

Ivy shook her head. She didn't like the way he was looking at her, as if he was expecting a certain answer. When she didn't give it, he seemed to relax.

More casually, he continued, 'Do your sisters not see

pictures that pop into their minds, then, the way you do?'

'I've never asked,' Ivy said. 'I'm the only artist. The only visual artist, I mean. Rose plays piano, as you know. She always loved the stories, and she believed them, more than any of us did, for a long time. But no, she's never said that she sees things.'

'And your other sisters? Did they believe the stories too?'

'Helen finds the subject distasteful and won't discuss it. She frightens easily. Once, she got angry with us for talking about it. And Kit thinks it's all balderdash.' She swallowed. 'I do too, of course. I don't want you to think that I'm trying to – to make people believe that I see things.'

'Oh, no, certainly not. You have claimed no such thing. But what I did not think about, not until now, is that some talents run in families.' He turned to her, the light from the window behind him making him a silhouette.

'Are you saying that I may actually have . . . ' She couldn't bring herself to say something so ridiculous. She must be misunderstanding him.

'I am of the opinion that most talents can be honed, in the right circumstances. I think your talents might be very useful to Great Britain, if we could learn to harness them. If you are interested, that is. It would mean leaving your position in Sheffield.'

Ivy smiled ruefully. 'I wouldn't miss it, and I don't think it would miss me.'

'And your family and friends would have to know nothing about your real work. Not Max, and not even your sisters and your parents. This is vital. You will still be a FANY, and you may say that you have been reassigned. Are you comfortable with that?'

There were FANY ambulance drivers on the continent, near the front lines. She'd just urged Max not to go there.

Mr Yardley repeated his question.

Ivy stood up straight, as if she were being called upon in school. 'I can keep a secret, if I have to.'

'The danger of discovery is both to the service you would be working for, and to you personally. Not everyone would react to your talents the way I have. If anyone – from any intelligence service, from the forces, anyone at all – asks, you work in the signals division and your work is very boring. If they ask you whether you have any special talents, you say you do not. If they suggest that you have anything like the Second Sight, you deny it. Do you understand?'

Ivy knew that there was war work that must be kept secret, of course. And if it was true that she had some sort of ability – what a thought! – then that would be an asset, and something to keep secret too. But if she wasn't allowed to speak to anyone about the possibility of the Second Sight, what did that leave for her to do?

'I understand, and will say nothing to anyone. But, sir, I'm not sure I understand what the job is.'

Mr Yardley rubbed his forehead as though it was itchy, and said, 'I'm not sure I do, either. For now, the main thing is just to learn what you are capable of. A day may arrive when I can tell you more about what might come next.' He paused. 'I hope to find someone who can teach you. If it can be taught. It is possible it will all come to nothing. It is also possible that you will learn things you don't want to learn. This is war work, Miss Sharp. It will be what it will be.'

Ivy thought of Kit, in occupied France, so silent. Of her father, teaching cadets and displaced students. Of her mother, bravely trying to find homes for children, and of the children who might never see their parents again. Of Rose, typing away. Of Helen milking terrifying cows and stoically waiting for her George to come home and marry her if he didn't die. Of Kurt and Karl, so far from home, trying to remember what their parents' faces looked like.

'Would it help?' Ivy asked in a small voice, 'if I were to try to see things? To learn to see things? Do you think it would help defeat Hitler?'

Mr Yardley smiled, a rare sight. He leaned forward over the desk.

'Let's find out. I am going to speak to some people and see what might be possible. Remember, say nothing at all to anyone.'

They shook hands, and Ivy went home, hoping that she wouldn't have to report back to Sheffield. But no word came, and she went back to driving for the horrible officers, and after a time she began to think that Mr Yardley had been humouring her, or teasing her, or that she had somehow misunderstood it all.

Then, in spring, a letter came to her in Sheffield. It was from Mr Yardley, and it contained a date and an address in London.

Ivy walked from King's Cross station. Taking the Tube would have saved her half an hour, but half an hour walking alone in London on a wet day, her cheeks bright with cold, was not an experience from which Ivy wanted to be saved. She hadn't seen the city since her return journey from France, a year and a half before, when the Blitz hadn't yet happened. Now, in March 1942 she saw the marks of it in hollowed-out and broken buildings, or scattered tumbles of bricks.

Still, there could never come a time when city streets beneath her heels failed to make her want to skip with joy. Paris or London: that was where people ought to live. When the war was over, Ivy thought, she would rent a flat. Perhaps something like the one in the stately mansion block just off Baker Street, the address Mr Yardley had given her.

She was wearing her FANY uniform. A doorman showed her into a bathroom, gleaming in modern black and white, and asked her to wait there. This was deflating, which might be the intention, Ivy supposed, or perhaps the place was simply too busy, too buzzing with secrets, for anywhere else to serve as a waiting room. Before long, he returned, and walked her down the hallway to a door.

The door shut behind her.

The room contained a table and two chairs, and not much else. A woman stood behind the desk, a cigarette between her fingers. Dark hair, neatly pinned, and a face like a school-teacher's.

'Hello,' Ivy said, inadequately.

'You're Ivy Sharp.'

'Yes, ma'am.'

The woman looked at her for a moment, then gestured with her chin that Ivy should take the chair nearest the door. She did so.

'I'm Miss Atkins. You came recommended. Good instincts, I'm told. *On me dit que vous parlez français.*'

Ivy was startled. 'Yes, I speak French. I learned it as a child, and lived there just before the war.'

'In French, please.'

Ivy repeated what she'd said, in French this time, which didn't help her nerves. Miss Atkins did not look impressed.

'We'll have to work on that accent. You lived with your sister Kit in Paris. I understand she's still there.'

'As far as I know, yes, ma'am.'

'And Rose is the one who drives an ambulance. Or is she packing parachutes?'

Ivy had the distinct impression that this interrogation was not aimed at getting information but at seeing how Ivy would phrase information that Miss Atkins already knew. 'I'm not sure exactly what she's doing, Miss Atkins. Typing, I believe.'

'Helen is in the Women's Land Army. And your mother is doing work with refugees and evacuees. And your father?'

'He's a history professor at Cambridge.'

Miss Atkins opened a folder and put a document in front of Ivy.

'This is the Official Secrets Act. Read it carefully, please. When you have finished, you may choose to sign it, and continue on with a training course. If you are found suitable for special employment, you may be sent overseas, and asked to do highly dangerous work, with a risk of death similar to that in combat. The worse risk will be capture, because you will be out of uniform, and may be executed or sent to a prison camp.'

Ivy understood that there was a question implied here; she nodded tightly.

Miss Atkins continued. 'Even among your colleagues, you will not be known by your given name; from now on, you will introduce yourself as Juliet.'

'Like Shakespeare,' Ivy said, because Miss Atkins had paused, and she had to say something.

'Like Shakespeare,' Miss Atkins agreed, with a small smile.

'I understand,' Ivy said. She was so cold, suddenly. There must have been some mistake; surely Mr Yardley had not intended this. She couldn't see how her talent – if it existed – factored into this sort of training at all. She thought about the best way to raise the possibility of a mistake; Miss Atkins hadn't mentioned Mr Yardley.

'The most important thing you will learn,' said Miss Atkins, 'is to keep your mouth shut.'

Ivy nodded. Then she read and signed the Official Secrets Act.

CHAPTER 11

Helen

Helen put one hand on her lower back and groaned as she straightened. The field seemed to stretch impossibly far. She was one of half a dozen women walking backwards through the furrows, planting seed potatoes, two women to each wooden tray. Her planting partner gave her a weary grin. Helen hardly had the energy to reciprocate.

It was important work and she liked being outside, even on a chilly March day. But walking bent over was wreaking havoc on her hips and back, which already ached all the time. It was to be expected, she supposed. She would have liked to ask another woman whether this was what pregnancy had been like for her, and how much worse it would get, and what surprises the next six months might have in store. But there was no one to ask, because she hadn't been able to summon the courage to tell anyone at the farm.

At first, she had hoped the problem would just go away. That she'd bleed and tell herself she had just been late. Then she had simply rusted into indecision, not able to move in any direction, while her body kept growing the baby inside her.

On the pale horizon, a new silhouette. Not one of the Land Army girls, and not the farmer. Helen recognized that slouch, the hands in the trouser pockets, well before Max was close enough to run to and hug. Which Helen did, hiding the tears that were streaming down her face, now that someone was here, now that she would finally be able to move.

'You got my letter,' she said into Max's ear as they held on to each other. 'I didn't expect you to come in person.'

'Of course. What are friends for? Can you get away now so we can talk?'

Helen shook her head. 'Another hour, and then it will be lunch.'

'Then put me to work.'

Max's shoes were sensible, by her standards, but they weren't farm boots. 'Go and tell Mrs Jensen that you're my visitor, and I'll see you shortly. I'm all right, really.'

It was easier to finish the planting, knowing that Max was here to rescue her. But no, that was silly. There was no rescuing from this.

'Do you want to keep it?' Max asked, brusque as usual, as they walked through the little apple grove beside the farmhouse.

'I do,' Helen said. 'I thought about it, of course, but I really do want to have this child, Max. Oh, my goodness, that's the first time I've said it aloud.'

'Then there's really only one choice. You can't stay here; you'll be showing soon. It won't be long before they all catch on, and send you home. You might as well go now.'

'I can't tell Mother and Father,' Helen said, knowing as she said it how childish it sounded, but it was true. She had always wanted to be a mother and wife, to have her own house with a little garden. Now everything had gone wrong, and George was away fighting, and she would somehow have to raise a child without him, without any income or home of her own. And yet, as awful as all of that was, it didn't compare with the looming prospect of saying the words to her parents.

'They'll work it out eventually, you know. You will have to tell them. Or will you pretend it's a foundling?'

Helen knew Max was teasing, but she didn't have the heart for it. 'They'll hate me,' she whispered.

'Oh, nonsense. Your mother is the most generous soul in England, and your father – well, I've never seen your father yell. Not once.'

'I'm not afraid he'll yell. I don't know what I'm afraid of. Oh, it's all so awful. Will you come with me?'

Max stopped walking and looked at her, her face concerned. She took Helen's hand. 'Of course I will. We'll go today. They won't let you keep working here, once they know. That's where we'll start. We'll tell your Mrs Jensen and then we'll go to Stoke Damson and tell your parents, and it'll be done. What about George? Does he know?'

Helen shook her head. 'I can't decide whether I want to tell him or not. Not until he's home, and can see her for himself.'

'Her?'

Helen smiled. 'I think she's a girl. It's silly, I know.'

'Not at all. As long as you're not disappointed if it turns out the other way.'

'I couldn't be disappointed,' Helen said, putting a hand on her belly.

It was more awful than Helen imagined. Telling Mrs Jensen. Watching her write 'pregnancy' on the 'reason for release' section of her record card. Refusing the offer of a doctor. Saying a hurried goodbye to the women she'd worked with for months. Everything seemed banal and routine, including the looks on everyone's faces as they made up their minds about her. She wanted to explain, to tell them about George, how they had known each other all their lives, how they were going to be married, but she could hear how flimsy the words would sound.

By late afternoon, she was sitting with her suitcase on her lap, in the passenger seat of Max's maroon Aston Martin. It was a sleek two-seater, with leather interiors the colour of milky tea, and looked utterly alien parked in the muddy farmyard.

Once they were on the road, with Max taking the bends too quickly, Helen tried to say something and found the wind took it out of her mouth. She cleared her throat and spoke louder.

'I'm sorry to pull you away from everything. It's just that I knew you were at home, because you'd been ill, and everyone else is off doing their war work.'

'Really, it's no bother. I've been bouncing off the walls of Father's house like a billiard ball. He says I need more time to recover, but I've been better for months. And now he's left, gone off to Canada for some political nonsense, so I can do as I like.'

'Are you going back to – where were you stationed?'

'Grendon Underwood. No, I don't think so. I felt just as cooped up there. But I met some people, and I think I can get something more interesting to do. Father believes he's my gateway to everything, but he doesn't stop to think. I know most of the people he knows, at least anyone who's ever come to the house while I've been there. I can make my own way. And I can find out what I need to know.'

'You sound like a spy,' Helen said, laughing.

'Do you know, I think he's trained me to be one, without even realizing it. I've learned how to keep secrets from him, and how to spy on him so I'd be aware of anything threatening my freedom. Oh, that sounds melodramatic, doesn't it? But in some way it's true. I know far more about his business than he realizes. *Your* father is developing a radical new theory about the Bayeux Tapestry, by the way, one that he thinks will have implications for the war, although I can't see how it would. There are all sorts of notes among my father's secret papers. Found them yesterday when I went looking for more interesting things.'

Helen made a face. 'I'd love to think it will distract him from my news. But you know, he's been working on theories about the tapestry since I was a child. It's his passion.'

'Yes, but this one sounds a little . . . well, never mind.'

'What do you mean?'

'I can't pretend I understood it all, but he seemed to be arguing that the whole thing was made before 1066.'

Of all her sisters, Helen had always been the one least interested in Father's work, and least likely to understand what he was talking about. Dates never stuck in her mind, and half the people in any given story seemed to have the same name. She could never make the facts come out in the right order, because Father and Kit always talked about them in bits and pieces, so it was impossible to keep the kings in line or remember who won which battle. But even Helen managed to keep the dates of the Norman invasion and Magna Carta in her head. At least, she thought she had.

She said, uncertainly, 'Before 1066? How would that be possible? The Norman invasion was in that year, wasn't it? And it portrays the invasion.'

'Maybe he's referring to the early parts of the story, before the invasion,' Max said, sounding unconvinced by her own argument. 'There's something in the notes about successive groups of women, adding on to each other's work. Maybe he's arguing that those sections of the tapestry were done beforehand, and it was finished later.'

'It isn't finished at all,' Helen said absent-mindedly. That much she remembered.

Max drove in silence for a moment, her face set. At last, she elaborated. 'I wonder whether your father's been . . . overworked lately. He seems tired and distracted. Oh, I don't mean he's really ill, but just, well, you know the way that Kit gets when she's working on something. He's like that too, isn't he? But it can't just be his work on the tapestry because he hasn't been home much, in recent months. Up in Scotland, so he says. You know that he and my father worked in intelligence of some kind in the last war. This business that has kept him away, after your great-aunt died – I think it's something else, really. Something hush-hush.'

Helen looked out at the fields flashing past, still more brown than green. It reminded her of a film strip, and she almost thought that she could see flashes of something else in the gaps between the images. With every hedgerow or crossroads, she saw her father, walking away from her, and he wouldn't turn around. No matter how much she called his name, he wouldn't turn around.

She felt ill. She'd managed to get a few months into this pregnancy without throwing up, but perhaps the moment was coming for her now. She closed her eyes and let the wind cool her cheeks.

'If it's hush-hush, then we're not meant to know,' she said.

They arrived just in time for tea, which was enough for four, not six. Helen spent the first few minutes arguing with her mother, insisting that she and Max didn't need to eat anything, although she was very hungry. She hoped that Father was at the university, that she would have a chance to tell Mother first, and then present a united front to Father. But the door to the sitting room banged and he came into the kitchen, asking what had happened, why Helen had come home so suddenly. Was she ill?

The boys came in just then, and Mother took one look at Helen's face and told them to take their sandwiches and go and eat them outside. They obliged, even though the day was damp and grey, leaving Max, Helen, Mother and Father all standing and looking at each other.

Helen had asked Max to stay, for moral support, but, in the moment, it didn't help at all. There was no making this easier.

'I'm not exactly ill,' she began. 'I've left the Women's Land Army because . . . because I'm going to have a baby.'

Mother gave a small gasp, but Father was silent, his face deepening to purple. Helen grasped the back of a kitchen chair and gripped it hard, just to hold on to something.

When Mother spoke at last, her voice was deep and quiet. 'Are you sure about it?'

Helen nodded.

Mother said, 'But is it . . . I thought you and George had . . . Who is the father?'

'Why, George, of course!' Helen protested. 'Before he left.' This was worse and worse: the four of them, all thinking of mechanics and timelines, occupying the same space, the same silence. 'We're going to be married,' she said. 'We wanted to wait until George could ask Father properly, but we've agreed. As soon as he comes home, we're going to be married.'

'Of course,' Mother said, recovering from her shock. 'You'll live here in the meantime, and help me with the boys. Are you feeling all right? Have you seen a doctor?'

'Not yet. I'm perfectly well.' She felt this was not the time for the litany of aches and indignities she'd wished she could complain about to someone, anyone.

Mother blinked a few times, as if adjusting her view of

the world. 'Well, you'll eat something, of course. Max, please do stay for tea. We'll open some tins.'

Max stirred beside her. 'Thank you, but I'd better go and see if I'm needed at the house. If there's anything I can help with, though—'

'I should have known,' Father said, very quietly, staring hard at Helen.

'What's that?' Mother asked, turning to him.

'How is it that I didn't know?' His face was still dark, his jowls set, his gaze iron.

Helen looked back at her childhood, at how she was never very good in school, at how she had no ambitions like Kit or talents like Ivy and Rose, at how she never had anything to talk to Father about. He must be asking himself how he could be the least bit surprised that a girl like that would end up the sad talk of the village, a burden and an embarrassment.

What would Ivy, Rose and Kit think, when she wrote to them? She didn't want to, for some reason. It would be too painful – not that they'd be ashamed or angry, but because they could not be here with her. Just a few months ago, she and Ivy had sat in this kitchen and glued strips of paper, like girls, and oh, God, Helen must have been pregnant then already. She wanted to keep it from everyone, as long as she could; they shouldn't have to bear the knowledge that she had made everything even more wrong and off-kilter than it already was, that they were missing their sister's first child.

Then there was Father, who probably would have liked to be able to go far away from her, or to send her away.

She couldn't look straight at him and felt ashamed of that, too. The wooden bars of the kitchen chair she was holding seemed to stretch up between them, like the walls of a prison. She blinked to clear her eyes, but they could not gain focus.

Now she seemed to see him, not standing and looking at her, but walking away from her. Refusing to turn back. Leaving her behind for good. The same vision she'd seen from the car. She shut her eyes tight, and shut out the vision. Banished it from her mind.

Father turned and left without eating, and Max went home, and Helen sat down at the kitchen table with her mother and had a long and tearful talk, her mother's hand on hers. The whole time, she tried to keep the images of her father out of her mind, because they were somehow horrible, though they were simple enough: Father in a dark, locked room. Aunt Kathleen, of all people, walking in a bleak field, under a bleak sky, and Father walking towards her. Father with his back turned, walking away from the house, from Helen.

She found that by concentrating very hard, she could put these images away from her and focus on her mother's face and on the cup of tea in front of her. But, by the time evening fell, she had a terrible headache.

CHAPTER 12

Ivy

At a railway station near Swindon, a driver collected Ivy in an Austin Seven that smelled of cleaning fluid and drove her to a red-brick manor house, surrounded by green lawns. It was older and larger than the Yardley house. The sort of place she'd always imagined she would live in, although how she would get to that life was an open question.

Among the dozen recruits was only one other woman, a lovely Frenchwoman in her forties with the code name Jacqueline. They shared a room, which helped Ivy feel a little less lonely and terrified at night. It also helped that she fell asleep as soon as her head hit the pillow.

In those first few days, Ivy kept watch on her fellow recruits for signs that anyone else had the Sight, or any other unusual abilities. All she was sure of was that they were all very clever. The instructors set them building aeroplanes out of Meccano, which was all right. She and her sisters had played with the toy construction set when they were young, and Kurt and Karl had inherited their box of jumbled metal strips and nuts and bolts when they moved in. She was afraid

116

the whole time that she would be the last recruit to finish, but she wasn't. They were given surprise quizzes about what the others in the house looked like, or what someone had said at breakfast, to teach them the value of observation. And there were countless interviews, always in French, mainly about Ivy's past, and about what she would be willing to do for her country.

Most of the time they spent running, or fighting dummies with sticks, or sitting in rooms being shown wireless sets and given lectures.

On the last day, half the recruits were gathered in the sitting room and were told that they had passed the course.

'Welcome to the Special Operations Executive,' said the commander, a brusque man with a worldly bearing. 'We are sending agents into occupied countries in Europe to encourage and support the Resistance. Your first task will be to write a series of letters to your family members, with dates stretching for several years into the future, so that they will believe you are safely working in a signalling facility here in England.'

He paused, and looked at Jacqueline and Ivy, who were sitting next to each other. 'We only recently began recruiting women, and most of them have had an accelerated course of training, because of the sort of work we expected them to do. But Jacqueline and Juliet, you are to proceed with the men on the full course. Enjoy your evening, everyone. Tomorrow you will be taken by bus to Scotland.'

The code names helped, a little. It was inconceivable that Ivy Sharp could garrote a man, but Juliet might. As Juliet, she learned to return the fighting teacher's gaze when he talked about gouging out an enemy's eyeballs with her thumbs. She was soon too sore and exhausted to imagine that life could be anything other than crawling through the mud, cleaning and reloading weapons, or hitting things or people. She felt beaten, in every way.

She had been to Scotland before, on the family visits to Aunt Kathleen, but this training school was in the Highlands, near the sea, miles from Glasgow. It was cold, and terrifying, climbing cliff faces suspended from ropes. Her feet slipped and her calluses bled. She had no visions, and there was surely nothing in her exhausted doodles at the end of the day that could be of any use to the war effort. She was simply in the lower end of the acceptable students. She had never been the cleverest one in a room, or the most talented, or the prettiest. But she had always been determined.

They learned how to wade through streams without making a sound, and how to mix explosives and hide them. They gave her earplugs, but that didn't prevent the ringing from the explosions and the gunshots. Ivy was awkward with weapons, always afraid she would make a mistake and kill someone. On the courses, when cardboard figures popped up to left and right she was always quick to respond, and she made a little guessing game out of it, the way she used to do with her sisters about traffic signals. But she wasn't very accurate, and she found it hard to pull the trigger twice, quickly, and keep moving.

Jacqueline, though, was the best shot of the group.

'I've already worked as a saboteur, in the Resistance,' Jacqueline confided in her one day, after Ivy had marvelled at how well she took to the training. 'I think that's why they sent me here. They couldn't very well say they only intend to use women as secretaries and flirts when I've already – well . . . '

She smiled at Ivy, and Ivy tried to look like someone who could take all this in her stride. She remembered Mr Yardley saying, *For now, the main thing is just to learn what you can do.*

And truth be told, she could do a lot more than she ever would have suspected.

One day, near the end of the course, they had to climb two separate firemen's ladders up the side of a cliff. As they watched the first of their colleagues struggle, Jacqueline said, 'I think you should go before me. Because if I see you succeed, that will help me, but if you see me fall, it'll just make it harder for you.'

Ivy said, 'We'll make it, all of us.'

'Unlikely. Some of us will be on our way to the School of Forgetting.'

A chill ran through Ivy. 'Where is that?'

'Nobody knows. Another posh house miles away from anywhere, I'd assume. But it has to exist, somewhere. Think about it. Not everyone passes the training, we know that. So where do the failures go? They can't just send us back to our homes and families. We know too much now. Codes, techniques, who the instructors are. No, if someone's not reliable enough to drop into France, they're not reliable enough to drop into King's Lynn or Swindon either.'

'Then what do they do with us?' Ivy's voice sounded high and childlike.

'They send us somewhere else, and give us something to keep us useful. Washing dishes. I don't know. Maybe they have techniques for erasing or confusing our memories. Maybe they just lock us in until the war ends.'

They both made it up the ladders, but three of the men did not. Those three were gone by the final day, when the recruits were told that they would be driven down to Manchester for parachute training.

'All except Jacqueline,' said a young man with slick, wavy blond hair whom none of them had ever seen before. He held a clipboard. 'You're to go straight to finishing school.'

Jacqueline looked puzzled, and said, 'But when will I do my parachute training?'

'You're to go to France by boat,' said the young officer. 'We're not in the business of dropping grandmothers out of aeroplanes.'

Finishing school was at a place called Beaulieu, on the southern coast of England, across the Solent from the Isle of Wight. When Ivy had survived her parachute training, she went there too, on her own because she'd been slow and was between groups.

Her only instruction was to dress in civilian clothing. When the black Austin Seven – a different one this time, without the smell of cleaning fluid – drew up at the railway station, she had a very strong feeling she should not get inside. For a moment she kept her feet planted to the platform, clutching her small bag like a woebegone schoolgirl, before deciding she was being silly. She reminded herself that she had been trained to kill, that it was wartime, that one didn't abandon one's post and go home because of a sick feeling on a cloudy day.

The evening was cold, and the ground was covered with yellow leaves. Ivy and two other women crouched behind an overturned log while Joan, the leader of their group, peered into the gloom beyond.

It was something of a relief to be doing this after sunset; a few more minutes and it would be too dark for anyone to spot them.

In the meantime, they watched the sentries, to get a sense of their patterns. Even though the recruits knew that these were only SOE staff dressed in SS uniforms, there was a part of Ivy's brain that believed what it saw.

They had been trained to recognize the uniforms, to tell Schutzstaffel from Abwehr, Abwehr from Milice. If they were caught in this exercise, they would give the names and cover stories they'd memorized. Ivy was no longer Ivy; she was not even Juliet, her code name within the SOE; her cover was Marie-Claire, an art student from Rennes. The only thing that made tonight different from a real mission in France was that there were no real bullets in the guns, and no cyanide pills in their pockets.

Ivy felt good. Night was falling, but she had already spent a night out in the darkness alone, and this was easier. Give her a quick fright over a slow one, any day. It was also easier than skinning a rabbit, which had turned her into a quivering child with tears in her eyes and vomit in her mouth, and given her a sore stomach for two days. Survival skills, they called it. One might be dropped into a remote and/or unfriendly area, on purpose or otherwise, and one had to be able to stay alive, alone, for days at a time. Which was all well and good, on paper.

Paper, for that matter, had also given her trouble.

Every agent in the field had to be able to cipher and decipher messages, to be transmitted by wireless operators to and from the SOE headquarters, which was on Baker Street, near the apartment where Ivy had been interviewed by Miss Atkins.

At Beaulieu, each recruit was told to select a favourite poem that they knew by heart. This was their poem, then, forever. Every time they wanted to send a message from the field, they'd choose five words at random from their poem. The order of the words would become a string of five numbers, to tell Baker Street which words they were using. Those five words became a transcription key: the alphabetical order of their letters became numbers, written at the top of a grid, and then one had to write the plain text into the grid, and then list out the columns by the key numbers, and arrange them in even groups of letters, which the wireless operator then had to send in Morse Code.

Ivy, luckily, was not being trained as a wireless operator, but she had to learn Morse all the same, and she had to learn to do her own ciphering and deciphering. Words became numbers, which became letters, which became numbers, and they all danced mockingly in her head. At one point, she overheard a visiting officer say to the coding instructor, 'Well, perhaps we don't want them overburdened with brains,' when the coding instructor suggested that Juliet's work was not up to snuff.

Ivy had never been bright, but she was determined, and she was good at guessing what teachers wanted. So she had always managed to get by. She could not actually understand algebra, but she could pass an algebra test. But at Beaulieu, for the first time in her life, she found herself in a classroom trying to learn, not merely to pass. Part-way through the process, she would look at the long string of meaningless letters and a dull, frozen absence would take hold of her brain and her pencils would snap between her fingers. It was the lurch from big to small that undid her, every time. She could rattle off the poem beautifully, but it all went blank and grey the moment she had to think about whether the word was 'among' or 'upon' in 'The moon was a ghostly galleon tossed upon cloudy seas'.

The coding instructor, who was apparently not as cavalier as his colleague about the superfluity of brains, felt the need to impress upon her that coding mistakes would leave the organization guessing about such things as where to safely drop an agent, or which network was compromised. It would get people killed. But Ivy couldn't seem to speed up; when she did, she'd stop, frozen by doubt halfway through. She would be aware, in that moment, that she had filled in the letters, but she couldn't explain how she'd done it. It reminded her of the way Rose used to stop sometimes in the middle of playing a piece on the piano, totally absorbed in one moment, then suddenly unaware of what came next.

But out in the woods, in the twilight, she knew exactly

what came next. Ivy was the lookout; everyone said she was the most observant. She knew that the sentry would pause and light a cigarette, lengthening his third lap around the house, creating a gap as the other sentry stayed on course.

She chose that lap as her moment to creep from one tree to the next, waving the rest of her team on behind. The ground was thick with brown leaves, and the slightest pressure would make them crackle like fireworks. She walked as they'd been trained, with the feet pointed straight ahead. No Charlie Chaplins. Even so, the leaves were so thick that she thought it best to avoid them. She stepped from one moss-covered rock to the next, gingerly putting a toe on a skinny, wobbly root when need be. But she made it, and knelt behind a large trunk.

The house on the other side of the sentries was smaller and older than the one in which the female recruits lived. There were lights in all of the windows, on both storeys. How many people inside? The least conspicuous approach was to slip past the guards and into the house, jimmying open a window. But if need be they could also incapacitate them (the recruits had lipsticks, rather than knives, to slash across a sentry's neck to represent a killing). The trick would be pretend-killing both guards without alerting anyone in the house.

If only she knew which window led into an empty room. This would be the moment for her supposed Second Sight to make itself useful. She thought she had a feeling about the second-storey window on the right, but thinking she had a feeling wasn't enough to risk failing this test and being sent to the School of Forgetting.

She turned back and whispered to Joan, who was a few feet behind, crouching behind a fallen log. 'We'll need time to listen at the windows, so we'll have to take the sentries out.'

Joan nodded. 'Lise, you take the one on the left. Juliet,

you take the one on the right. If you're taken, Celine and I will lie low and then see if we can get through.'

Ivy timed her movements with the sentry's, knowing that she had the advantage; he was half-lit by the house windows, and she was in darkness. Her heart beat hard, not out of fear but out of excitement. She had trained to do this, over and over again. She knew how to do it and she would.

One step, then another. On to the moss – and her foot slipped. She crashed into the leaves. Nothing had ever sounded so loud. She was frozen, her arms out, trying not to overbalance, willing her foot to stay where it was. She turned in place to see her colleagues, and to her relief she couldn't see them at all. They must have dropped low when they heard the sound.

The sentry should be shouting by now, or firing a blank into the air, or something. Was it possible they hadn't heard?

A hand went over her mouth and nose, cutting off all air, and someone strong was pulling her backwards.

CHAPTER 13

Ivy

Ivy made no noise as the gag went into her mouth and two men tied her wrists. They marched her through the dark woods with a gun at her back. This was strange; usually when an instructor or soldier posing as Gestapo or SS caught a recruit during a test they'd shout, raising the alarm. But the instructors always wanted to teach them to adapt. So she adapted, and made no noise, because noise could alarm the sentries and put her colleagues at risk. Just as she'd put them at risk already, with those damned leaves.

Tears blinded her and her nose started to run.

They marched her on to a gravel road, to a black car. They pushed her into the back seat, and they tied a blindfold over her eyes.

That was when Ivy started to think that, perhaps, these weren't instructors, or soldiers, or staff.

They took the blindfold off in an antiseptic room painted in hospital green, with no windows. She was on a chair and the two men from the woods were with her. They weren't wearing German uniforms, or any uniforms at all, which was worrying. If this was a test, they should be in disguise. Their suits didn't look like the ones the instructors usually wore when they posed as Gestapo. The German secret police were often in plain clothes, Ivy had been taught, although outside Germany they might also be found in SS uniforms.

The man who spoke did have a faint German accent, to her horror. His voice rang off the walls as though they were inside an oil tank.

'You have nothing to fear from us.'

Shouldn't she know? Shouldn't she be able to tell? The only instinct she had was terror. She told herself that it didn't matter whether this was a test or something else; she would follow her training. The only task was to hold out for forty-eight hours, to give the network time to realize she'd been compromised and make changes to all the safe houses, dead drops and missions. But she didn't have a network, and she knew about no safe houses or planned missions. There was very little information she could give up, which ought to make it easier.

'We already know all about the poem code,' said the one who hadn't spoken yet, an older man with a head like a bullet and close-cropped grey hair. 'And we know the names of every instructor at Beaulieu. We catch the English when they drop, and we ask them questions.'

She wanted to say, *then you need nothing from me*, but she was still gagged, and it was probably wisest to stay silent.

'We've recently made the acquaintance of a friend of yours,' said the younger man, the one with the German accent. 'You know her as Jacqueline. She has been very useful. A little too old for the job, perhaps.'

Ivy went cold. It was a cruel test, to refer to someone she knew, someone who wasn't even in training any more. How long would it have been since Jacqueline went over to France in her boat?

The older one said, 'Take off her gag.'

Forty-eight hours. She had to hold out for forty-eight hours, whether this was real or a test. She had to prove she could do it. She could talk, so long as she gave them nothing useful, nothing real.

'I don't know any Jacqueline,' she said, her mouth sore at the sides from the gag.

'Don't waste our time,' said the German. He pulled her by her jacket up out of the chair, and walked her over to the corner of the room. She didn't resist; the point was to drag it out. Her arms were stiff with cold or fear. He stopped her in front of a bucket of water, and pushed her to her knees. It happened so quickly she was mercifully unafraid for one moment, as his hand grabbed the hair on the back of her head, and as her face plunged into the cold water.

He was strong, and she did push against him, in a matter of moments, because she couldn't have stopped herself anyway. She bucked and wriggled and succeeded in getting her head out, and swiping his legs out from under him, but then the other man grabbed her by the shoulders and she was in again. Sputtering, her eyes stinging, breathing in water and choking on it. She lost all thought but light and dark, survival and death.

Then she was lying on her back, shaking. Freezing. Her head was wet, her shoulders were wet. She was breathing hard.

'What we want is someone who will help us,' said the German. 'We can protect your friends, when they go over. We can look the other way, even give them warnings. In exchange for just a little—'

Somehow the bucket was over her head again, she was drowning, even though she was still on the ground. She

127

could see the ceiling above her but she could feel the pressure sting in her nostrils. The hands that tried to shove the water off her face were not her hands; they were the hands of one of the other recruits who'd been in the woods, on the exercise. They were Joan's hands; she did not recognize them, but she knew them. She was in Joan's body, though she didn't even know Joan's real name. And Joan's head was in the bucket.

Sputtering and wiping her streaming nose, she rolled over to get to her knees, and her captors didn't stop her. They were backing away, giving her space. She knew this meant something, but it was all distant and she could not bring herself to care about it, or about anything except whatever force was taking her over. She needed to vomit out the water, but her body seemed frozen. Time was stuttering; she heard, in something stronger than memory, the German saying, *We can protect your friends when they go over*. She heard him saying *Jacqueline*.

Jacqueline's face, turned up to the sky. The face that had winked at Ivy after a blustering lecture from the demolitions instructor. The face that had blinked away a tear when no one was looking. The face that was so curious, so determined. Now blank. Ivy followed the vision down to her body, to the pale arm lying with a syringe stuck into it.

The needle was going into Ivy's arm; she felt the sting, felt death in her veins. She clawed at it, tried to pull it out, but her hands were not her own, and the vision was doubled, tripled. She was Ivy, she was Joan, she was Jacqueline. There was a smell of burning, of metal and chemicals. She was none of them, and all of them, but she had a single heart, and it was seizing and shuddering, struggling to keep breath in her lungs.

The German said, 'It's all right, you're all right. Well done.'

'Well done,' said the Englishman.

'Should we – there's a doctor—'

'Let's get her next door. Come on, Juliet. You'll be more comfortable in a moment.'

They lifted her, one under each arm, and soon she was in another room. She had a blanket over her, and she was sitting on a sagging sofa, shaking.

'You're all right,' she heard a third voice say, and she looked up, and saw Mr Yardley sitting across from her, wearing a comforting smile.

Then she vomited.

Ivy felt increasingly silly and embarrassed with every sip of bitter cocoa.

'You did well,' Mr Yardley said. 'You told them nothing. It's a difficult test.'

A test. The German and the older man were on her side, on the English side. Jacqueline had not been captured. It was only a test.

She found her voice. 'Does everyone have to go through that? The others . . . ' She couldn't continue, remembering how she had seen Joan's hands, felt the water fill Joan's throat.

Mr Yardley did not answer for a moment, as he was lighting a cigarette. He offered it to her, and ordinarily she would have been thrilled at the recognition of her status as an adult, a modern woman and a peer, but she didn't want it. Her hands would shake, and her throat was already raw. She used to smoke sometimes in Paris, with Kit and Max, but she'd given it up when she came back home. Mother wouldn't have approved.

So Mr Yardley kept the cigarette himself, closing his silver case and looking thoughtful.

'Every recruit goes through at least one such test. The design is different, though, for each of you. For most, the only goal is to ensure that the recruit can keep his head if captured and knows what to do if that happens. For you, though, I admit I was hoping the test would reveal something else. And I believe it was successful in that regard.' He paused and fixed her gaze with his own. 'Am I right?'

'I'm not sure what you mean, sir.'

She did, but she didn't want to. She didn't want to remember what had been in her head.

'You seemed to be . . . hallucinating, the officers said. Did you see something? With your gift?'

Her gift! If it was a gift, she would give it back. It did nothing at all most of the time, and then made her absolutely unfit during interrogation.

'I thought – I was thinking of my colleagues, and felt that they were being tortured too. And what they said about Jacqueline, well, it made me imagine—'

'Imagine? Or see with your mind's eye?'

'The latter, I suppose, sir. It seemed very real. It seemed to be happening both to her and to me, at once.'

He said, very casually, 'And what did you see?'

She tried to remember, tried to make the jumble of sensations into a story. 'Her face. She was dead. And there was a needle, in her arm.'

Her hand moved to her own arm, remembering the terrifying sting.

'What else? Where was she?'

Ivy shook her head. 'I don't know. I remember the smell of burning, of rot. Of old clothes. Something sharp, like soap. Other people around, other bodies, perhaps. I was thinking only of her face, of that needle.'

'And you saw the needle in your own arm?'

'Felt it and saw it, sir. But – I wasn't myself, at the time. What I mean to say is that I seemed to be Jacqueline, or another woman, as I was dying. Or, I thought I was dying.'

She paused, tried to collect her thoughts. 'What I *mean* to say is that I don't believe I foresaw my own death.'

'But perhaps the deaths of others. Now or in the future.'

She must have looked as stricken as she felt, because Mr Yardley added quickly, 'Jacqueline is fine. We had a message from her yesterday, with her security check. We only mentioned her during the test because it helps to have a believable scenario, with the real people one has worked with in the programme. We have nothing specific to fear from what you saw, but that doesn't mean it isn't real in some way. Was there anything else?'

'I also thought about Joan. Another recruit here. I thought she was also – with the water bucket. I thought she was going through the same thing I was.'

He nodded. 'That is indeed the case. But of course, you might have surmised that. Do you think that vision was your gift, or was it your imagination?'

She shook her head, and her hands shook too, and the cocoa sloshed in the cup. She'd burned the roof of her mouth on it. If it was not the gift, what was it? Hysterics? Or something that would, in Aunt Kathleen's words, land her in the county asylum? If it was not the gift, she was useless to the war effort, wasn't she?

'I don't think it was imagination, Mr Yardley.' She summoned all her courage and honour and said with honesty, 'But if it's a gift, I don't know how to use it.'

'Well, there I have some good news,' he said, stubbing out his cigarette and smiling as if they were discussing plans for a neighbourhood picnic. 'While you have been training, I have been looking for someone who might be able to help you learn your specialization. You may have wondered at my sending you off and then not checking in on you, but it couldn't be helped. I had to go to Canada to meet the man I hoped would become your teacher. I had to persuade a few people to let me have him. Tomorrow, you'll begin your next set of lessons, but you're the only student in this particular programme. At least, the only student so far.'

At that, a shadow crossed his face, and she wondered about it, but there were so many things to wonder about that she couldn't put any of it into words. She said, 'I do want to be useful, sir.'

CHAPTER 14

Ivy

In October 1942, Ivy moved into a small house in the woods, on the edges of the Beaulieu finishing school complex, a house that bore the designation Special Training School 22B.

Mrs Codd, the widowed housekeeper, took her bags and showed her to her room.

It wasn't until the following day that she met Grady Sinclair. She came down for breakfast and saw a ginger-haired young man slouching in a chair, his long legs stretched under the table, his tweed elbows on it, his long fingers interlaced. His eyes were bloodshot.

'You must be Mr Sinclair,' Ivy said.

'Yardley didn't exaggerate your gifts,' he said drily.

She blushed and sat opposite him, and cracked a soft-boiled egg.

'What did he tell you about me?' Mr Sinclair asked. He spoke with an American accent. No, Canadian. Mr Yardley had said he got the man from Canada.

Ivy swallowed. She had been so careful with the secret,

and she was always on alert for another test. 'That you would teach me to use . . . those gifts.'

She was expecting him to ask what she could do, and braced herself to try to make it seem as though her small collection of coincidences and imaginings might be of some use.

Instead, he asked, 'That's all?'

'That's all, Mr Sinclair.'

He unclasped his hands and put his fingers on the handle of his tea cup, but he didn't lift it. 'Did he tell you why?'

Ivy was confused. 'So that I can help in the war effort.'

'And how do you expect to do that?'

She hesitated. If she said the wrong thing, they might send her home to Cambridge untrained, unchanged. They might send her to the School of Forgetting. They might take her into a room with a bucket of water. 'I was hoping you could tell me.'

At that, he grinned, and not kindly. 'It seems we could be here for some time.'

Ivy looked down at her plate, chipped beige with the eggcup in the middle, a piece of toast on the side. She had no appetite and she wanted to be anywhere but here.

She felt very alone. Mr Yardley had told her that from now on she would receive no letters from her family. As instructed, she wrote to them to say that she was going to work as a driver for a signalling facility, and that the security there would mean she could not receive letters, but that she would send brief notes whenever she could, reassuring them of her welfare. The reason for this, Mr Yardley explained, was to arouse no suspicion when the day came that Ivy went abroad and stopped being able to receive letters; it would be obvious, if she suddenly failed to respond to family news in the pre-written responses she had created while in the first part of her training, back at Swindon.

That was, if she ever was sent abroad. If it weren't for her supposed talent, she would be there now, with the other recruits. Instead, she was here, useless, under the eyes of a stranger.

But this man, this breakfast table, would not defeat her, when she had survived so many trials.

'Every instructor I've had so far has expected me to drop out or fail, at every stage,' she said quietly. 'I have learned how to kill and climb and crawl through the mud. Although I may not seem very promising to look at, you will find me diligent and determined.'

He met her gaze for a moment, and then a smile cracked his face. 'All right, then. I've asked you my questions, and I've heard your answers. Do you have any questions for me?'

Ivy had too many questions and wasn't sure where to start. Wasn't sure which questions it was all right to ask. At last, she said, 'Mr Yardley says I am the only student in this programme. But I can't be the only person ever to have the Second Sight. My great-aunt used to tell me stories about it. And he thinks that you can teach me. So you must have known others. Or read about others. I suppose what I want to know is whether I'm . . . alone.'

He whistled softly. 'A big question. And one that deserves an answer. I'll tell you what I know.'

Ivy was so astonished at this that she sloshed her tea.

Grady Sinclair traced a pattern on the tablecloth with his fingertip, not looking at her.

'At the beginning of the war, the Nazis had already been recruiting astrologers and fortune-tellers for years. These people were mostly charlatans, of course, useful only for propaganda purposes. But the Nazis also did something new, something secret: they trained people with unusual talents. I don't know how many, or what they used them for. I don't know how many of them were genuine clairvoyants. But I do know that our side got wind of it, and got worried, before the Nazis shut it down.'

'Shut it down?'

'Do you remember when Rudolf Hess flew to Scotland in a private plane in May last year?'

She did remember – it had been in the newspapers. It was around the time Father had gone to Scotland himself, to see Aunt Kathleen before she died. Hess, the Deputy Führer, one of Hitler's top men, had flown a small plane to Scotland and been taken into custody.

She nodded. 'I don't know the details, but I remember it.'

'Well, Hess had this cockeyed idea that Britain could be persuaded to make peace with Germany. He's not the only Nazi who harbours that fantasy, but Hitler had to come up with some reason why Hess would go off and fly to the UK without permission. Hess was in the habit of consulting psychics, it seems. So that is where Hitler put the blame. The Reich has rounded up every two-bit actor with a spirit cabinet and shipped them off to wherever they ship people off to.'

Ivy was not sure what to make of this. 'Where do I come into it?'

'All those enemies Hitler has made among those with a mystical bent, like Hess, might be counted upon to work for their own interests. I believe that must be what Yardley has in mind. He's a politician, first and foremost. He's thinking about what happens after Hitler. *Communities of interest.*' Mr Sinclair said this last part with a bitter sneer.

This made little sense to Ivy. 'He said he wanted me to do war work. Actual war work, to use my talents to see things others couldn't. To gather intelligence. Troop movements, that sort of thing.'

'Is that what he said?'

Ivy thought back. 'Something like that, anyway. Why would he send me for SOE training otherwise?'

Mr Sinclair shrugged. 'Possibly so that he could test your ability to keep a secret. But I do suspect he would be very happy if we could use you in the field. It would be a useful demonstration.'

'You don't sound as if you share his hope.'

He scratched his head. 'You asked me whether you were alone. Of course you are not. It wasn't only the Germans who've taken an interest in unusual talents. But our side is always two steps behind. There was a bit of a push to train up our own people early in the war, to find people like you and me and put us to work. These efforts did not go well. I don't know what Roosevelt and Stalin have got up their sleeves, of course, but I believe the sum total of the Allied countries' genuine psychic ability in people of arguably sound mind is here at this breakfast table. There have been some unfortunate errors in judgement.'

Ivy thought for a moment. 'People like you and me, you said.'

'Yes.'

'Then you are—'

'I am an unfortunate error in judgement.'

His smile was different at either end, like a marionette with two masters.

The lessons began after breakfast.

The training room contained a table, chairs, and a filing cabinet. Mr Sinclair took a deck of cards out of the filing cabinet and sat on one side of the table, and gestured for her to take the opposite chair.

He flipped five cards down. They weren't playing cards; they were very plain, in black and white, and each of them bore a symbol: a circle, a plus sign, wavy lines, a square and a star.

'I'd like you to turn your chair around,' he said. 'Face the window, please.'

She did, and looked out on the square of brown and grey that was the world outside.

She heard him shuffle the cards, banging them against the table a couple of times. He cleared his throat. She could almost picture him, his sharp Adam's apple.

A few years before the war, Ivy had gone with the whole family – even Aunt Kathleen, who was visiting – to the cinema to see a film called *The Clairvoyant*. She could remember the chill that went through her when Claude Rains declared, 'I do not profess to be a superman. The powers I possess are possessed more or less by you all.'

More or less.

It was a bad memory, all told. Ivy had been tickled by the idea that everyone had psychic powers. After the film, back in the sitting room at Stoke Damson, she'd tried to make all her sisters play a parlour game of guessing playing cards. Just as she was doing with Mr Sinclair now.

'Focus on the cards,' he said. 'I'm going to flip one up at random and I want you to tell me which symbol you see in your mind's eye.'

She saw nothing in her mind's eye, just the series of five cards, which she could cycle through deliberately.

'Card One,' he said.

'I don't know.'

'Don't think about it, Miss Sharp. Just say whichever one comes to mind first.'

'Wavy lines.'

A pause.

'Card Two. Faster this time, please.'

'Circle.'

'Card Three.'

'Square.'

They were up to Card Fifty when he stopped, and said she could take a break. He was frowning over a tally sheet.

'Seven correct is not very good, is it?'

'How do you know you had seven correct?' He looked at her sharply, hopefully.

She pointed at the tally sheet.

He laughed. 'No, it's not very good. As bad as, or worse than, I might expect from someone guessing at random. Almost as though you were trying to *not* get them right. But that would be a very strange thing to do.'

Ivy felt she was being accused of something. 'Of course I was not trying to fail.'

'Were you second-guessing your choices? Because that would—' He stopped, seeing her face. 'It's the first session. Take half an hour, and we'll try again.'

She went for a walk. The guessing game in Stoke Damson back in 1935 had ended badly too. Helen had been furious with Ivy, saying that she had missed the whole point. 'Didn't you watch the film?' Helen had demanded. 'Don't you recall how the clairvoyant foresaw that mining disaster, all that suffering? Or how he predicted the crash? I can still see those terrible train tracks, rushing past. He saw awful things, and nobody believed him. I don't think you'd want that kind of talent.'

Helen hated anything frightening. She said that she just knew she was going to have bad dreams again, and she'd stormed off to the kitchen.

Father had followed Helen, to comfort her, while Aunt Kathleen told the remaining sisters that real Second Sight was no parlour trick. She told them her favourite story, about the town where all the men were sailors, and how, one day, three women each saw their respective husbands, standing against the horizon, up on the cliffs. Saying nothing, doing nothing, just standing there. And the following morning they found the husbands' bodies, all tangled up in a wreck, not far from shore.

How Ivy had loved the story then. She liked to get the shivers, to feel that something incredible was possible. But Helen was cold to her for days afterwards.

When Ivy returned to the house, Mr Sinclair had pinned five of the cards on the wall below the window, and her chair was set in front of it. He sat her in the chair and gave her a billiard cue and asked her to point to the cards, rather than say the words.

This time, she could hear from the slight slip of paper that he was drawing the cards from the deck after he announced them, rather than before.

'Card One.'

This time, after the fifty cards, he slipped the tally sheet into a drawer before she could turn around. But his face was disappointed.

They kept at it for weeks: not only the cards but other tests too. Every morning began with writing down her dreams in an exercise book. After breakfast, she had to watch ten minutes of film strip with random images and answer questions about them. Most days, she had an hour with her French tutor, a quiet middle-aged woman she met in another house nearby for a supervised session. A few days a week, she also had German lessons. Then back to the house with Mr Sinclair for the cards, or coloured blocks, or a passage of Shakespeare, or some other guessing game.

Once, she got up the courage to ask whether he had had any luck with the cards and games himself.

He lit a cigarette. '"He who can, does. He who cannot, teaches." That's George Bernard Shaw.'

There wasn't much to do in the house, which was probably why Grady Sinclair took long walks, two or three hours at a time. He'd come in with his cheeks wind-burned and his hands in his pockets, and Ivy would be reading or sketching on some scrap of paper and feeling lonely and sorry for herself. He never asked her to join him, and she suspected she wouldn't be able to keep up; he was tall, and had a fast stride.

Sometimes he wrote in a battered old notebook, and he never said what he was writing. Notes about how unsatisfactory she was, probably, but she would not have thought there was much to say about that.

They had dinner together on Christmas Eve, alone in the house, because Mrs Codd had gone home to her family. There was cold ham, sprouts, potatoes and turnips, and they prepared it together, in the kitchen.

'It must be hard for you, not being able to go to your family at Christmas,' he said.

'And for you.'

'I don't have any family left.'

'I'm sorry.'

'There's nothing to be sorry about. They were not good people. But you're close to yours, aren't you?'

'Very close.' She paused, and scraped the turnip peel into the bin. 'Or at least, we used to be. But all the Christmases have been quiet since the war began, of course. I doubt Rose will be able to get away; she couldn't last year.'

'And your other sisters?'

'Kit is in Paris. But Helen's in Stoke Damson, in our family home.' She paused. 'Or will probably be there, I suppose. She must be on the farm. I thought of her being there, at the house, because she was there just before I left for training.'

He stopped chopping the ends off the sprouts and looked at her curiously.

In the morning, he was reading the *Manchester Guardian*, as he always did, even though it was always a day or two old by the time it reached them. The sight of him with the paper in his hand made Ivy's stomach drop; he always made casual conversation about the news, and she knew it was full of tests. *Who do you think will win the Manchester Clayton by-election? How many casualties might result from the earthquake in Turkey?*

It was Christmas morning, and she was away from family, with nothing to celebrate and no real reason to be here. It was useless to go on pretending she had some sort of talent that might be useful to the war effort. She was good for nothing in this world but decoration – and not even much of that, she thought ruefully, pulling at her old green jumper and tucking her hair behind her ears.

But she was hungry. And Mr Sinclair had made them porridge, which was keeping hot under a tea cosy. She slid into her chair quietly, thinking that perhaps he'd keep reading and not quiz her, not today.

There was a present on her plate.

It was clearly a book, wrapped in green paper that looked as though it had wrapped at least one other gift before.

She stammered, 'I didn't – I didn't expect a gift.'

'It's all right,' he said, looking over his paper at her mischievously. 'I didn't either. Go on, open it. Your porridge is getting cold.'

It was a sketchbook, with a plain black cover and crisp new pages. A proper sketchbook. The sort of thing she had not given a second thought to, before the war. Now, with the paper rations, it seemed a gift for a princess.

'It's lovely,' she said.

'You can draw me a picture in it,' he said. 'If you really want to give me something.'

She made a face. 'The last time I gave someone art for Christmas it went badly for me.'

He had dropped hints that he knew the basic story of how

she had caught Yardley's attention, but he'd never asked her about it. Now, he folded his newspaper, and looked as though he was about to say something – when the doorbell rang.

She was on her third spoonful of porridge when he came back in, holding a telegram. But his face told her it wasn't bad news; he only looked puzzled.

'Miss Sharp, your sister Helen recently had a baby,' he said.

And then she nearly did choke. 'I beg your pardon?'

'A baby.' He held up the telegram. 'I made enquiries, about whether she was still working in the Land Army – because of what you said the other day. You had an instinct that she was at the house in Stoke Damson already, and then you disregarded it, and you see? You were right.' He grinned, and came close to her, and smacked the telegram on his palm in triumph. 'You were right!'

She shook her head. 'Helen can't have a baby. She isn't married.'

At that, he subdued himself and leaned on one of the empty chairs. There were four chairs at their table, but only ever the two of them, because Mrs Codd liked to eat by herself in the kitchen or go home to her family.

'Ah,' he said. 'I see. Well, maybe she got married since you saw her.'

'She can't have – her fiancé shipped out. Maybe there's a mix-up. Maybe it's another of the refugee children, or evacuees. My mother takes them in when she can.'

'I'm told she was very obviously pregnant through the summer. Our contact spoke with the town gossips.'

Her cheeks red with indignation, Ivy did a quick calculation. She'd seen George in December, before they'd had Christmas together. And now it was another Christmas. With a new baby. A niece or nephew! What would Mother and Father have said about it?

'Oh, poor Helen. Is it a boy or a girl? And can I write to her?'

'Impossible, I'm afraid. No communication with families, just the pre-written letters telling them you're all right. You know the rules. And I know nothing more than what I've told you.'

Ivy rubbed her temple. Helen, with a baby! And she could say nothing to her about it. Everything was broken and wrong.

'Let's go for a walk,' said Mr Sinclair. 'When you've finished your breakfast. I think it would do us both good.'

Tiny pinpricks of snow, not even big enough to catch gravity's attention, were meandering in the air. It was just cold enough to make Ivy glad of her scarf and mittens.

Mr Sinclair cleared his throat. 'I want to make a confession. The notebook I gave you. I've had it kicking around for years.'

'I couldn't have asked for a better gift, Mr Sinclair, really.'

'Perhaps you'd better call me Grady.'

She laughed bitterly, thinking that there could be no more certain sign that he wouldn't be her instructor much longer. 'All right.'

There was a silence, his steps in time with hers.

'I had an aunt who gave me a notebook every birthday,' he said. 'Because I was a journalist, I suppose. That one was too fancy to interview a policeman with, but I didn't want to get rid of it.'

'I didn't know you'd been a journalist. Were you good at it?'

'Very good.' Grady paused. 'I had an uncanny knack for knowing that something terrible was going to happen. Once, I took a notion to go for a walk in the train yard – this was in Winnipeg, where I used to live. And I spotted a man who was wanted for murder, being chased by two police officers. Just by happenstance.'

'That was your gift,' she said softly. 'Wasn't it?'

He didn't answer that. 'It didn't go well for the police officers that day. It didn't go well for anyone who was unlucky enough to have me find them. I witnessed more than my share of suicides and I stopped none of them.' Then, as if to lighten things, he said, 'Not that I didn't try. We brought in one of those horoscope columns, you know the sort; they became popular a few years before the war. They were written by a guy named Frank in the compositing room. Once, I changed a line in it, because I had this terrible feeling that it was going to make someone do something horrible. I can't even recall what it was now, something about "you cannot fail to meet with success on Thursday" or some nonsense. I doubt it made a difference, but I was downright superstitious. I had reason to be.'

It sounded like the opening to another story, but he stopped there, and said, 'You mentioned an aunt, once. The aunt who told you about the Second Sight.'

She laughed. 'Aunt Kathleen. A great-aunt, in fact. She died last year. You would have liked her. She loved to take long walks, too. She always had a dog, you see, and every one of them was named Barkley, in succession, like royalty. I think there were four Barkleys that I remember, and who knows how many before that.'

'And she gave you your first paint set.'

'Yes – did I tell you that? I don't remember. Oils. I thought they were terribly fancy and I was so afraid to use them. I still have a little left in every tube.'

'We're all so afraid to waste anything now.'

'Yes, but even before the war I was like that. Not because I was born thrifty, but because I waste and spoil so many things. You have no idea how many batches of scones I've

KATE HEARTFIELD

had to throw away in my life. When I was a child, I used to think that if I could be anything I wanted, I'd be a beautiful glass figurine, because nobody could want a beautiful glass figurine to do anything useful. Isn't that silly? I should have wished to be a car engine or something like that.'

He laughed, and stretched his long legs to get ahead of her, walking up to a fence. Beyond it was a frosted field where sheep sometimes grazed in warmer weather. But today there were no sheep, no people or animals anywhere, not even any birds calling.

He leaned out over the fence, not looking at her. Despite his laughter, he seemed troubled, divided, as if he was trying to make a hard decision, not letting her see him do it. Perhaps he'd brought her out here to tell her that the training was over, that she'd failed, that she was going away to the School of Forgetting. That would explain why today, of all days, he was talking to her, really talking to her, instead of trying to get her to make a prediction. She was hopeless; she was the glass figurine.

But on this Christmas morning that smelled of snow, it was hard for Ivy to believe that there was not some reason for hope. Hope that she would see her family again, that war would end, that children would be reunited with their parents in the places that had burned. If it was her lot to go home again, then at least she would not go home the same. Glass or not, she would find a way to get in someone's way. She knew that now, for the first time in her life.

She leaned on the fence next to him. 'I want to tell you that it isn't your fault. *I'm* not your fault. You've been a very good teacher.'

He looked at her, his expression grave. 'Have I?' His gaze held her.

Ivy would have looked away from his blue eyes, a month before. She didn't look away now. 'Why do you always ask

146

me whether I mean what I say? I always mean what I say. I'm not clever enough to lie properly.'

'What colour is my bicycle?'

She pulled back, frowning. 'You don't have—'

'Not here. Back home, in Canada. Picture a bicycle.'

Ivy closed her eyes.

'Now picture *my* bicycle.'

'I don't know what your bicycle looks like, Mr Sinclair.'

'Grady. And yes you do. What colour is it?'

Ivy hesitated. 'Black.'

'No. No. *Your* bicycle is black. You know what colour mine is, but you're just afraid to say it.'

'Blue,' Ivy whispered, not sure why she was frightened. She could see a blue bicycle, with no basket. Not the same blue as his eyes. Royal blue, scuffed. 'It has a tear across the seat, mended with tape.'

He said nothing, and she opened her eyes, and saw that he had reached out to grasp her arm but had stopped just short, so that his gloved hand was hovering like a claw an inch over the sleeve of her coat.

'Good,' he said hoarsely, and turned and walked away, leaving her standing at the fence, in the thickening snow, her eyes wet and her throat sore.

CHAPTER 15

Ivy

The following day, Grady's face was open and polite when she came down for breakfast. After he read his newspaper, they went into the classroom. He was going to keep trying, she realized, and steeled herself for another set of cards.

Instead, he left the chairs facing each other across the table, and he put a grainy photograph down in front of her of an unfamiliar house. Its door and windows made a grotesque face.

'Ivy, please tell me how many doors there are to this house. How many entrances, and where they are.'

She stared at him for a moment. 'I imagine there's at least one more in the back. But it's a large house. There might be more.'

'Don't imagine. Tell me what you see. I know this house, you see. I'll tell you whether you're right.'

Her cheeks were hot. She closed her eyes.

She tried to pick up the house and turn it in her mind, but there was no turning it. Another tack, then. She stopped thinking about the house. The bicycle, yesterday, had just come into her head. So what came into her head when she tried to empty it? A carriage house, yes, that might be right. There was some open ground, and then—

The seaside.

They were nowhere near the seaside. Her mind was supplying random images, that was all.

She opened her eyes. 'I don't know how many entrances there are.'

'You do.'

'I do not.'

'You opened your eyes because you were afraid of what you were seeing. I know how that is. Believe me. You're afraid that you can see the truth. Close your eyes again. The SOE has no use for a coward who will get agents killed.'

She scowled. None of this had been her idea.

'Fine. Do you want to know what I see? I see a rocky shore, and a great body of water. Blue as anything, and as wide as the world. And I see, rising out of it—' Her breath caught at what she saw. But there was nothing for it. He would understand, now, that she only had a vivid imagination, that was all. She might as well go back to driving in Sheffield. Better that than endangering people. 'I see tall fingers of steel,' she carried on, 'all sparking and blue, and green and purple lights at each tip, so high – and the fingers belong to a monster, with many heads, and every head is eyeless and mouthless, but they are screaming somehow anyway – and there's a woman in the water, floating—'

She opened her eyes, defiant, and saw the anger on his face. He was white with it.

'You can't do that,' he said. 'That's not what I asked you to do.'

'It is what I saw. What comes to my mind's eye, you see. Most of the time it's just rubbish, like that.'

'It's not rubbish. It's mine. That past is mine. I didn't give you permission to look into my past.'

She blinked the blur away. 'It was a monster. It was not a real—'

'It was Hydra. It's at the Farm in Canada, where your Mr Yardley found me. That's a rather dangerous secret, by the way.' His eyes burned as though he had a fever.

'A monster? You're teasing me.'

'Not a monster. A wireless installation. But because of the name, in my mind – it's my mind you were seeing, not the real world. That isn't what Hydra actually looks like. It's how I see it.'

She blinked, breathed, tried to make peace with this information. 'Then my gift – it's to read minds?'

He put his head in his hands, his fingers ruffling his red hair on his forehead, as they often did when he was tired. 'There was no one with you when you painted the picture that put the fear of the devil into Yardley.'

'And I still don't know why it did. These last few weeks, I've convinced myself it was a coincidence, that I happened to paint a woman's face that looked like a woman he knew. That my occasional lucky guesses were just that.' She paused. 'Tell me what you think. Please. Tell me what you think about me.'

He dropped his hands and looked up at her, his gaze open, defeated, calm. 'I was ready to accept that it was all coincidence, too. And then you mentioned those few words about your sister, that little slip of the subconscious. So I checked, and you were right about her. I wondered if, maybe, for your talent to kick in, there might be some need for emotional connection. You care about your sister, so that made it meaningful. It seemed obvious, when it occurred to me. I should have known, given my— I should have known this would never be as simple as a person sitting in a room reading cards through the back of their head . . . '

He paused. She could have filled in the gap. It was all starkly, horribly clear. But she did not. She waited for him to say it.

'So I thought, perhaps if *you and I* had a stronger connection . . . a friendship, I mean . . . if I let you get a little closer to me, you might be able to sense things about my life. It was an experiment. And it worked. You did it too well. It's possible that I could have been giving you an image – there are some stories about clairvoyants being able to *make* other people see things. But I've never had that happen before. And anyway, I didn't want you to see Hydra, and certainly not the way I see it. I wasn't even thinking about Hydra. The house that I showed you is in a different province, from a different part of my life.'

He swallowed.

She hated him in that moment, and hated herself for being so naïve. The Christmas present. His stories about his past. He had chosen to be kind, natural, human, only out of some deliberate attempt to trick her into performing like a trained dog.

She bit it back. It wasn't the first time that deception had been part of her training for the SOE. She was determined to become as hard and sharp as they needed her to be.

She focused on the practicalities and asked a practical question. 'Then if I want to be any use, I have to – what? Get to be friends with Adolf Hitler?'

'I don't know what it will take. But I know something's there. Maybe, now that we know how to tap into it, we can make it happen for other things. I am – like you, in some ways, I think. Not quite the same, but the kinds of things I see are particular to me. But there are examples of people who seem to cast a wider net. The woman you drew, for example.'

She let her surprise show on her face. 'What about her? Do you know who she is?'

He nodded. 'I'm under strict orders not to tell you this, you know.'

'But you're going to.'

'At this point, I don't think we're going to get anywhere by being dishonest with each other.'

They sat across from each other for a breath, two breaths.

Grady said, 'Her name was Ellen Merchant. I heard about her from those in Canada who were interested in these supernatural questions, and then, later, Yardley told me more about her, when he told me about you. She lived in a village near Newcastle. She called herself a medium, and Yardley was convinced she was the real deal. She used to write in to the papers about disasters and royal babies and all kinds of things. One day she had a vision about a bus crash, and she got into her car and raced to the area to try to stop it.'

'And did she?'

'There was no bus crash that day. Whether something she did stopped it, I don't know. But I don't see how it could have. I think she was simply wrong. And she paid the price for it. As she was racing down one of your English roads with the hedges on either side, a truck came straight at her and she died.'

Ivy felt cold. 'I didn't know this woman. I had no emotional connection to her.'

'No. So let's figure this out. Why did you draw her?'

She looked around the room, trying to think, to remember, avoiding the distraction of his face. 'I don't know. I was feeling mopey. Thinking about what lay ahead for me. Thinking about my own future. Then I saw this woman's face in the sky and the leaves.'

When he didn't answer, she looked at him, and for a split second she saw how stricken and horrified he was, before he tidied his expression up.

CHAPTER 16

Ivy

Mr Yardley was pleased when he came to visit in February. By then, Ivy had hit on a method for giving her mind's eye something to see, even when she didn't know the people involved.

It came easiest with anger and grief; when Grady showed her photographs of bombed houses in London, families weeping, she could tell him something about who had died or what else was in the area, and he could check the facts. About one-third of the time, she was right about something. The other times she saw nothing at all, or she saw images that she didn't understand.

'Am I just inventing these things?' she asked one day, in frustration.

'I think you're seeing the future,' he said grimly. 'Something about the future. Yours or someone else's.'

'But it's always just a face, or a suitcase, or a car or something. Nothing of any use to anyone.'

'We'll see,' he said.

The photographs that didn't make her cry were harder.

Sometimes she could get something by tapping into yearning, as she'd yearned for a new self that day she'd painted the medium she'd never met. Grady would show her a photograph of a beach, and she would imagine what it would be like to be on it on a beautiful sunny day, walking and eating an apple, and then she would tell him that at one end of the beach was a cottage with blue shutters on the windows, and he would allow himself the smallest of smiles.

She was able to show off to Mr Yardley right away, as she told him very plainly when he arrived that he had been delayed when his car broke down. It came to her in a flash, and she blurted it out confidently. A year before, she would have dismissed the notion as a guess or a fancy; now she knew it. And she was lucky: this wasn't some future event intruding on to the present, or whatever her errors really were.

He was stunned, and then so happy he went red in the face, and they opened the champagne he had brought. Grady got three glasses from the kitchen, and Ivy drew the curtains in the sitting room.

'I knew that when we had our breakthrough it would be a woman,' Mr Yardley said, after they'd had their first sip of champagne. 'No offence, Sinclair.'

'None taken,' Grady said, smiling.

'Why a woman, Mr Yardley?' Ivy asked.

'The feminine impulse to warn and to guide has taken this form, going back to the oldest times,' he said. 'The Oracle of Delphi was a woman. And there's a reason we call it Mother Nature. I believe your gift is part of nature. Not supernatural but essentially natural. A way of seeing the true nature of all things.'

'I've never been known for my maternal instincts,' she said.

'No, but you will be a wonderful aunt,' he said, and pulled out a photograph, of Helen holding a baby.

Ivy covered a gasp and stared at the photograph, holding it up to the light.

'Her name is Celia and she's the pride of the village. I understand your sister and George Bodley were married in secret just before he embarked.'

Ivy was puzzled: Helen would not have kept that from her sisters, even if she'd kept it from the rest of the world. A convenient story, then, to be regularized when George came home. If he came home.

She looked at the photograph again, and her practice kicked in unbidden, and she saw Helen crying, and young Karl giving her a hug, and then he was playing with the baby, with the wooden blocks that had once been Ivy's. It was all clear, a series of images like a film reel that had got stuck in the projector.

'I've kept an eye on Helen, when I can, to see whether she too will show signs of the family gift one of these days. It struck me that, in you and your three sisters, we can see the basic archetypes of the feminine,' Mr Yardley said, and Ivy looked up, blinking away the images. 'Helen, the nurturer. Rose, the pure maiden. Kit, the wise woman. And Ivy – Ivy who grows wild. The creative spirit, connecting the others.'

Something about this struck a loud wrong note for Ivy. She felt flattened, pinned against the wall. She and her sisters were not archetypes, to be praised when they conformed to a model and corrected when they didn't. Mr Yardley had known them all their lives, as real people, and now he spoke as if he'd read about them in a novel, or chosen them out of a catalogue. Where did his own daughter fit into this perfect set?

And what if Ivy were to choose to be something other than what he hoped for her? Her visions didn't feel creative; they felt destructive, tearing down the walls of her self, tearing down the world that everyone else could see and

touch. She was pulling herself off like a costume and disman-
tling reality like a stage set. She was on a pathway to oblivion,
just as surely as the medium whose face she'd painted had
once sped along a road to her death. Something terrifying
called to her, and she knew it was the transformation she'd
always wanted. There, she was nothing, and could be
anything. She would stand there naked and alone and she
would finally be – what? Time to find out.

If she were to tell Mr Yardley any of these thoughts, what
would he think of her? What choices would be incorrect
enough to make him lose faith in her, write her off as broken,
send her to the School of Forgetting? She was not the woman
he thought she was; but she was not going to stop becoming
the woman she could be.

So she kept her face a mask.

'Kit, the wise woman!' she chuckled, not quite a real
chuckle – she didn't look at Grady because he would know
her reaction was phoney and wonder about it, and that
would make her drop her mask. 'Don't ever let her hear you
say that, Mr Yardley, or we'll never hear the end of it.'

And then she really did drop her mask, because thinking
of Kit made her thoughts run, as always, to whether Kit was
still alive, whether she was hurt or afraid. She would have
appreciated an image then but her mind's eye was shut; she
saw only Kit's face smiling, Kit's face frowning, Kit's face
thinking when she believed no one was looking at her. It
fed her heartsickness only as fuel feeds a fire.

Mr Yardley did not notice. 'Wise women can be dangerous,'
he said, gazing into his glass, as if half talking to himself.
But then his expression cleared and he looked at her. 'I'm
very sure she can take care of herself, come what may.'

'And what is coming?' Grady asked. He was standing beside
the fireplace, a little behind Ivy's chair.

'Vichy France has made a stupendous error. They've been

deporting thousands of their own people. Sending them to Germany as forced labour. It's becoming impossible for anyone to believe that, if one just keeps one's head down, life can go on as before. And that means the Resistance is growing every day.'

'Then they'll need more weapons, and more radios,' Grady said. 'Are we giving them more?'

'We? We are doing our best, Mr Sinclair,' said Yardley drily. 'The rapid growth comes with its own problems, of course. More people means more spies, more slips, more chances our agents will be caught.' He pulled an envelope out of his pocket. 'How are you with photographs, Miss Sharp? Do you get anything from them?'

'Sometimes. Would you like me to have a look at one?'

'Several, if you're not too tired. If the champagne—'

She reached out her hand and took the stack.

A woman in a beret; she saw a child in a swing. She held it, tried to think of what it must be like to be a woman with a child, in war. Tried every emotion she could muster but saw nothing more.

She told Mr Yardley what she saw, and he nodded. She exhaled. The first test passed.

The second photograph was of a broad-shouldered, fair-haired man who clearly found himself handsome, a matinee idol with a blunt nose and a square jaw. Something hurt her about it: mailbags; blood on the wall. Blood on the name. A hand, tracing the name. This hand didn't belong to the handsome man in the photograph. This was an old hand, thin, scratching something into the wall.

She dropped the photograph and it floated to the carpeted floor.

'What did you see?' Yardley asked.

She put it into words. 'I saw letters. Bags of mail.'

'Good. Very good. The man in the photograph collects mail

from agents, sends it between France and England. Did you see any of the writing on the letters? Any people?'

'No. I'm sorry. I saw, also – I saw a name, or a word, but not on paper. Scratched into a wall. A hand, scratching a name.'

'And what was the name?'

She thought it had been her own.

'I don't know. I – it was covered in blood. The wall, I mean.'

'That's enough,' Grady said, striding forward and putting his empty glass down. 'You're really trying this? Again?'

Mr Yardley kept his face perfectly still, in the way that men of Ivy's father's generation had, lead in the jowls and steel in the eyes. 'Miss Sharp, perhaps you should take a break.'

'I don't need a break, sir.'

'Then would you be so kind as to leave us for a moment?'

'Ivy deserves to know what you're doing. She deserves to know that, when they showed me photographs like this, I falsely accused a man and ruined his life.'

Mr Yardley, still in his chair, tilted his face at last to look up at Grady. 'I am not a fool, unlike the men who tried to make use of you, Sinclair. I would never use the evidence gathered through this programme as the sole basis for taking action. For one thing, I would never risk the school's discovery in that way. If anyone in the government found out what we are really doing here, we would be shut down.'

'Then why put her through this?' Grady gestured at the photograph, still lying on the carpet.

'It tells me where to look, doesn't it?'

Ivy could not make the image in the photograph focus in her eyes. It was more than a test; Mr Yardley really wanted to know things about these people. Wanted to know – what? *Falsely accused*, Grady had said. Mr Yardley wanted to know whether these people were traitors. Whether the handsome man who passed along the mail was to be trusted.

She felt ill, and got to her feet because otherwise she thought she would tip forward on to the carpet. The two men looked at her, both of them wearing their concern on their faces. Grady put his hand on her arm. 'We're putting a stop to this right now.'

She said, 'I just need to lie down.'

'Here, the . . . sofa,' he said, and she smiled at the faint hesitation, because she always laughed at him when he called it a chesterfield, which seemed to be a Canadian catch-all.

'I'm all right. Really. Please, I'm just going to my room to lie down.'

Ivy walked as steadily and quickly as she could towards the stairs, and could feel Grady behind her wanting to follow, to make sure, but he didn't. She was glad to be on the stairs, behind a wall, and sank on to one of the steps halfway up until her head stopped spinning.

She overheard Mr Yardley speaking in a low, even tone that was somehow slightly different from any she'd ever heard him use before. The tone he used with other men, she supposed.

'Just because you failed, it doesn't mean she will. You have so little faith in your student.'

'I have the utmost faith in her. When she's ready—'

'Shall we ask Herr Hitler to wait, then? You are here to *make* her ready, with the utmost urgency. I didn't put you here so the two of you could play house.'

Ivy's face was burning, buried in her hands. She didn't hear the rest of their argument; she saw only red, black and white flashes, images she couldn't catch. She didn't open her eyes until she felt Grady's hand on her knee, heard him say her name.

'You need a doctor,' he said.

She wanted to shake her head, but was afraid of the consequences. So she opened her dry throat and said, 'No. Really.'

'He's gone now. The bully. I've half a mind—'

'He only wants to help. If it weren't for him, I wouldn't be here.'

'Well, then I suppose we must thank him for something. Come on.'

He put an arm around her and helped her to her feet, turned her on the stairs so that, with her hand on the railing and his arm around her waist, she made it up to her room. When she woke in bed in the middle of the night, he was dozing in the armchair. She thought she saw other people, standing in the corners of the room, but, when she blinked, they were gone.

By the time Ivy got better, Grady was suffering. He often got bad headaches, but this was one of the worst. For three days, she didn't see him. Then he was at breakfast one morning, pale, shadows under his eyes. He was flipping through the newspaper, running his fingers along the text as if studying for an exam.

'What is it?' she asked.

'Trying to see what happened.' He looked up, his face haggard. 'I always know when something bad is going to happen, you see. Usually I have some clue as to what it is.'

'What sort of thing?'

He said nothing for a while. Then, in a tight voice, 'In January, I kept having visions of a school on fire, of children dying, and I thought . . . well, I haven't ever told you, have I?'

She sank into her chair. 'Told me what?'

In a small, strangled voice, he said, 'When I was a child, I knew that there was going to be a fire in the schoolhouse where I was a student, and where my father taught. I begged him not to go to work, and I pretended to be sick, and stayed home with my mother. Nobody believed me, of course. But after – it happened, my mother blamed me.'

'But what could you have done?'

'Exactly.' He closed the paper. 'Exactly. And what could I have done about the fact that the Germans bombed Sandhurst Road School in London in January and killed thirty-eight children and six adults? These things happen in war, don't they? I feel them happening, or about to happen, and I wonder why some things and not others. There is human flesh burning somewhere in the world every minute of every day and I only feel it sometimes, and I stop it – never. I don't even know what I've been seeing these last few days. It's no use at all.'

She stood up, and went to him. Put her hand on his shoulder. She felt the heat coming off him, felt herself at home there.

He stood up, abruptly, breaking them apart.

'Yardley is right about one thing,' he said. 'The sooner we can get you into the field, the better.'

She didn't mention it when the anniversary came of the day she'd moved into Special Training School 22B. It was autumn again, of 1943, and she was still there, still waiting to seem like the perfect archetype of herself. Mr Yardley came once a month and he and Grady seemed to have reached some sort of détente. She didn't have to look at any more photographs of suspected spies; instead, she worked on filling in maps and building plans.

One day, Grady asked her to draw a building based on a photograph: a white building with a cupola. She didn't recognize it. It was not her best drawing; she had never been very good at perspective and found architecture stressful. One had

161

to be so exact, or else the whole thing came out wrong. The following day, he asked her to draw a building next to it – based on whatever came into her mind's eye.

Her mind's eye did not supply a building. Instead, she saw beermats, brown rings on wood. Smelled old beer. So she drew a small pub, a ground floor and one storey above, and as she drew she became more confident about what pieces of it looked like. And the following day, a grocer's. Then she heard someone walking up a creaking stairway, holding something heavy, saw a window with someone looking out of it, as though they didn't belong. She decided this was a hotel. There were, in fact, three small hotels in a row. Then a cinema, another pub, another hotel, a brick building with white ornamentation. She had a vision of a baptismal font, of dripping water, and she smelled stone. So she drew a small church.

Two weeks of this, and one morning Grady was waiting for her in the small driveway, leaning beside the open passenger door of a blue car.

He drove to Southampton, where Ivy had never been; her travel to Paris had been on the night ferry from London to Dunkirk, and the way home in 1940 had been via Nantes and a cargo ship to Cornwall.

With a gasp, she recognized the white building with the cupola that she had drawn. She held her breath as they drove slowly past the next building. A pub. It didn't look exactly like the one she'd drawn; it was smaller, a slightly different pattern of half-timbering, and the sign was all wrong. Next, though, was a grocer's, with the table of vegetables outside. Not exactly as she'd drawn it, but very close.

Then there was a blank, a pile of rubble. Southampton had been bombed heavily, early in the war.

'You drew hotels here,' Grady said.

'Yes. But look – it was a church. And churchyard.' She

pointed at the corners of walls, the arches, the broken tomb-
stones. 'Maybe it *will* be hotels.'

'No, they'll rebuild the church,' Grady said with a certainty
she didn't question. 'I think your mind just filled in a blank.'

'With hotels?' It was funny, but it was terrible.

He pulled the car over, and reached past her into the back
seat, pulled a briefcase up to the front. Inside was her sketchbook, page after page of buildings, showing the edges of the
buildings she'd drawn the day before.

He flipped past the invented hotels to the cinema, then
the other pub. Then a hotel. He put his finger on it.

'What do you think about this one? A real hotel or another
gap?'

She glanced out of the window instinctively, but couldn't
see it from where the car was parked. A woman clutching
packages walked past and glanced inside the car suspiciously.

'Ivy,' he said gently. 'You know what's there, don't you?'

'It's a tobacconist's,' she whispered, and rubbed her temple.
'He's got a big white beard, with yellowed stripes. I can see
him, Grady. I can smell his shop. If I can see it now, why
did I get it wrong a couple of days ago?'

It was odd, being in the car together, inches between their
arms. She was so used to only being with him in the house.
Used to being able to look straight at him. Here, looking
together at the sketchbook jammed awkwardly under the
gearshift, her eyesight only caught pieces of him, and her
other senses seemed to compensate. She heard him swallow,
as he was thinking. Noticed a tiny movement of his elbow
in his tweed jacket.

He started tapping his finger on his knee, under the steering
wheel. He often tapped his fingers when he was thinking.
He said, 'Maybe proximity matters. You remember what I
said about why I have visions of certain disasters and not
others? Why did I see the Sandhurst Road bombing and not,

I don't know, something happening in Sicily or Japan? You did better with the buildings next to the photograph I showed you. And now that you're here, you know what's down the road.'

'So the closer I get to what I know—'

'The fewer hotels.'

From then on, they referred to anything that seemed to be an invention of the mind as a 'hotel'.

The invasion of France was coming. The whole world knew it. The Allies had pushed back in North Africa and Italy, and the Soviet Union was turning the tide on the Eastern Front. To close in on Germany, it made sense to attack next in France, which meant landing somewhere on the coast.

The only question was where and when.

It would have been useful, Ivy was sure, for the Allies to have a clairvoyant on their side who could tell them what the weather would be on a given date, and whether the Germans would fall for a particular deception. To tell them whether the invasion would succeed. She was not that person; even after all her training, even now that her brain was bombarded by impressions and half-dreams, she could not tell anyone their future.

Perhaps it was better that they didn't have the future laid out like notes in a calendar, because what if the future held defeat? Better to fight on anyway. Grady seemed to see the future, more than the present, for all the good it did him. She saw how crumpled he was on his bad days, and was glad her own gift was kinder.

And, miracle of miracles, she was going to be able to put it to some use.

Mr Yardley explained that, when the invasion came, part of France would be occupied within weeks or, ideally, days. There were Resistance prisoners (including SOE agents) in

Gestapo custody in those areas. If things went well for the Allies, the Germans would be retreating as best they could in a landscape of broken rail lines and tumbled bridges, and they would face the dilemma of what to do with their prisoners. It was most likely that these prisoners – dozens or perhaps hundreds – would be shot immediately upon invasion.

That was where Ivy came in.

CHAPTER 17

Ivy

She was ready when the day came. More than ready, in fact. Ivy and Grady had spent so long practising using her mind's eye in the house that she knew her surroundings too vividly, and it made her slightly sick, like seeing all the veins in one's eye after looking at a bright light. She knew where Grady was, always. She knew where Mrs Cobb was. It was not as though she could see the rooms opened up like a doll's house; that would have been easier. Instead, it was a periodic intrusion of thoughts or memories or associations that were not her own. A flash of an inkwell turning over on to a man's photograph from the kitchen, or a flash of the sound of ice skates from the study. She saw, sometimes, their hands where her own hands should be, for a second or less.

Most of this she never mentioned to Grady.

When Mr Yardley came, though, he was refreshingly distinct. She had not spent day after day guessing at the shape of him through the walls.

He handed her a small briefcase and told her to open it.

Inside was some clothing, and she noticed the French

labels with a vertiginous certainty. This was it, then. The matchbox, and, inside, the cyanide pill. A small wad of French francs; she'd never seen the money printed by the Vichy government, and she took a moment to feel it between her fingers. They bore the images of a miner, a fisherman, a farmwoman. Working hard for the Fatherland.

There was a strip of white silk, with lists of code phrases, and an alphabet table in black and red letters.

'We don't use the poem codes any more,' Yardley explained. 'They led to too many radio conversations with Germans. This is the new way – we'll send a man tomorrow to show you how it's done. The silk can be sewn into your clothes, so no one will find it if you're searched.'

In two days' time, on May 8th, there would be a full moon, and Ivy would drop into France. Her first assignment would be to make contact with the Resistance circuit named Mechanic, and they would radio back to Baker Street to let them know she'd arrived.

Then she would make her way to a small village on the outskirts of Falaise, called La Codre. There was an old stone bank building in the village, which the Gestapo had taken over. They had a small 'house prison' in the basement: a collection of detention cells to hold Resistance fighters.

'It isn't the only prison in the area, but it's one we think will have the lowest security, because it's a small building in a village, and because of the offices overhead. We don't know how many cells there are, or how many prisoners. But we know there *are* prisoners there; our best efforts to trace some of our key agents led to it. There may be several dozen, despite the building's small size; all survivor reports suggest that every Gestapo prison is crowded these days.'

It seemed insurmountable, and it seemed a drop in the bucket. Sufficient perhaps for Mr Yardley to gather evidence of the practical value of her skills in wartime. And sufficient to get Ivy captured or killed. But that part, strangely, did not bother her. After all, one might easily die in any number of ways; she had a schoolfriend who had travelled to Spain to be a nurse, drunk a glass of water, and died of typhoid. At least this way, Ivy might do some good with her life, however short. She couldn't imagine a future, a goal after this war; there seemed to be a brick wall between her and a better world.

'Even if I manage to break them out of this place, what happens to the other prisons?'

'Let us worry about that. We used bombers to break some men out of a prison in February. There may be ways.' Mr Yardley rubbed his temple. 'But the house prison in La Codre is surrounded by civilians, since it's not really a jail at all. It seems to be off the books in some way; it doesn't appear in German communications and they don't even know we know about it. We suspect it's being used for prisoners of particular interest to someone, prisoners they don't want to ship off to the camps.' He coughed, seemingly realizing that this was not a good line of conversation to have with an agent about to risk capture behind enemy lines. 'As soon as you get to La Codre, study the movements of the guards, inside and outside. Use your gift to draw plans of the layout and find the best places to plant the explosives. We've been dropping explosives to the Mechanic circuit for months and have told them you will need some.'

'And when I go in . . . ' She paused. 'I go in on my own?'

'That's up to you, but no one can know what you're doing, not even your comrades, until D-Day comes.'

'And I suppose I can't know when that will be.'

'That's a question only you can answer,' Mr Yardley said, giving her a wry, questioning look. She shook her head.

'I don't see dates in my mind's eye. And I don't usually see the future – or, if I do, I don't understand it.'

'Not yet,' Grady said.

'Just be ready for the invasion to come at any time. The sooner you get to the prison and start work, the better.' He paused. 'And if you do work with any Resistance or SOE people, you have to be very sure they don't know how you're gathering your intelligence.'

'You're worried they'll drag me off to the asylum?' she half-joked.

His eyebrows lowered. 'It's a serious danger, I'm afraid. Didn't you follow the Helen Duncan trial?'

She looked at Grady. 'We've had to institute a rule. Newspapers are no longer allowed in the house.'

Yardley looked irritated. 'Well, we've just convicted a woman under the Witchcraft Act in this country, because she happened to mention in a séance that a ship had gone down, and the fact that that particular ship had gone down was still secret information. I'm fairly sure she was just a charlatan, but she paid for it all the same. If you're found to be telling secrets that you can't explain any other way, all of us are at risk. But when the time comes, when we gather enough evidence to explain to the right people in the right ways . . .'

He didn't finish the sentence.

They worked all through dinner and after, making plans.

When they had exhausted every question and themselves, Grady and Mr Yardley settled into an argument about the most likely landing spots on the coast. Ivy watched them, thinking that, soon, she would be on her own. Other than the painting of the woman and that silly cartoon, she had no evidence of her talent from her life before the SOE. Those flashes during the capture test, but they might have been her imagination. It was only here, with Grady, that she'd been able to harness it.

A thought occurred to her. Maybe being here with him made the difference.

That film, *The Clairvoyant*, the one she'd watched with her family back in 1935. The premise was that the Claude Rains character could only use his powers when the Jane Baxter character was near him. That she was a kind of battery, giving him power.

Ivy went through the kitchen, out of the back door and into the garden, to get some air. It was cold; she wrapped her cardigan around herself. But it cleared her head.

She heard Mr Yardley cough, behind her, and turned.

'I have one more thing to give you before you go,' he said. 'A good-luck charm of sorts.'

'I'll need all the luck I can get,' she said with a smile.

'Part one of the gift is a secret,' he said, 'since you have proven yourself so good at keeping them. Your father's work on the Bayeux Tapestry has always fascinated me; you know we share a love of history, and I've always found his analysis to be refreshingly open-minded. He recently developed a striking hypothesis. He believes the tapestry was made slightly in *advance* of the events it depicts, by clairvoyants. That it was a long-running exercise in short-term prophecy, carried out by Queen Matilda. A little like consulting the augurs before a battle, she would have her group of prophets add their visions to the record, so she could advise her husband on what to do next.'

Ivy was speechless. 'My father – he believes the Second Sight is real, then?'

'He shares your gift, Ivy. It is only in the last few years, though, that he's come to realize that.'

'Then is he doing war work too?'

'His work on the tapestry is important. I've encouraged him to focus on that. And besides, he – well, the one time he did try to use it, it did not go well for him. He warned the government about an event, with no explanation of how he knew it. When that event came to pass, he had a lot of explaining to do. It's his experience that has made me warn you, so often, about keeping your gift a secret from everyone. Friend or foe.'

She wiped a tear from her cheek, roughly. Why were her eyes welling up? She felt full to the brim of awful information, and heavy with responsibility. She wanted to talk to Father, but she didn't bother asking whether she could.

'A few years ago,' Mr Yardley continued, 'I happened upon a scrap of the Bayeux Tapestry at an auction. Just a little square, cut by an antiquarian who had access to it a few generations ago. I gave it to your father. Perhaps it inspired him to keep working on his research, because he developed his new theory not long after that. I found another piece, recently. Truth be told, I went hunting for it, and persuaded a collector to sell it to me. I wanted to give it to you, to take with you to France. To remind you that you are part of a lineage, a community. It can go in your pocket; it will mean nothing to anyone who searches you.'

He held out his cupped palm, and Ivy took the small bit of off-white linen with her thumb and forefinger.

They were there, in her mind's eye. Six women, seated around a large rectangular frame, their heads bent. One was embroidering the comet, and, when the others noticed, they peered at it, exclaiming. Ivy saw it in her head like a film, shining and strange.

She didn't like this vision; she had a sensation of lurching, of falling. Everything was bright, as if night had reversed itself. She'd never had a vision as overpowering as this; it pulled her in.

'Surely this should be somewhere safer than with an agent who is likely to be killed or captured,' she said, breathless.

'This is your birthright. There can be no safer guardian

than someone who understands the truth. Carry it with you and remember your duty to this lineage.' He stopped, while Ivy stared, speechless. Then he continued, in a more casual tone, 'Come back safely.' He patted her shoulder in a comradely fashion, and turned and went back through the kitchen door.

For a few minutes Ivy stood with the cloth in her hand, not wanting to drop it, not wanting to hold it. It bothered her somehow. Perhaps it was only that it was a desecration, a selfish, greedy act of destruction. Perhaps it was only nerves, on the night before she was to leave England, maybe forever. But she felt dizzy and shaken. Images flashed, so quickly and so brightly that she had to shut her eyes, and at last she put Mr Yardley's gift carefully into her skirt pocket.

After a few breaths, the feeling faded. She felt Grady's presence, and turned to look through the window, into the kitchen. He was there, leaning against the counter, smoking a cigarette and watching her. His expression was worried.

By the time she'd gone back through the door into the kitchen, he was gone.

In the sitting room, Mr Yardley was alone, reading. She heard Grady's step on the stairs. So she walked quickly up the stairs to meet him, suddenly desperate to understand.

'You were checking on me,' she said, part question, part accusation, part plea.

He stopped and turned, halfway up the staircase. 'I beg your pardon?'

'Just now, in the kitchen. If I can drop behind enemy lines, I can be trusted on my own in the back garden.'

He looked puzzled. 'I didn't check on you.'

'Grady, you said you'd be honest—'

He reached out to her hand, the one resting on the banister. His fingers circled her wrist and he said in a harsh whisper, 'Don't you think I *know* that I can't keep you safe? That I'm the one who's prepared you to go? That I wish I were going in your place?'

With her free hand, she pulled his head towards her, and kissed him. He kissed her back, bitterly and desperately, and then broke away and went up to his room before Mr Yardley could find them.

She asked him not to come to the airfield. Mr Yardley didn't come either.

But Miss Atkins was there. It was the first time Ivy had seen her since her interview for the SOE; she wondered what Miss Atkins thought about the fact that it had taken Ivy two years to train, or what she thought her specialisation was. They sat in a too-bright room as evening turned to night, waiting for the take-off time. Outside, there was constant noise; the airfield was full of people, of crates, of trucks moving things around.

'We're going to blind-drop you,' Miss Atkins said. 'With the invasion coming, there's a lot of activity, and a reception party means movement and lights, and all of that can draw attention. I know it's frightening, but it's amazing how much you can see by the light of the full moon. Or so all the agents say.'

Ivy nodded. Mr Yardley had told her this already. She would land alone in the darkness, and bury her parachute. Then she'd make her way to the safe house on the outskirts of Falaise. She had no map or compass, because, if she was searched, those things would give her away. She'd studied the map and knew how to navigate by the moon and stars, at least well enough to get her to the right road.

Miss Atkins checked Ivy's clothing one more time to make sure there was nothing that wasn't French. She wore wool stockings, a loose brown wool skirt with silk codes sewn into the lining, a beige button-up blouse, and a tweed jacket.

Then she stepped into the camouflage jumpsuit.

Miss Atkins surveyed her. It would have been a contrast, to anyone seeing them: Miss Atkins with her upswept hair perfect, her lipstick precise. She told Ivy that she had every confidence in her, but that it was all right to stop this mission here and now, and go home. Nobody would blame her.

Ivy gave Miss Atkins her powder compact and her keys for safe keeping, and she walked out into the night, where a Halifax bomber sat waiting.

There was something dangerously soporific about the sound of the engines. Ivy was not the only agent sitting in the guts of the bomber, but it was too loud to talk.

'Action stations!' someone called, and one by one the two other agents slid down to the hatch, the wind whistling cold. They nodded at Ivy, and Ivy nodded at them, and then the men dropped in silence.

She moved into position and waited for her moment to come. The plane smelled like paint and oil. She checked her parachute.

Her legs dangled out of the hatch, the same one they'd used to enter the plane. They were flying low, to avoid radar. She could see the landscape below, a quilt of fields, lined with trees, all clear in the light of the full moon.

She was dropping alone, into a field not big enough for the plane to land in, and hopefully not close enough to anything to attract attention. She was dressed as a civilian, and if she was captured she would be sent away to a camp to be tortured and killed. The so-called Ministry of Ungentlemanly Warfare could guarantee her nothing.

The tiny signal light turned green and she slipped down into the moonlight, her parachute popping into life, the noise of the bomber receding, the vast and silent world rising up to take her.

*

Jumping from below the radar took a matter of seconds.

Not much time to react to the fact that she was headed for a fence, with a cow on the far side of it.

The cow would move, surely. She wouldn't land *on* it.

Beside it, perhaps. It might kick her, or maul her – good lord, it was the sort with horns. Shouldn't it be inside, in the barn?

She pulled on the back two risers and rotated her body to try to face the way her chute was moving, but she was running out of time. Her feet slammed to earth and she crumpled and rolled as she had been taught, but one leg hit a rock, higher and harder than it should have. Pain shot through her leg. It took everything she had not to cry out. The field didn't belong to anyone the SOE knew and could trust – if it was even the right field at all; drops were frequently off-target. She could hope that whoever owned this farm would be on the side of the Resistance and happy to see an SOE agent. But her luck wasn't serving her well so far.

In the farmyard that held the cow, a dog ran up to the fence, barking its head off. The owners would come and investigate.

So Ivy crawled into the cover of some nearby trees, biting her lip. A cow – a bloody cow. She'd always been afraid of them; if it hadn't been for her fear of cows, she'd have gone off to the farm with Helen, and she never would have gone to Sheffield and taken up drawing again to fend off despair, and she never would have painted the image that had alarmed Mr Yardley, and she'd be safe on a farm somewhere now. She never would have met Grady or known that she could see things she shouldn't. She never would have gone behind enemy lines to break prisoners out of jail – the very idea! And here, in this moment when she'd thought herself fearless, a cow. And now her leg was hurt, and she'd be limping the five miles to the safe house, and would attract attention, and the whole enterprise was in danger. Because of a bloody cow. Outside, at night, for some reason.

She had to stifle a laugh, or something like a laugh. Far off, she could hear bombs. Did the pilot of the Halifax resent the fact that he'd had a lesser cargo than some to drop tonight? And for what?

Warm blood was creeping up the leg of her jumpsuit; she could see it like a shadow in the moonlight. She unzipped the front of her suit and wriggled out.

There was a little spade strapped to her injured leg, for burying her parachute and jumpsuit. She had a small knife on her belt, too, and with that she cut a strip of parachute silk and wrapped it around her ankle, tied it tight. There was nothing to be done about the tear in her stocking, or the blood. Ivy was fairly sure that, in addition to the long gash, her ankle was sprained. Not broken, she hoped. That square of rock – she could see it out there, pale and unbothered – must have been an old boundary stone, on just one side of the fence.

She knew how to find the nearby village and the address where she was supposed to make contact. She said the French pass phrase over in her mind, to still her thoughts: *Monsieur Bourget wishes to borrow a bicycle.*

The only problem was that she had to walk five miles to reach that address.

Ivy buried her parachute and jumpsuit, mainly working on her knees, and tried her best to make the ground look undisturbed. It was long, hard work, and by the end she was shivering from her own sweat in the night air. She found a stick that looked about the right length for a support, and walked a few steps. She could see the ribbon of road. A dozen steps in and she had to stop, tasting tears.

The dog, at least, had stopped barking.

She stopped to rest for a moment, and looked at the

farmhouse. But even if she waited until morning, her ankle injury was a giveaway; she'd have to come up with a cover story for it, but everyone would think of parachutes, on this night of the full moon.

She could still taste the whisky in her mouth from the flask they'd passed around on the plane. She walked as the world waited for dawn.

CHAPTER 18

Ivy

It was mid-morning and her ankle was throbbing when she noticed the young man walking in front of her, wheeling a bicycle. Where had he come from? At some point, he'd passed her, not surprising given her speed with this limp. But he was now keeping a steady pace, dawdling.

There were houses and shops dotted along the road; she was on the outskirts of Falaise now, approaching the town from the northeast. How odd to be walking into the town like any visitor, despite her limp. A small church, a large stone house, open cobbled streets. She was not far from the safe house now. A house with orange shutters, on an intersection with an odd angle. Almost there.

But the man with the bicycle, just ahead of her, made her nervous. She'd been trained that a good way to follow someone was to get in front of them; it was less likely to arouse suspicion, and, if you kept your wits about you, you'd be just as aware of the person's movements. This man had his head down and seemed genuinely lost in his own thoughts. Maybe she was overtrained, unaccustomed to being out in the real world.

Her mind's eye seemed sharper now than it had ever been. As she passed houses, impressions fought for her attention, like children pressing their noses to a glass window. Glimpses of people's lives.

And she was exhausted. She hadn't slept, and the effort of carrying on with her injured leg was draining. She'd removed the parachute silk bandage once the bleeding stopped, but it was clear her ankle was sprained, and there was a bloody gash on her stocking. Occasionally people gave her a glance of wary sympathy as she passed. It was not a large village, but people were walking into Falaise, or going to their work. The young man in front wasn't the only one with a bicycle. But she did wonder why he was wheeling it, rather than riding it.

She focused on her mind's eye, but all she could see was the ground rushing to meet her, over and over. The whoosh of her parachute. Her cheeks stung, perhaps from the wind – although, come to think of it, it hadn't been a very windy night.

The intersection with the funny angle lay ahead; she thought she could see the orange shutters.

And, in front of a tall building, two men in blue Milice uniforms.

Her mind's ear filled with unladylike language, she veered on to a cross-road. She followed it just long enough to duck behind a stone wall and came back to the main road. Beyond the building where the Milice still stood.

The man with the bicycle was waiting for her; he had apparently stopped to check the chain.

'It's not working properly,' he said, straightening up, and giving her a little smile.

He was about thirty, with thick, straight dark hair swept sideways, a lean face with sharp cheekbones. Something about it made her think of the paintings on the francs in her pocket.

Time to check that her French accent was passable, after years of practice at Beaulieu.

'My sympathies,' she said. 'They are uncooperative beasts. I'm afraid mine is a twisted wreck. That's how I got this.' She pointed to her ankle.

He looked at the ankle, then up at her. 'If you need to borrow one, you can have mine. I am sick of it. Or perhaps you know someone else who would like to borrow it?'

Her heart leapt into her mouth. They were a block from the safe house, and he seemed to have SOE training, or something like it.

She took the chance. 'Monsieur Bourget wishes to borrow a bicycle.'

His mouth twitched briefly, almost a smile, and he said, 'He still owes me five francs.'

The right response. Perhaps that was why she had seen the image of the francs, the picture of the miner with his pickaxe. She couldn't believe it; she didn't know what to say. For some reason, her cheek stung as though it had been slapped and she put her hand to it. She must have scraped it last night.

The trace of a smile left his face as he straightened up. 'Come with me.'

They passed the house with the orange shutters, and she said nothing. After a while, they came to a small tavern, with its windows still closed, and a staircase on the side of the building. He chained his bicycle to the bottom and went up the stairs, and she followed. The door had a padlock with a combination lock; he opened it.

It was a dim flat with a low ceiling – a single room with a bed at the far end, a sagging green sofa, a small table with two chairs. Photographs on the walls.

The man gestured her in and then shut the door behind him.

'You were looking for the house with orange shutters?'

She nodded, and here in the darkness her mind's eye had more to see. Images came at her in a barrage. Men in uniform pulling people in handcuffs. Someone slapping a face; she put her hand to her own cheek again. Then she saw the face of the man who'd been hit: a face she didn't recognize, under curly brown hair streaked with grey.

'It was raided last week,' he said. 'The Mechanic circuit is broken. I'm all that's left. If you had gone there, you would have found nothing, but you would have alerted the Milice. It's lucky for you I noticed your ankle before they did.'

She sagged a little, and he pointed to the sage-green sofa, on to which she sank gratefully. Her ankle was even more painful when she took the weight off, somehow, but at least she could catch her breath.

'We have to tell London,' she said. 'They must have communicated with Mechanic – they must have told them I was coming.'

'Then it's important that you lie low. You can stay here until it's safe. What was your mission?'

She hesitated. It was odd that he'd ask, but maybe he hadn't been trained with the same protocols she had.

'To help Mechanic. So I suppose that's you now.'

He nodded, and stuck out his hand. 'You can call me Léo.'

The sagging, faded couch smelled of Gauloises, although she didn't see him smoke. Still, she slept hard, after a meal of shiny red tinned meat and sliced bread.

He went out the following morning, leaving her to get her bearings.

Léo's flat didn't look as if a Resistance agent lived there, but then Ivy supposed that was the point. A few books, all in French. He was a photographer, and the walls were covered in black-and-white prints. Some showed bridges or buildings shot in a way that he probably thought was artistic but Ivy found frustrating: bits and pieces, framed oddly. Others showed people, particularly a young woman Ivy's age.

There might be something here she could use, some clue, to help him and her. She knew that. Still, it felt like a violation, to open his chest of drawers. She stood for a long time with her palm resting on a 1932 road map of France, thinking, leaving herself open to images. But nothing came, nothing but images of red road dust in sunshine, two women with their hair in scarves.

In the bottom drawer, there was a bright blue suitcase or briefcase that drew her eye. It was closed and latched but had no key. Perhaps there were papers inside, or a radio she could use. Would he have lied about that? If he had a radio after all, what would that mean? Her radio training had been brief, but she thought she could manage it. After staring at it for a long time, she unclipped the latches and lifted the lid.

And then nearly laughed out loud at how unlike the truth her own imaginings had been.

It was a gramophone, with a disc on the turntable. 'Rock Me' by Sister Rosetta Tharpe. She'd never heard of it, and quietly set the needle and played it.

A growling guitar, a voice as bright as a sword. She tapped her head, and wished she could dance.

She became aware, too slowly, of the V for victory beat beneath the music: short short short long. Beethoven's Fifth – the knock on the door. Léo was home.

She got up quickly, cringing at the reaction of her ankle, and unlatched the door.

Léo's face was unreadable. He closed the door behind him. 'Of course a British agent wouldn't respect my privacy.'

'It's better for the cover,' she said defiantly. 'If the neighbours hear music—'

'There are no neighbours.'

He went to the gramophone and lifted the needle reverently, and silence fell.

'You didn't train in England, then,' she said.

He shook his head. Then he put the canvas bag he was carrying on to the rickety table and pulled out gauze and iodine. 'Let's have a look at your leg,' he said. 'Then we can go. There's an agent not far from here who may be able to help you, find you a better place to stay. An agent with guns and supplies.'

Supplies. Like the explosives that Britain had dropped to Mechanic for months, the explosives that she was meant to use on the prison doors.

She obediently sat on the couch and pulled off her stockings, wincing as the wool came away from the scab. Her leg was worse than she'd realized: the wound was deep in places, and her ankle was visibly swollen.

The iodine stung, but it felt a bit better once he'd wrapped it.

'I don't suppose you have a pair of stockings in that bag,' she said.

At that, he chuckled, as if surprised into it.

She wasn't sure how far she'd be able to walk, but she couldn't waste time; the invasion could come any day, and she needed to get to the prison in La Codre and start working. So, when Léo asked if she could travel, she nodded, and gritted her teeth.

But as they descended the outdoor staircase she was shocked to see a black Citroën parked behind the building, battered but with a shining steel grille, and even more shocked when he opened the door for her.

'You have a car?' she asked. 'And petrol?'

'We take what we want,' he answered. 'Don't worry about it.'

The car smelled damp and musty, and Ivy felt a bit sick

as Léo drove out of town and turned on to a narrow road with hedges on either side. The ground was wet from recent rain, and mud spattered the windscreen from time to time. He seemed nervous.

'I'm sorry for going through your things,' she said. 'And listening to your gramophone.'

'If I had any secrets, believe me I wouldn't leave them lying in the drawers in that flat.'

Suddenly she saw the same man again, the one she'd seen when she was standing at the door. The man with the curly hair, the one who'd been slapped. But now he was happy, sitting in the sun, one knee bent, a cigarette in his hand.

This car didn't smell of cigarette smoke. Nor did Léo. But the flat had.

The image changed, and the young man now was talking to a man who looked familiar, a handsome man with fair hair. The matinee idol, from the photograph Yardley had shown her! The young curly-haired man was handing him a letter. For some reason, she wanted to stop him, to tell him not to be so trusting. To stop smiling.

Again, the image in her mind shifted. Now the curly-haired young man was dead, lying prone on concrete, blood spreading from a hole in his head.

She put her hand to her mouth.

'What is it?'

'Just a little car-sick.'

'Roll down the window, then.'

She didn't. She was thinking, trying to get her bearings. She asked, as lightly as she could, 'Do you remember who it was, singing that song you left on the gramophone? I'd never heard it before, and I'd like to find it again.'

Her whole body was freezing, suddenly. And he wasn't answering. He knew it was a test.

At last, he said, 'Several people have used that flat. I'm sorry. It wasn't my gramophone at all. I don't go in for that sort of music.'

The man on the ground had brown curly hair. She hadn't seen him in any of the photographs in the flat because he was the photographer. He was the real Léo. God, how obvious it was. The real Léo had given information to the fair-haired matinee idol, to the traitor. To a man who was passing information to the fascists, information like the locations of safe houses, and the code phrases British agents might use when they landed. How she wished she could *know* things, rather than just see things! She stared at the scene of his death in her mind's eye, while her physical eyes looked at the hand on the steering wheel.

The man who was not Léo turned the car down another small and dirty road, with nothing but farms on either side. She tried to remember the road map, and to fit the man's driving on to it, but it didn't matter anyway, did it? Wherever it was, it would be the Gestapo waiting for her. A fine job she'd done of it. Twisted her ankle on her drop, then limped right into a trap.

There was a leftward bend in the road, up ahead. He might have to slow a little. What choice did she have?

'I think I will open the window,' she said, and put her hand on the crank. She waited until he slowed for the turn, then moved her hand to the door handle, and flung herself out of the car.

She had practised dropping and rolling so much in parachute training, and the theory in her head worked quite well: cross your arms, tuck and roll, try to land on your back, not your head or arms.

In practice, it was not that simple. Her right shoulder hit the ground and her legs scraped along the gravel at the side of the road. Everything hurt and her head was ringing. But she got up and ran, as best she could on her bad ankle. She could hear the car ahead screeching to a stop.

She scrambled up and over the rise at the side of the road, fell into a shallow muddy stream the precise colour of Mother's milky tea. Everything stung and everything ached. She wiped dirty water out of her eyes, pushed her wet hair off her face, and looked at her surroundings.

Beyond the creek was a field planted with young green crops she didn't put a name to. There was a shed not too far into the field – the best place to hide before making a run for it, and beyond the field were woods. A good place to get lost.

But she knew that she couldn't get far on this ankle.

The stream meandered into the field, and there was a bridge over it, connecting a cow path. Hardly a bridge at all, really. Just a few flat planks. But there was room for her underneath it.

Ivy crawled, staying in the creek bed, and slithered under the bridge. There was barely enough room for her, and it was deep enough that most of her body was submerged. She stayed there, listening to the quiet sounds of a man hunting for her, a man who didn't bother to call her name, because the pretence was over. He went to the shed, and into the woods.

It wouldn't take long for him to check the bridge. She tried to get a sense of him with her mind's eye. As soon as she opened herself up to it, flashes of the man's life and thoughts overtook her: the anger, the slapped cheek, the man with the bloody hole in his head, the determined and triumphant face of the miner on the franc printed by the Vichy government. The face of that miner, that 'ideal worker', became her pursuer's face.

She could see what he was seeing: the woods, open and spare, no room to hide, but maybe he could glimpse something. A shape moving through the trees. A shadow flitting. She could imagine that. She could hold on to that image, hold it so hard she could believe in it.

With her mind still in the woods, Ivy wriggled out from under the bridge. She crawled through the field, back to the road, and crossed it, getting behind the little berm that seemed to line all the roads here. She kept moving.

The man called Léo never followed her. Had she bought herself some time, somehow, by making him see something in the woods? It seemed impossible.

How did she know what was possible and what was not, any more?

By nightfall, she was shaking. She found a little wooded area to rest, and examined her leg. The gash that she'd made when she dropped by parachute had reopened. There was fresh blood mixed with mud. Her whole body was coated with a residue of mud, and she was soaking wet, and very cold. There were fresh scratches on her leg too, and on the back of one hand. Her neck was stiff.

Somewhere, the phoney 'Léo' was probably telling his comrades about her. How hard would they look for her? Would they send out dogs? She remembered the dog at the farmhouse, how it had barked when she landed. She dreamed of a man with a pickaxe, and a man with a hole in his head.

CHAPTER 19

Ivy

Ivy learned that her gift, which seemed to be growing more powerful every day, was useful for one thing, at least: she was a very successful thief. She could sense when a kitchen was empty, and slip in and out for long enough to grab some bread, fruit or meat. It kept her alive, while she walked for three days, getting her bearings.

One day, she slipped into a kitchen and found an easel set up, a portrait of a dog half-finished, brushes in jars. She stared at it for a moment, remembering her old self like a character from a book, wondering whether she'd ever paint again. And then it struck her: without explosives or weapons, without help, she'd have to fall back on deception, if she had any hope at all.

Ivy pulled one of the Vichy five-franc notes out of her pocket, left it on the table, then packed up a few small blank canvases and some paints and brushes, turpentine, everything she would need. Even a portable wooden easel. It all fitted in the small, battered valise she took from a shelf. She wondered who the painter was, whether man or woman, whether they might have been friends in a different life. But she resisted the urge to try to see anything about them with her gift; best not to know.

That was when her luck changed for the better. She thought that the stream she'd hidden by might be a small river that had been marked on the maps she'd memorized, and after a while the patterns of roads fitted her memory. To her immense relief, she found that she wasn't very far from La Codre.

She had no explosives, no help, and the Gestapo would be looking for a woman of her description. But she would at least see the jail before she died. She would do that much for Grady, for Mr Yardley, for Father. For herself. For the young man with the curly hair, the real Léo, who had left her a song on his gramophone.

The village of La Codre looked as if it had come straight out of a storybook: creamy stone walls and brightly coloured half-timbering, lining a handful of narrow cobbled streets. There were flowerboxes and fruit trees; life carried on. But the faces of the people were drawn and wary.

It didn't take long to find the old bank, a three-storey red-brick building, next to an old hotel (she thought of Grady and smiled) and a bakery with apartments overhead. It was in the heart of the village, looking out on a little open circle with a dry fountain. Ivy sat on the stone wall of that fountain and opened her valise, took out a palette and paints.

One of the guards walked over to her, marching as if he were in the army. 'You can't sit there.'

She smiled at him. 'I'll stand, then, once I get my easel set up.'

'You're painting? Here?'

She gestured. 'It is one of the prettiest town squares in Normandy. Monet painted it. I make my living this way, you know. I sell my paintings back in Paris. Are you going to tell me I'm not allowed to paint?'

'You can't paint here. You can't paint this building.'

'You mean that building?' She pointed at the Gestapo offices. 'Oh, I'll face the other way. I find that quite ugly.'

She was opening herself up to him, trying to find an image, anything she might be able to use. All that came was a hand, gripping something, white knuckles and red blotches. Meanwhile, she stared up at him with the emptiest eyes she could summon, and he chose to believe what so many men had chosen to believe about her from the day she was born.

Ivy took her time with the canvas. It really was a picturesque view, framed by two window-boxes bursting with pink geraniums and dripping with ivy. Between stone walls, she could see a meandering road downhill, into the farmland that had sheltered her for days. And at the end of the road, rising out of the town of Falaise, the silhouette of the castle: a square shape with a round turret beside it. Right between the two houses, a perfect scene.

Her shelter now was an abandoned shack outside the village, where she ate what she stole and rested her ankle. It was still swollen, and very red around the wound, but there wasn't much she could do about that. The fake Léo had not been considerate enough to throw the iodine out of the car window when she jumped, and there was no pharmacy in La Codre. She didn't know how much time she had left before the invasion.

So, while she painted the scene in front of her eyes, she opened her mind to the building behind her. She saw flashes like negative images of the flowers and sunshine in front of her: sooty train carriages, weeping children, dour mothers watching their sons leave them. Sometimes she saw things that seemed incongruous, like a piece of chocolate cake, or a student writing a test, a pencil in his hand, clutched hard – and there it was. She saw more, understood more. The guard who had questioned her, the hand with the white knuckles; it was his hand, and he was writing a test. He was failing, sweat dropping on to the paper.

She thought of him from that moment onwards as the Schoolboy, and she started to get a sense of how near or far he was by the vividness of the image in her mind. When he was on duty in front of the door, it was strong. Just as she had once known when Grady was in the sitting room, she started to sense when the Schoolboy was inside on the ground floor, or when he was higher, up in the air – up in the offices. Sometimes he disappeared for a while without leaving the building, and she puzzled over this. It was not so much a vanishing as an intensifying: feeling without image, fear without sweat, just the sound of the breath in his lungs coming hard.

Those were the times he went downstairs, into the cells.

By the end of the week, she was repainting the flowers she'd already painted three times, and had nicknames and a mental photo album of all the staff. She had educated guesses for their roles: the two guards, an older man, a cleaner, a young records clerk or something of that nature, and several Gestapo agents. There was one woman, who ran strips of paper between her fingers, who wore a plain wedding ring that was too big for her now.

Stretching her awareness downwards, to the cells, she could see a stone staircase, with the iron grille at the bottom. It was the only part of the inside of the building she was sure of. Beyond it, she could catch only flashes bright and fleeting, like the time the film melted when Helen took her to see *Berkeley Square* at the Playhouse Cinema. It was too much for her mind.

When she tried too hard, she saw the inscription on the

wall. Sometimes she thought it was her own name, and sometimes it was a jumble of markings. Sometimes there was blood obscuring it. Whether she saw this only as a memory of what her gift had once shown her before, or whether it related to these cells, she couldn't say.

She had not been able to steal a gun, but her plan – if she could call it a plan – depended on silence anyway. She still had the small knife that had been on her belt when she dropped, for cutting away parachute straps in the event one got stuck on a tree. It was sharp and it would serve. She had stolen a pair of loose trousers that had belonged to a farm wife, in rough blue cotton, with an integral belt of the same fabric that pulled them to fit. Practical clothing for a no doubt practical woman whose belly had been many sizes in her life; when Ivy put the trousers on, she saw fields in sunshine, and smelled bread dough.

They had deep pockets, and she put in one of them the matchbox that held the scrap of the tapestry – her good-luck charm – and her cyanide pill.

Over and over in her memory, she replayed the training from Scotland two years before: the ways to kill a man with certainty and speed. She remembered the exercise at Beaulieu in breaking into a house, which had been interrupted by the false interrogation.

But all the windows on the ground floor had iron grilles embedded into the walls. She'd have to climb the stone walls and go into the back courtyard, then find a way up to a higher floor and break in that way.

Once she had a sense of the individual guards and agents, she started coming to the fountain earlier each day. Before eight o'clock there were always only four people she would have to worry about: two inside, and the two guards outside.

Taking two guards at once, outside, was a problem she couldn't solve. But if she could get inside, if luck and talent cooperated, she could kill the two agents and then it was just a matter of finding the key to the cells. Grady had spent months with her trying to see whether she could find a hidden object; sometimes she could. She would have to gamble that today would fall on the right side of sometimes.

Scrambling over the wall, even in the practical trousers, proved to be so hard that Ivy nearly gave up in despair at the first hurdle. As difficult as the training exercises had been, they had always been designed to be possible, and one knew that. There was no such guarantee here.

But eventually the toe of her shoe stuck into a divot in the mortar just long enough that she was able to scratch her fingers into a bit of mortar higher up. Then another push and she was there. Up on the wall.

There was no moon, just the electric lights from the Gestapo building, and the shadows were deep in the court-yard, so it took Ivy a few breaths to put a name to the great dark shape in one corner. A simple frame, a platform. A gallows.

A gallows, here behind what had been a bank.

She tasted metal as thick as a knife's blade as she decided to put the gallows to use.

With splinters in her hands and her ankle screaming, she climbed the top of the gallows frame, and leaned out to the nearest window. The bank had not bothered to put grilles on these windows, and not only because they were high up. The window was narrow; Ivy was a small person (smaller than ever these days, thanks to ration books and the long walks at Beaulieu) but she was not even sure she would fit.

The window was dark inside; the only lights were on the ground floor, and the one security light in the courtyard. They hadn't meant this place to be a prison, but they had turned it into one, because they could not occupy a square foot of the Earth without it turning into a prison.

The first blow with the knife-butt cracked the glass, and with her breath stuck in her chest she cleared it all away from the edges, until she was fairly sure she wouldn't cut herself to ribbons. All the same, when she squeezed through, the shoulders of her blouse tore and she felt a sting all along one arm. The opposite arm to the injured leg, which was a nice symmetry.

The room was dark, and smelled of paper and dust. Two long filing cabinets, a desk, a chair.

She could feel, almost too strongly, the two men in the front room, one floor below. She had given them all nick-names. These two were Poplar Trees and Stripes; the latter got his name because she kept seeing the fresh wounds that looked like the marks of flogging. She felt sick whenever he was in the building, and she hoped he would be the first one she encountered, because she thought it possible she could kill him.

She got her wish.

She felt him in her bones as he walked up the stairway, and she readied herself, but heard him open another door. The toilet, no doubt.

Ivy turned the handle of the door into the hallway as slowly and quietly as she'd ever done anything in her life.

There was a line of light at the bottom of the other door. She heard the toilet flush and when Stripes came out she was ready in the shadows, knife in hand.

In her head, she heard her instructor's voice. 'Killing a sentry silently is easily done with a knife from the rear. With your left forearm, strike violently on the left side of his neck, then instantly cover his mouth and nostrils with your left hand. At this moment, with your right hand, thrust the knife into his kidney. With the left hand still covering his mouth and nose, drag him backwards and downwards.'

There were no images in her mind as she killed him, just

a terrible blankness, as she tasted his fear and could not stop her breath from coming in time with the abortive lurches of his chest wall, until she let him slip to the ground nearly on top of her, blood covering her hand and arm. Her hands ached and she tried to remember whether she had made a lot of noise doing it; would it bring the one from downstairs?

Ivy stayed there with the body for long, long minutes, ready for the other one. Surely, even if there hadn't been enough noise to alert him, he'd investigate when his colleague didn't return from the toilet? But nothing. She began to feel it must be a trap, that Poplar Trees must be just around the corner on the stairs. She edged forward but saw nothing. In her mind's eye Poplar Trees was still a steady presence, downstairs, but it was hard to tell sometimes whether a lack of change in her mind's eye meant a lack of change in the real world.

She pulled the gun off the dead man's belt and checked it. Transferred the knife to her left hand. With the gun in hand at her hip as she was trained, she stepped on to the staircase, winced as it creaked. Shooting the other one would bring the outside guards, but it might be her only choice.

On the final step, she looked at the lighted room and saw him, and he saw her.

The shock registered on his face, and fear followed. Fear of her, because he didn't know what this intruder heralded, what her presence here might mean. Because he didn't know what she would do, and he had mere seconds to find out.

But Ivy knew. She was already submerged in the numbness of following her training; she just needed to keep herself there a little longer. When Poplar Trees stood and drew, her gun was already aimed from her hip.

Tap tap.

She shot Poplar Trees just as she had shot the dummies in Scotland and at Beaulieu. He slumped in blood. That part of it was not like the dummies. He was horrifically real, his limbs falling at unnatural angles, his eyes staring at sights she couldn't imagine.

The door opened and she slipped into the shadow behind the staircase as the Schoolboy came through, and saw the body, his back turned to her.

She felt the Schoolboy's fear, and out of a void came a series of images that nearly pushed her backwards. The Schoolboy, and a younger man, a child really, feverish and slick with sweat. The same child grown taller, looking out across a ruined landscape. She knew things about the child, and the man he would become.

She took three quick, limping steps to shove the point of her knife into his lower back, pointing upwards.

'Stay where you are,' she said in French, her voice coming breathless. 'I know exactly where your kidneys are, just as I know that your little brother has been sick for a while. I know he'll live, if you cooperate. If everything doesn't go well for me today, your brother will die, and not from his illness.'

With her injured ankle, she kicked the front door shut, ignoring the pain, and switched hands with the gun so she could throw the heavy bolt across the door.

'Get the key to the cells,' she said.

He walked stiffly towards a wall safe, and lifted the brass bar hanging from it – a combination lock. Letters, not numbers. She tried to see a word but nothing came into her head except, out of nowhere, the memory of dropping in the moonlight, avoiding the cow, the ground closer and closer. She was dizzy, from pain and nausea. She had killed two men.

He rolled each letter, his hands shaking. The word was RIND. She heard it in her mind, pronounced the German way, rhyming with hint. Remembering her few German lessons at Beaulieu, suddenly she understood why she'd been seeing a cow in her mind. Her talent, trying to help her, in its clumsy way. She almost laughed, but felt that if she started laughing, screaming and sobbing would follow. She swallowed it all, and kept the gun pointed at the Schoolboy. The lock popped off, and he opened the safe, pulled one, two, three keys off hooks.

She had more time to think about it this time, and she still had his family in her head. But her training was clear. A prisoner was a liability. Better to kill when necessary, swiftly. And better to save the bullets, and keep noise to a minimum.

She stepped forward, left arm raised to strike and grab his mouth, but the floor creaked under her and he turned. He twisted and flailed as she jammed the knife into his kidneys, and he screamed and burbled. She put her hand over his mouth, belatedly, as he went down, until his eyes closed and he lay still.

The walk down the staircase felt like walking into the belly of a ship in a storm. She had seen it, so many times, that she wasn't entirely sure she wasn't imagining it now, walking into her mind's eye while somewhere her body lay dying, or in a cell of its own, an illegible inscription on the wall.

Through a grille at the bottom of the stairs, and into a dim corridor, lit by an electric bulb. There were six doors leading off the corridor, heavy, windowless, and another at the end.

With shaking keys, she opened each one.

There were people stuffed inside each cell; they didn't move until Ivy said, 'I'm getting you out. Come on, we don't have much time.'

And then the corridor was full of people, all six doors open. She ushered them past. A man came out of the last door and watched the others leaving, and said, 'What about the vault?'

Nobody answered.

The prisoner grabbed the keys out of her hand and went to the last door in the corridor, a different design from the others. Fumbling, he opened it, then wheeled open an inner door.

A thin man took his hand and came out of a space too small to sit in. The prisoner helped the man walk and shouted at Ivy to go ahead. She did. But she was limping so much that she wasn't much faster than them. The others were ahead, at the front door, and too late she realized what would be waiting for them on the far side.

Two of the prisoners were down, blood on the floor, the crowd around them with nowhere to go, before she even realized she'd heard two shots. She still had the gun in her hand but there was a huddle of prisoners between her and the guard on the outside – and maybe he had help.

The prisoners pushed forward, nobody saying anything, and she followed as best she could, barely able to walk now. She had asked too much of her ankle and it was moments from giving up entirely.

At the door, momentarily blinded by daylight, she saw the final guard – she had thought of him as Ropes – lying on the stone step, blood pouring from his head. The prisoners were out in the courtyard, running.

She limped down after them and had reached the fountain wall when two shots came from behind, and she turned and saw him. Doubled over, his face grey, but the Schoolboy, still alive after all. Hatred in his eyes. A gun in his hand.

The prisoner from the vault went down and the man who had saved him went down too.

She didn't hear the shot that tore into her body and took her out of the world.

CHAPTER 20

Ivy

Ivy was alone in a cell when she woke up on a cot soaked with her own blood and stiff with the blood of others. The four concrete walls terrified her more than the pain in her leg, arm and shoulder; she wanted to claw at them, for all the good it would do.

Gradually, a sick awareness crept back. She had killed two men, at least; the Schoolboy might have bled to death by now, but probably not, given that he'd stood up long enough to shoot her. She must have missed the kidneys; she should have used a longer knife, and been less hesitant the moment before. A botched job. It couldn't be a very comfortable life for him, though. Or death, if it was death.

She tried to get a sense of whether he was nearby, but all that came into her mind was the memory of the men she had definitely killed. Two lives on her hands, forever. She didn't regret it, but she did regret that she hadn't bought freedom and life for everyone who had been in these cells. How many were down here again, now, like her? She hoped that the fact she was alone in her cell meant there were fewer prisoners now; there had to be. Surely some had got away?

She yelled, wordlessly, until her throat ached, and her face was wet with tears.

From the silence came a distant echo, of several voices. Damn it; the other cells were not empty. How many?

She tried to open her mind to whatever images the building held, but it hurt too much. She vomited clear liquid and closed her eyes.

She couldn't have said how long she was alone in that room. She moved from the blood-soaked cot to the floor, her ankle screaming, lying flat on her back. When a guard she didn't recognize opened the door, her whole body ached so badly she could barely sit up, and her mind's eye told her nothing. He put a shallow bowl on the floor; it stank of cabbage, though there were only a few strips floating in the grimy broth. She ignored it.

An hour or so later, the door opened again.

A different man, in a crisp SS uniform, with oak leaves on his lapels and a deep line between his eyebrows. He looked at her for a moment, at the room behind her. His face meant nothing to her and her mind called up no images. She didn't think he was one of the agents she'd come to know and given nicknames to, but she couldn't be sure.

The door shut behind him with a thud.

He spoke to her in English, with a perfect London accent, just slightly too perfect to be from anywhere. 'How are you, Marie-Claire? Or is it Juliet? Or would you rather tell me your real name?'

She said nothing. There was nothing to say; they might as well get it over with and kill her. Damn it – her cyanide pill. There was nothing in her pocket; they'd taken the matchbox and the money. And the little scrap of fabric, the piece of the tapestry that Mr Yardley had been so confident she would keep safe. It was in the matchbox too. They would probably throw it in the rubbish; how Father would hate that. But what Ivy cared most about, selfishly, was the cyanide pill.

It was all right. There were other ways to die.

She had been trained to hold out for forty-eight hours, to give her colleagues time to realize she'd been captured and change their habits. But she had no colleagues, no circuit, no one to compromise. They could ask her about Beaulieu, she supposed, but they had dozens of agents in custody already who had trained at Beaulieu.

They could ask her about Grady. But nobody knew about Grady, surely, and they wouldn't ask her directly.

'You think I don't know about the man you're trying to hide,' said the agent, and her gaze snapped up at him so sharply she hurt her neck.

The officer smiled and leaned down closer to her, looking slightly over her shoulder. 'I can see everyone you've brought with you. I only recognize one of them, though. This is very interesting.'

He seemed to be admitting to some sort of Second Sight. A trick? Surely it couldn't be true – he wouldn't talk about it so casually, and openly.

She studied his face. He was middle-aged, his jawline a little thick, his eyes clear blue like watery paint.

'Who are you?' she demanded, her voice rough. She remembered to speak French.

'You may call me *Oberführer*,' he said, in English. 'Or, if you feel more comfortable, you may call me Mr Teller. I hope we will be colleagues, after all.'

She shook her head, trying to clear it. She had been trained to keep to her cover story, to be a Frenchwoman.

'How did you know about the guard's younger brother? The one you told him was sick.'

She swallowed, said nothing.

He took a step forward, then squatted to look her in the eye. He pointed over her shoulder. 'I can see Gregory Yardley there, with you, clear as day. A strange coincidence, isn't it? I know Yardley from the old days, you see. We share certain . . . interests.'

Hearing his name out of this stranger's mouth set her world askew. Mr Yardley had sent her here, to this small prison among all the many hellholes in occupied Europe.

She stopped that line of thinking. The enemy wanted her to think her friends and colleagues had betrayed the cause. She stayed silent.

He straightened up. 'I am hopeful that our relationship will improve, but we are in a bit of a hurry now, thanks to you. So I am afraid we must accelerate things. That is out of my hands, unless you and I start having a conversation.'

Torture. There was no choice. She could try to talk, to drag it out, to lie and mislead, but her head was ringing and her stomach was sick, and she didn't trust herself. Better to stay silent, and take what came. Maybe it would all be faster this way.

She stared at him, until at last he knocked twice on the door, and then Ivy was held by two men and marched down the corridor towards the vault.

She resisted the urge to scream, to writhe, to yell; it would only cause distress to the other prisoners. With its sabotage, its weapons, its money, the SOE was fighting a morale war; this had been drilled into her. And she could cope. All she needed to do was die without talking. It was a small task now, ahead of her, and she could do it anywhere.

They closed the vault door on her, left her in near darkness, standing, braced against the walls to try to reduce the weight on her aching leg. It wasn't pitch dark; there were holes drilled high in the door. For air. She found that if she crunched herself into a foetal position she could sink to the floor.

There was something scratched in the wall beside her. She put her fingertips to it, felt them, read them. Two words, in English.

Hello, Ivy.

Time did not pass in the vault, except through Ivy's body passing through pain to numbness, and then to pins and needles, and then to a place where she was uncertain how to get back to her body, and every so often felt a spark of panic before it died in the airless chambers of her mind.

Sometimes she heard whispering, a man's voice, friendly and kind, but she couldn't put a name to it, or hear any of the words. A trick of the walls, carrying the voice of another prisoner, perhaps or, more likely, a hallucination.

Her mind's eye sharpened in that darkness. She saw every house in the village and everyone in it, but she didn't see them going about their business. She saw them standing and staring at her, occupying their bedrooms, gardens, offices and shops like actors on stages, staring into the house lights, each one waiting for the moment for the soliloquy. Some of them were dead. She saw the difference in their eyes, the way they stared, though the living didn't move or speak either.

Then after a while, they did begin to speak. Monologues that meant nothing to her, delivered with sudden and violent animation.

A woman said: *So I told the butcher that I would have his money by the following Tuesday, though I knew full well I would be gone by then, and he knew it too, I could tell by looking at him. But he wasn't going to say it so I wouldn't.*

A man said: *Three days, that baby lived. As many days as Jesus was dead.*

A girl said: *I would like to have a piano like that one.*

On and on, a cast of strangers, talking to no one, as if Ivy were in the shadows of a darkened theatre. None of it made any sense to her.

When the door opened at last, she put her arm up against the light.

They took her out, not to the room with the blood-soaked cot, but to another cell. This one empty too, but cleaner, and with no furniture except two concrete benches built into the walls, one on either side.

Teller was sitting on one of them.

He looked alarmed when the guard let her go and she limped in.

'We'll have a doctor in to see to that leg,' Teller said in French.

Behind her, the guard grunted cynically. He left, closing the door, which made Ivy jump.

Teller regarded her for a moment, with curiosity. He gestured all around her, and switched to English again.

'You're alone today. Interesting. An effect of solitary confinement. I noticed it with the vault's last occupant too.'

He crossed his legs, gestured for her to sit on the other bench, which she did, because it hurt to stand.

He continued, 'That man – the man you got killed – he could see the future, you know. He could predict it as if he'd been given tomorrow's newspaper. Extraordinary gifts. Imagine his final walk down the corridor, knowing that ahead of him lay his death and behind him, the vault. Hideous.'

Ivy tried to remember the stooped, spindly man who'd come out of the vault; she didn't think she'd even made eye contact with him. A clairvoyant, with that power, working with the Resistance or the SOE, and Yardley didn't know about him? No. Yardley had no doubt sent her here for a reason. It wasn't only that this particular jail was relatively easy to break into; it was because at least one of its prisoners interested him. Here at La Codre, he had hoped, she could do two things for him: she could prove the value of her gift, and, if she succeeded, she would add another clairvoyant to his recruits.

But now that clairvoyant was dead. There had been so much happening, so much to worry about. She'd seen him go down simply and quickly, right before the shot that hit her own shoulder. Somehow she didn't think he'd found his walk to death hideous, but what did she know?

The man had known about her, though. He'd written her name on his cell wall, found some shard of concrete and scratched it in. *Hello, Ivy.* He might have given her something more useful. But, having been in the vault, she knew no hope could survive in that place.

'He was going to tell us when the invasion would come, and where.' Teller said. 'He was very close to telling us. So you see, you robbed all of Europe when you robbed that man of his life. Our chance to defend ourselves against aggression, quickly and without unnecessary bloodshed.'

The people of the village had faded from her mind's eye, now that she was here in the light with another flesh-and-blood human. But she was still seeing images, superimposed on Teller's concerned face. Flickering images of anger, viciousness, his or someone else's.

His own face stayed calm, concerned.

'It is astonishing that the British government was ready to squander your gifts in this way,' he said. 'People like us are difficult to find. Most people with psychic abilities never learn to recognize them for what they are, much less put them to good use. And yet Yardley sent you by parachute into enemy territory – for what? To put some prisoners' lives at greater risk. We will soon find all of those who escaped in your little stunt, and they will not thank you for it.'

At that, she almost smiled. *All of those who escaped.* Then she'd been right, when she'd woken up in an empty cell, to hope that there was less crowding in this hellhole for a good reason.

Red light moved across his face and seemed to stretch his muscles into a scream. It made it easy to stay quiet, easy to remember there was no purpose in taking any crumb of survival from this man.

Before they put her back in the vault, though, they forced cabbage-smelling broth down her throat with a funnel, until she threw most of it up.

She went into the vault with words ringing in her ears, the last thing he said to her before he opened the door to call the guards. *I know you, Ivy Sharp. And I know the faces of everyone you love.*

CHAPTER 21

Ivy

Ivy had a very long time to wonder how he had discovered her name, and what else he knew. She ran her fingers over the words on the wall, but Teller had used her surname too. He said he could see the faces of all those she loved; perhaps it had only been a matter of detective work, once he knew to look for people Mr Yardley might have recruited.

Everyone she loved . . . most were in England, which gave them some protection. But Kit was in Paris, as far as Ivy knew. Just a short drive from here.

It had never occurred to Ivy that, by coming to France, she'd endanger Kit.

If only she could think straight; if only her leg were not aching; if only she weren't so dizzy.

The whispering began again, after the darkness had a few hours to settle into her blood and bone.

Blood and bone are your best friends now, said the voice. *That leg is infected.*

She put her hands to the four walls, trying to find some passage, some explanation.

You're just in my mind, she thought.

Yes, said the voice. *I'm just you, with a little hint of me, like a drop of paint in water. The voice of prophecy is leaky. That happens, you know. What we see and hear, sometimes we can make others see and hear. I've left behind what I could for you. A bit of my voice in your head. That, and the scratch on the wall. It isn't much but I know you will understand when I say I was not at my best.*

The man who had occupied the vault before her. The dead man.

I don't even know your name, she thought. *Are you the reason I was sent here?*

How should I know why you were sent here? My name doesn't matter. Nothing about me matters to you. You don't want to gather any more information now, Ivy. What you want to do now is die. As quickly as possible, before they make you work for them, or tell them anything. Because they will make you, eventually. You have to die first. You did that for me, and I can help you do it for yourself. I'll keep you company.

But they'll get to Kit, unless I warn her.

Warn her, then.

I don't know how.

She didn't die quickly enough.

In the vault, time stretched and shrank. Sometimes she was back in the Beaulieu house with Grady, sometimes home at Stoke Damson with her parents and her sisters. Sometimes she spent hours planning to break in to the La Codre jail, only to realize with triumph that she'd done it, that had already happened. Then she'd be confused; why was she in the jail, if she'd released everyone? Maybe she wasn't Ivy at all. Maybe she was an old man, with a gift for prophecy.

Most often, she remembered falling. There was nothing

at all around her, only sky. All she could hear, far off in the distance, was the barking dog.

After what felt like several days, perhaps even longer, the guard took her to a different cell, one she'd never seen before. It had a drain in the floor, and a tub full of soapy water.

Flashes came to her mind of the bucket, at Beaulieu, and her legs gave way.

In this room, there were no SOE agents pretending to be Gestapo. There was just a woman Ivy had never seen before. She wore a uniform, her hair tied up. She looked like a nurse, but she wasn't a nurse.

'Take your clothes off,' she said in perfect French.

Ivy did nothing.

The male guard was still behind her, and with obvious gusto he pulled her filthy blouse off, and her trousers. The woman held up one hand when she was in her bra and underwear, and gestured for the guard to leave. Ivy stood there shivering, although it wasn't cold. She would be cold soon. She would be cold as a corpse.

'You will get into the bath,' the woman said.

Ivy shook her head.

'Prisoners must be cleaned. Look at that leg.'

She looked down, and saw it was red, and swollen. Infected. Beyond the point at which soapy water would make much difference, but not far gone enough yet to kill her. The water might, though. If she struggled. If she forced them to do it.

A moment or two of bravery. That was all she needed. Just a moment or two. Then it would be over. Maybe once she was dead they would have no reason to go looking for Kit. Maybe Ivy's ghost could haunt Kit, the way the man in the vault haunted Ivy. Give her some warning. It was the best she could do.

She climbed into the bath, which was cold as ice. The soap

smelled sharp and hurt her leg and her shoulder, where the bullet had grazed her. She was still in her underwear, which was some comfort, that she would not be naked when she died.

The woman pushed her head down. It would be quick.

The trick would be to not let her pull her back up. To keep thrashing around, to force the bitch to keep holding her down. So Ivy struggled, and tried not to breathe. Her last breath – God let it be her last – came out in a stream of bubbles that blinded her. She saw the man in the vault, the small, old man, his eyes kind. She saw Teller's pale eyes. Her mother's, then, out of nowhere, brown flecked with gold, worry lines. Her mother's hands, helping her when she was ill, steadying her when she was at odds with herself, proud on her shoulders.

All she had to do was not breathe.

It was impossible. It built up, a terrible roaring ache, a pressure she couldn't bear. Ivy wriggled and kicked as much as she could until at last the world darkened and her lungs kicked like a knife. In that moment, she was afraid. Every part of her, terrified. She wanted to breathe, to take in the air outside on a golden day, to stand on a hillside, to feel a sun-warmed old fence beneath her hand, to dip a brush in paint, to hear Rose play her jangly old piano that hadn't been tuned since before the war, to put her arms around her father, to walk the streets of a great city, to sip champagne, to put the music of Rosetta Tharpe on to a turntable and take Grady's hand and pull him up to dance with her, to hold her tiny niece in her arms, to sit in a darkened cinema when the hush falls, to smell roast goose on Christmas Day, to sit in the opera, to walk through the halls of a museum in peacetime, with no one in uniform watching.

The brick wall broke.

The woman pulled her up, back into the bright world. But

her mouth and throat were full of water and now she was drowning, up in the air. A breath pushed at her nostrils, bringing more water with it, choking her. She was alive, for a fraction of a second, perhaps another. Shaking with cold and terror. Another breath and this time her chest got some of it, and the blackness around her temples cleared a little.

Back under the water. If she was weeping, there was no way to know. She was gasping now, her will exhausted, the animal body in control. Every gasp brought water, death, quicker this time. Better that way, she tried to think, but she couldn't believe it. No desires now. Just images. She was going to escape. She was away from this hell, with Grady at Beaulieu. He was standing in the garden, smoking, rubbing a finger on his bottom lip, which was red and dry. He looked worried. He saw her – she was outside the house, looking in, then she was inside, with him. The cigarette dropped out of his mouth and he put his hands on her shoulders.

She was back in the air. Soap stinging her eyes so that she couldn't see anything but red.

'Now you are clean,' someone said.

In the next interrogation, the room was full, though most of her brain knew that it was only her and Teller between those concrete walls. The walls themselves were covered with faces, moving images, grimacing at her. She kept looking for a film projector, which made Teller curious.

'Some people have a mind's ear,' he said. 'Some have a mind's eye. And some have neither, and they just know things. You're like me, aren't you? The way you think about things is by seeing them.'

She said nothing, so he slapped her face. Her eyes filled with shocked tears, though the pain was a respite from the other pain. Her clothes were finally dry but she would never be warm again. Her throat was still raw. Her leg ached all the worse for being clean, and her shoulder wound stung where her bra strap touched it. They hadn't bothered with iodine and plasters.

'I'm not a man of infinite patience,' he said mildly, still sitting on the bench, and then she realized that he hadn't slapped her at all. He hadn't moved. She was feeling the memory of the memory she'd picked up from Léo, perhaps, or a fresh wound – or maybe the guard had slapped her the last time he'd put her into the vault? Yes, that accounted for the sting, the bruise, but not the tears.

Teller said, 'You want what's best for your sisters, I know. Your sister Kit, for example. I have been aware of Kit for some time – we move in the same circles, you might say – but I had no idea how interesting her family is. I could, of course, give assurances that she will not be mistreated. Would you like such assurances?'

She nodded, and the room wobbled.

'But I would have to have something from you. You understand that. If, for example, you could tell me anything about the invasion. Just something small. A sign of goodwill.'

'I don't see the future,' she said, her lips thick with blood. 'Usually.'

'Usually. I see. You need assistance for that part, I imagine.' He put his hand into his pocket and pulled out a scrap of yellowed fabric and held it between thumb and forefinger, as if it was precious. 'The code on the silk was very helpful to us, but this, I think, may be even more helpful. We didn't recognize it at first. Not until I had a chance to touch it myself. This is why you're here, isn't it?'

The cloth. The little yellowed square that Mr Yardley had given her. Of course. They hadn't thrown it out. Teller had taken it.

'It's just a good-luck charm,' she said, uneasily.

He laughed. 'Try again. It's a scrap from the famous

embroidery that Queen Matilda made, nine hundred years ago. At least, tradition says it was Queen Matilda. And I know that to be true, because I have studied the tapestry myself. I know what it is. And I know what it does.'

What it does? How could a scrap of fabric do anything?

Truth be told, she had kept it in a matchbox for a reason. She had not enjoyed the sensation of touching it, when Mr Yardley gave it to her that night, in the garden at Beaulieu. But she had been so overwrought, about to fly to France, about to leave Grady. She hadn't thought that her vision had anything to do with the fabric itself, at least not more than what happened sometimes when she touched a photograph or a piece of clothing.

How much sharper her visions had been, since she came to France – since the night she started carrying that scrap with her. But that was ridiculous; he was trying to confuse her.

Teller leaned forward. 'Why have they sent you? What does England have planned for the tapestry?'

'Nothing. I told you. It's just a sentimental item.'

His focus was on the air around her, and his eyes darted. 'Oh, yes, I know all about your father's research. I've known about that for some time. It was learning about his theory of the tapestry as prophetic tool that first led me to study the item in person. But it did not occur to me to ask whether there was something more than analysis that brought him to that conclusion. Was it, shall we say, intuition? I see, I see. A gift that runs in your family.'

He stopped talking for a moment, and she noticed that she was shaking. Shivering. The air was so cold on her skin, and there were so many faces on the walls. Lines of German soldiers, watching her.

Teller said, 'Of course, I should have expected that if your father learned part of the truth, he learned all of it. I should have known that England would use the invasion to try to get its hands on it. But I did not foresee that they would send a girl.'

She shook her aching head. 'You're wrong.'

His smile was unnatural, a parody. 'I'll learn the truth eventually, you know. One way or another. I see some of your secrets and we will crack open the others before long. We have a connection now, and you will open up new vistas for my mind's eye. I would like you to do it willingly. You have a choice before you.'

'What *choice*?'

Teller held up the tapestry in the palm of his hand, as if it were a bird's egg. 'This scrap is evidence of a broken lineage, that we will stitch back together. You and I, and others like us. We will draw on each other, and on our inheritance, and with that strength we will put our God-given talents to use at last, in service of the greatest project humanity has ever attempted. You have the ability to put an end to this wasteful war. You are special. You are not to be shunned or feared or cast away. You should be a queen, and you will be. In the empire that we will build.'

She had heard that she was special before, but in a major key. Did Mr Yardley also think the tapestry had an effect on clairvoyants? Was that why he'd given it to her: to heighten her powers? She suspected not; she hadn't mentioned her visions or sensations to him, in the garden that night, and when he talked about Father's research he'd only mentioned the tapestry as proof of the existence of prophecy. But she never could be sure exactly what Mr Yardley knew about anything.

Another fragment of memory settled into place, like a puzzle piece: Mr Yardley saying this was the second cutting from the tapestry he'd found. She could hear his voice, in her mind, as clear as if he were in the room: *I gave it to your father. Perhaps it inspired him to keep working on his research, because he developed his new theory not long after that.*

Inspired him – or gave him visions? Was Father truly like her? What effect did that scrap have on him?

She must not think about her father, not now, lest she give something away. She tried to think of nothing, tried to benumb her mind, but all she saw was her home, her family: a summer afternoon, light coming through the sitting-room window, voices laughing. Father poring over a book on his chair, calling Kit over to show her something; Kit kneeling and frowning at the book, chattering away to Father. The old days, when they were still speaking to each other. When Kit was home.

Teller leaned back again, closing his hand over the bit of cloth. 'Your sister Kit has a real gift for historical research. Talent, or Second Sight? I wonder. Perhaps she's the one I should be talking to.'

'No,' Ivy said, quickly. She tried to think, to grasp at anything that would stop him from having Kit arrested. 'No, it's me. I can tell you what you need to know. I can tell you—' She stopped, looked at him, opened herself up like pulling open a wound. Visions of his life came flooding in, replacing her own memories. She stretched out her hand, flexed it, stared at it. 'I can tell you that that scar on your little finger came from when you hit a woman wearing glasses and broke them – there's a scar on her nose to match. She is dead now. She is—'

He stood up and the slap came for the second time, just as she had felt it moments before. When the guard came to walk her out, she couldn't see through her wet eyes, couldn't see where the blood was coming from as it dripped on the floor, marking her trail from cell to vault.

She'd angered him; she'd missed her chance to learn more. But she didn't care. She just wanted silence, and peace.

*

Kit reached out her hand from within the vault, and hugged her, closed her arms around her as Ivy stumbled in.

'They're coming for you, Kit,' Ivy sobbed. 'I can't help you now.'

She put her hands to her sister's face, and felt the embrace of cold concrete, in her vertical grave.

PART 3

JUNE TO DECEMBER 1944

CHAPTER 22

Kit

Kit has a dream that is not a dream; it's a story she's telling herself. Half-asleep in Lucienne's farmhouse, she remembers Aunt Kathleen telling her the story, years ago, on those weekend visits when Kit was studying in Edinburgh. But no, that did not happen, surely, because if it had Kit would have recalled it, when she got that strange letter from Father about his tapestry theory. Maybe it was Father who told her the story, then. Or maybe Kit's inventing it; maybe she's always known it. It unfolds before her mind's eye.

She sees Matilda, a young woman with dark hair, and bruises on her face. One of her suitors has taken offence at her rejection. William, the bastard Duke of Normandy, has no right to her body or his own anger, but he revels in both. Matilda's father, the Count of Flanders, will avenge her. She is descended from the kings of both England and France; an offence to her is no private matter. The count swears to take vengeance on this William, and Matilda, with her chin high and her shoulders back, waits for justice.

But Matilda's mother is not so sanguine. She comes to her daughter at night, when everything is quiet.

'Your father will not prevail,' says her mother. 'He will die at this duke's hand. I have seen it. God has sent me a vision.'

This is not the first vision Adela the Holy has told her daughter about. They have always come true; Matilda does not doubt this one. She thanks her mother, and she tries not to blame God.

'But that is not the only path,' her mother whispers. 'Marry this duke, as he asks, and help him to conquer a nation, and you will receive my gift. The gift of sight beyond the waking world. Tell your husband his own story, and he will make it come true. You will lead him to victory, and, when you have achieved it, God will send a star like the one he sent to the magi of old, to tell you he approves.'

Matilda cannot say, in the years after this, whether she chose to marry William to save her father's life, or because she believed that she might come to share her mother's gift. She does not see the future, not even after the wedding. But she is a daughter of kings, and she has married the man who beat her on the floor of her father's house, and she will not have her misery be in vain. She gives her lout of a husband a warship, and she finds him allies. And she finds others too: women and girls who are known in their towns and villages for telling fortunes or making good wagers. Nuns who have visions. Women only, because she doesn't trust men. She brings them all to her, and she asks them what they see. Some of them come from England, because she believes her husband's future lies there.

At first, it is disappointing. The women tell her so little: images and riddles. She finds a house for them, far away from travelled roads, so they will not be tempted to gossip about their duchess to anyone that matters.

It takes a long time. But the women talk to each other; they tell each other what they see, and it starts to make sense. Matilda puts a strip of linen in front of them, and she says: *Sew what you see. Begin at the beginning and tell the story of my husband, and don't stop, not even when you reach the present day. Keep going.*

The women spend a long time over every panel, talking and planning. The educated among them add words, in Latin. It takes years. They tell stories of families turned out of their homes, villages burned, children screaming for their mothers. But Matilda says all of this must be; it is destiny. Her destiny. She checks their progress from time to time, and she gives her husband advice. Wise advice, which seems prescient. When a terrible flaming star appears in the sky, just after Easter in the year 1066, she knows she was right not to doubt her mother's vision.

Bangs and shouts.

Groggy from dreams and imaginings, Kit takes a moment to realize that the German voices coming from the ground floor of the farmhouse are real. Official voices, making demands. Heavy footsteps.

Kit fumbles for the candle, lights it, and sees Maxine already at the bedroom door, listening, hesitating.

The door swings open and Lucienne stands there with her finger to her lips. Then she drops something into Max's hand. Two small keys; she puts both into her pockets.

Lucienne whispers, 'The Gestapo are between you and the bicycles. There's a motorcycle in the back shed. And there's a box under the floor there – they'll find it if they search. Take the money and find someone who can use it.'

'You're getting out, aren't you?' Max asks, in a tone that suggests she knows the answer.

'The boy's down there on his own,' Lucienne says, and then she is gone.

Max closes the bedroom door soundlessly, turns to Kit with a tight mouth. Then she points at the window.

They throw their clothes out first, and climb down in their pyjamas, clutching at a drainpipe and window frames. No noise from inside the house. Kit runs after Max, who's using a small key to open the padlock on the shed door.

Inside, dim shapes, mostly covered in oily sheets. The motorcycle in the middle has a large metal cylinder like a rubbish bin bolted to the back, just behind the second seat. Max rummages under a sheet, pulls out a coffee tin full of charcoal, opens a door on the cylinder and tips the charcoal in. It's a common sight these days, with no petrol available, but Kit's never driven on charcoal before.

Then Max pulls up the floorboard, and opens a shoebox. A wad of money, which she puts inside the headlight glass. She throws their rumpled clothing into the saddlebag.

As they roll the motorcycle out through the shed door into the darkness, they can hear raised voices from within the house. They lift the beast over a fence, and Kit says a silent farewell to her bicycle. What will happen to Lucienne? There will be no chance now to ask London about Ivy, not if the wireless operator is caught too – and if he isn't, he'll have to avoid the house.

Meanwhile, Max and Kit are free, thanks to Lucienne. Free to look for Ivy. She knows where Max is going to drive, without asking. Falaise. It's the only place that makes any sense. Lucienne said it was bombed, but better to go and see than to wonder and wait.

When they have walked for a few minutes down a track, Max stops and hops on, gesturing for Kit to get on behind her. There's a small metal handle on the seat between Kit's legs, so she doesn't have to grab on to Max.

A few tries with the kickstart and the engine grumbles to life, unbelievably loud in that stillness. Max peels off, without turning on the headlight, hurtling into darkness. The night is cold, but the moon is still almost full.

It's unreal, as if a small door has opened up in the universe and they've driven through it. She never expected to be alone with Max again, not after their argument, just before the German advance. When Kit said she was staying in Paris, Max said she would help Ivy get home safely. Of course she did. Without even thinking about it.

Two letters had got through from Max, to Paris. Had she sent any more? They were short, just to say that everyone was safe. Nothing that betrayed the slightest emotion, and not even any jokes. After that, letters were more difficult to get, once the Germans did away with the fiction of the free zone of Vichy France. Kit kept the letters, ran her fingers over Max's sloping handwriting. It was so lean and stylish, just like Max herself.

And now here they are, with the back of Max's pyjama shirt brushing Kit's knuckles. It's a bumpy ride, and Kit is soon exhausted from holding herself steady so she won't bump into Max.

'You know,' Kit says after a while, loud enough to be heard over the engine, 'I swore never to get on to a motorcycle with you after that time you swiped George Bodley's and nearly crashed it.'

'You can drive if you like!' Max yells back to her.

'I have, you know. In Arabia.'

'If we need to get to Mecca, I'll get behind you,' Max says. 'But I'm the one who knows the way to Falaise.'

In the darkness Max brakes suddenly, and Kit is thrown against her, one hand leaving the metal bar and bracing against Max's back. She stays like that a moment, catching her balance and her breath, feeling Max's warmth on her cold hand. The motorcycle has come to a stop inches before a chasm that was once a small bridge. Half of the bridge is lying in the little river below, now, wood and metal and stone broken.

'This explains why we haven't met any Germans on this route,' Max says cheerfully, while Kit is catching her breath. 'One for the Resistance.'

It takes them a long time to scramble down and ford the river on slippery rocks, carrying the heavy motorcycle between them, and by the end Kit is nearly weeping with exhaustion, bruised, her feet wet. They haven't brought anything to drink and she's parched, but doesn't trust the river water. She climbs back on behind Max, as the sky lightens.

Through the wood and around a bend, and they arrive in hell.

There's a smell of smoke, and the ruins of stone buildings are charred and black in the early morning light. The tops of the buildings are absent, and their walls jagged. Here and there, a wooden building has survived. There are no animals, no people. As they pass by a burned house, they see a body lying on the front step. A woman, face down. Dress half up her legs, a bloody gash on her head.

Kit bangs on Max's shoulder to tell her to stop, and she gets off, stumbles on sea legs towards the woman. She knows what she will see but she has to turn the body over, to be sure. The woman's face is waxy, her eyes open.

'There's no one here we can help,' Max says, standing behind her and walking the motorbike. 'We have to go on to Falaise. We must be almost there.'

Falaise, which was bombed too. Kit doesn't see the castle in her mind any more. She doesn't see anything but the face of the dead woman, her snub nose, her staring brown eyes, the wisp of grey hair coming out of her scorched headcloth. Are her family here among the rubble, or did they leave her body behind?

A village wiped out of existence because it lay on a route

the German army could take north to the beaches, to the front where the Allies are pushing forward. A sacrifice to liberation. If the Allies make it to this village, they will find nothing to liberate.

She walks on a little bit, to what must have been the heart of the village: a cobbled square with a round stone fountain wall, unbroken amid all the destruction. Kit leans against it, feeling it cold, real in her hands. Her hair has come loose on the motorcycle, and strands are sticking to her cheek. She brushes it back, trying to clear it.

To the left, a small alley leads between two bombed-out buildings. Two broken jaws of giant skulls. No eyes here but her own. Her gaze runs downhill, between the two stone husks, far into the distance.

Framed between the charred walls is a castle, a fairytale castle, exactly the shape she's been imagining for the last two days.

It's impossible.

'What is it?' Max is walking the motorcycle, looking at Kit's face.

Kit just points, her lips moving as if to form a prayer.

'Yes,' Max says. 'I knew we weren't far from Falaise. That's the conqueror's castle. The one we're looking for.'

'But this is what it looks like in my head. The exact angle. The silhouette. I don't see it close up, usually. I see it precisely from here.'

'What do you mean?'

'I mean that—' Kit chokes on air heavy with old smoke, and starts again. 'She must have been here. I saw what she saw, I think. I know, it's absolutely mad. But I can't think of any explanation, and I feel so – so sure.'

Max just stares at the castle for a moment, and looks back at Kit. 'If she was here, she must have left. We won't give up, Kit. I won't give up.'

Kit wants to fall into her but stops herself. She doesn't have the right. She wraps her arms around herself like bandages, keeping all her harm contained.

There's no sound on the air except the wind whispering, and something tapping: a stray piece of roof tile, clothes on a line, something. It resolves into a pattern. *One-two-three, four. One-two-three, four. One-two-three, four.*

V for victory.

Maybe all tapping sounds that way to her now.

'What is that?' Kit asks.

'What do you mean?'

'That sound.'

Max listens. 'I don't hear anything.'

Kit scowls, and walks towards a bombed-out building to the side of the square. It's coming from this direction, but she sees nothing moving. Just charred walls. Shapes without form.

The stone door frame is intact, columns topped with carved vines, though the door inside has burned and fallen out.

Inside the frame, a figure. Pale as smoke. Pale hair, pale skin, turning away.

Just like the figure she saw on the streets of Paris, and in her flat. Her sister, but here the vision is so insubstantial, she knows it can't be anything but a vision. A hallucination or a ghost.

'Ivy,' Kit breathes, and runs through the doorway. Inside, rubble. Piles of charred paper. Part of a desk. Roof beams and chunks of masonry. Oppressive, despite being open to the sky. She sees no one, of course.

She is tired of her mind's tricks, which have done her no good. These visions that have led her here, only to find rubble and the scent of death. Balling her fists, she throws back her head and screams.

'What do you see?' Max asks, softly, tentatively.

Kit lets her chin drop, her eyes closed. 'Nothing now. I thought I saw her. I thought I heard tapping, but now it's gone. It's all riddles and nonsense, Max. I'm afraid. So afraid.'

Even with her eyes closed, she feels Max stepping closer to her. She takes one of Kit's hands, gently. 'We'll face it together. Whatever the truth turns out to be. Wherever the trail leads.'

Kit opens her eyes, to grey daylight that feels harsher than the sun. It's the smoke in the air; it stings. But Max's hand is warm and real.

'The trail led us here.'

'Then let's see what it has to show us.'

Kit looks at Max's brown eyes, steady and strong. Despite everything. Kit avoided those eyes for years, even when they were friends, even before the rift between them. She knew even in her teens that looking at Max's eyes a second too long carried a risk, that Kit would then become part of their secret, a secret they both knew was wrong, perverse, shameful. She didn't want to be that for Max; she just wanted to be Kit to her. She wanted to always be Kit to her, and for Max always to be Max. Nothing else, nothing that could cause Max to regret knowing her, nothing that could cause Max pain with her father, with her friends, with anyone. Kit did not want to be an instrument of pain, and she feared there was no way to love a woman without becoming that.

She has never put any of this into words before. Here, in this hellscape, with the ghost of her sister always at the edges of her vision, every old fear seems flimsy and inconsequential. What does it matter if they hurt each other tomorrow? Tomorrow is a dream. Today is real, and today requires her to be the best she can. There is no room for anything but naked honesty in this moment. There is only Kit, and the people she loves, and what she is willing to do for them.

'I think,' Max says, 'that if you were led here, if you saw

her here, then we have to trust that. It must mean something. There is something here for us to find. We can at least bear witness – if that's all we can do.'

She means, of course, that Ivy might have died here.

Ivy probably landed with the last moon before D-Day, a month ago. Could she have been here during that time? Maybe she had spent weeks in this village. So close to Kit, a bicycle ride away, and yet Kit had seen no visions of her, had no hint she was here. Until two days ago – the day that this village and other parts of the Falaise area were bombed.

That cannot be a coincidence. Kit lets herself admit what she already believed: that the vision was real in some way, that it meant something. It might be a sign that Ivy had died. Or it might be a message from her. A plea, or a warning. Whatever it was, it had brought her here. It had also, as a side effect, taken her out of Paris. Could that have been the purpose?

Kit lets Max's hand drop and takes a deep breath, looking around the ruined landscape. 'Oh, Ivy,' she sighs. 'I wish I knew what you were trying to tell me.'

There it is again: a faint tapping, three short notes, one long. Morse code for victory. A sign of resistance. It may only be audible to her, but it is not her imagination.

It grows louder.

Kit takes a step, and another, while Max watches her patiently. She slowly paces the pile of rubble inside the ruined building, feeling like the old man who walks the fields near Stoke Damson with dowsing rods, looking for water or ley lines or God knows what. She can only follow the sound. Like a child in a game, she follows the tapping as it grows louder, obeying it, giving herself up to instinct.

At last, she reaches a spot where the tapping only grows quieter in any direction, when she tries to walk away from it. This is the loudest point. She doesn't see anything, but she feels Ivy here. It feels like wrapping her arms around her sister after a long time away.

Kit falls to her knees. Before she can think about it, she's pulling chunks of stone and wood aside, trying to get closer to the sound. Max is beside her, saying something, but Kit can't hear anything past the roar in her ears and the tapping.

She knows when she sees the hand reaching out of an opening, cracked concrete surrounding it, that it is Ivy's hand. A sense of homecoming, of relief.

The tapping stops.

Ivy has been here, buried under this rubble, since the day before yesterday.

Kit clutches the fingers.

Life in them. Warmth. A hint of responsive movement. She is sure it isn't only her imagination. Oh, let it be true.

Beside her, Max is scrabbling at bricks and cracked stones. Kit lets go of her sister's hand and joins her.

As they pull at the rubble, it soon becomes clear that much of it is too heavy to move, and a distressing amount is not rubble at all but concrete walls still in place.

Kit calls down to Ivy but hears no response, then again, and finally hears a faint, 'Yes, I'm here.'

Tears roll down Kit's cheeks. All the hope she's been suppressing flows out of her, and she puts her hands on the rubble to steady herself.

'You'll have to come up,' Max calls out, also on her hands and knees beside the hole. 'It's big enough, if we pull you. Reach your hands up. Both hands.'

They each grab one of Ivy's wrists and Kit grimaces at the strain, hands slipping and reddening Ivy's thin wrists, and she tries not to think about what this is doing to Ivy's bones and joints as she and Max pull, trying to get a grip on her elbows, her upper arms.

Kit is weeping with relief and terror as Ivy's head emerges, her blonde hair lank, her face thin and grey. But there's a small smile as she sees Kit, and then her eyes close.

They have to struggle with getting her shoulders through the gap. Ivy does her best to grab on to a chunk of cracked concrete to pull her legs up and through.

'You're safe,' Ivy whispers, eyes fluttering as she looks at Kit.

A laugh breaks out of Kit, and she wipes her nose. 'No, you are, you goose. You're safe. Everything's all right now.'

Nothing is all right. They are coated in a film of ash and dust, coughing, leaning together, and in the distance they can hear the guns. Kit holds her sister in her arms.

Ivy stays lucid long enough to insist on no hospitals, and something about the way she says it makes both Max and Kit take notice. Kit cradles Ivy's head while Max holds Ivy's hand. They are desperate, and alone. Kit clutches at her sister, as if she can will her not to die.

'I used to have a contact near Argentan,' Max says. 'A doctor.'

'Used to?'

'It's been a while, but, if he's still there and still alive, we can trust him.'

'We can't take her on the motorcycle like this, can we?'

They stand up and look around for a car they might use, but the only two left behind that they can see are burned husks.

'I'll be back in ninety minutes,' Max says, and she's leaping on to the motorcycle, then gone in a trail of smoke.

Kit walks the two steps back to Ivy, but by the time she reaches her she's lost consciousness.

CHAPTER 23

Kit

The doctor is a dashing young man who picks them up in his car. Max drives the motorcycle, and Kit drives the car, as the doctor is in the back tending to Ivy.

They only stop once, pulling over to the verge in a screech of dust, as a noisy convoy passes carrying German soldiers. Kit shrinks down in her seat, though they are not interested in her or the few other people on the streets; they're going north, to the coast, to fight the Allies. Truck after truck, some of them covered, some open and carrying young men in camouflage helmets, draped in ammunition belts that catch the late afternoon sun.

They reach the outskirts of Argentan at sunset. The doctor says the city has been bombed several times over the last two days, to slow down the Germans on their way to the coast. He lives in a small white house on a street that shows no signs of anything amiss, except a small suitcase lying open on the pavement, with a pink dress and a string of artificial pearls spilling out of it.

The doctor puts Ivy up in his guest room.

After he's made sure Ivy is comfortable, Dr Berthou makes Max and Kit acorn coffee in his kitchen, and takes a breath before telling them what they want to know, speaking in perfect English.

'Proper hydration and nutrition will go a long way. Luckily, the bullet wound in her shoulder is a mere graze.'

A bullet wound! Kit looks at Max, who looks steadily at the doctor.

'But the leg is infected,' Dr Berthou continues. 'I've treated the wound, but in her current condition I'm not sure her body can fight it off.' He pauses, chews his moustache. 'I had some other visitors yesterday. Visitors who may be able to get us penicillin. I think it's her best shot at avoiding amputation. Her best shot at living, to be perfectly frank.'

Kit stands up. 'Where are these visitors?'

'I'll go and ask them, if you're willing,' Dr Berthou says. 'I've given them my word that I will keep their location to myself.'

The visitors turn out to be three soldiers: an American, a Scotsman and a Frenchman, who dropped by parachute shortly before the invasion. Not only do they obtain penicillin for Ivy, thanks to their military connections, but they also give Kit and Max cots in the church basement where they're staying.

It's a pretty church; Gothic. Not Kit's period.

Max goes off to find them some soap, toothbrushes and hairbrushes.

All of Argentan's services have evacuated to the village of Aunou-le-Faucon, an hour's walk away, so Kit goes there and asks the woman in the makeshift post office if she can get a telegram to the Louvre. She'd like to tell them she'll be a few more weeks doing her research, so that they don't worry about her. And Evelyn, with all her contacts there, would learn that Kit was all right.

Evelyn knows everyone in Paris, or so it seems sometimes. Although she never talks much about her family life in the United States, she seems to have emerged from it with a kind of one-way independence; she's determined to take care of herself, and can be frustratingly private, but she shows a fierce devotion to her friends.

One story she did tell Kit, after a bottle of wine, was about a treasure she found when she was fifteen in the back garden of her house in North Dakota. A Victorian biscuit tin, with a young blonde woman on the cover in a pretty dress. Inside, Evelyn found rusted coins from the 1850s. The coins had bought her a bus ticket to New York City, and a new life, in which she had modelled her appearance on the woman on the tin. The tin itself she kept, although Kit never saw it.

'I keep all my treasures in it,' Evelyn said. 'It reminds me to survive. Because the person who buried that tin probably didn't.'

It was that buried treasure that had first given her the dream of becoming an archaeologist, which was why Kit had met her in Arabia years ago. But although her life might have started with a hoard, Evelyn was no miser. Her dedication to her friends often took the form of gifts, and generous ones at that. She gave Kit books: lovely old versions of Dickens and Walter Scott, the stories she had loved as a girl. Inscribed to her on the flyleaf, with Evelyn's pretty signature and *double entendre* above it.

Evelyn lived not far from where Sylvia Beach used to have her bookshop, Shakespeare and Company. Another of the Paris lesbians who all knew each other, or so it seemed at least, before the war. When Sylvia was interned, Evelyn had done what she could to make sure there was no threat to her shop. Sylvia is free now. Kit hasn't seen Sylvia or her lover in over a year, though, and the bookshop hasn't re-opened.

By the time she reaches the post office, Kit is feeling bad that she hasn't been able to tell Evelyn where she is, or when she'll be back. But the flustered woman in the post office says nothing is working, nobody knows anything. Perhaps another day.

So Kit walks back towards Argentan.

On one of the roads near the train tracks, there is window glass all over the road from a bomb-damaged building. A girl, not quite into her teens, is standing in the midst of it, holding a shard. She looks up at Kit.

'I can hear the planes,' the girl whispers.

Kit looks up into the blue sky. Silence. 'I don't hear anything.'

'They're coming,' the girl says. 'The planes are coming.'

She's holding the shard of glass like a dagger. It's filthy, and Kit's worried the girl will cut herself on it, so she approaches her and gently takes the shard, enfolding the girl's hands.

A woman calls, 'Françoise!' and runs towards them, taking the girl's arm and leading her away. Kit is left standing amid the broken glass. She looks at them walking briskly away from her, then turns back towards the church.

She finds Max chatting with the Scotsman in the church-yard. When the Scotsman walks off into the church, Max turns to Kit.

'Captain McGarel is a radio operator. I've asked him to include a message in his next transmission, to let London know that Ivy is alive. And that Lucienne may not be.'

'Lucienne seemed like a very resourceful person,' Kit says. 'Perhaps she'll be all right.'

'Perhaps.' Max taps her cigarette. 'She was my organizer. Our radio operator will have gone to ground or been caught. The most useful place for me now is probably here, with this team. McGarel and the others. They tell me there are many of these teams dropping in France, to support the invasion from behind enemy lines. New radios, new radio operators. Guns and medicine. They can use someone who knows the roads, I'm sure.'

'To do what, exactly?'

'Keep the Resistance supplied. Give the Germans trouble.'

Max has always been fearless, but her courage now is something Kit doesn't recognize. She watches Max hop up on to the cemetery wall, and after a moment she jumps up and joins her there. They're both wearing the same clothes they've been wearing since the day Max came and stood outside her flat in Paris. Max in her wide-legged, cuffed beige trousers, and the loose matching jacket. Kit in her plaid skirt and yellow cardigan. They wash their underwear and blouses from time to time and hang them to dry, wearing their pyjamas while they wait. Somehow, Max still looks glamorous and efficient. She looks like the sort of person who might very well go off and give the Germans trouble.

'I'll help as much as I can,' Kit says. 'I can't leave Ivy here alone, but if you need anyone, to, I don't know . . . catalogue things.'

Max smiles, and looks sideways at her. 'Are you still seeing your castle?'

Kit shakes her head.

'And the dog? The tapping? All gone?'

'So far as I can tell, everything I see and hear is what everyone else sees and hears.'

Max whistles. 'That was a queer thing, wasn't it?'

Kit isn't sure what to make of it now. When they found Ivy, she'd felt sure that Ivy had called to her, led her to La Codre so that Kit could rescue her. But the implications make her uncomfortable. She wants to poke at her own desire to believe in all of this, to be objective.

'The brain makes everything into stories,' she says. 'Like dreams.'

'Yes, but you knew things. Where to look. To go to Falaise.'

'Maybe. I saw a castle. You and Lucienne said it was the Falaise castle, so, when I saw the Falaise castle, I thought that was it.'

'But it was. Ivy was right there!'

'We always knew she was somewhere in the area. And what about the dog? The dog didn't lead us anywhere, remember?' Kit pauses. 'I've been trying to think whether anything might have played on my subconscious mind. Maybe, in Paris, I saw you in the street and didn't realize it, and that made me think of Ivy. Maybe I was just worried about her. Maybe I knew from years before that she would try something like this.'

'You were incredulous when I told you she'd come by parachute.'

Kit shrugs. 'Maybe it's all coincidence.'

Max looks at her. 'You don't believe that.'

'Belief and fact are not always aligned.'

'No. No, they are not.' Max stubs out her cigarette on the wall beside her. 'I never told you how I knew that Ivy was in France.'

'I assumed you couldn't tell me that.'

Max shrugs. 'I was never told. Not exactly. A few years ago, at Christmas, my father had Ivy to the house for a private chat. He told me about it beforehand, so I wouldn't get curious, I suppose. He said something vague about your mother's work with the refugees. It seemed natural enough and I wasn't surprised he didn't invite me to the chat. I went out, so it wouldn't be awkward.'

'You're still not getting along, then?'

'It's a détente. He leaves me to my life and I leave him to his. If he chooses to believe that I've reformed, that I'm not a Sapphic any more, well, fine. If he asks me, I'll tell him the truth. He never asks.'

Kit has recently wondered what Mr Yardley thinks about *her*, about Kit, given that she and Max once shared a flat. At the time, the thought hadn't occurred to her that he would make that connection, and, after all, Ivy had been there as a kind of chaperone.

'So was it your father who told Ivy about the – what is it called?'

'The Special Operations Executive.' Max sighs. 'He must have. One day not long after that, a colleague of his came to the house, and played tennis with me while he was waiting for Father to come home. He said I would do marvellously with some very special war work. It was a line, of course, but eventually I went to London to see about it. Father found out after my interview, and railed at me. He said I was too reckless and selfish, that I would put everyone else at risk. I said that surely that was for the trainers to decide; they could send me away, if I was unsuitable. So then he said that was precisely what he expected to happen: that I would embarrass myself, and embarrass him into the bargain.'

'Oh, Max. I'm sure he was only worried about you, but he didn't have to be so beastly about it.'

'He would have to be a different man not to be beastly,' Max said. 'Anyway, I did very well on the training, as it happened. Out in the countryside, very hush-hush. But I did not take very well to the rule that we weren't allowed to leave the premises without permission.'

Kit brings her legs up to sit cross-legged on the wall, to get more comfortable. 'You got into trouble.'

'I did not. I managed it perfectly. Slipped in and out without anyone being the wiser.'

Kit wonders what the mischief was, and whether it was

a woman. She has no right to wonder about it, no right to be bothered.

Max carries on with her story. 'As I was hiding in a coal shed early one morning, I overheard two instructors talking about a student with the code name Juliet. A young blonde artist, which they found very amusing. She had been sent somewhere for special training and never heard from again, ha ha. One of them said she was a protégée of Yardley's. And I remembered the meeting, after Christmas.'

'*Special training*,' Kit repeats, thinking.

'Yes. At the time, I decided it was probably a stalling tactic of my father's. Ivy might have gone to him asking to be put to use – you know how she is, how she always wants to be glamorous and important. He found a position for her, feeling badly because of his friendship with your father. He put her in some invented special training to make sure she never went over. To save her life. This was my theory.'

'And you never found out? Never spoke with Ivy?'

'No, because I was sent over myself not long after that. He certainly took no measures to stop *me* from killing myself.' Max drums her fingers on the wall. 'But Kit, I wonder. This is going to sound ridiculous, but I wonder whether they might have trained Ivy to – I don't know. It does seem as if she managed to get a message to you, somehow.'

'It does indeed sound ridiculous. But I can't say I didn't feel it strongly at the time, that she was communicating with me. I don't know. Perhaps it's only that my mind went to that because of all the stories Aunt Kathleen used to tell us, and how we all played at being clairvoyants when we were children.'

Kit is still holding the shard of window glass in one hand, and she traces a pattern with it into the stone, scratching lines that mean nothing.

'My father's always been interested in folklore, magic, all

that business,' Max says. 'He's said some odd things, since the war started.'

'What sorts of odd things?'

'Oh, I don't recall exactly. Just some comments here and there about primeval wisdom, more things in heaven and earth, *et cetera*. I don't know. I can't say I was very interested in asking him to elaborate on his thoughts. We could barely stand to be in the same room together. And now we can't ask him.' Max kicks the wall with her oxfords. 'But I do know we'll be able to ask Ivy soon enough. She's going to get well.'

'And how do you know that? Don't tell me you've got magical powers now too.'

'I know it because I won't accept any alternatives.'

On this beautiful June day, Kit believes it. There are no planes in the blue sky, and they cannot hear the guns at the coast, cannot even hear the trucks now. She thinks of the girl who heard the planes no one else could hear, and wonders when she'll be proven right. But for now, she's alive, and Ivy is alive, and Max is alive.

'I haven't said thank you,' Kit says. 'For coming to see me in Paris. For trying to find Ivy, when you have so much important work to do. I know it wasn't easy. After everything. It means a lot.'

'No bother at all,' Max says brusquely, hopping off the wall and brushing her trousers off, although her supernatural ability to come through anything without the slightest wrinkle on her clothing is still serving her. 'Now excuse me, Kit – I have to go and see about blowing up some Nazis.'

CHAPTER 24

Helen

Helen walks down the aisle of St John's, under the stern gazes of the faded frescoes, until she meets the equally stern gaze of the vicar. He's standing at the door, saying goodbye to all the parishioners. Mother smiles and thanks him, says a few words, but Helen is too numb to say anything.

She doesn't even care that he's looking at Celia and wondering about the marriage story that's gone around. Helen isn't wearing a ring, because that would feel like a lie, and anyway it is entirely reasonable to assume that the bride of a soldier might not have a proper ring yet, especially if she got married in a register office. All of it is plausible; all of it looks all right. Last week, she cared about that. Today, all she can think about is Father.

It's been days since they came to take him away, and here she is at church, as if nothing at all is wrong. The Sharps are irregular churchgoers, but Mother wanted to go today.

'And how are the boys? Kurt and Karl?' the vicar asks.

'Doing very well, thank you. Karl will be taller than me soon, if you can believe it.'

'And do give my regards to Professor Sharp. He's travelling again, is he?'

'He's very busy lately,' Mother says. Helen notices that she doesn't quite lie to the vicar. She wants to scream.

But she doesn't. She gives the vicar the best smile she can manage, and then they're out in the summer sunshine.

'I prayed for your father,' Mother says, when they've walked down the path far enough to be out of earshot of the other families walking home.

'Of course,' Helen barks. She didn't mean to bark. 'I did too, but I'd like to do something more than pray.'

'There's nothing to be done, Helen. Rupert told me that he's been asked to go and answer some questions. I imagine that they need his expertise, perhaps on a matter of history, or perhaps on something to do with the work he did in the last war. Whatever it is, it's none of our business. It will take as long as it takes.'

Surely Mother doesn't truly believe that's all there is to it. The government would not have sent men to the house to collect him if they only wanted Father to answer questions. She remembers what she overheard Mr Yardley saying on Thursday, about bringing suspicion on the house. About not being able to help him this time. She remembers, years ago, Max telling her of her father's theories about the tapestry, how he seemed to think it might be useful for the war effort.

Helen had put that out of her mind, as she put so many things out of her mind. Sometimes she wonders whether that's why she gets so many headaches lately: the concentration it takes to keep out the fears, worries and imaginings.

'And what if he needs our help?'

'The way we can help him best is to do as we always have in this family: get on with things, and do the best we can for others. We have a lot to be grateful for, Helen, and a lot to do. There's no need to borrow trouble. I'm sure your father is fine.'

Helen has only ever wanted everything to be fine; it has been her sole ambition, her whole life. A family, a home, laughter and firelight and food.

Every inch of this village reminds her of George. How they went everywhere together, in the days when it seemed he would never declare his feelings. Everyone said he was madly in love with Helen, and had been since childhood – everyone except George himself. As they entered their twenties, she worried that he took her for granted, that he was waiting for someone better to come along. When it came to getting his job with the post office, or dealing with all his brothers, George was always bold, never embarrassed. If he wanted something, he simply went after it. Therefore, she thought, he must not have wanted Helen. He must not have realized that they would be perfect together, that they had always been happy in each other's company and they always would be.

Between the way things were and the way things ought to be, there was a chasm she couldn't cross. She didn't know how to make the world arrange itself properly.

She felt like a fool for walking out with him, as if people might think she was following him around like a puppy. So she started avoiding him, being busy when he came around. He caught up with her one day after church, though. On this very road. He was walking his motorcycle; he hadn't been at the service.

And that day, a group of his friends laughed and teased him about her, as they walked past them on this very road. That was the day George finally said angrily, 'I wish they'd stop. It's hard enough to try to get you to come out with me lately.'

The determined expression on his face had been so eloquent that Helen was shocked into laughing, out of sheer joy. He thought that she was laughing at him, and he'd driven off on his motorcycle with her running after him, dishevelled, her hat flying off on to the road, yelling his name.

She'd never known Stoke Damson without George in it, and now he's far away, fighting, and the friends who teased him are too, and some of them aren't coming back. How foolish her past anxieties look to her now.

As far as anyone in Stoke Damson knows, her father is a respected professor who sometimes goes away to attend to family matters, or to advise the government on some area on which he has expertise – *didn't he do something with intelligence in the last war?* Everything looks fine. But that isn't enough. It has to *be* fine. And she knows in her soul that it is not.

Mother goes to bring the boys home from a neighbour's, and Helen is alone in the house, except for Celia, who's so sleepy that she goes down for her nap immediately. Helen doesn't hesitate. Father's privacy has always been sacrosanct, but she knows, deep in her bones, that he needs her help now.

She opens the door to his study and takes in the sight. It looks smaller and shabbier all of a sudden. Papers on the desk, framed photos of the tapestry on the wall.

The drawer in the middle of his desk is locked. It takes her only a moment to guess where he'd hide the key: Aelfgyva. She doesn't know why, exactly, but it seems the likeliest spot. And indeed, there it is: a tiny brass key resting on top of the frame of the section that shows Aelfgyva, the mystery woman Father and Kit used to chatter about.

The drawer contains a notebook, written in her father's hand. She opens it gingerly. This might be a violation too far. But what else can she do? His handwriting is difficult to read, even more so than it's always been. There are long sections about the tapestry, asking himself questions, or arriving at conclusions. Some of the latter are all in caps, underlined, with exclamation marks. She would not have expected Father to use exclamation marks about anything.

Whatever this is, it will take her a long read to understand, if she ever can. She tucks the notebook under one arm and pulls out a stack of loose typewritten pages from the drawer.

They're all letters. Each is addressed to a different recipient, and she recognizes none of them. The letters have different dates but similar content: advice to students about some difficulty in their studies. Of course Father would keep these in a locked drawer; he was always scrupulous about privacy.

They're carbon copies, Helen realizes, from the unevenness of the type. There are twenty-two altogether.

Two are not written to students. One is to Mother, from 1941. A few lines of reassurance that some unexplained "they" will be done with Father soon. Something to do with his business in Scotland, after Aunt Kathleen died, perhaps.

The last letter is from May 20, 1944. Less than a month ago. It's written to a man whose name she doesn't recognize.

> *Sir,*
>
> *You may remember that in 1941, you told me that it was a remarkable coincidence that I seemed to have guessed at certain events yet to come in Scotland. Perhaps you will think it strange that such a coincidence could occur twice in one man's lifetime, so I write with some reluctance, but my duty to my country means I cannot stay silent. I am confident that the French town of Falaise and its environs will soon be the target of a heavy bombing campaign. Not only could this event*

result in heavy loss of innocent life, but it could impede the movement of Allied forces from the coast toward the interior, if they happen to land in Normandy or Brittany, whenever those landings might occur. I leave the strategy to you and your colleagues, of course, but having become aware of what I believe to be an enemy plan, I could not live with my conscience if I kept that to myself.
Yours very faithfully,
Rupert Sharp.

This has to be it. Somehow, Father came across information that was useful to the government. She shoves the stack of letters into the notebook and rushes out of the study, closing the door behind her. Just then, the two boys come running into the sitting room, with Mother behind them, looking pleasantly flustered.

'What is it, Helen? What have you got?'

'Something of Max's,' Helen lies, her cheeks warm. 'I'm going to take it over to the Yardleys', in case she comes home one weekend and wants it.'

'What, now?'

'I won't be long. Will you keep an eye on Celia for me? She's sleeping upstairs.'

She doesn't wait for an answer, just strides out of the house, down the path to the bridge over the stream, and right up to the Yardley house.

It has always intimidated her, but she ignores that today. She takes a moment to tuck in any stray hair and check that her skirt and blouse are straight. Then she raps with the silver lion door knocker and waits.

It's a long time before the door opens, and a young woman she doesn't recognize opens it. She greets Helen with a German accent. A refugee, wearing a maid's uniform. It shouldn't be her job to open the door, but perhaps there aren't any other servants left in the house, with everyone gone off to war work or fighting abroad.

'I'd like to see Mr Yardley please, if he's at home. My name is Helen Sharp. I'm a neighbour.'

It occurs to her, belatedly, to wonder whether he's at home at all. He's a busy man, but it's Sunday afternoon.

The woman nods, looking perplexed, and takes Helen into a large, bright room with modern paintings on the walls. It's at least ten minutes before Mr Yardley comes through the door, in a waistcoat and shirtsleeves, concern on his face.

'Helen, my dear,' he says. 'I hope nothing's wrong? Everyone well?'

'Yes, everyone is well. That is – except for Father.' She rushes on, knowing that if she stops, she'll lose her nerve. 'He's still not home. I know you spoke with him just before the officers came. I wondered if you might be able to tell me where they took him and why, and how I might help him.'

Mr Yardley's face is grave. He sits on the sofa opposite her. 'What do you have there, Helen?'

She looks down at the notebook in her lap, the letters visible where she shoved them inside the cover. 'I think he wrote to someone in the government, telling them about some sort of . . . prediction. Evidence he had about an enemy plan. I don't know why the police didn't search his office. They would have found this.'

'Your father is not under arrest, my dear. A branch of military intelligence simply wants to have him consult on a certain matter. Because of his expertise.'

'His expertise in medieval art?'

'You might be surprised.' He cocks his head. 'Why do you think he's detained, Helen? Did something make you worry, or did you have a feeling?'

She feels a headache coming on, a fog around her eyes. 'It was the look on his face when they came to take him, I suppose. He seemed resigned, somehow. And this letter explains it, doesn't it? Was he right? About the bombing?'

'In a way. The Allied forces bombed Falaise, shortly after the D-Day landings, to cut off the German supply line. He knew in May, when he made the misguided decision to write to a friend in the War Office, that the bombing would happen. But he got it wrong. It wasn't the Luftwaffe that would bomb it.'

Her hands are gripping the notebook so hard that it's quivering. She says, in a quiet voice, 'Please tell me, Mr Yardley. Maybe I can help.'

After a long pause, Mr Yardley says, 'I will tell you what I can, Helen. Your father made a prediction, back in 1941, about a certain plane that came down in Scotland. When he was visiting your aunt. She and he had a shared premonition, which turned out to be true. Naturally, the government was interested in what he knew, and asked him to help them get to the bottom of it. I was able to persuade them it was a coincidence. But now that he's made another successful prediction, I don't think I could persuade them of that again.' He leaned forward, elbows on knees. 'That is why you and I must not breathe a word of this to anyone. They are treating him with respect, asking him to help them again, by answering questions, or applying his expertise – I don't know exactly what. It is not jail, nor anything like jail. But I am afraid it would be, if he were to refuse their request.'

Helen's headache is getting worse. 'But how long will they keep him?'

He spreads his hands wide. 'Difficult to say. This time, with it being the second incident, I should think at least the length of the war. They can't send him back home, not if they can't explain where he's getting his information. One coincidence can be believed, but two accurate predictions? The odds are difficult to explain away.'

All the air goes out of Helen. 'He's not a spy.'

'No, of course he is not.'

She speaks very slowly, as if some better, more rational thought might come and save her mid-sentence. 'Then you believe he has some sort of power? The Second Sight? Something like that? Oh, Mr Yardley, I see now that my father might well believe that. Some of the things he's said – perhaps it's the war, and Aunt Kathleen's stories – I don't know. But surely you don't believe it yourself.'

Mr Yardley opens a silver cigarette case on the side table and lights one, offering the case to Helen, who refuses. He leans back, folds one leg over the other. 'You found these papers in his office, did you?'

'Yes, sir. I would not snoop, ordinarily.'

'Of course not. Mitigating circumstances. But I wonder, Helen, how did you know there was something to be found? How did you know where to look?'

She starts to object that she knew nothing, but she remembers how the location of the little brass key came to her in a flash, and her certainty that there was something in Father's office. She rubs her temple. 'I just thought there might be something there.'

He watches her for a moment. 'Your father is very lucky to have such courageous and talented daughters. How is this: I will try to argue his case again. I will keep you apprised of progress; you must come for tea when I'm home, and bring your daughter if you like.'

Helen nods. 'Thank you. Oh, thank you, Mr Yardley. You're very kind.'

'I must warn you, though, that in order to make it seem that your father is an ordinary man with no foreknowledge, he may have to pretend to be – I hate to say it – a crank, a crackpot. It may damage his reputation.'

'I would rather my father be safe at home where he ought to be, no matter what other people think,' Helen says firmly. 'I will do whatever I can to help him come back to us. The war has separated me from my sisters, but it will not take my father from me.'

CHAPTER 25

Kit

There are no more bombings in Argentan, for the time being.
Every night, Kit and Max listen to the radio in the church
basement. The Allies have always been closing in on
Cherbourg, will always be closing in on Cherbourg. It's excruciating, and every day Kit half-expects to hear that the
Germans have driven the Allies back into the sea, that the
war will stretch on for years and years, that there will never
be peace. She can't even remember what peace feels like.

Kit doesn't want to go far from Ivy, so she does what she
can to help nearby, working at an aid station that's been set
up in a local school, to help people find food and supplies,
or safe shelter, or missing family members. Her joke to Max
about cataloguing turns out to be not far off the mark, as
most of the work is keeping track of who needs what and
where they might be able to get it.

As for Max, she is busy doing something with the team
of soldiers, something she won't tell Kit about.

Kit sits by her sister's bedside when she can, but Ivy sleeps,
or stares at the ceiling. She won't tell Kit much, only asks

nonsensical questions, sometimes about Father, or about the tapestry.

The advances made by the penicillin in Ivy's body, like those of the Allies in France, were dramatic at first, but have seemingly stalled now. The Louvre has probably given up on Kit. Evelyn probably has too. Possibly for the best; it isn't as if she and Evelyn are going to spend their lives together. Only the war. Assuming there is life after war.

One morning, as Kit goes to visit Ivy, the doctor meets her at the gate, waving her closer.

'What is it? Is Ivy worse?'

He shakes his head. 'Much better. I think the infection's finally broken. But she's well enough to be getting restless. Thrashing around in the night, even though she no longer has a fever. I think it's her mind that needs our attention now.'

With everything Ivy must have been through, Kit thinks it's a wonder she's only thrashing.

'What can I do for her, doctor?'

'Just go in and visit. I won't tut about you staying too long, not this time. Some connection with the outside world might do her good.'

Ivy is indeed sitting up in bed when Kit opens her door. She's wearing a teal shirtdress that Kit has never seen before; the doctor must have got it for her. The clothes Ivy was wearing in the bombed prison cell were fit only to be burned.

Kit props up Ivy's pillows and sits on her customary chair, and takes her sister's hand.

'You're better than ever, the doctor says.'

Ivy nods. 'My shoulder's all right. The leg aches a bit. Kit, I have to get out of here.'

'Won't be long now. How did you manage to get yourself so banged up?'

Ivy turns her face away, pulls her hand out of Kit's. 'Please don't interrogate me. It doesn't really matter how. What matters is that I have a job to do. Will you help me? The doctor has been telling me about the invasion but I need to know a very specific thing, Will you find out if the tapestry is safe, in Bayeux? It's under Allied control now, isn't it?'

'The tapestry? The Bayeux Tapestry? Ivy, of all things to be worried about. It's perfectly safe.'

'The Allies have it? And they'll protect it?'

Kit hesitates, and decides on the truth. But how much of the truth? She remembers Evelyn's warning, that Himmler will try to move it to Paris.

'It's not in Bayeux. It's still in occupied France, in a château south of here. It was moved there a few years ago. But it's under the protection of the Louvre, and the château is marked, so the bombers will avoid it. All right? Nothing to worry about.'

Ivy shakes her head violently. 'No. No. Oh, I hoped I was wrong. I've seen him, in my dreams. And I've seen the tapestry – I've seen it all, you know. All of them, the women, making it. But today I can see *him*, with trucks and guns and – oh Kit, he's going to take it out of France and then we'll never be able to stop them. I've seen what he's going to do with it and it's terrible, Kit.'

A half-remembered dream comes back to Kit, about Queen Matilda and her tapestry. It's been on Ivy's feverish mind; perhaps that's why it was on Kit's.

'I don't think even the Nazis want to destroy the tapestry,' Kit reassures her.

'No, you don't understand. He's going to use it. It makes him stronger – helps him to see things. He's used it to find so many in the Resistance already, Kit, and now he's using it to predict where our soldiers are, to stop the invasion. I've seen the future that he sees – a future where men like him know exactly what other people are doing, what they're thinking, what they will do, where they will go – a future where the Nazis control everything.'

Putting her hand on her sister's, Kit says gently, 'I think everything's been a bit jumbled in your dreams. It's the fever. Just rest and everything will come clear in your mind soon.'

'You don't believe me, then. You won't help me.'

'Ivy, think it through, slowly and carefully. The Nazis want the tapestry, of course, as they want everything. Just because they are pirates and thieves. But I think they have other things to worry about just now. Surely they won't bother with that.'

'You're wrong. They know it's important. They said Father had a theory about it.'

Kit shrinks back. The letter, still tucked into a drawer in her dresser in Paris. The last letter she had from Father, in 1940, telling her that he thought he'd found the explanation for Aelfgyva, one that fitted the available evidence. How her eyes had stung reading it, how she'd decided that her father's insistence on making the world make sense had finally tipped over into the opposite.

Uncertainly, Kit says, 'Father has many theories.'

'Did he ever tell you he thought the tapestry was created *before* 1066?' Ivy asks.

Kit bristles. 'So he told you too, did he? What nonsense. Besides, what does it have to do with anything? Did the Nazis really bring that up with you? They must have been trying to scare you, to show they know things about your family. Don't you think that's something they would do?'

Ivy nods uncertainly. 'But there's something else. It seems to have an effect. Physically. I had a scrap of it—'

'A scrap of the tapestry? Are you sure?'

'It was a gift. Father had one too. Mr Yardley gave it to him a few years ago, and it was around that time that he came up with the theory. Maybe the tapestry triggered something in him. I didn't think much of it, but the one time I touched it myself, I felt things. Saw things. I think that being around others with the gift makes it stronger somehow. Being with Grady, being with . . . and the tapestry. It connects me to them. The women who made it.'

Kit can barely make sense of this string of thoughts. She doesn't know who Grady is.

'Maybe it was just a scrap of cloth. There can't be that many snippets of it out there. Good lord, it's like the True Cross.'

Ivy shakes her head, her blonde curls messy. 'No. I've seen it. I've touched it. I believe it does affect people like me.'

'People like you,' Kit whispers, making fists with her hands, making one last effort not to understand.

Ivy grabs her arm. 'People like you too. You found me, Kit. *How* did you find me?'

Helplessly, Kit says, 'I saw you. In Paris. Or, I thought I saw you. And I saw some other things, heard some things. It all led me to you. It's a long story.'

Ivy lies back again, looking at Kit's face. 'I have a long story of my own. And it's not over yet, Kit. There are Nazis who want to find more people like us. Put us to *use*. There's a Nazi who has been using the tapestry to sharpen his Second Sight. He can only see so far, you know, like all of us. I've been watching him, in my dreams. On his own, he's only been able to see the Resistance. He couldn't predict the invasion. But if he gathers more of us, if he builds more connections, using the tapestry . . . Kit, I can see his plans in my mind, as plain as day. The places where he's going to bomb long lines of Allied soldiers, destroy them all from above the way they might have at Dunkirk. I can see the traps he's going to lay, the all-seeing fortress he is going to create around their empire, and within it. He sees things – camps full of people, starving and sick, lining up to go to their deaths. How much more efficient it will be, he thinks, once they can find the bad apples by simply thinking about it. I have a connection to him now, you see. I have to stop him before it's too late.'

Whether the Sight exists or not, Ivy believes it does, and it seems someone who tortured her does too. Of course. Kit well knows how many of the Nazis are obsessed with the occult, following Heinrich Himmler's lead. Himmler's convinced that old legends and folklore must represent some literal golden age, that it must all be true on some level. She's met or heard of archaeologists who were sent after the Holy Grail and Thor's hammer, and historians sent to record the chanting of witches in the bogs of Finland. In the last few years the Nazis in Paris have been quieter about it, since Adolf Hitler has proven mercurial in that as in all things, but there are still many among Evelyn's contacts in Paris who will slaver over anything they think is mystical.

'Your captors believed you have the Second Sight,' Kit says, holding on to things she can admit are possible. 'And they believe the tapestry has some sort of supernatural power. So they're going to move it out of France, while they still can. Is that right?'

'Yes. It's going to happen today. I've seen it, in my dreams. I hoped I was wrong, but now . . . Where exactly is the tapestry?'

Maybe Kit shouldn't tell her, shouldn't encourage her. Not now, while she's still recovering. But Ivy's face is fierce; she's different from the girl she used to be. She's a grown woman, who's passed through fire, and she deserves respect and honesty. And Kit doesn't believe she's deluded.

'It's in the Château de Sourches, about a couple of hours by car from here – if we had a car.'

'And if the Germans were going to move it – how would they do that? Who would be involved?'

'We've managed to play the Nazis off against each other to some extent, when it comes to all the artwork and artefacts we've stashed in little museums around the country. There's the Ahnenerbe: those are Himmler's scholars, some respected archaeologists among them, but all tainted by his obsession with the occult and the mystical. Then there's the Kunstschutz, which is the supposed art protection organization, although art protection tends to be another word for art theft in the Reich. The Kunstschutz generally does protest against artwork being moved around, so that's allowed everything to stay where it is, for now. With the invasion, though, there are bound to be more efforts to move everything back to Paris, and the Kunstschutz won't be able to object if there's an argument that the artefacts are in actual danger elsewhere. If the Ahnenerbe wins that argument, they'll just go and get whatever they want. Including the tapestry.'

'And they're a branch of the SS, aren't they?' Ivy asks, darkly.

Kit nods.

'I see,' Ivy says. 'So the SS will take it, and they'll get it to Paris, and then they'll move it to Berlin, because Paris will be unsafe. Or maybe they won't even bother with that. Maybe they'll get it to Paris and just keep going. To where?'

'Probably Himmler's castle. Himmler is a collector of artefacts that he can fit into a story of a once-and-future Nordic empire. He wants the tapestry because it shows a Norman duke, descended from Norsemen, who might as well be Germans, in his world view. Crossing the Channel and conquering England, setting fire to the houses, harrowing the towns, imposing a new culture, a new history, a new language. He wants to hang it in his castle for all his SS lackeys to see, to inspire them to create their own empire where pure-blooded Germanic heroes rule over anyone else not burned to ash in the process.'

'All right. So if Himmler is likely to take it to his castle, then we know their plans.'

Kit speaks softly, trying to keep her own emotions in check around her ailing sister. 'Ivy, you can't risk your life.'

'My life?' Ivy laughs a little. 'There's only one thing I want to do with my life now, and that's use it to take out as many Nazis as I can, starting with one in particular. I refuse to let him take it, Kit. I have seen that future. It's the future you're talking about, the future Himmler wants – the fascist empire stretching from ocean to ocean to ocean. And, in that empire, everything we do and think and plan will be known in advance. There will be no refuge. Don't you see? There's a man who can make this happen, and the tapestry can help him do it. If he's going to take the tapestry today, I have to get to it first.'

Get to it? Kit is struck by her sister's passion, but worried about her capacity to reason in her current state. 'The tapestry's very big, you know,' she says. 'Even if it's still at the Château de Sourches, you can't just fit it under your jacket.'

'I *know* that,' Ivy says, the little sister for a moment. Then her expression hardens. 'I'll kill anyone who tries to take it. I know how, you know. I've done it before. You may understand Himmler's research interests, but I understand the way he tortures and kills people. I learned all about them in training, and I learned all about them in La Codre.'

A stone rises in Kit's throat and she keeps herself very still, because if she moves to hug Ivy, she'll break down.

'Are you going to help me or not?' Ivy asks, coldly. 'Do you believe that I know what I'm talking about?'

The woman staring back at Kit is the same woman she saw in the streets of Paris. The expression is the same: it has steel in it. Kit nods.

'I will help you.'

CHAPTER 26

Kit

Max tells Kit to take the motorcycle. She doesn't ask why Kit and Ivy are hell-bent on getting to the Château de Sources. She doesn't ask why Ivy doesn't come into the church herself, why she stays out in the churchyard, pacing, as if she's allergic to the stone walls. Max just leaves them to look at the map while she tops up the motorcycle's charcoal.

The day is warming up. The roads are dry, and they should make good time. Kit looks up, at a blue sky without any birds in it.

'Tell me about this château,' Ivy says, peering over Kit's shoulder at the map.

'What, the Château de Sources? I've never been there. It was built at the time of Louis XV. I think it belonged to the Duchess of Tourzel, who was the governess of the royal children, imprisoned during the Revolution.'

'Huh. All right, I can picture it now. And, somewhere inside, there's the tapestry.'

'Yes. It's probably somewhere in the cellars, in a chest or

case, wound up or folded. I'm not sure which. It's all one piece, not broken up like the replica we went to see when we were children. It was in Bayeux until a few years ago. The Ahnenerbe sent a team there to photograph it, early in the war.'

'A team?' Ivy glares at her. 'What team? Who was on it?'

'I try not to learn any more about the Nazis than I need to.'

Evelyn learns all she can, though. Kit remembers the warning Evelyn gave her about the tapestry, how touching it had been that Evelyn remembered her father's interest in it.

'And would it have been that team that moved the tapestry?' Ivy demands.

Kit shakes her head. 'No, the Kunstschutz, the so-called art protection organization. They weren't happy about the Ahnenerbe disturbing the tapestry over and over for their photographs and inspections. The Kunstschutz managed to move it to the Château de Sourches, where the Louvre already had a storage facility. More remote. An attempt to make it a little more difficult for Himmler's thugs to paw it and fawn over it.'

'It didn't stop them,' Ivy declares. 'And it's not going to stop them from taking it today and using it. I'm telling you, Kit, this tapestry – they see it as a weapon. And it is. It could win the war for them, give them power beyond Hitler's wildest dreams.'

This feverish certainty of Ivy's makes Kit feel ill. She half-believes her – after all, Kit can't explain everything that's happened. But she wants desperately to retreat into reason and sense. The tapestry as a weapon? It's always been a comfort in their lives, a constant presence, like fairytales at bedtime. Kit remembers the day she walked into the Reading museum, staring up at those multicoloured horses, at mysterious Aelfgyva, with her father at her side, telling her stories.

'Don't you think it's possible that all Himmler wants is to hang it in his castle and bloviate about how the Conqueror used his Germanic superiority to reunite wayward England with the Germanic race, or some such nonsense?'

Ivy shakes her head vigorously. 'They can make all that up, even if they don't have the artefact itself. They could make their own replica, come to that. It's not just a trophy. It has power.'

'Well, all trophies do have power. Why does it matter that the Rosetta Stone is in the British Museum? Because the French stole it from Egypt, and we took it from the French. A spoil of war. We could give it back, and keep a replica. But if it's our artefact, it's our story. And stories can make people go along with just about anything.'

'This is more than that!' Ivy's nearly yelling now. 'I'm telling you, a man has been using this tapestry to gain power. A clairvoyant, like me, like you, but on the German side. The Allied invasion gives him the perfect excuse to steal it, to pretend he's only moving it. But instead he's going to draw on its power to show him everything he wants to know. The more he uses it, the more powerful he will get. Maybe there are others like him. The Allies' plans, the Resistance, everyone hiding from them, every thought of every citizen – it will all be laid bare.'

Kit's never seen her sister's face like this, drawn with pain, her eyes seeming to focus on things that aren't there.

'Ivy, I'm worried,' Kit says, gently. 'I'm worried about you. About these things you're telling me – but, even more, about everything you're not telling me.' She bites the bullet, broaches the subject that makes her go cold: the way Ivy keeps saying that Kit is a clairvoyant too. 'Max thinks you were sending me messages. It certainly felt as if you were.'

'I was. I was thinking of you, pleading that you would be safe. I was worried about you. So I brought you into danger, by trying to save you.'

'But you were the one doing it, whatever it was. Not me. You.'

Ivy shakes her head. 'People who have their own gifts are more receptive. Ordinarily, I can't make anyone see things. But sometimes – with some people – you can sort of share visions. Or send a warning, or a farewell. Those dead sailors on the cliffs that Aunt Kathleen used to talk about, do you remember? Saying goodbye to their wives when their wives didn't even know yet that their husbands were dead. But not everyone sees that sort of thing. Some people have a talent. I didn't know about mine, until Mr Yardley noticed something odd about one of my paintings.'

'Max told me that her father recruited you for – whatever it is that you do.'

'Not much gets past Max.' Ivy looks at Kit with red, exhausted eyes, and grins wanly. 'By the way, you two seem to be getting along better.'

Kit sniffs. Ordinarily she'd glower at Ivy for the implication, but she's grateful for the respite from the conversation about terrible visions and powers.

'We are. We're friends. I'm glad we're friends again. And I never told you that I'm very sorry you were caught up in that. It must have made things difficult.'

'It didn't make anything difficult for me at all. Max helped me get home. Max is a very impressive person.'

'I know that.'

'Do you?'

As if summoned, Max walks across the churchyard. She hands Kit the key to the motorcycle, along with two shoulder-bags.

'You'll find corned beef sandwiches and a canteen in each.

This one is for Ivy, and this one is for you. And there are scarves, for your hair. Yours was an awful rat's nest after the last ride.'

Kit laughs, takes the scarf, and in return, hands her some money, folded. 'Will you give this to Dr Berthou?'

Max takes it, cautiously. 'You didn't leave it yourself?'

'He was with a patient,' Kit says. 'I didn't want to leave it lying around.'

This is partly true, but it's more true that she didn't want him to object to Ivy leaving when she is still not entirely well. Kit objects to this herself, but she believes Ivy when she says she'll go, one way or another, alone or not. She's never seen Ivy like this, and she realizes she doesn't really know her sister at all. Maybe no one knows anyone.

Max tucks the money into her jacket pocket.

'We have to leave now,' Ivy says.

'If all goes well,' Kit tells Max, 'I hope to have the motor-cycle back by tonight.'

'It should go back to Lucienne anyway, if . . . eventually. Keep it as long as you need it. I'll find my own way around.'

'You do seem to have a way of getting your hands on everything you need.'

'Not everything,' Max says, turning away, but then she turns back again and winks, to show that Kit doesn't need to worry, there aren't any desperate gazes coming her way. Maybe not ever again. Maybe they've exorcised that now. And Kit can go back to Paris, drink cognac with unbreakable Evelyn on Saturday nights.

'Please don't get yourself killed, Max,' Kit says, out of nowhere, surprising herself.

'You can't tell me what to do,' Max replies, and she's walking away towards the church steps, her hands in her trouser pockets.

Despite the fact that they want to get to the Château de Sourches as quickly as possible, Kit avoids the main roads and railway lines. Evidence of Allied bombing is all around them; they pass a burned shell of a village and a broken bridge. It is slow going, because the motorcycle refuses to accelerate for some reason, so by the time it gets up to speed after a turn or intersection it's time to slow down again for the next one.

At least the roads are quiet. Eerily so. They take narrow paths, through forest broken up here and there by pasture and small farms. It was unpleasantly cool this morning when she walked to Dr Berthou's house, but, as the day wears on, Kit is grateful for the breeze and the dappling of trees over-head.

There's an odd effect from the growl of the engine and the wind in her ears; after a while it starts to sound like wailing.

At last, they drive down a straight brown road towards a château that rises from a landscape of green lawns and tidy tree-lined alleys. There are no cars or bicycles anywhere, and only the occasional horse. Kit feels as though she and Ivy are riding their noisy motorcycle into a colour photograph, lit to perfection by the afternoon sun.

On the lawn, large white letters spell out a plea to the Allied bombers: MUSEE LOUVRE.

CHAPTER 27

Kit

They park the motorcycle in the woods, a few minutes' walk away from the château, so they can approach unheard and unseen. But there are no signs of any German presence, no military vehicles in the drive. All the same, she can feel Ivy's agitation.

The building itself is a massive, symmetrical pile of creamy stone with a grey roof. A woman of about fifty in a black dress answers the door, looking puzzled.

Kit can't recall the names of anyone who works here, so she says, '*Bonjour, madame.* I'm Kit Sharp, from the Louvre. I work with Monsieur Jaujard.'

The woman peers at her. 'Is Monsieur Bazin expecting you?'

Kit has met Germain Bazin, a middle-aged curator, once or twice; he spends a lot of time in Paris. And he might remember her.

'I'm here on a matter of some secrecy, and some urgency. I believe he'll see me, if you wouldn't mind asking him.'

The woman looks apologetic. 'It's just that he's only just

returned from Paris, and he injured his leg. Come in, please, and I'll see what can be done.'

'Thank you,' says Kit.

Ivy quickly adds, 'Please tell him it's about the tapestry. It's in danger. Immediate danger.'

The woman in black turns back to them with a frown. 'Bombs?'

'Nazis,' Ivy says.

'We believe the Ahnenerbe is going to try to take it,' Kit explains, now that Ivy's chosen to show their cards.

'All right, come this way.'

She leads them through several rooms filled with crates, canvases stacked against the wall. Their shoes click on marble, then wood, then a fine old carpet. Finally, she asks them to sit in a large salon lined with a jumble of paintings and boxes.

'She didn't say it's gone,' Ivy says, stalking the room as if it might be hidden there.

Kit drops her voice to a whisper. 'Is it the sort of thing that you . . . can find?'

'Given enough time,' Ivy says confidently. 'But I don't know how much time we have. I can't feel *him* any more. It would be downstairs, you said?'

Kit nods. 'Protected from bombs.'

'I saw a staircase back that way,' Ivy says, and to Kit's surprise and horror she walks back out the way they came.

She doesn't want to get separated from Ivy, but if Bazin comes into the room someone ought to be here. As she's hesitating, the door opens, and Bazin comes in. He's on crutches, his face shining with exertion, his mouth tight. But he smiles when he sees her.

'How are you, Miss Sharp? This is an unexpected pleasure. I so seldom see you when I'm in Paris.'

She strides over and shakes his hand, and gestures to the sofa. They sit next to each other, turned to be able to talk.

'I'm so sorry to disturb you. I didn't know about your leg.'

'An ill-timed leap over a barrier in the Paris Métro, as it happens. It's not broken, but I spend most of my time working from sofas and beds these days. Shall I ask for some tea? Some coffee?'

She holds up her hand. 'No, please don't go to the trouble. It's possible time is of the essence.' She lowers her voice. 'Can we speak freely here?'

He nods. 'I don't believe there are any listening devices. I wouldn't use the telephone for anything of import, though. My assistant tells me this is about the embroidery from Bayeux? The one commonly called Queen Matilda's Tapestry?'

'Yes. It's here, isn't it? I mean, it's still here?'

'I think it would be difficult to steal. We can check the basement, if you like.'

She shakes her head. 'That's quite all right. When they move it, it won't be by stealth.'

'Move it!' He looks alarmed. 'An official order to move it? I can't imagine Jaujard approving such a thing.'

This is the moment for Kit to decide whether to risk her career – whether to risk the tapestry itself – on Ivy's hunch. Even if Ivy really is clairvoyant, she could still be wrong. What Lucienne said, about gut feelings and evidence, echoes in her memory. Surely Ivy has shown her evidence. Surely Ivy *is* evidence.

Monsieur Bazin fills the silence while she hesitates. 'Is this about Teller's inspections? He's seemed happy enough to access it here.'

She goes cold. 'Who is that?'

'He's in the Ahnenerbe. An officer in the SS. For more than a year, he's been coming here to open up the crate and check the tapestry, every week or two. Insists on going down alone. He doesn't unroll it, so it's causing no great damage, although I'd rather not give moisture and moths the chance, but what can we do? I assumed he wanted to make sure it was still here. And now he wants to move it?'

An SS officer who's been accessing the tapestry, alone, every week or two. Just as Ivy said. Kit shouldn't have doubted her. If Ivy says the tapestry holds some sort of power, she might be right about that too.

Kit makes her choice.

'The Ahnenerbe have permission to move it to the Louvre,' she says, matter-of-factly. 'Today. They managed to convince the Kunstschutz that it was too dangerous to leave it here, so close to the fighting.'

It's not quite a lie. Let him believe she knows this through ordinary means; that she learned it at the Louvre and has come here to stop it.

He shakes his head. 'Safety, my foot. One doesn't move a priceless artefact through a country full of ambushes, bombing raids and explosives because of *safety*. If they move it to the Louvre, the next stop will be Berlin. But what can we do? You say they're coming today?'

She's moved, suddenly, by her colleague's anger. So often, passive defence has felt *too* passive, and it's been easy to forget that people all over the country have been working, sometimes alone, in whatever ways they can.

'That is the information I have. We must get the tapestry to another position. It doesn't have to be far. Anywhere we can hide it when the SS comes. You have a truck, or a cart?'

He nods. 'But no one to help, and I am as you see . . . '

The roar of car engines outside is like a hand around Kit's heart. She stands up, all the blood rushing out of her head.

They're here. The SS. She and Ivy were too late. And Ivy is somewhere in the basement.

They're banging at the front entrance now, shouting. She can hear the footsteps of the woman in black. Bazin gestures to a door into an adjoining room, and Kit slips through it, leaving the door open a crack. Five men come in, all in the uniforms that the SS and Gestapo wear.

She moves back, one step, praying the old château has quiet floors.

A middle-aged man with watery blue eyes asks Bazin, 'Has anyone been here today?'

She can hear Bazin, though she can't see him, over on the sofa. 'No, *Oberführer*, no one has been here for months, except for you. I've had no instructions. No visits and no authorizations.'

Except for you. This is the man, then. Teller. The SS officer who has been visiting the tapestry every week or two for a year. Is this someone Ivy met, in that prison? How hideous to think of her face to face with these men.

'And no one else has asked you about the tapestry recently? Authorized or otherwise?'

'Of course not. As you can see, I am indisposed. Why are you gentlemen here? What does the Gestapo want with artefacts?'

He is drawing it out. To give Kit a chance to get away? Or just to make it as difficult as possible for the Nazis? Kit should get to Ivy, but what will she tell her?

Teller speaks, in a sickeningly reasonable tone. 'As you know, the tapestry has been the subject of exhaustive study in the last few years. That research has determined that the tapestry is a testament to the glory of the German people. To keep it safe from enemy bombardment, it will be taken east, to a more secure location. It will be on temporary display in Paris.'

Very temporary, Kit suspects.

'This is quite irregular,' Bazin argues. 'I can't let you take it without authorization.'

'You have my authorization, and that of the Kunstschutz,' says a man Kit can't see, whose French is untinged by German.

'But I have no authorization from Jacques Jaujard at the Louvre, who must be consulted about every movement of artefacts,' replies Bazin. 'You know these men cannot just burst in here with guns—'

'Enough of these games,' says one of the Germans. 'Tell us where it is.'

'I am not able to give you that information,' Bazin retorts. 'I must follow procedure, or anything that happens to the tapestry will be my responsibility. I thought the purpose of your Kunstschutz was to preserve art, not destroy it. It is a dangerous time to be transporting artworks through this part of France. I hear that there are Resistance fighters everywhere.'

Kit hears the slight sneer in his voice. Good for Bazin. But it's pointless, and he knows it's pointless. All he can do is delay. In the meantime, she needs to warn Ivy, to get her out of the building.

She draws away from the door, and looks around. She hears one more voice before she leaves the jumbled room. The voice of the man with the watery eyes.

'I'd wager there is a lot of degenerate art in this rathole. If a good Germanic artefact burns along the way, some would consider it a cost worth paying. Either we take the tapestry, or we burn this place to the ground. Your choice.'

She slips behind some boxes and sees a staircase, going down.

At the bottom of the stairs is an open area filled with huge, crated paintings. Dozens and dozens of them, guarded by statues in ghostly drop-cloths. Several small rooms open off this area, and one long whitewashed corridor, with an arched ceiling.

'Ivy,' she whispers, but hears nothing.

She walks the whole length of the corridor, flooded with electric light, and pokes her head into each door along it.

Crates of all dimensions, piled deep, stamped with numbers and letters. At the end of the corridor is another, smaller stairway, leading back up to the ground floor.

One final room, and she catches sight of Ivy at last. Kit whispers her name and ducks behind more of the veiled statues and sees her sister standing next to a square wooden box, more solidly constructed than the crates around it. About four feet square.

It can only be the tapestry. The object of her father's obsession for all those years, just inside that box. In all that time he has never seen it himself, only the replica and photographs. Centuries ago, he told her, they used to hang it around the nave of Bayeux Cathedral on holidays, for everyone to see the story. It survived civil wars, revolution and occupation, and now here it is, wrapped around a spindle, inside a box, like a spool from a giant's sewing kit, stowed in the basement of a musty château.

'Ivy,' she says again, and a flicker of annoyance in her sister's face shows she heard.

Maybe Ivy can feel that it was made by clairvoyants, but Kit feels nothing but awe. Awe at the thing's very ordinariness, at the plainness of the box, at the practical stewardship of men like Bazin.

How long do they have before the Gestapo come down? In his current mood, Bazin seems likely to lead them all over the house first, injured leg be damned. Still, it won't take forever. Few other items are the right size and shape.

There's no need for them to set fire to the place, though God knows they might do it anyway. She puts her hand to the box, picturing the panel on the linen inside, the one showing the men setting fire to a house. Invaders. Father always thought they weren't Normans at all, but British men, making sure that the conquerors would find their conquest barren. Four years ago, when the Nazis marched into Paris, they found a cold and echoing Louvre. Give them the waste-land they desire. Let them think all the light has gone out of the world, so they won't run to extinguish it where it hides, far and quiet and deep, waiting to greet a better dawn.

But darkened museums only ever offered a temporary reprieve. The Nazis have had years to shine their torches into every corner and grab what they want. And now they fear the days of their empire are numbered; now they have reason to bring the torches close.

'Ivy,' she says again, looking up into her sister's face.

Ivy has her eyes shut, and one finger from each hand on the box.

'Ivy, we have to get out. They're here. The Germans. They've come for it.'

At that, Ivy's eyes fly open. She comes around to Kit and puts her hands on her shoulders. 'Who is it? Who's here?' She searches Kit's face for a moment, then says, 'He's here. I knew he'd come.'

The Gestapo are on the staircase already, the one on the far side of the corridor, the one that Kit took. She and Ivy have one chance to use the other staircase to leave.

'Get out,' Ivy says.

'I'm not leaving you here. Ivy, there are four men with guns. We'll watch and wait. We'll find a chance. This isn't it.'

Ivy isn't listening. She's leaning on the box, her eyes closed again.

Kit can hear the men speaking in German, giving instruc-tions. They're on their way. They'll have no excuse to set the château on fire, at least. A mere matter of minutes, and they'll have what they want. And Kit and Ivy will be sent to a cell, or to a camp, or shot on sight.

She can almost smell the fire; no, she *can* smell fire. She can hear it crackling. Surely not. Surely they wouldn't set a fire here, despite their bluster – it makes no sense.

The light in the room is changing, reddening. She's pulling on Ivy's sleeve. They'll be seen, now, but better to be seen and have a chance to run, to live. The Nazis will leave too. They must.

With a terrible whoosh, the corridor fills with dark red clouds.

It's so hot that Kit is pushed back as if by a windstorm, and she knocks Ivy away from the box that holds the tapestry. But Ivy's eyes are still closed and she just stumbles as if she's drunk, holds up her hands to keep Kit away. The look on her face is quiet, determined.

The men are shouting: one's barking orders, one's screaming in pain.

There's no window in the room. No way out, other than that corridor. No way out but through. They'll be burned, but if they can keep moving, maybe they have a chance to get out alive.

The scarf Max gave her, to tie around her hair, is still knotted around her neck. Kit pushes it up to cover her mouth and grabs Ivy by the front of her dress, yanks her towards her and arranges her scarf the same way. Ivy is like a dead weight but she doesn't resist. Kit pulls her sister as she walks backward towards the inferno. She can feel her lungs struggling, the heat on her skin, her stockings like sandpaper, the sweat running down her back.

Then it's gone.

The light changes in the room, from red to blue, and the air at her back is blessedly ordinary. Kit lets her sister go and turns to look at the corridor. There's no fire and no sign of fire. Nothing charred, not a single flame. Nothing destroyed.

The sight of it throws her back into the room just as the fire itself had. 'Ivy,' she whispers, through a throat that still doesn't believe it hasn't been breathing smoke.

Ivy is on the ground, her back against the box that holds

the tapestry. Something is very wrong. Her head is tilted back and her mouth is making odd, fish-like gasps, as if she's drowning, and her arms are straight out at her sides, pushing away something Kit can't see.

Footsteps and voices. She grabs Ivy under the arms and pulls her out into the corridor.

To the right, she sees the Gestapo men at the entrance to one of the rooms, their backs to the corridor. They're talking loudly, giving each other instructions as they look for the tapestry.

The one exception is Teller, the SS officer. He's standing in the corridor, turned towards Kit and Ivy, but his eyes are shut. The look on his face is the same sort of determination that Ivy had on hers a moment ago, but he has a slight smile she didn't.

The eyes open. Those pale blue eyes, like clear water. They are focused, not on Kit and Ivy, but on something behind them. He doesn't move.

Kit takes her chance. She pulls Ivy to her feet and to her immense relief Ivy is conscious enough to stumble along as Kit pulls her up the smaller staircase, and up to the ground floor. They nearly barrel into the woman in black, who simply steps aside with a nearly silent swoosh of her dress, and then they're at the front door.

The sunlight seems painful, somehow; the expanse of perfect green a simulacrum. Nothing seems real. Kit holds Ivy's hand and urges her along, but Ivy is stumbling so much now that Kit can barely keep her moving. By the time they reach the gates, it's clear she can go no further.

They left the motorcycle in the woods. A five-minute walk at most, but Ivy can't walk that far, not until she has a chance to catch her breath at least.

Outside the walls of the estate, out of view of the château, tall grasses and wildflowers hide them from the road. Ivy falls on to her knees, coughing. When she finally catches her breath and her body stops convulsing, she lies back, Kit cradling her head in her lap. Ivy's eyes are red and her lips are so pale they're nearly blue. She has tears on her cheeks.

Kit whispers, 'I should never have let you leave the doctor's house.'

Ivy croaks, 'No, this is nothing. It's just a trick. He's like us.'

Kit chews her lip, uncertain what that means, uncertain about everything. How can she keep her sister safe from drowning in air? From fire that burns one minute and not the next?

Ivy grabs her blouse, pulls her close. 'This was a trap,' she whispers.

Footsteps.

A dozen men in uniform walk towards them from three directions. The only one not pointing a gun is the man with the pale blue eyes.

The truck they put the sisters into is open in the back, so Kit can see the other truck, behind them, where the Germans put the tapestry. She watches them load it and put the cover on to the truck bed. Ivy doesn't seem interested. Her eyes are closed, and she leans back against the wooden rail, not fighting the fact that there's a loop of rope connecting the rail to the restraints on both her hands and Kit's.

It's a slow, bumpy ride east. Three SS men sit in the back with them, their guns on their laps. They don't jeer or make jokes. When Kit asks them where the truck is headed, they say nothing. Teller told Monsieur Bazin that they had orders to take the tapestry to the Louvre; Kit clings to this. Maybe they are on the way to Paris. Maybe they'll interrogate her and then return her to her life and work. After all, they wouldn't bring the tapestry to an internment camp, and the tapestry and the sisters seem to be travelling together. Teller wants them; if he didn't, they'd probably be dead by now.

This was a trap, Ivy said. Those visions she had of the tapestry – could Teller have sent them to her? Luring her to the château exactly when he wanted her there? He has Ivy *and* the tapestry now; he has everything.

It's hard to judge time or distance on that journey that seems to go on forever. The convoy avoids towns, and she can't see any landmarks she knows, only the occasional church spire in the distance. There is no castle in her imagination now to guide her, nothing but the hard, real world. Her armpits are sweaty, and her nose has been itchy for hours. She already knows, in her heart, that they have gone past Paris.

Her mind's eye has always been able to call maps to mind, and she does it now, closing her eyes against the waning sun. They wouldn't bring the tapestry to a camp. If they're not going to Paris, then where? Himmler's castle, where he keeps all his prizes, is near Düsseldorf. Towards the north of Germany; they'll go through Belgium. Surely she'll know when they cross the border?

But, just as she is thinking this, the trucks judder to a halt. They're in a wooded area, isolated and quiet. A good place for killing people. Somewhere nearby, soldiers are talking. Ivy, beside her, still doesn't open her eyes, but she's breathing regularly, almost as if she's sleeping. Kit cranes to look over the front of the truck, but all she can see is a dreary wall of overgrown beige brick, with narrow doorways at regular intervals opening into darkness.

CHAPTER 28

Helen

Helen puts the towel on the bed and the baby on the towel. Celia's kicking her feet, smiling and cooing, and Helen stands there with the clean nappy in one hand, and suddenly last night's dream washes over her, as if just being here in the bedroom has resurrected it. It's nothing definite, just a bad feeling; less about the dream itself than its residue.

She's always been prone to nightmares. Sleep is a battleground. When she was a child, she used to lie in bed afraid of not being able to sleep; the prospect of everyone else in the house being silent, being *gone* to a place she didn't want to go, was terrifying. And then, of course, she couldn't sleep. When she did, she had nightmares.

Eventually, Helen got better at closing off the doors in her mind, where the monsters might come through. But it's worse again now. It began when she came home from the Land Army; she thought it might have been the pregnancy. Now, Celia is a toddler, but Helen's nightmares have not improved. They're always worse the nights after she sees Mr Yardley.

Try as she might to forget them, the dreams come back

to her in pieces throughout the day. Shards of shrapnel working their way to the surface. A few days ago, she was mending Kurt's bicycle with him when suddenly she recalled a nightmare image of George, grinning madly, a knife in his hand. Her dear sweet George, who made a clay house for toads and was so gentle and kind to Kurt and Karl. But she couldn't forget the look on his face, even though she knew it was all in her mind, her fears and emotions twisting her world into a weird travesty.

She went straight to her dresser and pulled out George's latest letter. Ran her fingers over it as if there was some secret message there. He can tell her so little, and she suspects he tells her even less than he's allowed to, to spare her. She doesn't even know where he is. The one compensation is that the letters are poetic and romantic, filled with phrases George would be embarrassed to say in person. All it does is remind her that he might be dead tomorrow – he might be dead now, for all she knows. Any day could be the day the telegram comes.

She sends him the same news she writes to Rose: about Kurt and Karl, and how tall they're getting, and how well they're doing in school. About Mother's ability to have the most hilarious adventures simply going to the butcher or checking up on a friend. About Celia, her darling, who has never met her father.

Helen feels very alone, accompanied only by an overwhelming sense of grief. Grief with no target.

Mother is in Cornwall, visiting an old friend who's dying slowly. Helen is looking after Kurt and Karl as well as Celia, which she does frequently. She misses adult company – or rather, she is sick of communing with the inside of her own head.

Whatever her dream was last night, it's left her not even wanting to be near the bed. If she thinks about it for a moment she'll probably remember what it was – but she doesn't want to remember. If it isn't George being monstrous, it'll be Ivy stuck in a box, or Father weeping, or some other horrifying nonsense. The worst dreams aren't about anyone in the family at all, or anyone she knows. One recurring dream takes place in a house she doesn't recognize, yet she knows every inch of it. It seems to have more rooms than is likely, long corridors that lead nowhere, and panels that open to show people standing behind them as if they were playing hide and seek, but they aren't smiling.

Helen would do anything to be rid of the dreams. Once, she drank two glasses of Mother's cooking sherry before bed, to try to quiet them, but she had worse dreams than ever, and woke in a cold sweat in the middle of the night.

Sometimes Celia wakes her in the middle of a dream, and it freezes in her mind, vividly. She almost prefers that, though, to the days when she's forgotten the contents of her dream but the sickening fear from it lingers, ready to put its cold fingers on her at any time.

Helen finishes changing the child's nappy and lifts her high. She's getting heavy. The joy of her life, although two years ago she thought it meant her life was over. It turns out a person can survive embarrassment. A person can survive a lot of things.

She goes down to the kitchen, where Karl is sitting at the table, bent over a maths problem. It's the weekend, but she's given him her old textbook to work on, because he has been having trouble with it at school. He's mature for twelve, or at least, more mature than she remembers being at that age. It bothers him that he struggles. But she hates to see him inside like this. It's a fine, breezy July afternoon.

'Why don't you go outside and play with your brother? It won't be long before dinner, and you look as if you could use a break.'

He looks up at her with a sheepish smile. 'Kurt's off playing football and I'm no good at it anyway. I don't mind. I want to work out how they got this solution. Do you think you could have a look?'

Helen bounces Celia on her hip. 'Oh, I'm no good to you, I'm afraid. I don't remember a thing in that book. It's all Greek to me now.'

He nods amiably. 'It's all right. It's just this one question. I can't see how they got the answer that's in the book.'

'It's always possible the book is wrong.'

'Maybe.' He smiles, cocks his head. 'My father always said that there is no such thing as wrong. Just an interesting interpretation.'

It breaks her heart. His parents haven't seen him in five years, if they're even still alive.

'I think your father and mine would get on,' she says, and glances at the clock. She's due at Mr Yardley's.

The sight of the exercises laid out on Mr Yardley's coffee table makes Helen want to lie down and never get back up again. She's already sick and exhausted, and there's the stack of ink blots, and the notepaper, the photographs, the coloured pencils. The blindfold: she hates that most of all.

Mr Yardley takes Celia, bouncing her in his arms in a way that would have amazed Helen a few months ago. He does it to put Helen at ease, but she still can't help marvelling that this important man is a friend to her child.

'Any news about Father?' It is always the first thing she says.

He smiles. 'I think you're going to be seeing him very soon.'

She lets out a heavy breath. 'Oh, really? That is wonderful news.'

'I want to ask you, Helen, whether you'll continue with these sessions after he comes home. I know they're difficult for you, but it's important that we understand how the visions work, and what their limitations are. If we're to protect your family from further dangers.'

Helen does not see the logic in this. Surely the visions are the reason Father's in trouble in the first place? The best thing for everyone would be to put these old stories out of their minds, and stop trying to do unnatural things.

She tries to think of something to say that will be honest but won't dissuade Mr Yardley from helping her family.

'I'm afraid I'm not much good to you, since I haven't shown any signs of the Second Sight.'

'Haven't you?'

He puts Celia down, and goes behind his desk. He pulls out a beautiful doll, of the Victorian kind, porcelain with blonde curls, and puts it in front of Celia, who grabs it and immediately starts banging it on the floor in a way that makes Helen wince. Mr Yardley seems unbothered. He sits on the chair behind the coffee table, and gestures for Helen to take the sofa opposite.

'Let's begin with the blindfold,' he says cheerfully.

She swallows with a dry throat and picks up the hateful black band. Once it's in place, she grabs for a pencil and puts the point against the drawing paper, waiting for some unseen force to move her hand. She never gets more than a wild scribble, but he keeps the results anyway, carefully locked in a drawer.

'Where is Celia?' Mr Yardley asks.

This is a game they've played before. She hates to cheat, but of course she knows exactly where her daughter is; any mother would. She's picked up tiny sounds; she knows how her daughter behaves.

'She's gone behind the desk,' Helen says. 'She's left the doll and she's hiding from it.'

'And where is your mother?'

'Cornwall.'

'No, Helen, tell me what you see.'

She frowns. She does have a picture of Mother, in her mind, but it's an imagining. She's folding a sheet, outside, under a clothes line; something Helen has seen her do a thousand times. She reports this to Mr Yardley, for all the good it will do. There's no way to test it.

The sounds of the room echo strangely – the ticking of the grandfather clock, and Celia cooing at her doll. It's as if the ceilings have stretched taller, the walls become hard stone rather than wood and plaster. She's cold, suddenly, and very afraid.

The next question is quiet.

'Where is Ivy?'

Helen gasps. A bright light comes over her vision, like whitewash. The pencil breaks in her hand.

She yanks the blindfold off. There's a photograph of her sister there on the coffee table, from years ago. Mr Yardley has shown her this before, and she doesn't understand why. Surely Ivy has nothing to do with anything. Mr Yardley has explained that the Sight usually seems to show people visions of those close to them. Making her picture her family members, at a time when they're so separated, seems cruel.

She gets up and goes over to Celia, checking on her to cover up how upset she is.

'Did you see something, Helen?'

'Nothing.'

There's a pause. 'I do appreciate how difficult this is. Why don't we go downstairs for our tea today? I have a surprise I think you'll like.'

Walking through the Yardley home with Celia in her arms always makes Helen feel out of place, even now that she comes here every few days. She will never feel comfortable here. There are real paintings on the walls, and little pedestals everywhere with Mr Yardley's pots and sculptures on them. Just going down the curving staircase makes her feel as if she's in a museum. It's a wonder Celia's never broken anything.

Helen waits at the bottom, and Mr Yardley goes ahead of her and opens the door into one of the large rooms on the ground floor. There's a Turkish carpet and a long oval table, and a man standing at one of the tall sunny windows, looking out at the lawn. He turns when she comes in.

Father. Her knees buckle from relief.

He turns to her. 'Helen. Gregory told me that you've been helping him, while I've been away. Thank you.'

She isn't sure what to say. 'You're home, then? They've let you come home?'

'Yes. Gregory was good enough to send someone for me, and I thought it best that you and I talk here. About how we might work together now that I'm home.'

Helen is speechless. She looks to Mr Yardley and then to Father. Celia is heavy in her arms; she hitches the toddler up on her hip. What kind of work could they do? Maybe there's a statement they need her to make, to explain the predictions Father made to the government. Maybe the university is asking questions about his absence.

At last, she asks, 'What do you need me to do?'

'Together, we might be able to see more,' Father says, walking towards her.

Understanding breaks through. 'I can't see anything. I can't – I won't. Father, you'll be taken again. Mr Yardley, please tell him. As you told him before. He can't risk telling anyone anything again, not if he doesn't have a way to explain how he knows it.'

'Certainly. Secrecy is of the essence. But if he could see more clearly, we might be able to gather the evidence we need, now and after the war,' Mr Yardley says. 'The family connection is exciting. I don't have access to everyone – the branches of His

Majesty's Government are not always cooperative. And so we can't test this with Rose. Or with your other sisters. Not yet. But we can see what the two of you can find out.'

Helen is out of words. She shakes her head, violently.

After a while, Father steps close to her and speaks gently. 'Let's leave it for now. Let's go home. I want to check some things in my notes.'

CHAPTER 29

Ivy

Sometimes, Ivy believes she is back in the vault in La Codre. Sometimes she wonders whether she ever left. She is alone in the darkness, and the damp smell of stone wall surrounds her. But those walls are farther away – when she makes a sound, to make sure she's still alive, that she exists in the world, it echoes. And her solitude is complete, this time. There are no ghosts here, or, if there are, they don't talk to Ivy. There are no names carved on the walls.

But there are pictures. Broken landscapes. Shadows creeping, absorbing the shapes of children. Faces grimacing, watching her, accusing her. She has become almost accustomed to these faces; they give her someone to talk to in the long hours. And, as terrible as they are, they are only after-images of the worse visions she has when she is with Teller.

At unpredictable intervals, two soldiers come and take her, shackled, into a long corridor, to the sessions with Teller and Kit.

Ivy regards all this distantly, as she regards everything

distantly, thanks to her regular appointments with two other soldiers, the ones who put the needle into her arm. At first, the needle triggered memories of memories, the visions she had at Beaulieu a lifetime ago. Maybe it was not Jacqueline's execution she was seeing then, but her own. She found this somewhat comforting, but whatever poison is in the needle has not killed her yet. It keeps her at one remove, so that reality seems as flat as the faces on the wall.

Early on, it wore off enough to allow her to make an attempt to trick the soldiers' minds, to make them see her in one part of the room, when she was really in another. It worked, for a little while, but it took painful concentration, and she only made it part of the way down the hall before her body and her illusion collapsed. After that, they came more frequently, kept the drugs in her veins at a steady flow.

It's always an hour or so after the dose that they take her to Teller. The room contains two chairs, both bolted to the floor, on either side of a table. The Bayeux Tapestry is spread on it, with one end still wrapped on its spindle, like a giant spool of thread on its side.

Kit is always there already, shackled to her chair, with soldiers waiting on either side of her. Like Ivy, Kit is dressed in a plain off-white dress, loose as a nightshirt. Another day that Kit has chosen not to hang herself with that dress, so Ivy doesn't either. She stays alive so that Kit won't be alone.

Kit always looks defiant, and she always looks hard at Ivy when she comes in, as if she's examining her. Ivy doesn't always look directly back. It's too painful, like staring at the sun. She allows Kit to look her over, then takes her position opposite her, while Teller walks around them, like a schoolmaster.

Her chair is close enough to the tapestry that she can sometimes catch a bit of its mothball odour, underneath the antiseptic smells of whatever prison they are keeping her in.

She could reach out and touch it, if she weren't bound to the chair.

Today Teller begins, as he usually does, by pointing at the tapestry. 'Shall I tell you what I see?'

'Go to hell,' Kit mutters.

'I see women,' Teller says. 'I see them sewing.'

It always begins this way, with insults and a story.

'We're still in France, aren't we?' Kit says, resisting. 'How far from Paris?'

'The women are embroidering with red, yellow and blue thread. They are telling each other what they see. One says, *I see the horses, being loaded on to the ships.*'

Kit's voice, louder. 'I know we're in France. I can almost see it. East of Paris. Close to Belgium. That's right, isn't it?'

'We are in Normandy, with the women, where, all around, people are preparing the ships for the invasion force.' Teller's voice is insistent, but not angry. He never gets angry.

Ivy closes her eyes tight, to stop Teller from putting images into her mind. Her head is heavy, and his voice seems to travel through water. The scene on the cloth is seared into her vision, those blues and yellows, the reds gone brown like bloodstains. She can feel the nubs of the stitches on her fingertips, although her hands are folded in her lap.

Ivy knows the scene because she stitched it herself, or at least that is what her memory tells her. She was a woman with indigestion and a soft belly who stitched that mail coat, being carried by soldiers. She was a young woman, thin and anxious, who counted the bundle of swords she saw in her visions, to be sure to get it exact.

Ivy sees what those women saw. On the road east of Caen, nine centuries before, men carry newly forged weapons to the coast of Normandy. Enough to stock hundreds of ships. She smells the fear of the wide-eyed horses and hears the incessant banging of the anvils. Chokes on the dust of fresh timber floating in the summer air.

William, the bastard duke, runs his cruel hands over the tapestry, its colours still bright. How his mouth curls as he stares at the flaming star.

He waits until the star appears in the sky, and he does not wonder at it, because he knew it was coming. Then and only then, he prepares his fleet. When it is ready, he waits again. He is a patient man; he has studied the border of the tapestry, and taken note of where the lions of Leo appear, and where the scales of Libra. He knows precisely at which time of year he must sail. And so he tells his vassals he is waiting for a good wind; for two months he tells them this. Wars are always made of lies.

The women thought they were clever, not showing him that his enemy would fight other enemies in September and be exhausted and depleted on his arrival. William doesn't need to know that. He sees what they sewed on the margins, consciously or otherwise, and he knows precisely when everything must occur.

He sails in the ship his wife had built for him.

It begins that way, on the roads east of Caen. She hears Teller relating this, like a gramophone playing in another room; she doesn't need to hear it because she sees it.

And when he tells a new story, she sees that too. On the same roads, centuries later, a new army sits. Squat metal beasts and terrible guns. Not the full strength they might have had, no, because Hitler relies on bad information. But Teller's information is impeccable. He sees where the bombs will fall, on the city of Caen, the smell of stone dust hanging in the summer air. Wails and screams and blood. Children with dusty faces, lying on the street.

He sees this and Ivy sees it with him, her visions strengthening his, and his strengthening hers. She sees it all in terrible detail. Ivy opens her eyes to try to replace the visions with reality, but in the glare of the artificial light it all crowds together. Squirming on her chair, she pulls away from the tapestry, but there is nowhere to go; they've bound her to the chair, and there is no escape for her except the next needle.

Kit is sitting like a rag doll in the opposite chair, her head hanging down. But Ivy can see that she's still breathing; her too-thin chest is moving.

'Thank you both,' says Teller, leaning back, a sheen of sweat on his satisfied face. 'When the enemy bombs the town, I'll make sure there are no German forces there. We'll stay well clear of the area, and then we'll be ready to fight.'

'You can't hold off the liberation of France forever,' Kit says, weakly, lifting her head. 'I've seen the forces on both sides and so have you. You can see the future. You just don't want to.'

Ivy lets her own head hang to one side and looks at her sister with something that would be curiosity, if the drugs weren't so thick in her system. She doesn't think Kit is drugged, or at least not drugged as much. She seems sharper, more like herself. Ivy sometimes thinks that she, Ivy, isn't here at all, that she's only a figment of the imaginations of the sister who loves her and the jailer who controls her.

Teller's attitude towards Kit is, always, polite in a way that Kit must find maddening.

'I can delay the advance, and I already have, thanks to you. We have made it slow and bloody, have we not?' He puts a hand out and rests it lightly on the tapestry. 'How many such objects do you think there are in the world that are imbued with the visions of prophets? I am patient, you see. Like Duke William, I am patient, and I know things happen in their own time. Like Duke William, I am ready to play my part when that moment comes. We aren't just seeing the future here, you and I. We're making it happen. We make it inevitable.'

He smiles at Kit, and Kit spits at him, though her spittle doesn't get close enough to land. That draws a smile out of Ivy. How spirited Kit is, even now, though she's so gaunt and her eyes are sunken.

Ivy would like to make her sister proud.

As she walks back to her cell, between two soldiers, all she can see is lines of young men who look just like Grady, walking warily through a beautiful orchard, quiet until the roar of the tanks surrounds them.

Everything will burn. France rings with the sound of bombs and shells. Out of that evil symphony a new order will rise, an order that shapes the future and the past into a single story, sung to a single song.

The soldiers lie in the mud. Grady is there, his face turned away from her.

She whispers his name, and would reach out to touch him, but her hands are shackled. She wants to turn his face towards hers, to see him one more time.

The next dose deadens Ivy. Lying on the floor of her cell, she's a ghost within four whitewashed walls, an echo of herself. She has no idea how many hours or days pass; it could even be weeks. None of this is happening.

But Ivy is not dead. She's in the shadowlands, where the ghosts live, and she lives with them.

There's no such thing as ghosts.

The voice comes sharply, roughly, nothing like the whispers or the flames. It's Grady's voice.

Ivy sits up, slowly, keeping her eyes on the vision. He's sitting too, cross-legged, holding her hand. Grady's hand is on hers; she sees his freckles. Feels the touch between them as if it's something real.

Somewhere high above all of this, her mind floats, aware. She tries to ignore what it's telling her: that if she is seeing Grady, then Grady is dead.

I am not dead, he says. She looks into his face. His eyes. *I am not dead. I am here to tell you to stop listening to that goddamned Nazi.*

She thinks: *I am seeing your ghost. I am seeing the sailor on the cliffs.*

I can tell you with some certainty that, while Southampton has its charms, it is not heaven, and it would seem very unfair to the virtuous if this is hell. I'm alive. You're alive. You just need to remember it, so that you will come home to me. Please.

She knows this expression, on his face. It's the one he puts on when he wants to look as if he isn't worried about her.

What does my bicycle look like?

How wonderful it would be to be back in the house in Beaulieu, with him. Sitting near him and listening to his blunt questions, under his unwavering gaze. At the time she wanted to be gone, to be off, proving herself.

That Ivy was alive. How she mourns her.

What does my bicycle look like?

He won't be put off. Not even now. Those eyes are still on her. His hands are holding hers, though there is no warmth in the touch.

It comes to her: an image of his bicycle. So ordinary. It speaks of days spent working and loving, of a world in which people do things other than kill, survive and die. Of blue skies, not orange ones. Of laughter, not screams.

She tries to hold the vision, but it's gone already. In Grady's arms, she's weeping, with nothing in her vision now but tears.

You can see what you choose to see, he says.

*

The following day, in the tapestry room, she gets the nerve to look into Kit's eyes.

Something grabs her, even through the drugs. She can hear Teller beginning his story, but when she holds Kit's eyes she can keep the visions at bay. Holding each other's gaze, Ivy and Kit create a vision Teller doesn't want them to see, moment by moment. Ivy sees the face of a woman, carved out of stone, like the statue on the side of a church.

The woman's stone lips form words, the same words Grady said. *You can see what you choose to see.*

The face is familiar. Kit knows it, and Ivy knows it through Kit. As they stare at each other, they both realize that the stone woman is the same figure they've seen stitched on to the tapestry, the face Father has peered at for so many hours of his life. The face of Aelfgyva, the mother of a boy who should have been king. She is not stone or stitching now, but a real woman, with sunspots on her cheeks and a cut on her finger. A widow, and a mother. She cares only about one thing now. Her son.

Matilda knows full well what will happen, if Aelfgyva presses her son's claim. She has seen it; her weird women have already started to stitch it on to linen. Brief glory for the boy, and early death, followed by a bloody anarchy. Matilda shows the tapestry to Aelfgyva, shows her the scene with her own actions in it. Aelfgyva runs her hands over it. She has not asked the bishop for his help yet, but she intends to. She wants to press her claim. No one knows this but her; she is not a woman who trusts people.

Matilda, watching her face, asks the women to tell Aelfgyva the story of what happens next.

'You see all this?' Aelfgyva asks when she has heard it all. 'Is it inevitable, then?'

An old woman with long grey hair shakes her head. 'There is always another path. Cast off your ambitions, and your son will live. Your story, as far as the world knows, stops here. Your choice. You can see what you choose to see.'

The old woman points with one knobby finger at the half-finished panel, at the words, where Aelfgyva and a certain cleric . . .

Aelfgyva has to think about it. She goes out to the coast, glares across the sea towards the land her son will claim, if she takes that path. A path that leads to her son's early death, for the sake of a dynasty, an idea, a bloodline. The story on the tapestry could be her son's, or it could be something else. Her boy could live. Not an easy life, perhaps, but a life.

All that is visible is a hazy horizon. All she can hear is the roar of the waves.

A deafening roar, a relentless roar. A train on its tracks, drumming its beat. The steaming breath of an iron dragon.

Ivy can barely hear the sound of Teller's voice under the roar of the train. Chugging along, implacable. Usually, hearing a train puts her to sleep, but this one wakes her up. Not even the drugs can silence it.

Teller asks her what she sees, and this causes her to try to focus on his face. To her delight, he looks afraid.

'I hear trains,' she says.

Uncertainty flickers in his eyes. 'There are no trains passing nearby. I hear nothing.'

'You will.' She leans forward, straining her shackles. 'You hear them, don't you, Kit? You know that railway platform as well as I do. The Pantin railway station, in Paris.'

Kit says nothing; her face is stricken.

Ivy twists to look at their tormentor. 'Don't you see them, Teller? Don't you see the wives and husbands, and children and parents, crowded on the platform? There in those pens – I know you can see them. Those are my colleagues. Resisters, the ones you haven't killed yet. Some of the ones you were able to find with your mind's eye, who've been in prison all this time. I recognize some of the agents I trained with. I grieve for them.'

His face betrays him; he is seeing it too.

'You don't sound as if you're grieving,' he says.

Her voice comes as a harsh whisper. 'No? Perhaps I've absorbed too much of you, here in this room. You don't find it pleasing to watch their loved ones strain to pass them a note, a final few words of love? You don't enjoy seeing the anguish on the faces of their children? You know where they're going, just as I do. They're all being shipped out of France, to terrible camps. I see them. Oh, I see them.'

The roar of the trains is so loud in the room now that the spindle holding the tapestry shakes.

Despite her hoarse throat, she gets out the last thing she wants to say to him. 'I know why these trains are coming, roaring past us, going east. Because Paris is about to fall, and you and your comrades are taking your last chance to inflict vengeance on those who resisted you. It is your last blow. A desperate one, a cruel one, a petty one. And you and I both know that these trains are coming soon. Because I have chosen to see them. And now you see them too. This will happen. It hasn't happened yet, but it will.'

Exhausted, she leans back against the hard chair to which she is shackled. She does not see the fighting around Caen now. Another vision has taken hold, of both of them. A vision of a terrible future, full of grief and hope, which drives away all other visions. She has shown him he has reason to despair.

The trains have gone quiet. For a long time, Teller stands in silence at the end of the table, staring at the tapestry that he believes must tell the same story every day, the story of a victory long ago.

'It is not our last blow,' he says.

293

Then he takes the few steps over to Kit. Ivy cries out as she sees it happen, twice; she doesn't know which moment is the real event and which is the premonition. He flicks a penknife in his hand and slashes Kit across the face.

CHAPTER 30

Rose

At three o'clock in the morning, the grounds of Bletchley Park teem with bodies, a lake of moving shadows.

Rose Sharp stops a few steps from the door of her decoding hut. She lets her eyes adjust. So little light bleeds through the blackout curtains, and there is no moon. And her feet have yet to learn the path from Block F to the dining hall in the big house. Most of her years at Bletchley Park have been spent in a different building, and sometimes she stumbles at night, her head filled with decryptions.

At least she can be guided by the streams of people, like schools of fish, heading either to the food or back from it. Chattering in low voices about anything but work or singing softly. She can hear them tonight, women's voices, singing 'The Lambeth Walk'. It reminds her of the night she met Harry Frederick, at Father's party.

The tune turns the whispers in Rose's head into static, and she leans against the wall of the nearest hut.

'Miss Sharp!' someone calls out. 'Are you all right?'

She pushes her glasses higher on her nose, looks up into

a familiar assemblage of kind eyes and scrappy brown moustache.

Harry Frederick himself.

Harry and Rose worked at different huts for the first few years. Even now, they don't work side by side; Harry works in the Newmanry, while Rose works in the Testery, though the two cryptanalysis stations cooperate.

It's been weeks since she saw him, or anyone else she knew from before the war, although she had indeed recognized a few Cambridge people here, as Harry had told her she would. But there are so many people working at Bletchley Park – thousands of strangers, most of them women. She hasn't exactly made friends – there isn't time for that – but after a while she had started to feel at home. Bletchley is its own little world. People often call each other by their Christian names. When the stockings started to run scarce, some of the girls at Bletchley defiantly wore mismatched ones, which led to a fashion for colourful stockings. Those girls remind Rose of the horses on the Bayeux Tapestry, with their legs in varied colours and patterns.

There it is – the tapestry again, intruding on her thoughts.

She smiles up at him, weakly. 'I'm fine. Thank you, though.'

'You're not fine. None of us is fine. It's three-thirty in the morning and you've been working for days straight. Have you got any leave coming up?'

'I was due for a week in May, but of course—'

'Ah, of course.'

In the lead-up to D-Day, all leave across Bletchley Park had been cancelled. Everyone was, and continues to be, terribly busy. Rose has only a rough idea of the scope of the business, of all the army, navy, air force, diplomatic and other codes in German, Japanese and who knows what else.

In her years in Hut 6 they'd worked to crack the Enigma

code, by hand and with the help of the 'bombe' machines, great structures of spinning wheels that could run through possibilities faster than any human code-breaker could.

And now Rose is working with another machine: Colossus. It is able to strip one layer of ciphering off the messages that come via teleprinter rather than Morse, messages that the German command and much of the army use. But, after it strips off that layer, code-breakers still have to do the rest.

Hut 6 consisted mainly of women. The Testery's code-breakers are largely men, except Rose. Rose, a civilian, is in awe of the women who work the Colossus machine for them, in their smart Wren uniforms.

And she has a secret.

She doesn't break code by running through possibilities or spotting patterns – not really. She lets the patterns come to her. Rose has a knack with the strips of paper left in the basket, the ones that no one else has been able to crack. The dead ducks. When things are a bit quiet – always a relative state – Rose works on a dead duck. Sometimes they speak to her, in a sense.

But this particular dead duck is giving her a new sort of headache. It isn't just speaking to her; it's yelling. She knows exactly what it will say when decrypted. She just can't work out *how*. And she doesn't trust her instinct, because her instinct is telling her something that can't be true: that the message is connected not only with the tapestry her father has been obsessed with for years, but also with her sisters. With Ivy, and with Kit. How could it be about either of them, never mind both? It doesn't say their names, but she feels it strongly.

Which means her feelings must be leading her astray. Anxiety about her family, intruding on her work.

'When's the last time you were home?' Harry demands.

'Oh, it must be a year and a half now. I went home for

a few days soon after Helen had her baby. But I'm really quite all right. It's just a dead duck that's got into my head.'

'Some of them are more frustrating than others.'

She nods. 'It came through Colossus all right, and I have the funniest feeling about it. What I mean is – well, I think I know what it might say, but I couldn't tell you what the words of it are. Oh, that makes no sense.'

He thinks for a while. 'Will you wait here? I'll just be a moment.'

She agrees, and sits on the stairs at a hut entrance. Everything is dark, and the shadows that flit past could be anyone. But there is safety in darkness. A bomb fell on the Park back in 1940, and everyone says that Bletchley is overdue for another, even if the Germans haven't learned what is happening here – and it seems unbelievable that they haven't. And now those terrible flying bombs are falling everywhere.

Rose thinks of Helen and the children at home, how frightened they must be. Of Ivy driving around her terrible majors in Sheffield – no, that's not right, she's at a signalling facility now. Of Mother, with her charges all over the country, and Father with his students gone off to the front to die. She can hardly bear to think of Kit, in Paris, and what dangers she might be in. No wonder she's imagining Nazi messages about her sisters, at a time like this.

The hut door opens, and Harry comes out again. It is quieter now that most people on their meal break have made their way into the dining hall. Harry sits next to her on the step, and shows her a blue-and-white-wrapped bar of Cadbury's ration chocolate.

'I keep it in a drawer for emergencies,' he says sombrely.

Rose smiles, and takes the square he breaks off for her, and chews it gratefully. She can hardly remember now what Cadbury's chocolate tasted like before the war. Perhaps it wasn't that different, though when they changed to the ration recipe Ivy wrote to Rose that she 'flopped down by the fire and put a pillow over my head in despair'.

It has been some time now since Ivy's last letter. A month, at least, and that one was very short, almost perfunctory. It hadn't sounded like Ivy at all, though it was in her hand-writing. Usually Rose can hear her sisters' voices in her mind when she reads their letters, but this one was silent, mere marks on paper.

Unlike the dead duck message.

'Do you think you ought to tell me what you believe it says?' Harry asks, gently. 'What I mean is, are lives in danger?'

Rose thinks, then shakes her head. It is a message about the Bayeux Tapestry: that it must be moved out to a place of greater safety, that the fortress is not acceptable, that the experiments can continue in Germany, that her sisters can come too. It's probably something else entirely. Mere house-keeping, that her mind caught some part of, and has woven a fantasy around. And yet – it bothers her. It could be code words, perhaps.

'I don't think it's anything serious. In fact I suspect it's just my mind playing tricks. How could I possibly know what it says, if I can't work it out? The only explanation that makes any sense is that my subconscious remembers another message and something rings a bell in this one. Something like that.'

He nods, and silently offers her the bar of chocolate for another piece, but she shakes her head.

'I always say that code-breaking is as much instinct and feeling as anything else,' Harry says. 'Did you ever hear about how angry Turing got with Jack Good for taking a nap?' He looks at her with a twinkle in his eye.

'No, I haven't heard that story.'

'Well, I can't say whether he just wanted to get Turing's

goat, but Jack claimed that he dreamed the answer to a stubborn cipher they'd been working on. When he woke up, he tried it, and it worked.'

His voice is low; this story, even more than the chocolate, is a kindly gesture and a bit of a risk. Nobody talks about work unless it's strictly necessary, though he hasn't told her any specifics. They have all signed the Official Secrets Act, and nobody quite knows what would happen to someone who blabbed – they couldn't very well send you packing, knowing what you know, but nobody wants to find out.

'And you know about the Herivel tip,' he said, his voice lower still.

She nods; it's a pattern, a general tendency that lazy German operators have of using particular settings.

He says, 'John Herivel swears he came up with that as he was sitting in front of his landlady's fire, just daydreaming. Just a thought that popped into his head. Sometimes our brains are working on the problems we give them when we don't realize it. And we may not ever see precisely how we made the connection.'

Rose learned long ago that the key to playing a difficult piece on the piano without making a mistake is not to think about it, only to hear the music and let her fingers pick it out. All it takes is a brief moment of analysis for her brain to shut the whole thing down like a stick in a bicycle wheel.

She sighs. 'Thank you, Harry. I'm sure if there's something there, it will come clear to me.'

'I could work on the dead duck, if you like. Are there any words you think likely to appear?'

She grimaces. 'It's silly.'

'Sillier than some of the soldier talk we've intercepted? With their girlfriends' names? Come now, you never know what ridiculous thing might be a code word they're using.'

'Tapestry,' she blurts. 'And fortress. And moving, or

securing . . . But I'm not sure which German word it uses for either thing. Possibly . . . possibly a mention of sisters.'

His eyebrows dip down under the rim of his glasses. 'So you know what it says, but you don't know . . . what the words are.'

She looks back at him, then smiles and ducks her head. 'I don't really know either thing. As you say, I'm probably just tired.'

Harry stretches out his legs. They sit there in the darkness for a moment, in silence.

'Well,' he says at last, 'I stand by what I said about instincts. I'll have a crack at your dead duck. If it's speaking to you, I suspect someone will be able to work it out. And I'll make sure to send you flowers when we do.'

'Send me flowers?' She straightens up, alarmed.

'It's been more than two months since D-Day. It's busy, but it will stay busy now for a while. I think we can arrange some leave for you, and get you back here in fighting form.'

She says nothing, looking down at her hands, the finger-nails bitten right down.

He continues, softly, 'Don't forget what happened to Good and to Herivel. It was only once they got some proper rest that they solved things. Maybe it'll come to you in your sleep. But you can't get a proper rest here, on these terrible shifts. You're still billeted with that woman who made you sleep on the plywood board over the tub, aren't you?'

She gives him a rueful half-smile. 'That was only for a little while, while her cousin was visiting.'

'All the same, your own bed in your own home would do wonders, I'm sure. It'll be nice to see your parents. And Helen. You'll give my regards to your father, won't you?'

A hard thing gets in the way in Rose's throat. Suddenly she feels very certain that the message is about her family, that she needs to get home, urgently.

She looks up at the glasses of the young man who is being so kind to her, and says, 'If you think it will be all right, I will go home. For a short while.'

Rose knows something is wrong before she even opens the door. There's a heavy atmosphere, like the hour before a storm. As always, she uses the back door, the one that leads into the kitchen; the front door of the Sharp house has always been for visitors. She expects to find the house empty, or everyone gathered discussing some tragedy. But Helen is pacing the kitchen with Celia in her arms, as if everything's normal. The kitchen is sunny and warm; the boys' laughter drifts down from upstairs.

It's so incongruous with Rose's instincts that she's taken aback and stands in the doorway for a moment getting her bearings. She pushes her glasses up on her nose.

'I didn't know you were coming!' Helen exclaims, and manages to hug Rose with the child between them.

Rose sets down a small suitcase and sits at the table that has been in this kitchen for as long as either of them can remember. 'It wasn't planned. I just wanted to see you all.'

'What is it, darling? What's happened?'

'I'm fine. But how is everyone here?'

Helen turns around to put Celia down with some building blocks. Something about it gives Rose the feeling that Helen's hiding her face, that she is worried. But, when she stands back up again, her expression is bright. She looks gorgeous and healthy, her light brown hair, longer than Rose's, curling on her shoulders.

'Everyone is fine here,' Helen says. 'Wait until you see how tall the boys are getting. Mother is busy, as usual. She's out today. And Father is all right. He's home.'

'Ah, he's not teaching today?'

Something like confusion passes over Helen's face, and

then she says, 'No, he's not teaching today. He's been . . . well, he's been stuck in that little room of his doing research for hours today, and yesterday. I'm glad you're here. It'll brighten him up.'

'Shall I tell him I'm here?'

'No, stay here with me for a moment.' Helen bites her lip. 'I hardly ever get you all to myself.'

There's something behind that, but Helen is a fortress when she wants to be, and Rose knows there's no use in trying to make her open up. Rose was never good at making anyone open up. She doesn't have Kit's humour or Ivy's charm.

'What about Ivy?' Rose asks. 'I get her letters but they're so short. Not like her at all. And I don't suppose you've heard anything from Kit.'

'No news,' Helen says sharply. 'We would have told you, if there was anything.'

'Would you? I don't want you to spare me, Helen, if anything does happen.' Rose pauses, tries to think of a graceful way to introduce her question, and fails. 'What about George? Have you had . . . any news?'

'I had a letter from him not long ago. He doesn't say much, of course. Nothing about the war, I mean.'

'No, of course not. But he's all right.'

'He was when he wrote.' A shadow passes over Helen's face. 'Did you come home just to quiz me?'

Rose looks at her feet. 'I'm sorry. I just had a bad feeling.'

'Exhaustion, I'd say,' Helen grumbles. 'Why they work typists so hard and give them so little leave, I don't understand. Typists! As though the war would stop if some assistant to the minister can't dictate a letter. How long are you home for?'

'A few days.'

'Well, do you mind if I start on lunch? The boys will come running through the door hungry any minute. Wait until you see them, Rose.'

'I can only imagine.' Rose crouches by Celia. 'She's absolutely gorgeous, Helen. A year and a half, is she?'

'Nearly two.'

'And are people being terrible about it?'

Helen sniffs. 'Not really. Do you remember Mrs Beresford?'

'Oh, that old wasp. What has she said?'

'The funny thing is that she gave me a way out. She was probing, once I started to show, and suggested that perhaps George and I had held a secret wedding before he went back over. I'm afraid I didn't correct her. It was cowardly, but now that seems to be the common understanding.'

'And how are Mother and Father about it now?'

'Oh, they dote on Celia. They've come around, I think. I never would have imagined they would accept such a thing. But people can surprise you, can't they? Mother even said something the other day that made me think she knows about Kit – Kit falling in love with girls, I mean. Which is funny, because Kit never wanted to talk about it, while Ivy came home full of stories, trying to shock me with all the flirtations she'd had with both girls and boys. But of course she never breathed a word of that around Mother.'

'People see more than it seems.'

'Yes.'

'Mmm.' Helen looks at Rose. 'And how about you? No young man yet? I imagine the competition must be fierce among the typists.'

'No, I'm not interested in romance at all.'

'Oh, once you meet someone nice, your tune will change.'

'I don't think so. What can I do to help make dinner?'

'I won't hear of it. You're here to relax. How was the train?'

'Full of Home Guard men. I had to sit on my suitcase.'

Rose sits at the table while Helen bustles at the sink, rinsing runner beans. This very ordinary conversation feels as though it's happening in another place, or as if they're on stage, pretending that everything is all right. Every part of her body knows that it isn't. There's something wrong: the tightness in Helen's shoulders. The way she didn't run to tell the boys and Father that Rose is here.

There's a knock, on the front door; they can barely hear it from the kitchen.

'Who can that be?' Rose asks. She gets up from her chair.

Helen, the colander in her hands, freezes like a frightened animal.

For a moment, neither of them moves. Perhaps Helen's worried it will be news of George. Perhaps that's what Rose's bad feeling was.

Rose walks through the door to the sitting room, and then into the little front hall. She'll save Helen from dealing with the bad news in front of strangers, even if she can't save her from anything else.

But Father is already at the front door, and the man standing there on the step with his hat in his hand doesn't look as if he's delivering a telegram.

Father turns when he hears her, slowly, like a man older than he is. His expression goes from wary to startled. 'Rose, good heavens, where did you come from?'

'Just came home. In through the kitchen.' She smiles at him and then turns politely to the ginger-haired man, who is looking from one of them to the other and back again.

'I'm sorry to intrude,' he says in a flat accent, American or Canadian, Rose thinks. 'My name is Grady Sinclair. I'm a friend of Ivy's. May I come in?'

CHAPTER 31

Helen

Helen watches in amazement as Rose nods along to what any sane person ought to reject as nonsense. Mr Sinclair says that he is worried about Ivy, that he has reason to worry because he saw a vision of her, and she seemed to be asking for his help.

'Forgive me, sir,' the young man goes on. 'But I thought, from some things that Mr Yardley has told me, that you might have certain . . . instincts as well. If Ivy is in danger, I thought you might know something about it.'

Rose just looks from one man to the other, as if they're talking about the weather. She seems to accept this situation almost gratefully. Perhaps she knew about Father's theories, or his notebooks. As usual, Helen is the odd one out. She grips the arms of her chair, remembering the sickening white that overtook her vision when she wore the blindfold, when Mr Yardley asked her where Ivy was.

'I don't know anything, and I haven't seen anything,' Father says, abruptly. 'I have been worried, of course. I had a feeling. Whenever one of those letters came. But that's all. What does Yardley know about it?'

Mr Sinclair hesitates. 'I have signed the Official Secrets Act. I'm probably committing a crime by being here at all. But she is trying to tell me something. I'm sure of that.'

Until now, the idea of the Second Sight as something real has been confined to herself, to her father, and to Mr Yardley's ideas. To hear a stranger give it credence makes Helen panicky.

Father leans back in his chair, thinking. 'Well, the obvious thing would be to wire the signalling facility where she works, or to go there directly. You know Gregory Yardley, do you? I imagine he would know how to get in touch with her. We can go over there now – I believe he's at home.'

Mr Sinclair shakes his head. 'I telephoned Yardley right away, but I got the brush-off. He – I don't think he knows where she is.'

'Well, it ought to be easy enough for someone with authority to find out,' Father says. 'Even if we can't know, we should be able to get her a message.'

'She's not at a signalling facility,' Rose says suddenly. Her face is white. 'She's in France.'

'What?' Father demands. 'How do you know?'

He looks back at Mr Sinclair, who doesn't seem surprised by Rose's comment at all. The acknowledgement written on his face makes Father shut his eyes for a moment, seeking privacy, or a vision, or strength.

'Rose?' Helen says with a quaver in her voice. 'What is going on? Why are you here, really?'

Rose bites her lip. 'I can't say where this information comes from, but I know about a message from a Nazi officer in Germany to one in France. I think it says something about Ivy and Kit, and about the tapestry. Your tapestry, Father. Now I feel certain. Ivy is with the tapestry. They have her and Kit, somewhere. Does that make any sense, Mr Sinclair?'

'You mean the Bayeux Tapestry?' Grady Sinclair asks, confused. 'I know about your work on it, of course, Professor Sharp, but why would it be wherever Ivy is?'

Father looks very grey and small in his chair. 'Because the tapestry has a kind of amplifying effect on the Sight. It was made by clairvoyants, and, as each of them added their visions to it, it accumulated something of their power along with it. A story that grew and added to itself. I have experienced this myself, here, with a mere scrap of it. It's possible Ivy knew this, and sought it out in France. But how? I have never told her.'

Mr Sinclair hesitates, looking pained. 'Perhaps Mr Yardley did.'

There's silence. Helen watches Father's face go from grey to purple, the same sign of anger she once saw when she came home and told him she was going to have a baby. This time, after a moment, he speaks, very quietly.

'Do you mean that Gregory Yardley knows that Ivy is in France?'

Mr Sinclair nods slowly. 'He sent her to me for training, and then – you must appreciate that this is secret information—'

Father's voice is barely above a whisper. 'My friend trained my daughter and sent her to France. Unbeknownst to me. This is what you are telling me.'

Nobody says anything for a moment. Then Father waves his hand.

'Well, in any case, I have never told Gregory about the effect the tapestry has on me. He does know that it was made by clairvoyants – I did tell him that. Either he or Ivy might have discovered its effects, I suppose. But this doesn't make sense. I've tried to find out the state of the tapestry myself, of course, with the invasion. There are rumours that the Germans removed it from where they were keeping it.

One of Gregory's colleagues raised the question in the House of Commons a few weeks ago, and the war secretary said it was likely in a store with other artefacts. That's the only update I've heard on the matter. Kit might know, of course. I wonder.'

Mr Sinclair clears his throat. 'When I was working with Ivy, one thing we learned is that our talents seemed heightened around each other.'

He's blushing, for reasons Helen thinks she can guess. She's become a stranger in her sisters' lives. How did that happen? It was Kit first, before the war. To think that Ivy's been training to use the Second Sight – the same exercises that Mr Yardley gave to Helen, perhaps. To think that she's in France. It doesn't seem possible. Helen wants to close her eyes and wake up in 1938, and do everything over. She wants to banish this nightmare, extinguish it so it can never worm its way into reality ever again.

Mr Sinclair, apparently aware of his blushing, tries to explain himself. 'What I mean is that clairvoyants seem to, well, amplify each other – exactly as you are saying about the tapestry, Mr Sharp. We are stronger in the presence of others like us. Or perhaps, even of the prophecies others have made. That's one reason I came here. I thought that perhaps, even if you didn't know yet about Ivy, we might be able to find out. Together.'

Her father immediately goes into professor mode. 'Rose, you had a feeling about a message – have you had any experience with the Sight before?'

'I don't think so. But perhaps I just didn't recognize it for what it was.'

'Well, let's assume you've got the talent. Excellent. That makes three of us. Helen?'

She looks at her father, startled. 'Yes?'

'You and Gregory Yardley were training. He said you

showed promise. I have left it alone, because you seemed not to want to talk about it, but if you do have a talent for it . . .'

'No,' she says, curtly, and stands up. She can't stay in her chair another minute; her whole body is rebelling. She wants to run. 'I don't have a talent, and I don't want anything to do with it. All of this has only brought us sorrow. Father, if you take it into your head that Ivy is somewhere and you go and tell – whoever you would tell – they'll take you away again, and this time for good. I know they will. If she's really in France, if she's really in trouble, surely someone knows. The people who sent her.'

'I don't think they do,' Mr Sinclair says quietly. 'I think we are the only hope Ivy has now. She told me so, herself.'

Father stands up. 'All right, then. There's no time to argue any more. Rose, do you have anything on paper?'

Rose pulls a folded paper out of her breast pocket. 'I wrote down the message. I can't show it—'

'Of course not. Just hold on to it. I'm going to get the bit of tapestry, and I'll hold that. Anything else we can use – a photograph of Ivy, perhaps.'

Helen watches as the three of them arrange their chairs close to each other, each of them with something in their hand, and that hand clasped with the person next to them. It looks like a séance or a prayer circle, not like the sitting room in Stoke Damson in the middle of the afternoon.

Upstairs, Celia is sleeping. She might cry out at any moment, and Helen could go up to her, and be ordinary again. She could pretend that everything is fine. She could keep her eyes open so that she never sees that horrible white, never feels the terror she can't name.

That terror was the answer to 'where is Ivy now?' That terror is what her sister is living through. And maybe Kit too; Rose seems to think so. Helen doesn't have to understand it. She only has to love her sisters enough to look the terror in the eye.

Helen walks into the dining room and picks up another chair. She brings it back and sets it down so that the three-point circle becomes a four-point diamond. The others look up, move their chairs to accommodate her, and take her hands. Her father hasn't held her hand since she was a little girl; it feels strange.

Across from her, Mr Sinclair gives her a comradely nod. How odd it must be for him, holding the hand of the father and sister of the woman he loves. Because he loves Ivy, that much is clear. He's come here to save her.

Helen takes a breath, and closes her eyes.

The whiteness surrounds her immediately, and she's gasping. She sees Kit, with a bloody gash across her face. Sees her father, as a young man, walking up a hill, exhausted, filthy, blood on his shoulder. Brick buildings breaking out of the forest. There are soldiers everywhere, some trudging, some screaming on the ground, and the sound of shelling. Her father goes up to one of the soldiers on the ground and turns him over.

It's George. Her beloved George, his eyes staring at nothing.

Helen screams.

Everyone around her is screaming too. She's no longer holding her father's hand, or Rose's. Kit is on one side of her, screaming, and Ivy is on the other. They're surrounded by figures, people Helen doesn't recognize, in medieval clothing. A needle is going into Kit's arm; another into Ivy's arm. Now it's going into Helen's.

She pulls her hands out of her sisters' to bat away the needle, and falls off her chair on to the floor.

Father is there, standing over her. His face is stricken.

'I'm all right,' Helen says, taking his hand and getting to her feet.

Rose is still in her chair, staring straight ahead as if frozen. Mr Sinclair is looking at all of them with an ashen face.

Once Helen is back in her chair, Father paces. 'Did we all see the same things? The needles – the cut on Kit's face?'

'I did,' Rose says, her voice rough.

'And I, though I didn't know that was Kit,' Mr Sinclair says.

Father looks confused. 'But I saw a time I remember from the last war. Was that only me, then?'

'No,' Helen says. 'I saw that. I saw you, in uniform, in a wooded area. And there were other soldiers. And . . . '

She doesn't say George's name. She looks at her father, and it's written on his face that he saw him lying there, his brown eyes staring. There's no space in this moment for grief; if she acknowledges it, if she says the words, she'll collapse.

'I've been dreaming about that battle,' Father says at last, turning from her and putting his hand to his temple. 'From a long time ago. That might be why it showed up now. An old memory.'

Rose stands up, with victory on her face. 'No. It's more than that. I can see the connection now. I know what the message says. This fortress, the one you remember – where is it?'

'Near St Quentin. East of Paris.'

'I know it,' Rose says, excitedly. 'I know all of it now. It's Himmler, saying that the tapestry cannot stay where it is in the fortress, that they must move it into Germany, to a place of greater safety, and that the sisters should accompany it. That's Kit and Ivy. We know where they are.'

Father walks to the coat rack and takes his hat. 'I'm going over to see Gregory.'

*

The rest of them follow Father like a pack of determined ducks, over the bridge and across the lawn; Helen pushes Celia in the pram. When they get there, they meet Mr Yardley on his front step, just leaving for London.

'You sent my daughter to France,' Father says, without a greeting.

Mr Yardley's eyes widen. He looks at the group behind Father, gives Mr Sinclair a wary nod of recognition. 'We should go in,' he says, looking around, even though they're out in the open, surrounded by wide lawn, where no one could be listening. 'Or if we could postpone this—'

'There is no time.' Father barrels forward. 'Did you know she's been taken prisoner? How long has she been missing?'

Mr Yardley takes a moment before responding. 'We heard from her three days ago. She's meeting her schedules.'

Mr Sinclair steps towards him, his shoes crunching on the white gravel of the drive. 'You know as well as I do that the Germans capture our wireless operators. They could have learned Ivy's security checks somehow. Or are there even security checks on the messages?'

'There are.'

'Then why do you look so uncertain?'

'Because there is another agent who has relayed . . . concerns. Who believes that Ivy hasn't been seen. I should not say anything more.' He pauses.

'It's Max, isn't it?' Helen is certain of it; there is something in Mr Yardley's twisted expression, and she has a memory of Max picking her up from the farm two years ago, and talking about her plans to do something more exciting, the people she knew. 'Max is in France too.'

Mr Yardley recovers his self-assurance. 'We should not be having this conversation. In fact, we are not having it any longer.'

Helen knows that there is only one argument that will

convince him to take a chance. 'We've seen her. We know where Ivy is. And Kit too. Two clairvoyants who could be working for England. Who knows what we might learn from them, if we could bring them home alive?'

When that day comes, she will not tell this man anything, and she'll tell her sisters not to either.

But Mr Yardley can't be sure of that. She can see him wavering; he doesn't want to risk anyone else finding out about Ivy, about Father, about Grady Sinclair, any of it. His reputation would be at risk, and all the work he's done. He's asking himself whether that risk is worth the cost of recovering two clairvoyants, one of them the most talented and well trained he knows. Helen watches him consider these questions as though she's reading his mind.

'You've seen them,' he whispers to Father. 'A vision?'

'We all have,' Helen answers. 'All four of us.'

Mr Yardley looks behind her to Rose, standing there little and defiant, with the pins falling out of her hair. To Mr Sinclair with his hands in his pockets. To Father, who has been his friend for decades. She watches him calculate.

'We can't send a message if I can't tell my colleagues how I know the information,' he says.

'Oh, hogwash,' Mr Sinclair says, startling Helen. 'Nobody ever knows everything from beginning to end; how we know the information won't be the business of the person you ask to send it. The only problem is who to send it to. Who will be willing and able to act on it? This Max – is he—'

'She,' Mr Yardley says. 'She is my daughter. I don't think she'll be able to help us. She's just a courier.'

'Give us Maxine's code name, Gregory,' Father says, his voice low and deceptively calm. 'You owe us that much. We'll take it from there.'

At this, Mr Yardley looks at his friend with dignity. 'Ivy willingly chose to serve King and country, as we all have, using whatever talents we have at our disposal. I don't owe you anything, and neither does she. My daughter certainly does not.'

Helen is angry. She doesn't get angry very often; usually it frightens her, to feel out of control. But today she's just grateful for something that can give her the strength she needs. She stands on the drive, pushes the pram away from her a few inches, and balls up her fists, scrunches her eyes closed. Someone says something, but she doesn't pay it any attention. She is going to take what she needs, to protect her family. She opens herself up to all of it – the red rage, the white fear, the black grief – and there are tears flowing down her face when she opens her eyes; but her head, for the first time in months, is perfectly clear.

'We can go now, Father,' she says. 'I know what Max's code name is.'

Father and Mr Sinclair go to London in the Morris Minor, and Rose falls asleep on the sofa. Helen doesn't sleep, knowing that Kit and Ivy are in danger, knowing that every time she closes her eyes she'll see George's staring eyes. She sits quietly, with the light of one lamp beside the bed, reading the same page of a novel over and over.

At some point she must have dozed, because she becomes aware that she's lost time. The house has the unmistakable silence of the smallest hours, just the faint ticking of a clock in the hall. Helen's head is better, clearer. She closes the book and stays still for several minutes in the dark house. She smells a storm. There's a distant note of thunder, and the baby starts to cry.

Helen walks over and lifts her out of her cot. She's dry, maybe just hungry. But as soon as Helen puts her to her shoulder Celia falls quiet again, the weight of her head and the light breath on Helen's neck sure signs that she's fallen asleep. Helen walks back and forth, feeling stable now, feeling calm. She's made some kind of peace, in her sleep. But with what?

Something about the blackout curtain bothers her, suddenly. It's heavy pink fabric, double-lined. She feels that if she were to flick it aside she'd see someone hiding there. But it's only the window, and darkness outside. She knows that.

With the child still on her shoulder, Helen walks to the window, draws it aside just a little. Not enough that the small lamp would put them in danger; there hasn't been an air raid recently anyway. She just has to see.

There's no moon tonight, and it's perfectly dark outside. She thinks she sees something, someone. She stands there looking out from a bedroom window, the same way she did when the men came to take Father away.

Father's not there now, but someone else is. A familiar silhouette. As her eyes adjust, it becomes clearer. The shape of the shoulders of the uniform, the fall of the trousers. But he still stands the way he always did. Not like a soldier at all. Like a boy with a message.

'George,' she whispers to the window.

Yes, comes his voice in her mind.

'Are you alive?'

No.

She knew it already. She saw him lying dead in the shared vision and she knew it was real, even though it had nothing to do with Ivy, or Kit, or Father. Maybe not even that region of France. The moment she opened herself up to the Sight, it showed her the one thing she wanted desperately to know.

For whatever reason, she is not surprised to learn that she is seeing her lover in the way women once saw shipwrecked sailors. Better to learn this way than through the dreaded telegram. She's glad, at least, that she found the strength to open her eyes, to look, so that George could visit.

Helen bounces the toddler a little, though Celia is still sleeping soundly. She speaks to the man who would have been her husband.

'Would you like to come in?'

CHAPTER 32

Kit

Teller brings Kit in separately, the next time. Her cheek is still raw, the cut healing ragged. He straps her to the chair and shows her a photograph of Ivy. It's hard to tell in black and white, but Ivy looks wet, her thin dress clinging to her. There's blood on Ivy's shoulder, in the photograph, and one eye is swollen shut.

Is this recent, or from whatever horrors they inflicted on Ivy in La Codre? She can't tell; she can't bring her mind's eye to see it. She wants it to be nothing but shapes on paper, not her sister at all. Her sister is raucous laughter, and a slight frown line between the brows, and passionate friendships and fleeting ambitions.

Kit swallows all the vicious words she wants to say. She won't give him even that. She won't say anything.

When the visions begin, she says Ivy's name in her mind, over and over. She sees nothing. Only a pale sky. Like grey stone. She turns herself to stone, like the nun's head she held in her hands, what seems like a lifetime ago. Only it wasn't a nun's head at all. It was just a woman in a wimple,

318

a woman who could have been a queen. Aelfgyva, who chose her own future.

Kit remains as still as stone, until Teller pulls the shackles off and orders her to stand up.

He doesn't cut her, this time. Instead, he puts her back in the cell. And then he starves her.

When she starts to realize what's happening, when the hunger caves in on itself and she feels no pain but can't stand up properly, she tells herself it's a blessing. A slower death than she would have wanted, but at least she can't be used against her will any more. But how can she die, and leave Ivy here alone?

She doesn't know how many days pass, but she is still alive when they push a bowl of broth through her door, and she does not even think. She pours it down her throat. Tears streaming down her cheeks. Then she retches it all up.

A few more cycles of this – days at a time – and Teller brings her back for more.

This time, she can't stop the visions. But they aren't much good to Teller. She sees Canadian soldiers walking in the ruins of La Codre, sees tricolour flags hanging from the window of her neighbour's flat in Paris.

'They're coming,' she says at last, the first words she's spoken in a fortnight, or more.

She speaks it in triumph, but Teller only smiles. 'Do you think we will leave Paris for them? There will be no Paris, now, thanks to you. It will be smoke and ashes. We are ready; the orders have come. All that remains is for me to choose the opportune moment. A demonstration the world will not forget.'

Kit isn't sure whether Evelyn is a vision or not, at first. She must be real, surely, because she's talking to the guard at the door to Kit's cell. The guards never talk to any of the other visions who stalk Kit's cell.

From where Kit is lying, on the cot in a corner, Evelyn seems incredibly tall, a giantess, a shadow cast by the sunset of the world. She's wearing a trim suit and smells of her usual perfume, created by a clever manufacturer a few years ago out of whatever he could find in a Paris warehouse when the shortages hit. She is made out of war, which is why Kit wanted to be with her; she was incorruptible because there was nothing in her to corrupt. A woman Kit wouldn't feel guilty for kissing.

Kit reaches out to Evelyn, to test whether she's real.

Evelyn reaches back.

'I think this scar will suit you,' she says. 'Your face was too perfect before.'

Kit grabs Evelyn's hand, holds all her fingers in a bundle. 'You're here,' she whispers. 'How? Have they got you too?'

Evelyn pulls Kit up to a sitting position, and then joins her on the cot, tucking one ankle behind the other. She's wearing lovely high-heeled shoes, but they're scuffed at the edges. Not even Evelyn can get everything; not any more.

'Teller and I are old friends. Since before the war. You know I used to work closely with the Ahnenerbe. When you met me, in Arabia. I knew him back then. I've kept all my contacts. How do you suppose I've been able to help people, all these years? Help you, with your letters and false papers? Keeping you out of the internment camp, for God's sake? It comes at a price, you know. And Teller has chosen this moment to collect.'

Despite the lightness in her voice, there are tight lines around Evelyn's mouth. Underneath the wartime perfume is a note of sweat. She's afraid, Kit realizes. She didn't know it was possible for Evelyn to be afraid. She tries to make sense of all the words Evelyn has said – so many words; she hasn't spoken to anyone in so long – but she can only understand the emotion. Evelyn is afraid; she is here, and she is afraid.

'Have they threatened you?'

Evelyn shrugs. 'Every conversation with a Nazi comes with a reward and a threat. I'm in no danger. I can take care of myself. It's you I'm worried about. You need to understand your situation.'

'I do understand it. I'm a prisoner. I don't know how much you know—'

'I know everything,' Evelyn interrupts her. 'I know about the letter your father sent you, years ago, telling you that he had a new theory about the tapestry. At the time, it seemed a good bargain. A useless, crackpot theory to exchange for whatever I needed at the time. Safety and comfort and another day drawing breath. I didn't think twice.'

Kit pulls her hands back, shrinks away from her. Her subconscious mind is faster than her thoughts. At least there aren't any drugs in her at the moment – one up-side of Teller leaving her to starve alone for days between sessions – but she's ill and in pain, and that makes everything else seem unreal. Her eyes see the cell floor, the painted concrete, the little drain. Her mind's eye sees Evelyn, digging into her dresser drawer, pulling out the letter, copying it down.

Betrayal.

Kit tries to speak, then coughs.

'Do you need water? I can ask for anything you need. Oh, Kit, you're so thin.'

She waves this away. 'You told the Germans about my father's letter? Why? Why would you do such a thing?'

'I've always had a good eye for what's valuable.' Evelyn's lip quivers, just for a moment, a crack in the façade. 'Men like Teller want to know everything about everything. He's rather brilliant, you know. He only asked that I pass along anything that touched on his areas of interest, and when I could find something that seemed to do no one any harm

– oh, don't look at me like that. I'm not a prostitute. I fell for you in the old-fashioned way. I really did. I loved you. More than you ever loved me.'

'Go to hell. Don't talk to me about love. You were spying on me. Get out. Get out of here!'

'No. I wasn't, really. Just passing along anything that seemed of interest, anything that seemed it wouldn't harm anyone, and might be something that would save a life. He just wanted to be informed about your movements, your projects at the Louvre. Until recently, both were very boring.'

'And passing along my private letters. God, Evelyn. Do you understand what you did? That must be how he learned there was a connection, between the tapestry and people like us – why he started studying it. Do you even know why we're here, my sister and I?'

Evelyn, for once, looks nervous. 'I know what I need to know. You're useful, Kit.' She puts a hand on Kit's leg, tentatively. The heat of it makes Kit's skin crawl, and a shudder runs through her leg. Evelyn lifts her hand, places it back in her lap as though she's putting away a tool or an instrument. She continues, in a reasonable tone, 'That's good, you know. Being useful is the best way to survive.'

'Some things are more important than survival.'

'No,' Evelyn says, her voice hoarse. 'Survival is the only thing there is. Everything else is a fairytale. Martyrs are not remembered by the dead. It's easy to die for a cause, but it doesn't help those who must keep going, after.'

She says it with such passion that Kit feels she's glimpsing Evelyn's true thoughts, for once, if she can even be sure what that is. If Evelyn even knows herself.

But when Evelyn goes on, in a lower voice, the spark has gone out of her eyes. 'Teller wants me to persuade you to cooperate. And I do think you should. But what he isn't telling you is that he's disobeyed Reichsführer Himmler's orders to bring the tapestry, and you and your sister, straight to Germany.'

'So we *are* still in France. I thought so.'

She has come to believe in her visions, but all the same it feels comforting to have them confirmed. She hasn't seen daylight in weeks; her world is one of humming electric lights and booted footsteps, and sometimes it seems impossible that anything else exists, anywhere.

'Yes,' Evelyn confirms. 'We are in France. Teller moved the tapestry east, past Paris, but stopped here, before the border, because he wants to use you and the tapestry to stop the invasion. He's put Himmler off with excuses about safety, about the condition of the tapestry, about you or Ivy being injured – I don't know what else. He wants to prove that he can still win the war. Here with you, with whatever work you're doing. Do you think that he can?'

Kit says nothing. Even if she knew the answer to that, she wouldn't tell Evelyn.

After a moment, Evelyn carries on. 'Kit, everyone is saying the Allies can't be kept at bay forever. They'll take all of France eventually. Slowing them down only means more cities and towns bombed. More people dead. For what?'

Evelyn has always had a way of talking that makes Kit want to agree – or to accept that she already does. She tries her best to resist this, through the haze of pain and fear. Tries to dig down to Evelyn's real goal.

'You're telling me not to cooperate, then? What a coincidence. That was already my plan. Thank you for coming, Evelyn. Lovely to see you.'

'Come off it, Kit. I'm telling you what you need to know. Himmler will send his own men for the tapestry, and soon. All you have to do is stay alive until he does. And then you'll be away from France, safe in Germany. Himmler wants to make peace with the Allies; most of them do, you know.

There was an attempt on Hitler's life last month, a coup that very nearly succeeded. Even those loyal to him have lost their appetite for war. We must think now about what comes after.'

'I think about that every day, and in those fantasies, let me tell you, I am never in Himmler's castle.'

'It will be safe there, after the war. The Allies will leave Germany alone, I'm sure. And you'll be able to carry on with your research. Real research, not your little monographs that no one will ever read, but something exciting, with the tapestry. So you see, there's no point in going down as a martyr now. Trying to force Teller's hand. He told me that he had to hurt you, that he might have to hurt you more, to get Ivy to cooperate. He says Ivy is more valuable to him. But obviously I do not feel the same.'

It's hard to believe that Evelyn's gaze means anything other than adoration for Kit, but Kit sees through it now. She sees another Evelyn, an angry and worried Evelyn, an Evelyn who does not want to be alone and does not know how to be otherwise. An Evelyn who doesn't know what it means to be alive.

'You're right about one thing,' Kit says, her voice sounding weaker than she feels. 'If I stay alive, I will be safe, because the Allies will come for the tapestry. Soon.'

'Nobody knows where it is!' Evelyn snaps. 'Everyone at the Louvre thinks it's there, in the basement. The paperwork says so. And God knows, paperwork is reality. Nobody knows where it is, where you are. Nobody is coming here, not until it's all over.'

Kit shrugs. 'Then the sooner it's all over, the better.'

As she says it, she feels that there's something false, something wrong. Not a lie; for once Evelyn is telling the truth. It's not anything she can see or hear or smell, just a certainty. Someone is coming. Someone does know where she is.

Kit closes her eyes, and when Evelyn starts to speak, Kit

puts her hand to her lips to shush her. She needs to concentrate, to understand.

Max.

Max's face, half-turned on the motorcycle. Her face when she loaded her gun in Argentan. Her face on the street opposite Kit's flat, serious and anxious. Max's face, that night she tried to tell Kit she loved her, that night Kit should have had the courage to listen. Max always did listen to Kit: when Kit was telling her about her plans to go to Edinburgh to study, or ten years before that, about the rock Kit found on the beach at Brighton that she was convinced was a fossil. A thousand other moments, a thousand movements of those dark eyebrows, that wry mouth. The curve of the cheek and the pinch near the end of her nose.

Max, looking into her eyes, grinning at her. Max is on her way.

Kit starts to laugh. She laughs so hard she knows Ivy can hear her.

She laughs with her eyes shut, so that all she can see is Max's face, and she knows Ivy can see it too. What a relief and a joy to be rid of language at last, to tell her sister everything she needs to know. To hide nothing, and be afraid of nothing. To stop being afraid of herself.

If there were words for what Kit shares with Ivy, they would be:

Don't worry.

She's coming.

Get ready.

Kit doesn't stop until she retches, and she doesn't stop even then, until the guard opens the door, wondering what's going on. Evelyn's face is stricken.

'I think she's gone mad,' Evelyn says. 'I think she needs a doctor.'

Kit's doubled over, still sitting on the cot, but through a

curtain of her own hair she watches the guard saunter over. A boy in a uniform. As he bends down to look at Kit, his nose wrinkles because she's vomited on the floor.

Kit stands up, fast, head-butting the guard as she does so.

He goes down, right in the vomit. Kit's knee is on his chest and her hand searches for his gun. She doesn't hesitate. One shot into the temple, and he's gone. All the fear and hatred and love has left his eyes before the sound of the shot stops ringing. Kit's hand is shaking. She's shot a gun before; it was Evelyn who taught her, back in Arabia. She's never killed. Not until now.

The silence after the gunshot cannot last. They'll come. It's a matter of seconds.

Kit turns the gun on Evelyn. She's two feet away; close enough to try to grab the gun. So close that it's hard for Kit to focus on anything, even if her head weren't ringing from the blow she just gave the guard. So she looks at Evelyn's hands, the hands that have touched every part of her. The cheek that she has kissed with morning tea. The eyes that have seen her trying not to cry, on the days when the war got to her. The hair spread out on her pillow.

Evelyn sent the man of nightmares after Ivy.

They stand facing each other like two rivals in a duel, and they exchange some kind of understanding between them, a eulogy for the past and the future. How pitiful and grasping Evelyn is. How much harm she has done through her cowardice. But she doesn't have any hold over the Sharp sisters any more; she doesn't know anything the SS doesn't know already. Maybe Kit ought to shoot her anyway – it's more mercy than the Resistance would show her – but her finger can't seem to pull the trigger for a second time.

There's commotion outside, but the footsteps aren't running into Kit's cell, but past it. She catches bits and pieces of what the men are yelling, about numbers and weapons, something about a fire.

'I think you'll have to go to Himmler's castle without me,' Kit says.

It's difficult to see anything clearly, when she's alone, and not in the same room as the tapestry. The next few minutes are a crowd of possibilities. Kit sees a door like the one to her own cell, shut; she sees her own hand pressing it. A locked door.

She searches the guard again, his body still warm, and finds the key. The key to her own cell and, she hopes, Ivy's.

And now what? Patience, she tells herself, calming her breath. Gives herself time to listen to her own instincts. It feels like stepping off a cliff, but it isn't. It's just one step in front of the other.

It's good luck that the door to Kit's cell opens into a short, out-of-the-way passage where she can see the main corridor, full of noise and motion. She had no idea how many people were stationed in this fortress, or even how big it is. Her visions have given her the impression that this is only part of a series of fortifications, but when she tries to see the whole, or get a sense of the people within, everything goes hazy.

The only thing clear in her mind now is Ivy.

Her sister is in two places at once; it's an odd sensation, but Kit is certain of it. Ivy is up on the third floor of the fortress, halfway out a window, with a door locked behind her, and a grenade in her hand. Testing Teller's orders not to shoot her, while the soldiers watching her from the ground feel their own lives are at stake.

But Ivy is also in her cell. Kit follows that certainty like a thread in a labyrinth, choosing to trust it, because it's the less impossible scenario of the two. It takes what feels like hours, sneaking down passageways, waiting for the moments when no one is watching. Kit has never had to trust her instincts this much, and it's enervating, like groping through an unfamiliar house in the dark, all her senses vigilant.

When she gets to the right door, there is no guard near it. Another piece of good luck. She fumbles with the key she took off the guard.

An explosion, somewhere close, sends her reeling against the wall of the corridor. Surely this can't be the Allies attacking? She hadn't thought they were this far east yet.

When the door swings open, her heart falls. Ivy is there, lying on the floor, her upper body splayed against the wall. Her eyes are staring, unblinking.

No, Kit thinks, and runs to her sister, falling at her feet. She says Ivy's name, in her head or aloud; she can't say which.

And slowly, slowly, Ivy turns and focuses on her, though her gaze is unsteady and her head lolls as if she has lost the strength to hold it up.

'It's time to go,' Kit urges her, putting one arm under her sister and trying to lift her. 'There's something happening – did you hear that? Some attack. I think it's Max, though how or why—'

'Of course it's Max,' Ivy says. 'They've tried to kill me now. In the other room. They know I'm not real there. They're coming.'

She strains to stand up, and with Kit's help she gets to her feet. It's a slow walk out to the corridor, excruciating with every second. When they reach a fork, Kit can hear the men running towards them. She steers Ivy the other way, urging her onwards, swearing under her breath.

Ivy digs in her heels. 'No,' Ivy says. 'We have to go the other way.'

'We can't. It isn't safe.'

'They'll be dead in a moment.'

She says it with such cold certainty that Kit hesitates, and then she hears someone coming from the direction they're headed. They're caught. Is Evelyn in one of those groups, yelling orders, telling them that Kit is free?

She couldn't bring herself to shoot Evelyn; she seemed to pose no threat now that she had no more secrets to betray, and Kit is no murderer. She let Evelyn run, let her seek out a hole somewhere to survive in. Maybe it was the wrong choice.

Nothing for it now but to trust in Ivy.

Kit follows her sister towards the shouting and the gunfire. Down a corridor, towards a bend near what looks like the front wall of the fortress. There's a small window there, the first one she's seen here, that she can recall. At least before the end she'll see sunlight. At least they'll face whatever comes together—

They are thrown backwards, and Kit can't hear anything. Just ringing. Dust and chunks of stone are falling on them from the walls and ceilings, and there's a terrible roar like an earthquake, and then the light changes as if a great sea has swept away the humming electric lights and replaced them with clear daylight.

The wall in front of them is ripped in half, the result of whatever explosive is still ringing in Kit's ears. Ivy limps towards it, and Kit follows her, hearing groans from a pile of rubble nearby.

They clamber out over the pile of stone and into the world. Not pausing to think, to look behind them, just walking as fast as they can in these broken bodies towards freedom. In front of them is a grassy area, with a few trees, and the trees get thicker beyond. They can be safe there, maybe. They can hide.

A German army truck comes growling towards them and

Kit pulls Ivy down, on to the pile of stone, bruising and scraping them both. It's no good, though. They must have been seen. The truck stops. There are four figures in the cargo bed, with guns.

She thinks she hears Max's voice, telling her to run. But there's nowhere to go, just the broken fortress behind them, which seems to stretch beyond her sight in both directions, and the truck in front of them.

'Kit!'

It *is* Max's voice. Surely this is real? Kit focuses on the waving figure in the cargo bed of the truck. Despite the coveralls and the wool cap, despite the Sten gun in her hand, it's Max.

Max leans over the railing in the back and screams at her. 'Come on, get in, you ninnies!'

Kit obeys, choking on what might be laughter, or sobs, or just stone dust and unexpected hope. She helps Ivy up into the back and then climbs up after her. There's a large crate in the back, which takes up half the cargo bed. Behind it, Max and three other people are hanging on to the metal ribs that stretch over the bed, that would hold up a canvas cover if there was one.

A young woman doesn't bother even nodding at Kit, and neither does a teenage boy who looks familiar. They're both standing on watch, guns at the ready.

But the other person is, to Kit's delight and relief, Lucienne. Lucienne helps Ivy to a seat on the plank bench.

As the truck lurches into motion, Kit wraps her arms around Max, holding on to her like a drowning woman.

'Ssh. You're all right, both of you, now,' Max says.

'But the tapestry,' Kit says. 'They've got it.'

As she says it, she knows it's wrong. She feels it, there in the crate, loaded into the truck behind Max. Max's face is triumphant.

'You got it,' Kit whispers, staring at Max. 'You took it from them. How?'

'A few explosives followed by a gun to the head does wonders,' Lucienne answers.

'I can't believe it,' Kit says, marvelling. 'I can't believe you managed this.'

'Oh, this is just the beginning,' Max says, and winks. 'Wait until you see what's happening in Paris.'

Kit falls on to her behind on the plank that serves as a bench in the back of the truck, next to Ivy. Lucienne and the other two stay standing, and now Kit recognizes the boy from the farmhouse.

There's blood on Kit's loose, prison-issue dress, and she realizes it's coming from her right palm. She spreads her hands out to see the damage. Several filthy gashes, but nothing too serious.

Max, sitting beside her, takes each of Kit's hands in her own. She bends her head, her dark curls falling forward. She kisses the right palm, right in the centre, despite the blood and grime. Then the left palm, a kiss on skin that has never been kissed before. Max leaves her face in Kit's hand for a moment, and Kit feels everything there is to feel, lets it wash her, lets it wash everything. She doesn't care that they aren't alone, that everyone can see how they feel. It's only one long, shuddering breath, but, by the end of it, Kit knows that the part of herself that she's kept locked and bolted all these years has been blasted open by this goddamned war. She has been living too long as unexploded ordnance. There is nothing left now to tiptoe around, no frightening change of feelings to avoid. It's already happened to them, whatever comes next.

She catches Lucienne looking at her, with an expression more compassionate than any Kit might have expected her to keep in her arsenal.

But the older woman only says, 'Keep your eyes out, and you'll find pistols under the bench. We might not be through the worst of it yet.' She looks away. 'And you'll find a first-aid kit for those hands under there too.'

CHAPTER 33

Kit

They drive fast on back roads, taking frequent turns that throw Kit into Max or into the railing. She can't say which of them chose to sit just a little closer to the other than necessary, but they stay that way, the nearness an acknowledgement of the unspoken. Kit never wants to be further from her than this.

'Don't worry,' Max says after a turn that presses Kit against her. 'Étienne is the best driver I know. And he grew up here in Picardy. He's taking us to a safe house, once we're sure we haven't been followed.'

'No,' Ivy says, her face pale. 'You have to take the tapestry to the Louvre.'

'The Louvre!' Max is astonished. 'Ivy, surely that's exactly where they'll look. Most of the Louvre staff already think that it's there. Whoever took you and the tapestry out here will expect you to take it there, won't he?'

She leaves a pause. Kit doesn't want to say his name ever again, if she can help it. But he's still out there, and he won't give up easily. He can sniff them out like a bloodhound.

'Oberführer Teller,' Kit says. 'He's in the Ahnenerbe, in the SS. He'll be following us, or his men will. He has the same sorts of talents that Ivy and I have, and he knows us well now. That means they'll pick up our trail quickly, no matter where we go. We have no chance of hiding it.'

Max considers this and doesn't ask about it further. 'But he's not our only problem. Himmler's instructed an SS team to get the tapestry out of France.'

'How do you know what Himmler's up to?' Kit asks.

'I got a message from England,' Max explains. 'Through a wireless operator. They intercepted instructions from Himmler to Carl Oberg. The message says, "Move the tapestry to a place of safety." We weren't sure we would beat them to St Quentin. We thought you might already be gone by the time we got there.'

Carl Oberg. The head of the SS in France.

Kit frowns. 'When did Himmler send this message?'

'August 18th. Three days ago. The same day the uprising began, so I suppose they've been busy. But once the SS learns the tapestry is at large, surely Oberg will make that his priority, given Himmler's instructions.'

Ivy interrupts, her voice stern and impatient. She looks exhausted. 'If you take us to the safe house, Teller will find us, kill us, and take the tapestry far from France. I know he will. I can see it. Kit, can't you see it?'

Her sister's gaze is hard and terrible. Kit can't see anything now, here in the open, with the wind drawing tears from her eyes. Despite the tapestry being so close, there in the crate. Perhaps she doesn't want to. She's spent long enough in that unseen world; she wants to be here, with Max's knee an inch from her own, with the hard reality of wood and metal saving them from those unrelenting white walls, and the shadow people that stain them.

'If you see it, Ivy, that's good enough for me,' she says at last. 'But is there anywhere other than the Louvre?'

'We have to go there,' Ivy insists. 'It will be safe if we go there.'

Max looks troubled. She believes in Ivy's visions; she believed in them before Kit did. But she clearly isn't convinced by her argument. 'And what about you?' Max demands. 'Will *you* be safe? Both of you? Can you tell me that?'

Ivy looks away, saying nothing.

Max sighs and then shoots a questioning glance at Kit.

But it's Lucienne who speaks next, in her dry, pragmatic way. 'I say Paris is the best place for it. It's going to be free of fascists in a day or two.'

Kit gasps. 'What, really? Are the Allies that close?'

'Not yet. Some say they're not coming, that they're going past the city to Germany. But if they don't come soon they'll find that Paris has liberated itself, which will be embarrassing for Eisenhower.' A twitch of Lucienne's mouth suggests she likes the prospect. 'The police turned against the occupiers a few days ago, finally, and the German bureaucrats have been fleeing the city like rats. The French fascists are pissing themselves in fear, as they should.'

Jean-Pierre sniggers, his admiration for Lucienne written all over his young face.

'But the army's still there,' Max says. 'If we drive the tapestry into Paris, we're driving it into a war zone. The fascists may talk of a ceasefire, but it's a ruse.'

'All of France is a war zone,' Lucienne retorts. 'And the remaining Nazis will be so busy saving their own skins, in and around Paris, that they won't bother with us. The basement of the Louvre is a safer place than most, all things considered. If we can get it there.'

And that's it: the decision is made. Max bangs on the side

of the truck to tell the driver to stop, and she hops out to tell him the new plan. The rest of them spend the next three hours gazing at the dusty road behind them, waiting for pursuers to appear.

Ivy and Kit take turns changing into clothing that Max brought them, with Max and Lucienne holding up a coat around them to make a screen. It isn't easy getting dressed in the back of a moving truck, but soon they're both wearing trousers and tops, with cardigans. The first proper clothing they've worn in weeks.

Max gives them each a pistol, and Ivy looks at it with an appraising eye, and holds it in her lap.

Lucienne makes a plan for what to do if they encounter a checkpoint, a plan that involves a lot of shooting and hoping for the best. But they are never stopped. On the outskirts of the city, any German soldiers they see just wave them through, if they acknowledge them at all. The soldiers all seem to be on the move, or about to move. They stand around tanks or hang off the backs of trucks. One more apparently German truck isn't something any of them have the stomach to check out, it seems.

Deeper into the city, they hear gunfire, from different directions, like storms converging.

Tricolour flags hang from windows and lampposts, many of them home-made out of dyed sheets. On the pavement, there are people walking with purpose but without destination, carrying weapons openly. Kit catches the gaze of two young women who pass by, in shorts, bare-legged, holding Sten guns at their hips.

Kit smiles. She wants to shout, to dance, to throw a grenade, to climb on to something and wave a flag. She leans across the bed of the truck and takes Ivy's hand, and feels her there with her, solid and alive. She smiles at her, and Ivy's smile in response is damaged but genuine.

The truck slows and comes to a groaning stop, and Kit's heart stops with it. Is it a checkpoint after all? She stands and peers over the tapestry crate, over the front of the truck. No soldiers. Just women and children, in the street. They're prying up paving stones with pickaxes and piling up furniture.

They're making a barricade.

Lucienne and Max both hop down and walk over to talk to one of the women. After a few moments, Lucienne picks up a small bucket of paint and a brush and walks back to the truck. Kit can just make out what she paints on each olive-green door, in dripping white: the letters FFI.

'French Forces of the Interior,' Max says, with a little smile, as she takes her place beside Kit again. 'To show everyone that this truck has been commandeered. We're entering Resistance territory now.'

But, as they take a meandering path to avoid the barricades, they soon find that the battle lines are drawn street by street.

'The people at the barricade said that Dietrich von Choltitz, the new commander of Paris, is still entrenched in his headquarters at the Hôtel Meurice,' Max tells Kit quietly as the truck grinds its way down an alley. 'Just down the street from the Louvre. So we can't hope to avoid a lot of soldiers being in the area. But the good news is, on this side of the Louvre, the Rue de Rivoli is in Resistance hands. We might be able to get there without ever encountering any Wehrmacht.'

As the truck approaches the Canal Saint-Martin, though, Kit gets an uneasy feeling. Everything is too quiet; there's one rat-a-tat of gunfire, but she can't see where it's coming from. Then a loud boom of artillery.

She urges the driver on with her mind. *Don't stop here; we're sitting ducks.*

The bridge is in front of them. A little bridge, just over the canal.

Kit looks at Ivy to see if she shares her unease, but her sister has her eyes closed, one hand hanging on to one of the steel ribs over the cargo bed.

Max climbs up on the railing, and then over on to the side. She's clinging to the steel ribs, and she knocks on the window. Then she yells, 'Don't stop here. We're sitting ducks. Go around, to the left, to where the canal is covered over. We can't risk crossing at a bridge.'

Then she's back in the cargo bed, her light jacket swinging with her stride, the lapels hanging open. She has a pistol at her waist.

Giving Max an arm to help her back on to her seat, Kit doesn't bother asking why she said it in those exact words. She holds Max's arm for a little longer than necessary, to steady her as the truck backs up.

It takes long minutes, but Étienne, the driver seems to finally find an open street to take them west into the heart of Paris. With each yard, though, the gunfire grows louder, a great scattered symphony of it. It's a narrow street, lined with apartment blocks, and Kit catches sight of some silhouettes on the rooftops: snipers, watching for German soldiers out in the square ahead. *Crack crack crack.*

'Damn it,' Max says under her breath. She's moving a leg, up and down, restlessly.

They have to find a way through. Kit closes her eyes, like Ivy, and tries to picture the map of Paris, but she sees nothing, and closing her eyes just makes her feel imprisoned, swallowed up. She wants to see.

Without giving herself or anyone else time to talk her out of it, she sticks her pistol into her belt and scrambles up on to the crate that holds the tapestry.

'Get down,' Lucienne hisses, but Kit ignores her. She

crouches on top of the crate, keeping her head down, and stares into the open ground of the Place de la République, which is still festooned with swastikas.

Several tanks sit there, guns firing. Kit can see a truck beside the statue at its centre of the square, and can make out the helmets of soldiers using it as cover. There's no barricade between this street and the square, but there is a sniper on the ground, lying on his stomach, shooting towards the army position.

With a shriek, a shot ricochets off the pavement beside him, but the man doesn't move; he keeps firing. There are a few others, kneeling closer to the buildings and firing in the same direction: a black man with grey stubble on his thin jaw and a loose shirt that looks as if it fitted him better before rationing; a white woman wearing a yellow print dress with one bloody knee; a boy not old enough to join the war in any way but this, in a flat cap. They all look so ordinary, but they hold their guns like extensions of themselves.

A roar out of nowhere; Kit can't see where it's coming from. She twists and sees a truck roll past on the intersection behind them. It looks a lot like the one Kit and her friends are in, but this one has German troops in the back.

Max, Lucienne and Jean-Pierre are already shooting at them; Jean-Pierre looks more like a child than ever, with a gun in his hand, but his jaw is set. He's seconds away from a bullet ripping into him, taking his life. Kit can see it, her fears so close that they're visible, but she can't tell whether it's the Sight or just normal anxiety.

At a sign from Max she goes flat on the tapestry, yells at Ivy to get down, but Ivy doesn't move. A shot rings off some part of the truck. Kit draws her pistol and shoots, but she's a terrible shot and her hands are shaking. All the same, one of the Germans grabs his chest and tumbles out of the truck, shot by Max or by one of the people on the rooftops. Up in a window, an old woman aims her gun at the Germans, but the Germans aim back, and Kit pleads with God or fate or someone that the bullet won't find its target.

A sound like an axe-thwack makes the crate under Kit shudder. Her hand is stinging; she looks down and sees a long splinter embedded in it. The corner of the crate has a fresh bullet wound, the pale wood poking out in all directions.

And they're cut off. In front of them, the Place de la République with its tanks; behind them, a truck full of Wehrmacht soldiers.

The tapestry is not safe here; the Germans will destroy it if they don't take it. She lies flat on it, holding on to the edge as if she can somehow protect it with her body. Then someone takes her hand and Kit looks up to see Ivy in front of her, staring into her eyes. With her other hand on the crate, Ivy whispers, 'They'll look behind them and see something. What do they see, Kit? Help me; I can't see anything but *him*.'

How she would take that vision from her if she could. Kit doesn't see Teller, doesn't feel him, and she knows what a mercy that is. She doesn't share Ivy's connection with him, or Ivy's ability to make the world see her imaginings. It is not something Kit understands, or wants. Kit sees only the past and the present, only the things that have happened.

What arrogance, she hears in her mind, and realizes with a start that it's Aunt Kathleen's voice, those Glaswegian vowels blowing through Kit's thoughts like a cold wind. *What pride, to believe that what you see in the past is all anyone might find there, to believe that the present is something you can reach out and touch. Haven't you learned enough humility by now to keep an open mind? You and your father, two peas in a pod.*

Father will be broken if the tapestry is lost. If Ivy doesn't come home to him. That future is too painful to accept, and she doesn't have to accept it. The future is being made right now, here. With her eyes closed, Kit clears her mind. She thinks of the tapestry, inches below her, and the women who foresaw the invasion and harrowing of Britain, who chose which parts to tell and which to keep secret. How much of that future did they make? What futures did they unmake?

Crack crack crack.

'What do they see, Kit?' Ivy asks, her voice singsong, as if she's a child playing a game.

Kit screws her eyes tighter shut. She sees it: ordinary women, in sundresses, and ordinary men in loose torn shirts, rising on a beast painted in the colours of war.

'The Resistance has stolen a tank,' Kit answers her. 'They see a tank behind them.'

Ivy's hand grips hers harder.

The German truck starts moving. The troops keep shooting as it goes, but within moments it's past. Kit turns and looks into the street ahead of them to see whether the people there are all right. To her joy, she sees the three people emerge from alcoves and doorways to retake their places: the boy, the woman, the man. They turn and start firing into the square as if nothing has happened. In the square, a tank's on fire; someone in the Resistance had thrown a well-aimed petrol bomb.

The sniper who was lying in the street is still there, perfectly still. Too still. There's a shout, and two women run towards him holding a white flag with a red cross. To treat his wounds, Kit thinks, and maybe they do too, but when they get there and turn him over there's no life in him. They pull his gun off him briskly and hold it out like an offering; a man runs to take it from them, to use in the fight.

'We need to go further south,' Ivy says to Max, with

great certainty in her voice. 'Now, before more of them come.'

Max nods and goes out to relay the message to Étienne, while Kit climbs down and sits on the bench, ignoring Lucienne's glare.

She hasn't asked what happened to Lucienne after the Germans came to the farmhouse, but now she sees flashes of it: a prisoner shot, Lucienne turning her head. Kit glances away, not wanting to intrude, not knowing how much strength she has to see someone else's pain today. Not like her sister, who seems capable of absorbing every terrible thing and then sending it back out into the world a hundred-fold.

When Ivy takes her place on the bench, she sits very still. Her eyes are open now, but her hands are in her lap, and she looks like a well-behaved student waiting for an exam. But she's alive, and they're all alive, and the tapestry is still safe in their hands.

They creep through the narrowest streets they can find, the ones not big enough to merit barricades or Nazi positions. Every time they pass a tricolour made of dyed bedsheets, Kit's heart lifts.

Change in the air, electric as a coming storm. The fascists are going to lose.

As if to prove her intuition right, the truck turns into the Rue de Rivoli and they see a long line of barricades, one at every intersection, some made of sandbags, some of felled trees, some of bricks, stones and furniture. At every one, the citizens of Paris stand with their guns pointed west.

Lucienne hops out again and walks down the line, until they lose sight of her.

'Every fascist in this city is going to be focused on saving his own skin today,' Max says, filling the silence. 'Maybe they won't bother with the tapestry.'

'They'll come,' Ivy says. 'They're already on their way. We have to get there first, before they do.'

Kit reaches over and takes her hand, tries to see what she's seeing, but her mind's eye sees only what's around her. 'Who's coming?'

'Oberg's men. He contacted Teller two hours ago to advise him he was on his way, this morning, but Teller told them to go to the Louvre as fast as they could, to stop us, to wait for him there.'

'How many?' Max asks sharply. 'Where are they now?'

Ivy shrugs. 'I didn't see that part.'

'But you saw Teller talking to Oberg?' Max asks, awe in her voice.

'In a way. He's always with me now,' Ivy says, looking away. 'I've been trying to keep an eye on him, while we drove.'

'We should find another place to hide it, for now,' Max says.

Kit shakes her head. 'If Ivy can see him, he can see her. There's no hiding. All we can do is try to get there as fast as we can. What the hell is Lucienne up to?'

Lucienne, already walking back towards them, heaves a long breath and then leans against the side of the truck. She's tired, Kit realizes; she's in ill health. 'The Resistance holds the Rue de Rivoli for perhaps a few hundred metres past the Hotel de Ville,' Lucienne explains. 'But after that there's a no man's land between the Resistance and the Nazis, who are entrenched around the Hôtel Meurice. The Louvre is in the middle of that no man's land.'

Étienne pokes his head out of the window, and Kit gets her first glimpse of him: a round-faced man, with hard lines on his face, too old to be shipped off to a factory to work.

'We can't get past these barricades,' he says. 'Should we go down along the river?'

Lucienne looks at Ivy, who nods, and she relays this to Lucienne.

The truck turns left, straight towards Notre-Dame cathedral, then right along the Seine.

One moment and then another, Kit thinks. No time to waste. Try to forget that the SS are heading towards the same spot. Get the tapestry into the museum, by hook or by crook. Once it's inside, Kit thinks she can hide it well enough, even in an almost empty museum, to at least slow down the searchers. She knows the little rooms down in the basement where they won't find it easily, at least not until Teller arrives to help. All she has to do is hold the SS at bay until Paris is free – not even that long. Just until freedom creeps far enough up the Rue de Rivoli.

On the Seine, there are no boats. When the east façade of the Louvre comes into view, Kit gets up and bangs on the window, gestures for Étienne to turn into the first entrance from the south side.

This is a narrow postern entrance, but it's wide enough to admit trucks; Kit knows this because she watched the convoy of trucks leaving through it in 1939, loaded with rolled-up paintings and crated sculptures. Someone has left the heavy doors open, as though they're expected, but there could be a million reasons why they're open. Especially today. Kit looks up, searches for the tricolour, but doesn't see it anywhere here. Jaujard's priority would be the few remaining pieces in the museum, and the people who work here; he wouldn't poke the Nazis in the eye for no purpose, not until he was sure the museum was beyond their reach.

Through the passage and into the square internal courtyard at the heart of the Louvre, bounded by enormous palace wings on all four sides.

There's no one there. Kit should feel relieved, but it unsettles her. With guns or without, German or French – no one at all. She has never seen this gleaming grey courtyard completely empty. Everyone in Paris is either holding a gun or hiding; there is no way to simply *exist* anywhere in Paris today. And, though they can hear the fighting, it is not close; Kit thinks even the Rue de Rivoli, on the far side of the museum from where they came in, must be quiet at the moment. No incursions into the no man's land.

The iron lampposts are dwarfed by the four wings of the museum all around them, the imposing walls of what was once an impossibly big palace. The truck lumbers towards the central wing on the east side of the square courtyard, where there's a door. She tries to get a sense of whether there's anyone inside, and finally her Sight seems to help her; she's certain there is. Probably Jaujard and at least a few others, here to keep watch on the remaining treasures and the building itself, to safeguard it from whatever comes.

Kit's feet hit the flagstones with shin-splitting speed before the truck comes to a halt.

'I'll get someone to come and unload it!' she yells. 'They'll listen to me. They'll hurry. You keep watch. Max, keep an eye on Ivy.'

One step, and another. A sense of being watched. The postern door screaming on its hinges. Slowly, despairingly, she stops and turns.

From every cranny of the old palace, uniformed figures step out, holding rifles.

They're surrounded, trapped in the square courtyard. A dozen SS men, at least.

Lucienne, Max and Jean-Pierre have their pistols pointed in three directions, but the moment one of them shoots, they'll have bullets coming their way from several more.

Whatever it is that one of the SS men shouts, in French, it does not penetrate Kit's consciousness. The words bounce off the walls of the Louvre, ring all around the courtyard, and fade. All she can think about is that some of them will die in the next minute, hour, day. Max, or Ivy, or Lucienne, or young Jean-Pierre, or, Étienne. Let it be Kit herself, and only her.

But praying doesn't stop Ivy from walking towards the truck, with her arms spread wide, her little pink cardigan stretched like fairy wings. The men point their guns at her. Then suddenly the ground beneath them changes.

Kit thinks it's snow, at first. Snow in August. The flagstones of the Louvre courtyard go white, covered in some sort of film. But then, from underneath that film, shapes rise up. Uneven, lumpy, unmistakable.

Corpses. They are standing in a field of corpses, laid row on row. There is a head between Kit's feet and she freezes, not wanting to move for fear that she'll trip and fall on them. She can see the noses poking up beneath the winding sheets, the crossed arms. Some are children.

It's clear that the SS men are seeing it too. They look all around, start moving to try to free themselves from the nightmare. One of them trips, and falls, and that seems to be enough for the others. They start firing at the bodies, ripping holes in the winding sheets, defiling the corpses.

But there is no blood where they shoot. Instead, blood blooms like shadows on their own grey-green uniforms. The guns jump out of their hands and fall, right through the bodies and clatter on the stones. One is still going off.

Max and Ivy are still standing. Kit focuses all her energy on Ivy, trying to help her maintain this. She tries to see what Ivy sees; tries to tell Ivy a story so that Ivy can tell that story to the world. The story is an accusation, and the charge is murder. These men have killed, adults and children, and they have sent more to their deaths. Let them see it all at once. Let them stop pretending that their present exists separate from their past. Let them reach out and touch their futures.

The men whose uniforms are dark with blood clasp their

hands behind their backs, as if they've tied themselves to poles, and they back up a little, postures ramrod-straight. They've closed their eyes. They've met their executioner, though within or without reality Kit isn't sure. She tries to get inside the vision, to keep it real for them, to do with her mind what she would do with a weapon given half a chance. She keeps her eyes open but stands straight, ready for judgment. Let judgment come.

Ivy steps forward, and catches her toe on something. A stone, a body, nothing at all. She falters.

Kit knows what the soldier is going to do before he does it. There's a break in his vision and he's confused, terrified. The gun is not far. There on the ground. All he has to do is reach for it . . .

By the time he opens his eyes, Kit is running at him. She sees the hollow of his cheek, a cut where he shaved. He's young. He's going to kill her sister. She can see it, thirty seconds ahead: the gun in his boyish hands, Ivy's rib cage shattered, red blood on the pink cardigan.

So she runs at him, to make him turn the gun on her instead.

Two short raps come from the right and the soldier falls back, his gaze skyward. Max is running too, her pistol in her hand.

Ivy's illusion is losing its grip on the soldiers' minds. The blood fades from the soldiers' chests and they're alive again, scrambling for their guns. One of them picks up a long gun and whacks Max on the head with it as she's running at him. Max goes down.

But the corpses are still there, as solid as the truck and the boots and the guns. When Max falls into them, they wake up.

Kit is screaming. *Max, Max!* But her cry is lost in the noise of a thousand people getting to their feet.

They're standing, now, and their winding sheets are

flying into the wind, away from them. They have guns in their hands. Sten guns and pistols. The guns go off, a cannonade of small arms echoing in that vast place. The soldiers turn wildly, trying to see what is real and what isn't.

One of the SS men rushes at Ivy, finally realizing where the danger lies. He has no gun but he grabs her and she grabs him, pulling at his clothing, trying to get him out of her way.

Kit draws her pistol. She doesn't need steady hands. All she needs is to see a future in which the bullet goes into the soldier's throat, and make that future real. There's a spray of blood as he falls. The pavement around her is bare, dry, ordinary stone. She looks back at Ivy.

Ivy is stumbling backwards, into a mist, which is all that's left of the fighters she conjured. They're gone.

Or, almost gone. A small group of fighters is still there. Not illusions at all, but Resistance, come to their aid. Their guns are still pointing at the soldiers. One of the bullets hits and another Nazi goes down, in a very real way, with a bullet between his eyes. *Crack crack crack.* A last fusillade and then the courtyard is free of living Nazis.

Kit has never been more afraid than in those few steps towards the shape lying on the ground, alone, the pavement around her marked only with her own blood.

She puts her hand on Max's shoulder and nearly weeps with joy. The lift and fall of Max's breath.

Max rolls over of her own accord. There's a gash in her forehead, but her eyes are focused and her breath steady. Kit would kiss her, if she had the right.

'I'm all right, Kit.'

Kit sits with her for a moment while Max gets her bearings.

'They're gone,' Kit says.

Then she feels it, another absence, a wrong absence. She's up on her feet, looking, before Max speaks.

'Where's Ivy?'

CHAPTER 34

Ivy

Nobody bothers Ivy as she walks down the Rue de Rivoli. Past the tanks in the Tuileries Gardens, across the bare street. Past the guardhouses, where the soldiers glance at her without turning their heads. To their eyes, she is wearing a German uniform; she is one of the Wehrmacht auxiliaries, and she works at a telephone desk inside the Hôtel Meurice. They recognize her. They have no reason to fear her.

There are several things about the lobby of the Hôtel Meurice that rattle her. First, there's the marble everywhere, on the floor, and the pillars. The glass everywhere: chandeliers, mirrors. She's been so long confined by white walls that all this dazzle makes her jumpy.

Besides, it's full of people.

Ivy had the impression, from Lucienne's confidence, that the Germans were on the run, that only an unfortunate, doomed rump is left behind in Paris to face the Allies. But, whatever the situation across the city, the Hôtel Meurice is full of grey uniforms and red faces. There's a clink of glass and metal from the hotel restaurant, and a dozen murmured conversations bounce off the marble walls.

Luckily, she doesn't have to spend much time on the ground floor. She can sense Teller, can almost see through his eyes. She knows where she has to go. The staircase brings her up to a dim hallway; by this time in the late afternoon, the lights in the wall sconces should be on. But the power must be off.

Out in the city the guns seem very close, and very many. The afternoon is wearing on; will there be a bombing raid tonight?

Ivy pauses in front of Suite 213. There's no need to open the door. Beyond it is a room with brocade on the walls and heavy yellow curtains pulled back to show the view over the Tuileries, towards the Seine. On one side of the room is a large desk, its gleaming wood covered with maps and papers, a telephone, books and notes. A man stands behind the desk, gripping the back of the chair.

She searches for images from his mind but sees nothing but fires burning and bombs falling, cities in ruins. Wincing, she examines him instead the way Teller sees him. Dietrich von Choltitz, loyal German soldier through two wars, getting a little pudgy now along the jaw. A prudent man, who gets out of everything with his life and his job intact. He looks after himself.

Now here is Teller's mind, impatient, ready to do whatever it takes to – oh, she thinks, stepping back as she realizes how his mind has changed. He no longer wants to stop the Allies; he doesn't think they can be stopped. All he wants now is the tapestry before Himmler gets his hands on it. All of Himmler's mad obsessions with runes, incantations and ghost stories do not make him qualified. Himmler is not a clairvoyant himself, and he is incapable of building the society that must come, after the harrowing of the Earth.

So Teller must take it, now, and he must take Ivy and Kit too, somewhere their friends can't find them. He will be more careful this time. She can feel him searching for her; by keeping herself very still, by imagining herself as part of the hallway, no more a presence than the carpet or the wallpaper, she eludes him. She listens without letting her own thoughts or judgements shape what either of the men hears or sees. She listens, and they talk.

'The Führer will undoubtedly order you to destroy Paris,' Teller says. 'You must be ready to carry this out.'

With great force of mind, Ivy keeps herself from reacting, keeps her horror and panic at bay. Again, she sees the burning, the broken buildings. Sevastopol. She knows its name, though she's never been there. Choltitz has, and he and his comrades left it in ruins.

'Thank you for your advice, *Oberführer*,' Choltitz says drily. 'I am already making preparations.'

'Oh?' Teller's tone is light. 'Before receiving the order? Are you a prophet?'

'He has hinted his desires to me already,' Choltitz responds grimly. 'He wants to make sure that, when the Allies come, they find nothing but ruins. To teach the world a lesson, using the people of this city as an example. We will finally take our revenge for the dead of Hamburg, Düsseldorf, Lübeck, and all the rest.'

The city in his mind shifts, again and again; she sees men on bridges, watching the sky. Rotterdam. The bombers overhead, the smoke and blood and fire. How many cities has this man watched burn? But he feels nothing for them. The fires fill his mind and have burned away all remorse, all empathy.

Always, eventually, the fire comes from above, Choltitz thinks. The only trick is to be standing in the right place when that happens.

Teller sees his thoughts. 'Then we must ensure that whatever we wish to save from this, for the glory of the Reich, gets out of the city now.'

'Take what you wish, Teller. Take art, jewels, women, whatever you want, and go. That's my advice.'

'I'm not talking about loot, General. I am here to do my part to save the Germanic treasures from whatever may come. I have orders to collect the Tapestry of Queen Matilda from where it sits in the Louvre. Just down the street.'

She feels Teller point out of the balcony, over to the left, to where Ivy left her sister and Max and the others. She does not reach out her mind to see whether they're all right; she keeps herself steady, still, absorbing the present moment just as it is, here on the other side of this door. She can stay very still and small; she can force herself. In the vault, in those long hours after the bombs came and brought the Gestapo headquarters down on top of her, she found that she could leave her body behind, like a chrysalis, and that way she didn't mind not being able to move her leg, scratch her nose or push the hair out of her eyes. It would have driven her to screaming horror, if she had not been able to make her body totally inert, to imagine herself as something other than what she was. She had a long time to practise that, there.

It occurs to her for the first time to wonder how Teller practised that skill; how he was able to counter her fire with water, back at the Château de Sourches. What form has his training taken, all on his own, with his only peers his prisoners, when he can catch them? A flicker of empathy flares in the back of her mind, and she carefully tamps it down; she senses Teller sensing it, being on alert.

Teller is arguing with Choltitz. 'These orders come from Himmler himself. From the Reichsführer, do you understand? We are to remove the tapestry and take it to a place of safety.'

Teller does not say that he has no intention of handing the tapestry over to Himmler.

'Go and get it, then,' Choltitz says. 'I will not stand in your way.'

'I would happily do so, but I find that since I was last in Paris you have allowed the Resistance to take over a large section of the Rue de Rivoli. They may have advanced as far as the Louvre by now. I require at least thirty men to carry out these orders. You command the Wehrmacht in Paris, do you not? This should be a trifle for you.'

Thirty men, sent to the Louvre. To get the tapestry. She must not be anxious; she must not try to stop it. Not yet. Ivy waits and listens; she makes a box around herself, knowing that soon she will be free.

Choltitz laughs. 'My dear Teller, you are surely joking. How did you get to the Hôtel Meurice today? Did you not see what my troops are up against out there? If I am to survive here long enough to mine all the bridges, all the buildings, before the Allies arrive, and prepare the operation and get you and me out of here alive, I need every man working on that day and night. I won't piss away men and resources on trips to the museum.'

Teller is not a man to give up. He cannot make people do what he wants, not yet. But he can show them things. Trick them with imaginings. All he needs to do is see where Choltitz can be threatened, how he can be moved.

This is Ivy's moment. While Teller is focused on Choltitz, on conjuring visions for him, Ivy conjures visions of her own. She shows the general a future, one in which he lives, and his family lives, and he is not prosecuted by the Allies when they come. No, more than that – why hold back? She shows him a vision in which he's called a hero, the saviour of Paris.

She almost laughs in triumph. There, shining in the air

above the smoking ruin of the general's mind, is the future she has created for him. She can feel it becoming more real, minute by minute. Feel the seeds of doubt and disobedience growing in his mind. After all, it may well be impossible to carry out the destruction of Paris in the time that remains. Choltitz knows very well what it takes to level a city. Let Hitler send the Luftwaffe, if he really means it.

She feels the change in the room; feels even the soldiers throughout the hotel unnerved by new doubts.

Teller feels it too; he feels *her*.

Ivy's eyes spring open.

'Do as you see fit,' Teller snipes at Choltitz. 'While we argue, the Resistance could be securing their position in the Louvre. Every minute here is a minute lost.'

Ivy barely has time to duck into the entrance alcove to another room, a few steps down the hallway. She pulls her pistol. Then the door to Suite 213 opens, and to her surprise a different SS man walks out, one she doesn't recognize. He was there in the room, but was of so little consequence to Teller that she didn't see him in her mind's eye.

She keeps herself still as Teller himself steps into the doorway. Slows her breath. Thinks about absolutely nothing.

Aims her gun at his heart.

Tap tap.

She doesn't see him fall. Instead, she sees a future.

Paris levelled, just as Choltitz imagined, from above. The Eiffel Tower surrounded by flattened, blackened remains. Kit lying bleeding in an alley, staring at the hazy sky. When the sky clears, Ivy is home in England. Not home, no. In the sitting room at Stoke Damson, Mother is teaching little girls comportment, and how to obey their husbands. She passes around a photograph – Helen's photograph – and instructs each little girl in turn to spit on it. Mother says, *I have seen at first hand how fornication destroys a woman. Do not let it happen to you.*

Where is Father? Where is Rose? Ivy feels the absence of them, though she doesn't see their corpses. They've gone, into some black night where she can't follow. They resisted; they paid a price.

Ivy stands in the sitting room and pleads for Grady to come to her, to help her understand this. But Grady is not speaking to her; she can't hear his voice. She sees him, as if through smoked glass. He is teaching at a technical college, teaching young men in suits the proper way to write for the state newspaper. He's looking over the shoulder of a dark-haired young man, watching him writing with a pencil. Something is broken in Grady's eyes. He touches the man on the shoulder and closes those eyes, seeing the student with his inner vision instead. Learning what he can about him. Hours later, the student is walking home, down a dark street, and two strangers come upon him and take him away. Gone forever. The desk in the classroom is empty, the next day, with JEW written on it in red paint.

She doesn't believe this future. It isn't real. It's a trick; it's Teller's mind. All she needs to do is stop seeing it, but she can't. It's all around her; how can she get back to the hotel hallway, to the SS man who is lifting her gun to shoot her, to the yells and the running footsteps, to Choltitz climbing out on to his balcony, taking his chances that outside is safer than in, if someone is shooting in the hallway?

All of that is there, somewhere, but she can't clear her vision and get back to it. Somehow she has left her body in the present while her mind wanders in the future. Why bother getting back at all? The present leads to this reality. She has remade the present before, shaped it to her imaginings, but how can she shape the future? Isn't it written? Isn't it as plain as the past, to those who can see it?

Women, sitting in a damp room, nine hundred years ago. Stitching their visions on to cloth. One of them chose; one of them pricked her finger, and looked at the blood. *Aelfgyva,* said the woman across from her. *Don't bleed on it, or it'll be the devil to get out. Look, I'm working on the part where the bishop told you to start working on the tapestry. Where a certain cleric and Aelfgyva. You're part of the story now as a picture. Don't go making yourself part of it as a stain.*

No. She hears the word in her mind, like a gunshot. *No. That is not the story of Aelfgyva.*

How do you know? she asks Teller. She can feel him dying, feel him grasping for the threads of the story, to tangle her in them, so that they will both die believing in the future he sees. That they will bring this future into the world as their souls go out of it.

He screams at her. *I know the truth because I have seen it! And so have you! Aelfgyva was not an embroiderer. She was the mother of the young heir, the one who gave up her ambitions to save his life. The one who chose her son's future.*

No, Ivy says. *I see another story. Look.*

Now the women are bickering over what to show in the scene. One of them asks the other whether it's wise to show the mother of King Edward having a scandalous affair with a priest, years before. Simply because they know it, because they can see it, that isn't reason enough to tell the world.

It is real, before her eyes. She sees the women, smells the dye on the thread, hears the barking of dogs outside.

But wait, Ivy says, relentless. *I see yet another story.* The women put a different history into the tapestry, to explain events, to teach Matilda the past as well as the future. They show Aelfgyva, not King Edward's mother, but that woman's great rival. The spurned first wife of King Canute. When Canute died, she sent a cleric to Normandy, carrying a letter for Edward's brother, another claimant for the throne, inviting him to come to England. And the moment he arrived he was killed. *If only he'd had the gift of prophecy,* the women joke, telling each other this story, their needles sliding through the linen.

Teller screams in her mind. *You cannot change the past!*

But I can change what we see there, Ivy says. *Did you think it was only here and now that we can create false visions? What imaginings have you conjured without even knowing it, in the world of nine hundred years ago? What imaginings have I conjured, and shown you?*

She is jolted back to the present as Teller's mind lets go of hers. The visions vanish. Nothing but reality around her: Teller's dying body on the ground; his comrade's gun raised, the running footsteps on the staircase. In less than a second, she has travelled with Teller to futures and to pasts. She wants none of it; she rejects it, and him, and all that he is.

When Ivy opens her mouth to scream, the SS man hears the whistle of a bomb overhead. His arm falters and he looks up; she shoots him dead. She runs down the stairs, still screaming, past Germans running too, trying to get out of the building or at least under a table or something, some-where, where this bomb will not hit them. They believe in the bomb. And, for the few minutes it takes to run out of the Hôtel Meurice and towards the Resistance lines, Ivy believes in it too.

CHAPTER 35

Kit

Kit walks up the monumental staircase just inside the main entrance to the Louvre, like any visitor. It's nine o'clock in the morning on November 11th, Armistice Day, and the museum hasn't opened yet, but there are schoolchildren here already by special invitation, walking up the stairs with as much joy and reverence as Kit, if with a little more energy.

The great alcove at the top of the stairs is still empty. Before the war, the statue known as the Winged Victory of Samothrace stood here, but it was sent out to a château with all the other art that could be moved. Although the museum is open to visitors, the upper floors of the Louvre are still empty – with one exception.

Kit slows her steps as she turns to the left and enters the Salle des Sept Mètres, where the Bayeux Tapestry is on display.

There ought to be no surprises here for her. It was partly in order to plan this exhibition that Kit stayed behind in Paris, when Ivy took a concussed Max home to England to recover – returning the favour of 1940, as Ivy put it. It may be that Ivy is grateful for a reason to leave France and its ghosts behind; Kit wants to do the same, soon. Travel still isn't easy, but it isn't impossible. She's run out of reasons to stay away from home.

But first, she has work to do here.

At long last, she has finished her monograph. Gathered all her notes and papers and written the stories of women carved out of stone, how their sculptures were chosen and designed. A few people might read it, and that is enough. It's a beginning. She feels there's some truth in it.

When she wasn't working on the monograph, she helped plan the horseshoe-shaped wooden frame that will hold the long embroidery, so that it can stretch down one wall of the Salle des Sept Mètres and curve around to come back down the other. It's a perfect fit, as if the space was born for it, although soon the tapestry will be back in Bayeux where everyone agrees it belongs, for the sake of long tradition if nothing else.

Kit went to every meeting and did every bit of work she could, consulting on the wording of the pamphlets and posters. But she avoided any task that would have required her to see or touch the tapestry itself. The last time she had seen it was in the fortress, with Teller.

No visions plague her now as she approaches, cautiously. Lit by a long skylight, the tapestry looks more brilliant here than under the electric lights of her dungeons. It is not a trophy or a triumph but a commemoration of war, while war rages on. It is sad in the way that churches are sad, and transcendent in the way that churches are transcendent, when people gather in them to sing. When she was young, Kit used to believe that the tears that sprang to her eyes in church were proof of the existence of God; now she believes that the songs didn't connect her to something sacred; they created it. If God exists, she thinks, it is people gathered together to make something beautiful. She wants no other theology.

But here in the Louvre, no one is singing. Even the children talk only in whispers. The voices Kit hears are those of women who died long ago, and she can't quite catch what they're saying.

Since Ivy left, she's had fewer brushes with the Sight. A funny feeling, now and again. A tendency to look over her shoulder. Sometimes she sees a person staring at her from across the street and she wants to ask whether anyone else can see them, but she doesn't. Sometimes she has dreams that hold on to her all day.

Walking down the centre of the room, she takes it in, on alert in case anything attacks her mind's eye. There's nothing but people looking at the tapestry, and the very real and solid room.

Halfway down the left-hand side, in the middle of a jumble of children, she sees a young woman, with blonde curls and a jaunty purple cap. Kit pauses. She looks familiar, feels familiar.

Ivy turns to her, and smiles.

Smiling back, Kit takes a few steps towards her, but the children shift and jostle and then Ivy's gone. The children part as Kit approaches the tapestry. It's the section that shows Aelfgyva in some sort of building, with 'a certain cleric' striking her, blessing her, caressing her; everyone who sees it interprets it differently. But the children aren't interested in her; they're giggling at the man with the droopy genitals in the margins below. Kit smiles too.

She waits until the children have moved a few steps farther along, and then she reaches out, with some trepidation, towards Aelfgyva's face, like a parody of the mysterious cleric. Her fingers touch the glass cover that protects the tapestry, and she feels nothing. Only some kind of prayer.

*

It's snowing when Kit walks up the road to the house at Stoke Damson six weeks later, suitcase in her hand, wool cap on her head.

'You're late,' Ivy says, flinging the kitchen door open. 'We've been keeping dinner warm for hours.'

They embrace on the doorstep, and behind them, Helen says, 'It's been closer to ten minutes. Don't listen to her.'

Then she's inside the kitchen, which seems terribly small, probably because she's squashed between Helen, Ivy and Rose, all of them hugging her at once. Helen plants a kiss on her forehead and Rose clings to her as if she's going to cry. But nobody does cry; instead, they laugh. Mother looks Kit up and down as if inspecting her, for what, Kit can't imagine.

Father is the one who looks most likely to cry, and that makes Kit unsteady. After all these silent years between them, all the arguments, she doesn't quite know what to say to him. She knows he's had some experience with the Sight, but she doesn't know what; nobody wants to put anything specific in letters.

'It's good to see you,' he says. 'The crossing was all right?'

'Yes, it was fine. A bit of chaos but that's only to be expected.'

'I want to hear all about the exhibition of the tapestry,' he says, and Kit remembers that he's never seen it, never touched more than a scrap of it. Maybe some day they can travel to Bayeux together.

'But that can wait,' Father says, as if he's read her thoughts. 'Come on and meet the boys.'

The boys turn out to be Kurt and Karl, who are standing behind their chairs in the dining room, waiting for everyone. And Grady Sinclair, a young Canadian man who gives her a big grin when he shakes her hand.

'Ivy never stops talking about you,' he says. 'I'm so glad

the family could all be together. Rose nearly didn't get leave to come, which would have been a shame.'

Rose brings in a steaming dish. 'I'm only here for two days, but I intend to make the most of it. Kit, I hope you don't intend to sleep while you're here!'

'Oh, give her space,' Helen says, bringing in a beautiful toddler. 'This is Celia. Celia, meet your Aunt Kit.'

Kit takes in the sight and gives Helen a look that conveys how sad she is about George; she doesn't say it aloud, in case either of them breaks down.

When they're all seated, some on chairs borrowed from the sitting room and Father's study, passing bowls of vegetables around, Mother says, 'Since Rose is only here for a short time, we should discuss this family's talent for the Second Sight, and make sure we're all in agreement about how to use it from now on.'

In the silence that follows, Kit, shocked, looks from face to face – from the refugee boys to Father, from Rose to Helen. Nobody else seems surprised.

'Oh, Kit,' Mother says, seeing her expression. 'Just because I seem to have no talent for clairvoyance myself, that doesn't mean I can't see what's in front of my nose. Your father has told me some things, including that our Karl has displayed an aptitude himself. Helen is working with him to help him understand it better.'

Karl nods, as if she's talking about a book report or a mathematics exam.

'It's fascinating,' says Mr Sinclair, helping himself to the potatoes. 'Mr Yardley thinks that the talent runs in families. He wants to find bloodlines – indeed he has an entire theory about the tapestry itself being a record of bloodlines as much as anything.'

'It's nonsense,' says Father.

'Oh, it is most assuredly hogwash,' Grady agrees. 'You see,

Kit, what Professor Sharp and I think is that it doesn't run in families in any physiological sense. It's just that, when one clairvoyant is around another, it seems to trigger their talents, enhance them. Even reading about another's visions seems to have an effect – which of course explains the tapestry. There are lines connecting us, but they are lines of – I don't know how to put it.'

'Stories,' Ivy says, sitting beside him. 'The connections are stories. Stories of the past and of the future.'

Then Ivy looks up at Kit, and for a moment they share a vision. Teller is in the room with them, briefly, standing in the corner. Watching them jealously. From Ivy's expression, Kit guesses that Teller is frequently in the room with her, whatever room she happens to be in.

But Ivy's expression brightens, by force of will. She looks at Grady, who smiles back, and takes her hand briefly. Kit notices that this doesn't surprise anyone either; she wonders whether Grady has declared his intentions, whether he's asked Father for permission. In any case, Father seems to like him.

'As for Gregory Yardley,' says Father, 'we are no longer speaking to that man, and I would advise you to do the same, Kit.'

Kit is taken aback; she never did speak to Max's father if she could help it, but he and her own father have been friends for years.

'He wants to find all the clairvoyants in England to trace their bloodlines, to prove his theory,' Helen explains, her mouth twisting as if she's just eaten something bad. 'He calls us, the four of us sisters, "the mothers of history".'

Rose chimes in. 'What we've decided – Helen and I – is to act as if there never was any Second Sight in this family. Everything can be explained some other way, can't it? We simply aren't cooperating with Mr Yardley or his plans.'

Mother nods. 'But there's no reason not to use one's talents as seems fitting, to help the war effort, or any other good work. Is there, Rupert?'

'As long as we're careful,' he agrees from the opposite end of the table. 'I don't advise writing letters to His Majesty's Government warning him about Nazis flying their aeroplanes into Scottish fields near your aunt's house, or predicting the bombing of the town where your daughter is in Gestapo custody.' His expression is wry, pained; he looks older than Kit imagined he would be even after all these years. 'I have promised your mother, Kit, that I will focus my own talents on research. I would be very grateful for any help or advice you might care to give, while you're here.'

Kit doesn't quite know what to say to this. She nods, and smiles. There will be arguments in their future; they may be irreconcilable. But the arguments of the past, at least, are buried.

'How long are you staying, Kit?' Rose asks.

Kit clears her throat. 'That depends. On a few things.'

The night is very dark, but the waxing moon silvers the surface of the little stream that divides the Sharp house from the Yardley estate. Kit is in her coat but it's not very cold, and the snow has stopped, leaving just a bit of shine on the wooden bridge: she holds the railing as she walks up its slope. Because she's watching her step, she realizes Max is approaching the bridge from the other side only when they're a few feet away from each other.

They both laugh, as Max joins her in the middle of the bridge.

'I didn't want to go to bed without seeing you,' Kit says. 'But I didn't want to disturb your household, either. I wasn't sure what to do. Throw stones at your window as you did with that girl you liked in Cambridge.'

Truth be told, she isn't sure what she would say to Max's father, given everything she's been told. But she had to see Max.

'You could throw stones if you like,' Max says. 'I'm not sure you'd hit my window, though. Your aim has always been terrible.'

They stand in the middle of the bridge where they used to drop sticks into the water, where Ivy once saved Max's life. Kit isn't sure what to say. In Paris, after the liberation, it didn't seem right to tell Max how she felt, as if it might be attributed to the general euphoria, or to sympathy for Max, or gratitude for all the times Max helped her and her sister. Even now, Kit is always thinking about how her desire for Max might be misinterpreted, twisted into something ugly, cast aside as something trivial. She once thought she would prefer to live with that desire whole and beautiful, and entirely private, rather than risk anything happening to it. Risk never seeing Max again. It was better to hold on to what she had, and keep it safe, a little flame within her that no wind could ever blow out.

But tonight she is out in the cold dark world, because safety isn't enough any more. There is no hiding from the world, or from herself. In the dining room, as her family talked and laughed and ate, she kept seeing shapes in the shadows, in the corners of the room. Ghosts whose names she knows, and some she hasn't been introduced to yet. Possibilities and regrets. It is going to be strange, living in a house full of clairvoyants, she realizes. In Paris, she could keep the Second Sight at bay. Here, she'll have to learn to live with it.

For the moment, she lets herself be a little uncomfortable, a little uncertain of the future. This moment is real. She will hold on to this for weeks, months, years. The presence of Max beside her, looking at the same stream, lit by the same moon. The moment feels inevitable, as does what must come next. Kit doesn't need to rush it. It will come. It must come.

If Kit could go back to 1940, what would she say and do to make this present different? But Kit in 1940 was not the same person she is now.

And Max in 1940 was different too. Too young to understand what she felt for Kit, too excited by the possibility of inviting danger into their comfortable life. Now they'd had enough danger for a lifetime, surely even for Max.

Max says, 'I'm going away for a while. I don't know exactly where yet. But there may be work I can do in Asia. War work.'

Not enough danger for Max, then. And there is nothing inevitable about this night, or anything that happens after it.

They aren't looking at each other; they lean over the railing of the bridge and look into the water.

When Kit has absorbed the blow, she says only, 'I'm sure you'd be an asset anywhere.'

Max says, 'Are you going back to Paris?'

'I haven't decided yet. Ivy will be all right here, with her Mr Sinclair.'

'Oh, yes, he's lovely.'

'And Father is all right. Helen is grieving, but she has her little girl. Mother's always fine. Rose – I have never seen Rose so confident and content, strangely enough. I don't think they need me here. I always feel that I'm liable to cause more damage than anything else.' She pauses, gathers a tiny bit of courage. 'There would be work for you in Paris too, you know. If you wanted.'

'I can't, Kit,' Max says, immediately and matter-of-fact. 'It's too hard, being around you.'

Kit swallows. 'Of course. I know there are bad memories.'

'All my memories of you are good. It's the future that hurts.'

While Kit considers this, a cloud goes over the moon, and the shadows gather, and the water below them goes dark. There's no light on their path, only this step, the next step, and the next. This moment, when she could still turn and say goodnight, and go back to the house.

Instead, she says, 'I can see the future, you know.'

A tiny laugh breaks out of Max. 'I'd forgotten. What do you see?'

Kit turns to her, leaning one elbow on the bridge, watching her face. It's Max who waits, frozen, as if nervous. Max, who's never nervous.

'I see you,' Kit whispers, and puts one hand on Max's shoulder, to turn her towards her.

Their mouths are already open when they come together, like people gasping for air. Kit's hands cup the back of Max's head, her curls running through her fingers, as all the time that has gone before and all the time that lies ahead reshapes itself. For the rest of her life, Kit will not be able to hear an owl call without remembering the call that came as she was kissing Max on that bridge, as the clouds scattered, and the moon came out.

Author's Note and Acknowledgements

Most of the characters in this novel are invented. Given that the Second World War is recent family history for many (including me), I was cautious about representing real individuals, beyond the occasional reference to off-page figures such as Heinrich Himmler, Carl Oberg, Rudolf Hess, Jacques Jaujard and Helen Duncan. Two on-page exceptions are the brief scenes with Vera Atkins at the SOE, and Germain Bazin at the Château de Sourches. In those cases, I have tried not to extrapolate too much beyond what we know of the facts of their lives.

The third exception is Dietrich von Choltitz at the Hôtel Meurice. It did indeed happen that two SS men came to ask for his help in retrieving the Bayeux Tapestry from the Louvre during the Paris uprising, but my rendering of that conversation is an invention. A few days after that, Choltitz did ignore Hitler's order to destroy Paris. In his memoir, Choltitz portrays himself as the saviour of Paris, but to what extent he even had the capability to carry the order out is still a subject of research and analysis.

There is some inconsistency in my sources about which date the SS turned up to speak to Choltitz about the tapestry. I've gone with August 21st, which seemed the best attested and the likeliest, given the context of how far the uprising had advanced, but some accounts have it as August 22nd or August 20th.

Although the other characters are fictional, real people who resisted the Nazi regime inspired this book. To take one example, Rose Valland, a French art historian who quietly recorded the location of looted artworks so they could be recovered after the war, was one inspiration for the character of Kit.

The movements of the Bayeux Tapestry follow the historical record, with one exception: as far as we know, the tapestry stayed in the Louvre after the Gestapo removed it from the Château de Sourches; the period it spent in a fortress in St Quentin is my invention.

As for the tapestry itself, the theory that it was sewn by Queen Matilda or her ladies, or commissioned by her, is not widely held today but was once common, and it was often referred to as 'Queen Matilda's Tapestry' in the 1940s. The identity and significance of Aelfgyva is still a mystery and many historians have outlined the evidence in favour of various women. Rupert Sharp's identification of Aelfgyva with Agatha, mother of Edgar, is just my own pet hunch.

Harry Frederick, the codebreaker at Bletchley Park, is invented, but the stories about Jack Good and John Herivel are real.

The woman with the code name Jacqueline, who trains with Ivy, is an invented person, loosely based on two of the earliest SOE agents, Yvonne Rudellat and Andrée Borrel. They were both ultimately captured, like many SOE agents; Rudellat died of typhus in the Bergen-Belsen camp, and Borrel was killed in the Natzweiler-Struthof camp. The depiction of SOE training follows known historical records as much as I could.

Lucienne and the Mechanic circuit are invented, but the collapse of the SOE and Resistance circuits because of agents being captured, turned or killed was all too real.

The village of La Codre and its Gestapo office, including Mr Teller, are my invention, but the conditions are based on descriptions of other Gestapo house prisons – often a few cells built into repurposed buildings. The fascists in France did shoot Resistance prisoners *en masse* after Operation Overlord began in June 1944, and there was a partly successful SOE operation to break prisoners out of Amiens prison in February 1944. The doctor and team of soldiers in Argentan are my invention, but the three soldiers would have been one of the so-called Jedburgh international teams that dropped into France in the summer of 1944. The final deportation of political prisoners by train from Paris, which Ivy sees as a vision, did happen as Paris was rising up.

Grady Sinclair is invented, but the so-called Farm where he worked in Canada, now known to history as Camp X, was real, including the Hydra communications array. I live not far from there now.

I'm very grateful to the many historians whose books and articles informed my research, including my own grandfather's memoirs of his service and life during the war. Any errors and distortions are my own.

My immense gratitude as well to my editor, Jane Johnson, who saw what this book could be and helped me get it there with her usual perspicacity and good humour. Linda McQueen did this book an invaluable service with her copy edit, and I'm so grateful for her careful work. Thanks as well to Colin Lindsay and Ember Randall, for providing very useful feedback on an early draft.

As always, many thanks to my writer friends who have provided support of various kinds, especially the Codex writers community. And to all my family, especially my partner Brent for always making space for my writing no matter what, and my son Xavier, the best brainstorming partner I could ever have.

Finally, thank you to my wonderful agent, Jennie Goloboy, and to everyone at HarperVoyager UK for bringing this book into the world. My thanks in particular to Chloe Gough, Ajebowale Roberts, Kate Fogg, Robyn Watts, Emily Chan, Fleur Clarke, Philippa Cotton, Harriet Williams, Holly Martin, Erin White and Zoe Shine, and to Toby James for the wonderful cover design.